STAR TREK®
TESTS OF COURAGE™

▲ ▲ ▲

With a Special Introduction
by GEORGE TAKEI

STAR TREK: TESTS OF COURAGE

STAR TREK is a registered trademark of Paramount Pictures. Published by DC Comics under exclusive license from Paramount Pictures, the trademark owner. Copyright © 1994, Paramount Pictures. All Rights Reserved. Originally published in single magazine form by DC Comics as STAR TREK 35-40. Copyright © 1992 Paramount Pictures. All Rights Reserved. The stories, characters, and incidents featured in this publication are entirely fictional.

DC Comics, 1325 Avenue of the Americas, New York, NY 10019
A division of Warner Bros. - A Time Warner Entertainment Company
Printed in Canada. First Printing.   ISBN # 1-56389-151-4

Cover painting by Sonia G. Hillios   Publication design by Veronica Carlin

STAR TREK®

TESTS OF COURAGE™

HOWARD WEINSTEIN
WRITER

ROD WHIGHAM
GORDON PURCELL
PENCILLERS

ARNE STARR
CARLOS GARZON
INKERS

ROBERT PINAHA
LETTERER

TOM McCRAW
COLORIST

INTRODUCTION BY GEORGE TAKEI

AFTERWORD BY HOWARD WEINSTEIN

BASED ON STAR TREK
CREATED BY GENE RODDENBERRY

My Cup Runneth Over

An Introduction

By George Takei

My cup runneth over. I have a bounty of blessings to the point of overflowing, an abundance of fortune too good to keep contained. But the problem with such a brimming cup is that when it runs over, it creates a terrible, dribbly mess. I now have a wet mess on my hands.

Instead of boldly going where no one has gone before, as I have been doing now for almost thirty years, I have for the past year been carefully going in reverse, peering and sniffing at memories from where one has already been in life. You see, I have been engaged in that time-honored actors' rite of passage called writing my autobiography.

In rummaging around in the attic of my life, I have discovered that I've been blessed with an overflowingly huge and eclectic treasure trove. But like most attics, mine is a chaotic mess. It contains memories that range from a barbed wire internment camp in Arkansas to the star-spangled splendor of the inaugural festivities of two United States presidents. I've found bits and pieces from experiences such as picking strawberries in the fields of

California to loading trucks in the factory docks of Long Island City, New York. There were shining gleanings from the climb up to the top of Mt. Fuji in Japan and the agonizing ecstasy of finishing the 26.2 mile London Marathon on Westminster Bridge above the River Thames. I found luminescent jewels, treasured remembrances from the Edinburgh International Arts Festival in Scotland where I played a marooned Japanese soldier in an award-winning production all the way to becoming the 23rd-century captain of a starship on a sound stage at Paramount Studios in Hollywood. I have the glow of history from putting my hand print in wet cement in the landmark forecourt of Mann's Chinese Theater on Hollywood Boulevard to being a guest at an epochal event in human history, the "roll out" of the first space shuttle at Edwards Air Force Base in the high plains of the Mojave Desert. And in between these incandescent lights, I found in the dark recesses, painful hidden memories. What I discovered in the overabundant attic of my life is a big and bountiful but dismayingly disorganized collection of the bits and pieces of a blessed life. To arrange them all in some coherent, presentable form has been my challenge. And I had to have it finished by February 1, 1994 — my deadline.

To make this challenge daunting, my agent came up with a tantalizing film project. It wasn't just another production that I could easily pass on. It was written by an old friend and colleague, Peter David. I had collaborated with him on a comic book a few years back. But for this film, ominously titled *Oblivion*, Peter created a role too deliciously irresistible to keep me sorting out the miscellanea of my life for an autobiography. The part was a serio-comic role of an alcoholic town doctor in a wild western town on an alien planet. Pure Peter David! I couldn't say no. No way. And miss out on a Peter David madness? Absolutely not! And so, my life got messier. Then they told me it was to shoot on location in Bucharest, Romania! Of all places! My life got ridiculously, exotically messier. I had to get a new deadline for my autobiography. My editor, Kevin Ryan, accommodated me with an extension to March 15.

I finished the film and returned to the autobiography determined to make some sense out of the growing disarray and meet my new deadline of March 15. Then another friend and colleague called. During the course of this blessed life, I have collected an abundance of friends and colleagues as well. This one was Bob Greenberger, at DC Comics, with whom I had worked before.

"Hi, George," he greeted me in his usual sprightly way. "How'd you like to write the intro to a collection of stories by your old friend and colleague Howie Weinstein?" My cup was starting to dribble again. Dear friends and colleagues continue to bless me and make a mess of my already disorderly life.

But then, Howie is a good friend from way back — more than a decade. We met at some long-ago *Star Trek* convention in some long-ago city... I think it was Baltimore, or was it Cleveland? I can't recall. It's all part of that abundantly jumbled mess of convention memories. But Howie comes dancing through that mass like the Eveready Bunny, marching relentlessly, clanging his cymbals noisily, a supercharged bundle of kinetic energy. Absolutely unforgettable and completely irresistible! How could anyone say no to Howie? He charms with the sparkle of his wit and holds you mesmerized with the effervescence of his ideas. He sets the spirit soaring with the wonder of his tales told in that whimsical dancing voice of his. He sprinkles them throughout with unexpected details of the *Star Trek* universe. That floppy disc memory of his can retrieve data with the speed of at least warp three. He is a person you not only cannot say no to but irresistibly cannot help saying yes to. He is actually a sprite disguised as a science-fiction writer.

And what a writer! This series of his stories under the collective title *Tests of Courage* is a colossal adventure with the sweep of events ripped from the headlines of today's newspapers. It's Bosnia. It's South Africa. It's the Israelis and the Palestinians. It's North Korea and all of the madness of our ebbing 20th century shot out into the galaxies of the next millennium.

It's also a human drama of old friendships and the testing of new relationships, of the obsession with power and the search for the coexistence of infinite diversity in infinite combinations. And for me personally, it is an enormously satisfying tale of the emergence of the indomitable team of two starship captains working in dynamic concert with each other — the grizzled war horse, James Tiberius Kirk, and a new leader stepping out on his own from Kirk's tutelage, Hikaru Sulu. It's a strong bond between them with subtle undercurrents, a true and recognizable relationship that Howie captures with keen sensitivity. And it is a powerful team Kirk and Sulu make, a teaming that whets the appetite for more such galactic partnerships. Howie Weinstein is a storyteller of compelling power and delicate nuances. With *Tests of Courage*, he has written a rip-snorting blast of a space opera.

Yes, Howie is a friend to whom I always say "yes." And yes, he is a colleague who always makes a mess of my already abundantly blessed life. My abundance runneth over.

I called the editor of my autobiography to discuss another extension of that March 15 deadline. I told him that Shakespeare warned that March 15 was an unpropitious date. "The ides of March," he called it. Awful things happened on that date — especially to Julius Caesar. I asked that he move the deadline away from such an unpleasant date — farther away to a nicer one. He agreed and extended it to April 1.

I wonder if he's trying to tell me something with the new deadline. But I'm not complaining. When you have an overflowing cup, you keep busy cleaning up the mess you have. But it's great to take a break from it occasionally and go off on a pure galactic adventure with a good friend and colleague — especially when the hero is the dashing Captain Sulu. I just have to have the mess cleaned up by April Fool's Day.

(Editor's Note: As of this writing George's deadline has been extended – to May 15.)

So nigh is grandeur to our dust,

So near is god to man.

When Duty whispers low,

Thou Must,

The Youth replies, I can.

Ralph Waldo Emerson
"Voluntaries"

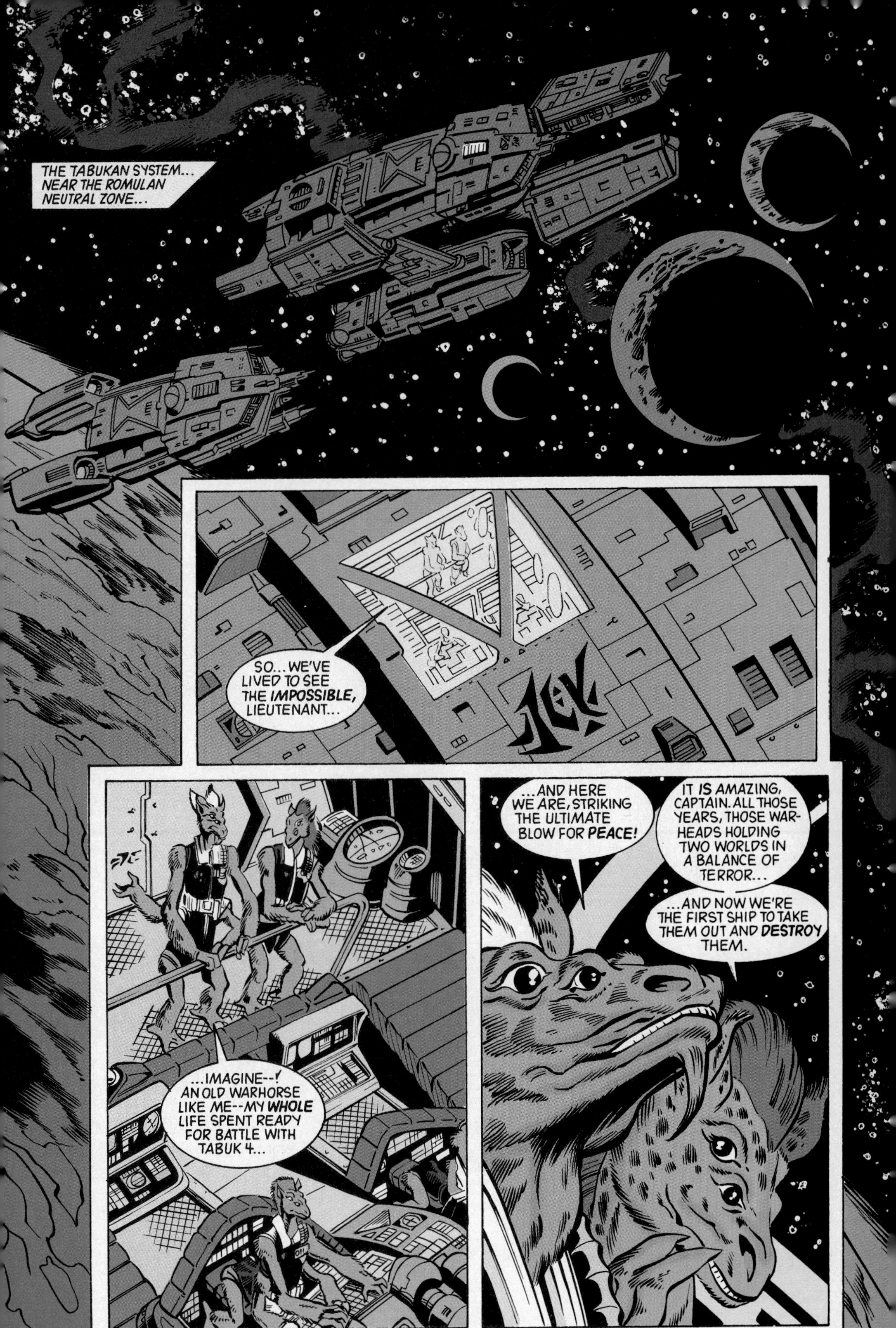
THE TABUKAN SYSTEM... NEAR THE ROMULAN NEUTRAL ZONE...
SO... WE'VE LIVED TO SEE THE IMPOSSIBLE, LIEUTENANT...
...IMAGINE--! AN OLD WARHORSE LIKE ME--MY WHOLE LIFE SPENT READY FOR BATTLE WITH TABUK 4...
...AND HERE WE ARE, STRIKING THE ULTIMATE BLOW FOR PEACE!
IT IS AMAZING, CAPTAIN. ALL THOSE YEARS, THOSE WAR-HEADS HOLDING TWO WORLDS IN A BALANCE OF TERROR...
...AND NOW WE'RE THE FIRST SHIP TO TAKE THEM OUT AND DESTROY THEM.

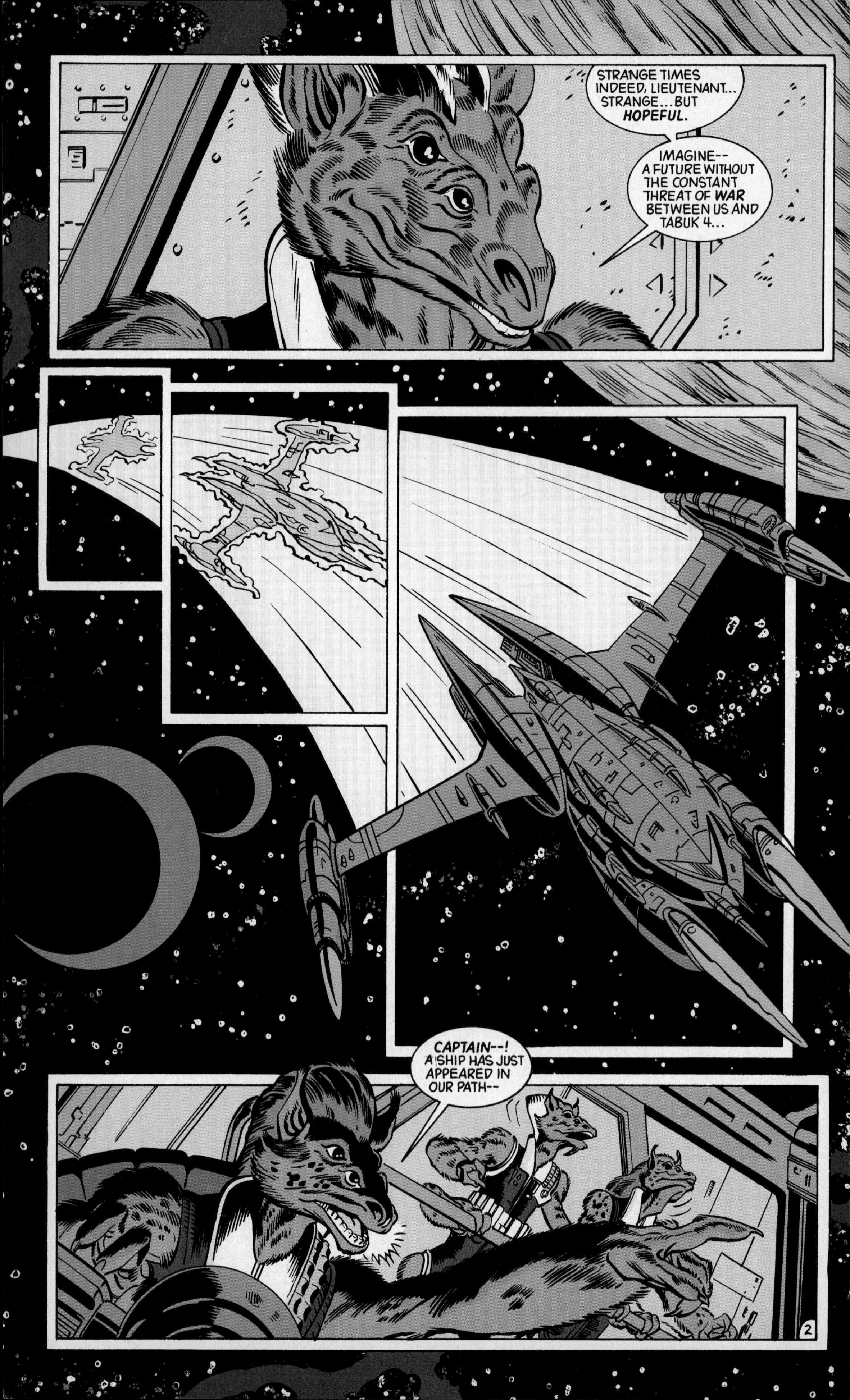

STRANGE TIMES INDEED, LIEUTENANT... STRANGE... BUT HOPEFUL.
IMAGINE-- A FUTURE WITHOUT THE CONSTANT THREAT OF WAR BETWEEN US AND TABUK 4...
CAPTAIN--! A SHIP HAS JUST APPEARED IN OUR PATH--

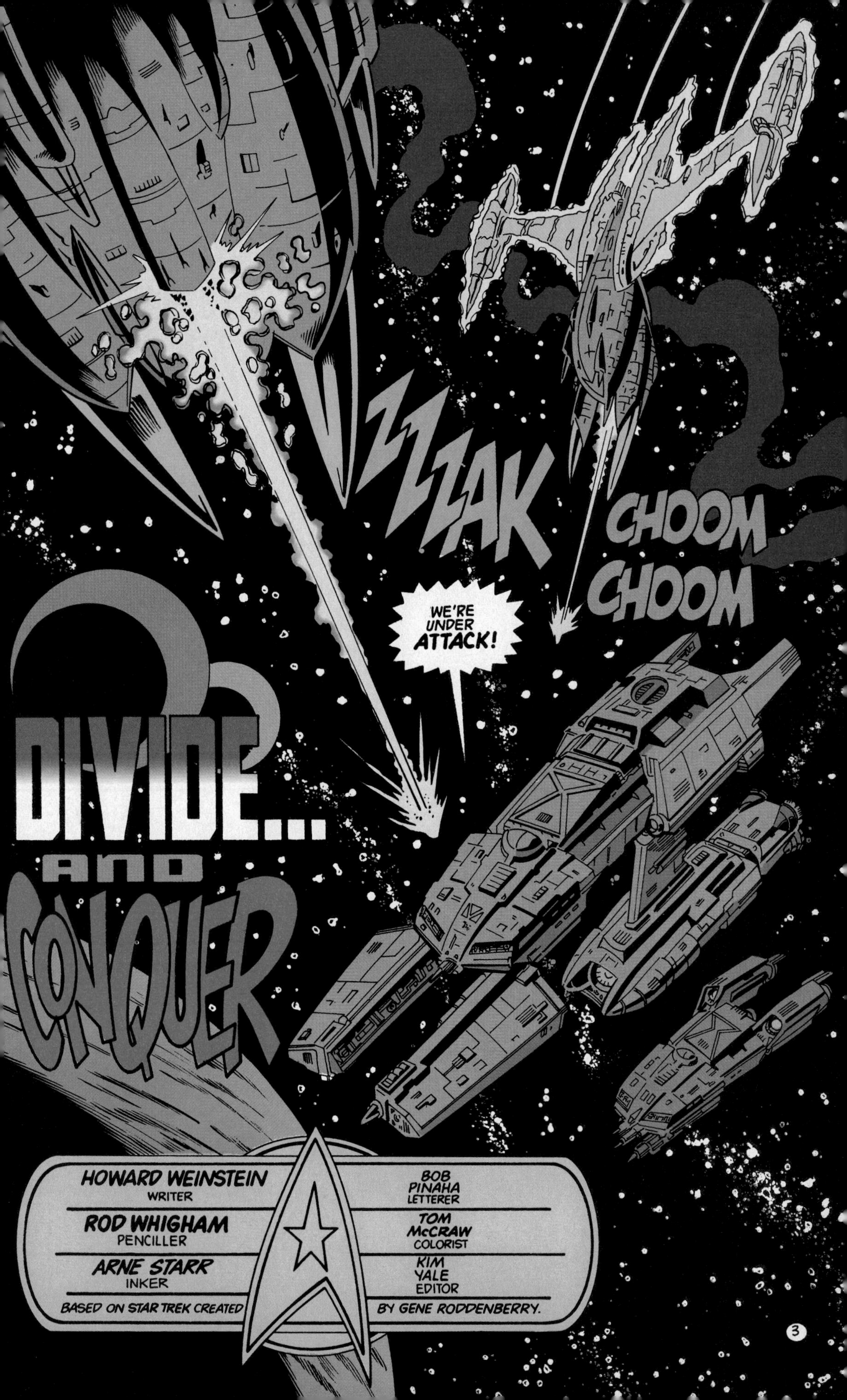
ZZZZAK
CHOOM
CHOOM
WE'RE UNDER ATTACK!
DIVIDE... AND CONQUER
HOWARD WEINSTEIN
WRITER
ROD WHIGHAM
PENCILLER
ARNE STARR
INKER
BOB PINAHA
LETTERER
TOM McCRAW
COLORIST
KIM YALE
EDITOR
BASED ON STAR TREK CREATED BY GENE RODDENBERRY.
3

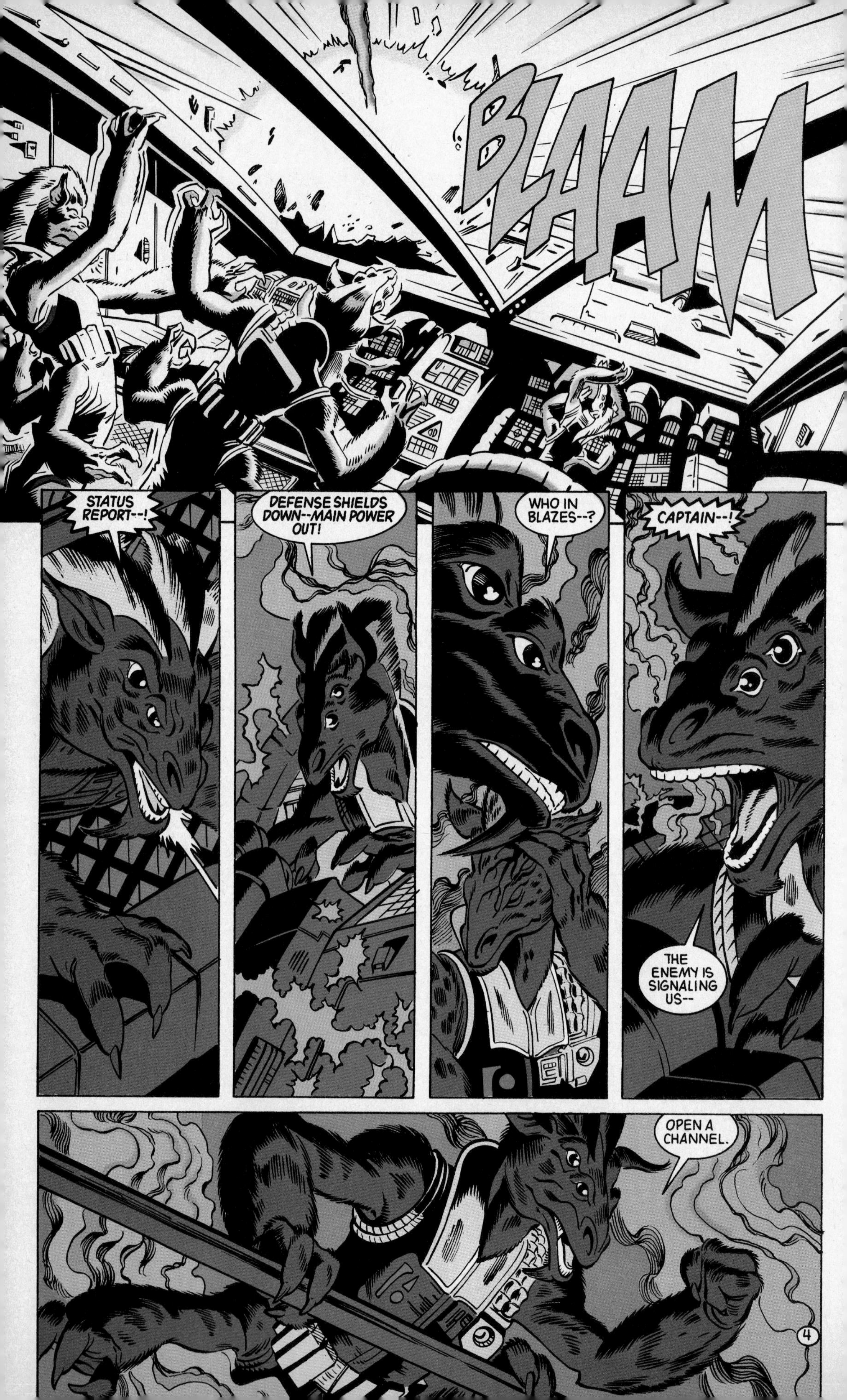
BLAAM
STATUS REPORT--!
DEFENSE SHIELDS DOWN--MAIN POWER OUT!
WHO IN BLAZES--?
CAPTAIN--!
THE ENEMY IS SIGNALING US--
OPEN A CHANNEL.
4

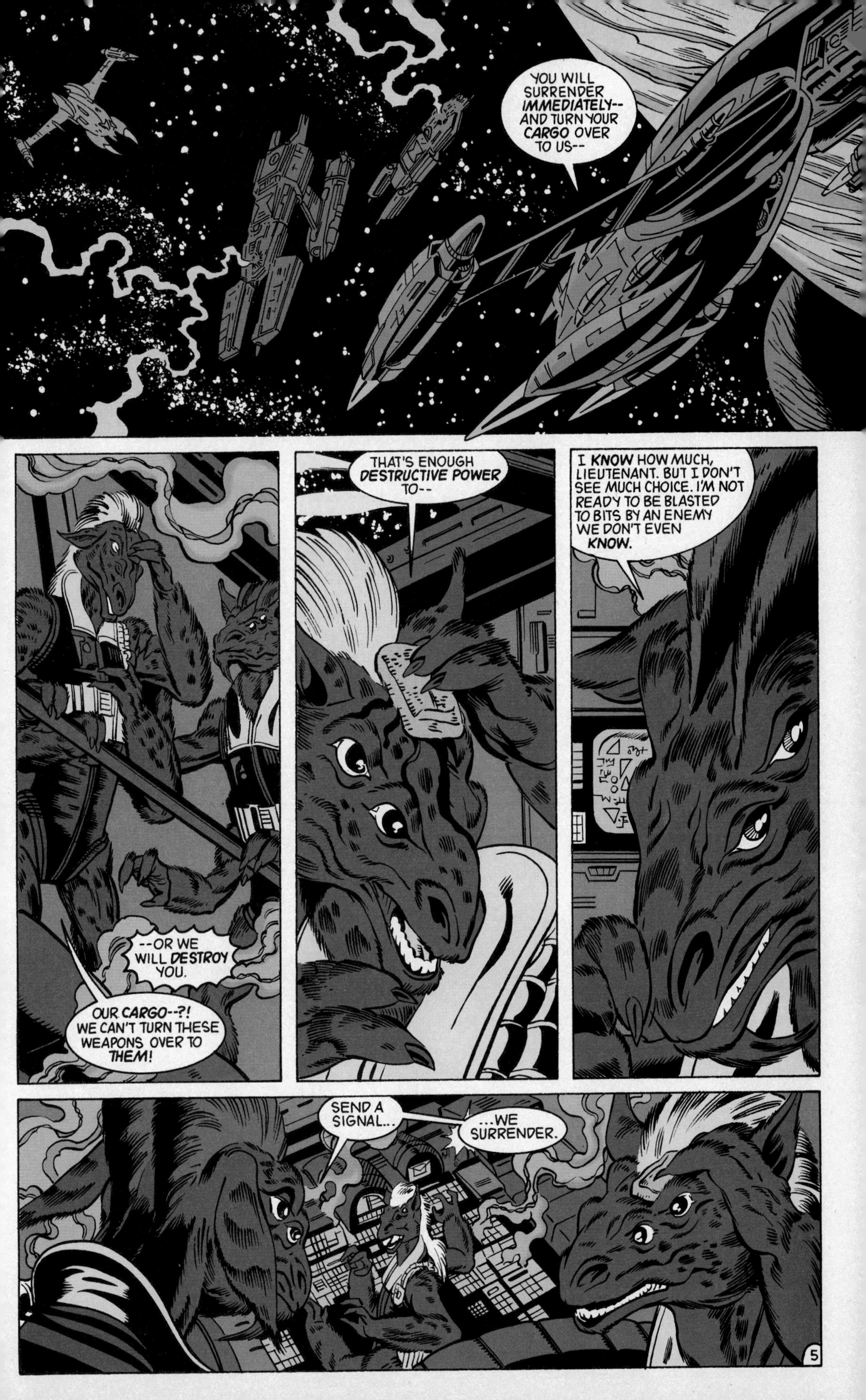

YOU WILL SURRENDER IMMEDIATELY-- AND TURN YOUR CARGO OVER TO US--
--OR WE WILL DESTROY YOU.
OUR CARGO--?! WE CAN'T TURN THESE WEAPONS OVER TO THEM!
THAT'S ENOUGH DESTRUCTIVE POWER TO--
I KNOW HOW MUCH, LIEUTENANT. BUT I DON'T SEE MUCH CHOICE. I'M NOT READY TO BE BLASTED TO BITS BY AN ENEMY WE DON'T EVEN KNOW.
SEND A SIGNAL...
...WE SURRENDER.
5

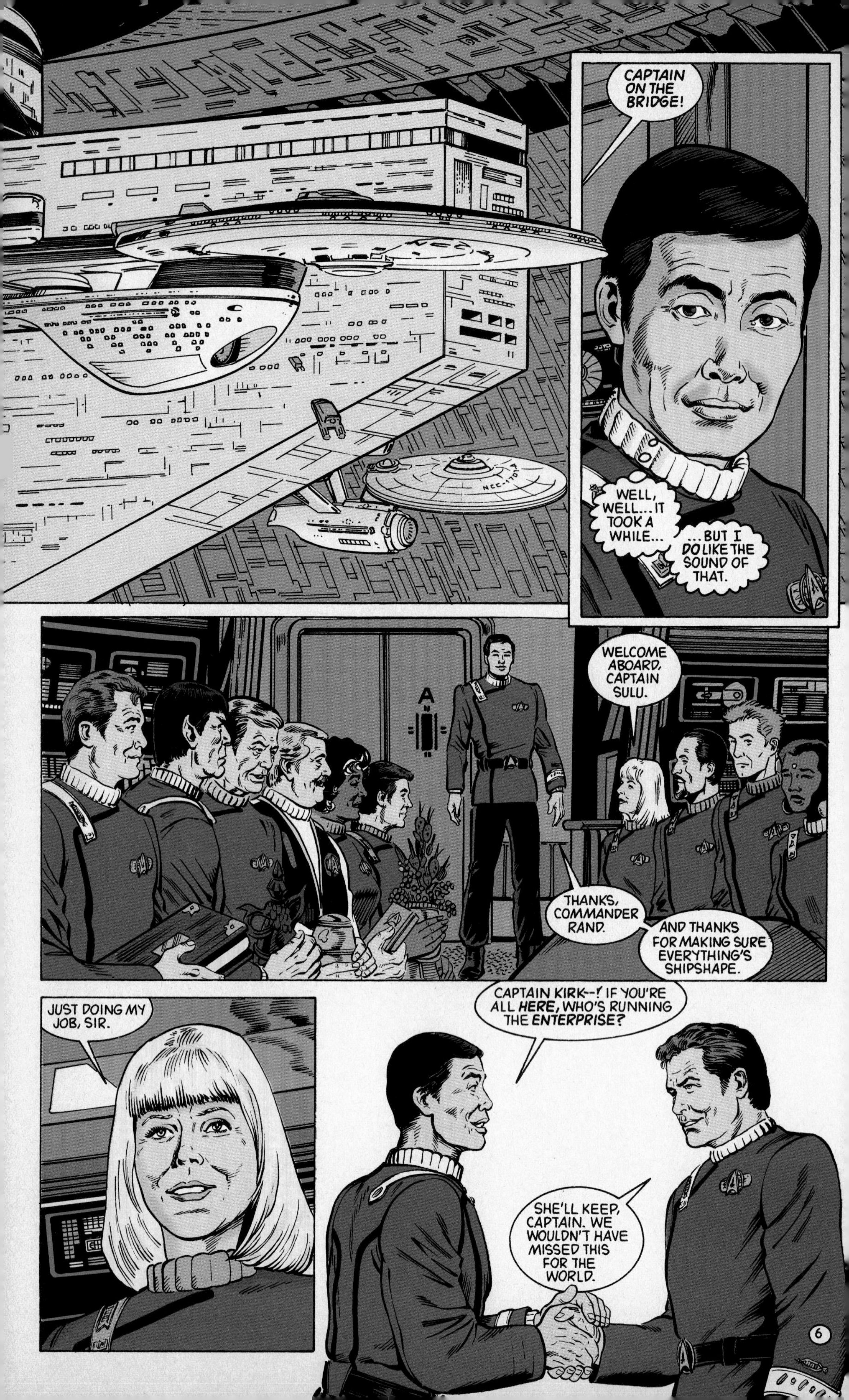
CAPTAIN ON THE BRIDGE!
WELL, WELL... IT TOOK A WHILE...
...BUT I DO LIKE THE SOUND OF THAT.
WELCOME ABOARD, CAPTAIN SULU.
THANKS, COMMANDER RAND.
AND THANKS FOR MAKING SURE EVERYTHING'S SHIPSHAPE.
JUST DOING MY JOB, SIR.
CAPTAIN KIRK--! IF YOU'RE ALL HERE, WHO'S RUNNING THE ENTERPRISE?
SHE'LL KEEP, CAPTAIN. WE WOULDN'T HAVE MISSED THIS FOR THE WORLD.

AYE. AND WE COULDNA LET Y' LEAVE WITHOUT A FEW GIFTS T'REMEMBER US BY, LADDIE.

Uh, SCOTTY-- THAT'S *CAPTAIN* LADDIE.

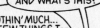

AND WHAT'S THIS?

OH, NOTHIN' MUCH... JUST A FEW THINGS I-- uhh--*"BORROWED"* FROM *EXCELSIOR'S* ENGINES DURING M'BRIEF SERVICE WITH CAPTAIN STYLES.

HA-HAA- AH-AH-AH AH--!

Y'WON'T BE *NEEDIN'* THESE SINCE THEY REPLACED THOSE TRANS-WARP BEASTIES WITH *REAL* ENGINES. BUT I THOUGHT Y'SHOULD *KEEP 'EM* AS A REMINDER O' THE *WISDOM O'STAYIN'* ON BONNIE TERMS WITH Y'R *CHIEF ENGINEER.*

I DON'T KNOW ABOUT THIS, DOC. IT LOOKS LIKE OUR NEW CAPTAIN NEEDS *KIRK* TO SHOW HIM WHERE THE CENTER SEAT IS.

≡A-HEM≡ GOT A PROBLEM--

--ENGINEER LUKAS?

Uhh--*NO,* COMMANDER RAND... NO PROBLEM AT ALL.

GOOD. BECAUSE NOT ONLY DOES CAPTAIN SULU *KNOW* HIS WAY TO THE COMMAND SEAT--

--*BUT*--AFTER SERVING WITH *CAPTAIN KIRK*--

--ONCE HE SITS DOWN, HE'LL *ALSO* KNOW WHAT TO *DO!*

7

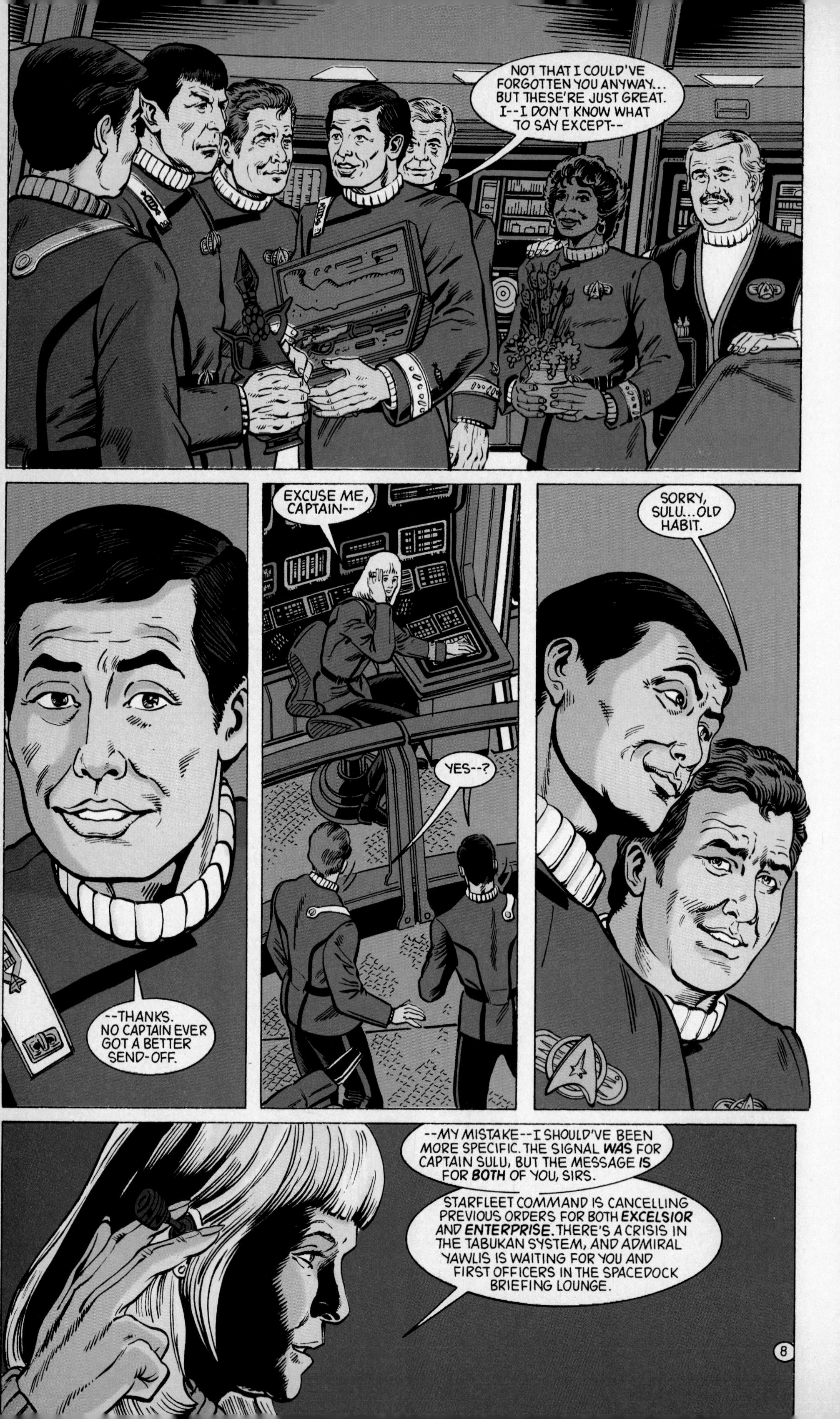
NOT THAT I COULD'VE FORGOTTEN YOU ANYWAY... BUT THESE'RE JUST GREAT. I--I DON'T KNOW WHAT TO SAY EXCEPT--
--THANKS. NO CAPTAIN EVER GOT A BETTER SEND-OFF.
EXCUSE ME, CAPTAIN--
YES--?
SORRY, SULU...OLD HABIT.
--MY MISTAKE--I SHOULD'VE BEEN MORE SPECIFIC. THE SIGNAL WAS FOR CAPTAIN SULU, BUT THE MESSAGE IS FOR BOTH OF YOU, SIRS.
STARFLEET COMMAND IS CANCELLING PREVIOUS ORDERS FOR BOTH EXCELSIOR AND ENTERPRISE. THERE'S A CRISIS IN THE TABUKAN SYSTEM, AND ADMIRAL YAWLIS IS WAITING FOR YOU AND FIRST OFFICERS IN THE SPACEDOCK BRIEFING LOUNGE.

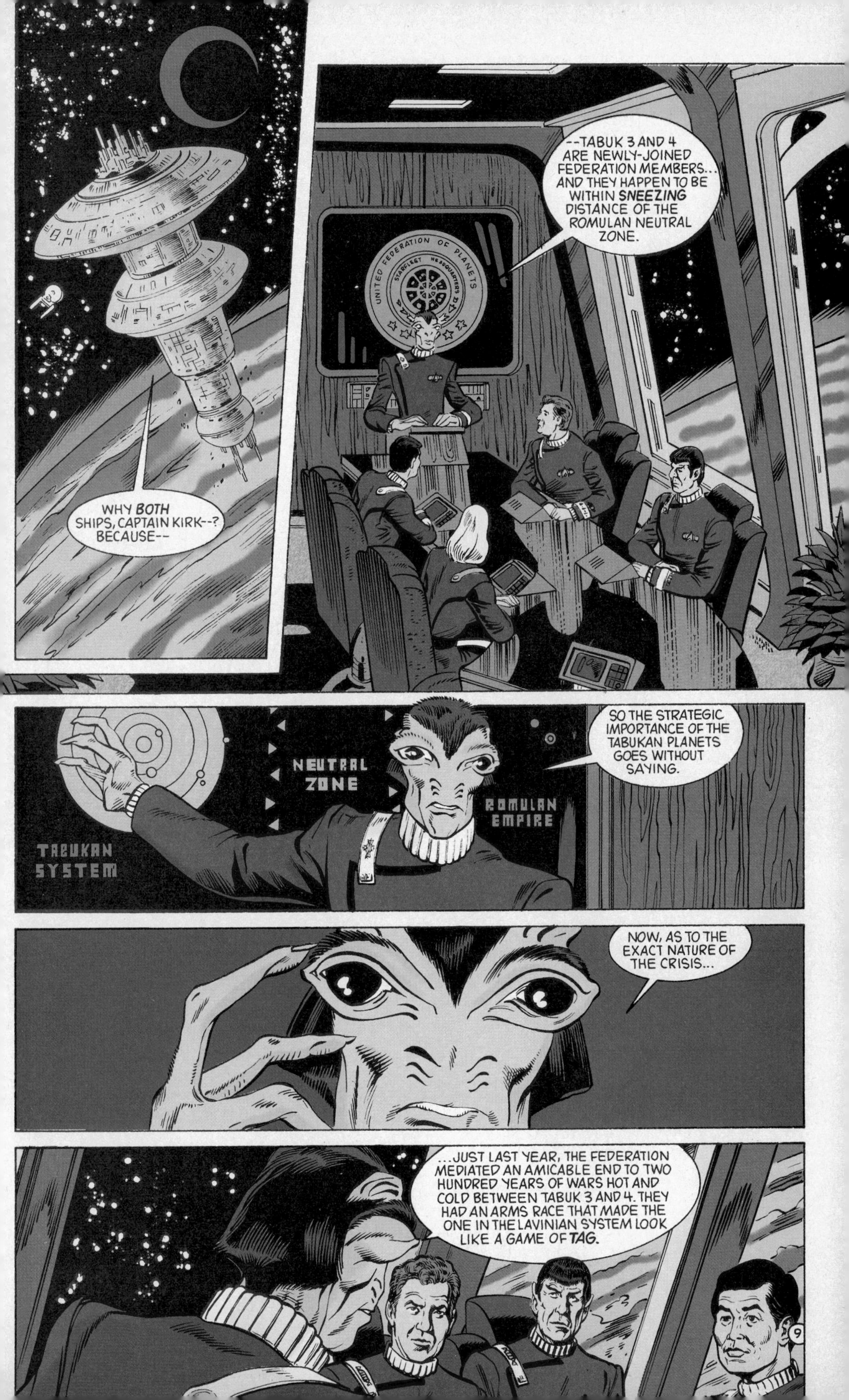
WHY BOTH SHIPS, CAPTAIN KIRK--? BECAUSE--
--TABUK 3 AND 4 ARE NEWLY-JOINED FEDERATION MEMBERS... AND THEY HAPPEN TO BE WITHIN SNEEZING DISTANCE OF THE ROMULAN NEUTRAL ZONE.
UNITED FEDERATION OF PLANETS
STARFLEET HEADQUARTERS
NEUTRAL ZONE
ROMULAN EMPIRE
TABUKAN SYSTEM
SO THE STRATEGIC IMPORTANCE OF THE TABUKAN PLANETS GOES WITHOUT SAYING.
NOW, AS TO THE EXACT NATURE OF THE CRISIS...
...JUST LAST YEAR, THE FEDERATION MEDIATED AN AMICABLE END TO TWO HUNDRED YEARS OF WARS HOT AND COLD BETWEEN TABUK 3 AND 4. THEY HAD AN ARMS RACE THAT MADE THE ONE IN THE LAVINIAN SYSTEM LOOK LIKE A GAME OF TAG.

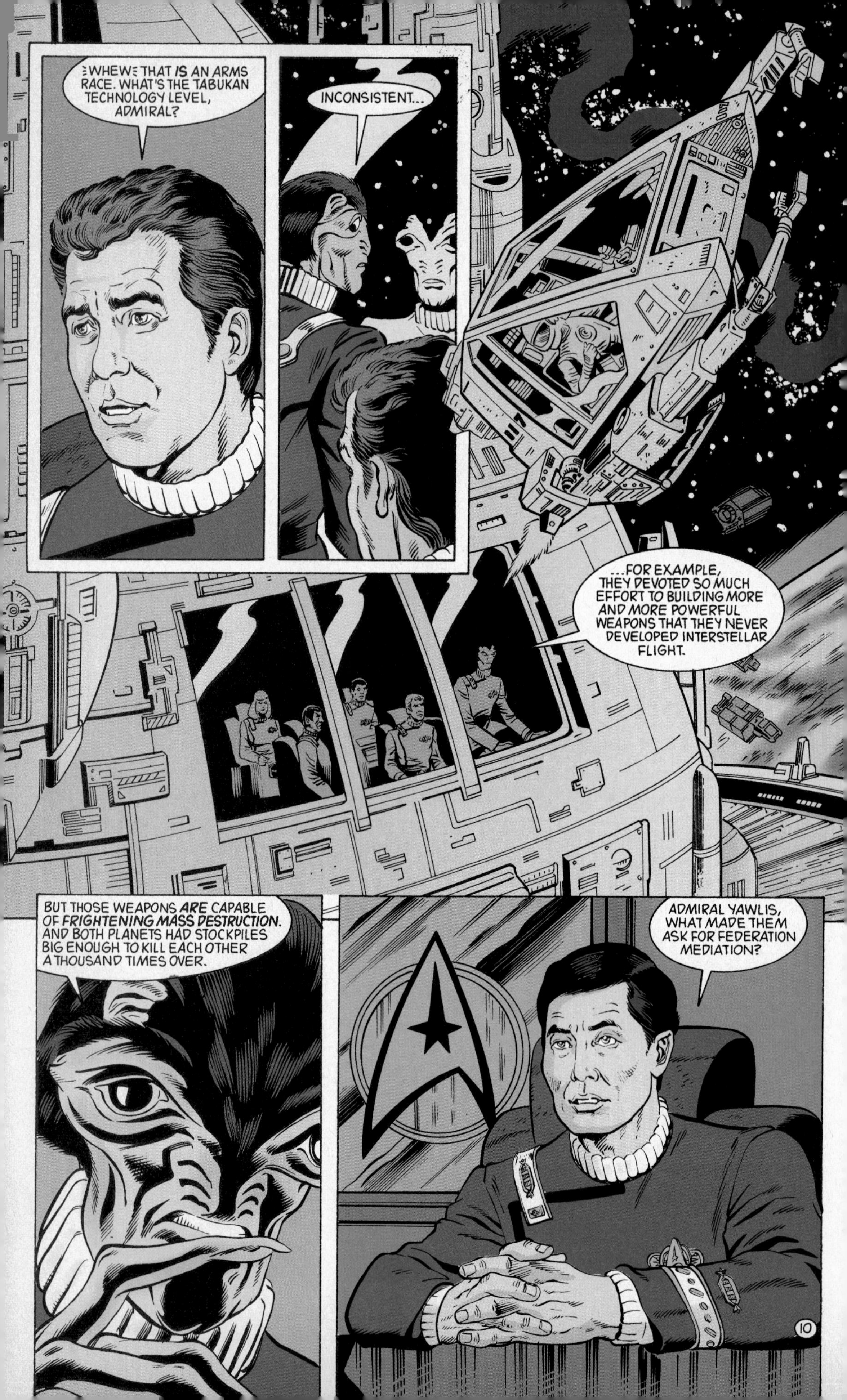

=WHEW= THAT IS AN ARMS RACE. WHAT'S THE TABUKAN TECHNOLOGY LEVEL, ADMIRAL?
INCONSISTENT...
...FOR EXAMPLE, THEY DEVOTED SO MUCH EFFORT TO BUILDING MORE AND MORE POWERFUL WEAPONS THAT THEY NEVER DEVELOPED INTERSTELLAR FLIGHT.
BUT THOSE WEAPONS ARE CAPABLE OF FRIGHTENING MASS DESTRUCTION. AND BOTH PLANETS HAD STOCKPILES BIG ENOUGH TO KILL EACH OTHER A THOUSAND TIMES OVER.
ADMIRAL YAWLIS, WHAT MADE THEM ASK FOR FEDERATION MEDIATION?
10

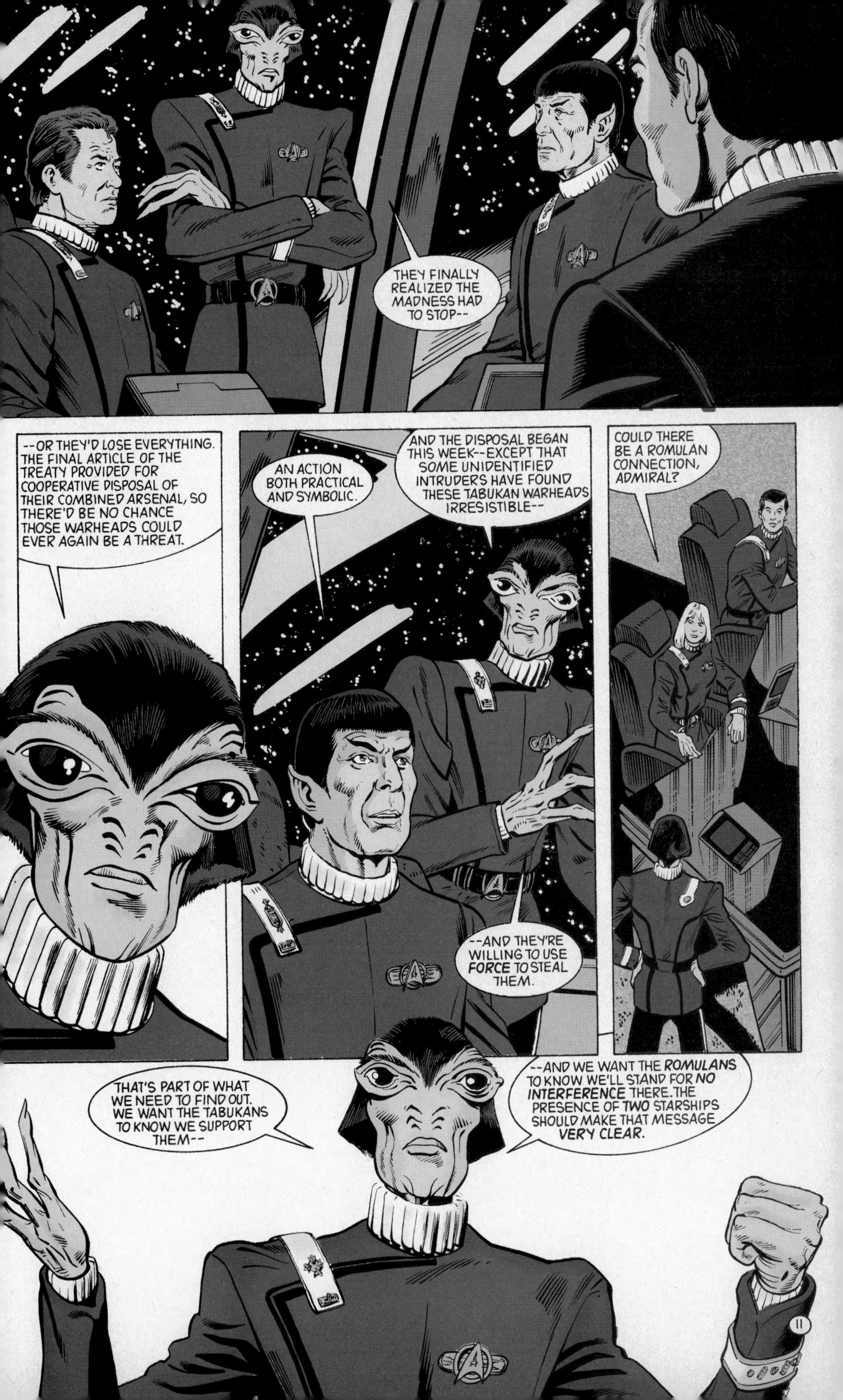
THEY FINALLY REALIZED THE MADNESS HAD TO STOP--
--OR THEY'D LOSE EVERYTHING. THE FINAL ARTICLE OF THE TREATY PROVIDED FOR COOPERATIVE DISPOSAL OF THEIR COMBINED ARSENAL, SO THERE'D BE NO CHANCE THOSE WARHEADS COULD EVER AGAIN BE A THREAT.
AN ACTION BOTH PRACTICAL AND SYMBOLIC.
AND THE DISPOSAL BEGAN THIS WEEK--EXCEPT THAT SOME UNIDENTIFIED INTRUDERS HAVE FOUND THESE TABUKAN WARHEADS IRRESISTIBLE--
--AND THEY'RE WILLING TO USE FORCE TO STEAL THEM.
COULD THERE BE A ROMULAN CONNECTION, ADMIRAL?
THAT'S PART OF WHAT WE NEED TO FIND OUT. WE WANT THE TABUKANS TO KNOW WE SUPPORT THEM--
--AND WE WANT THE ROMULANS TO KNOW WE'LL STAND FOR NO INTERFERENCE THERE. THE PRESENCE OF TWO STARSHIPS SHOULD MAKE THAT MESSAGE VERY CLEAR.
11

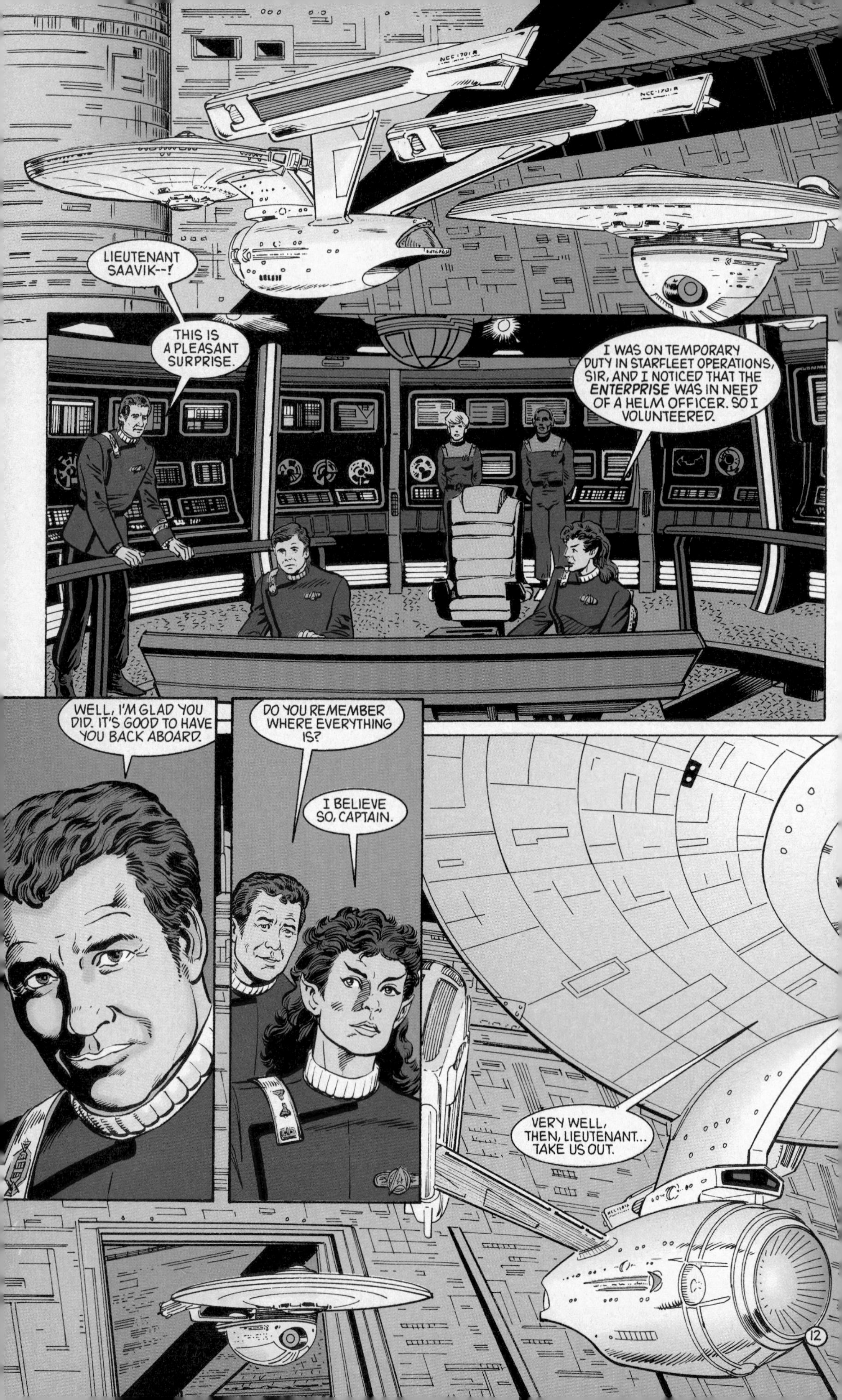
LIEUTENANT SAAVIK--!
THIS IS A PLEASANT SURPRISE.
I WAS ON TEMPORARY DUTY IN STARFLEET OPERATIONS, SIR, AND I NOTICED THAT THE ENTERPRISE WAS IN NEED OF A HELM OFFICER. SO I VOLUNTEERED.
WELL, I'M GLAD YOU DID. IT'S GOOD TO HAVE YOU BACK ABOARD.
DO YOU REMEMBER WHERE EVERYTHING IS?
I BELIEVE SO, CAPTAIN.
VERY WELL, THEN, LIEUTENANT... TAKE US OUT.
12

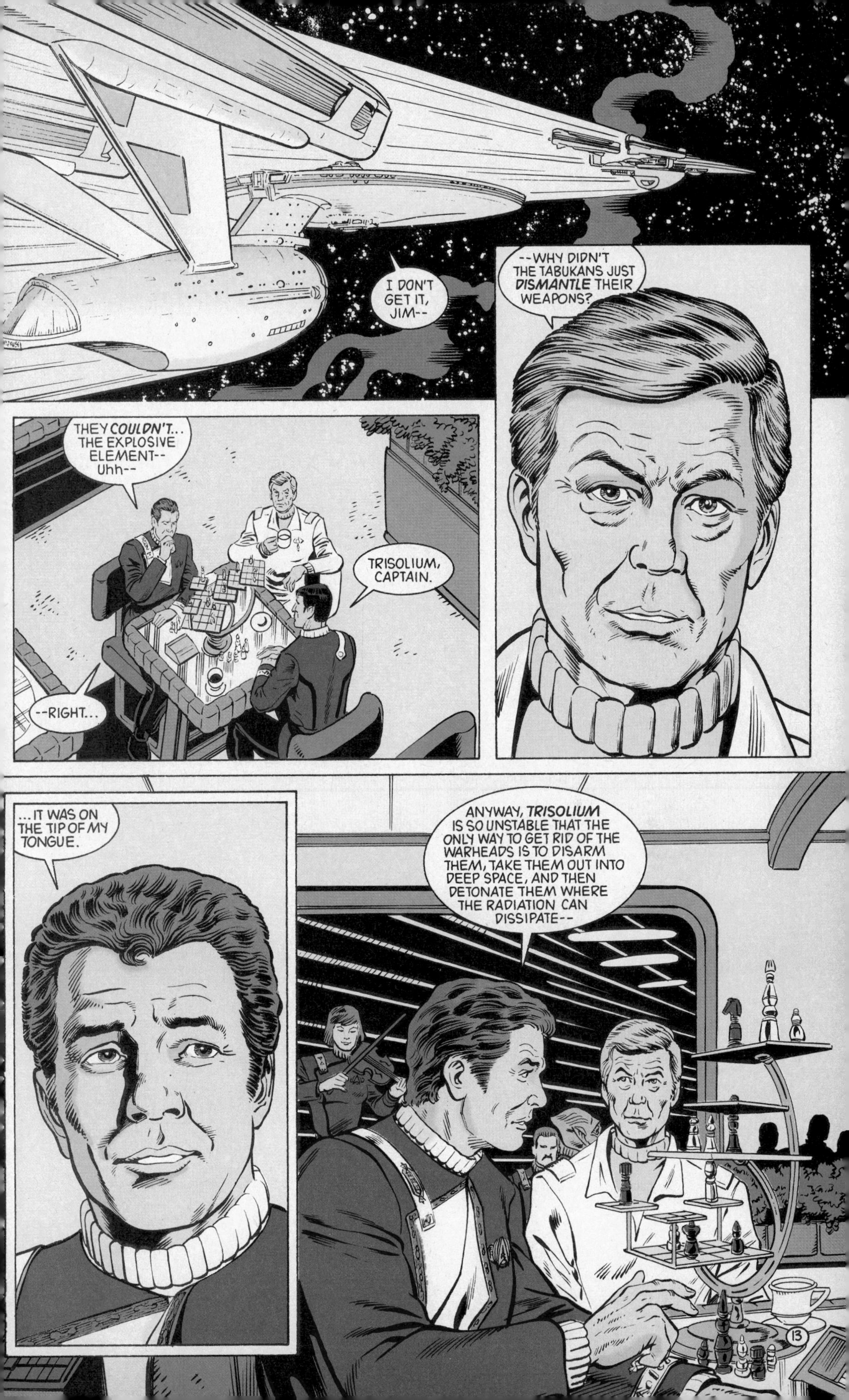
I DON'T GET IT, JIM--
--WHY DIDN'T THE TABUKANS JUST DISMANTLE THEIR WEAPONS?
THEY COULDN'T... THE EXPLOSIVE ELEMENT-- Uhh--
TRISOLIUM, CAPTAIN.
--RIGHT...
...IT WAS ON THE TIP OF MY TONGUE.
ANYWAY, TRISOLIUM IS SO UNSTABLE THAT THE ONLY WAY TO GET RID OF THE WARHEADS IS TO DISARM THEM, TAKE THEM OUT INTO DEEP SPACE, AND THEN DETONATE THEM WHERE THE RADIATION CAN DISSIPATE--
13

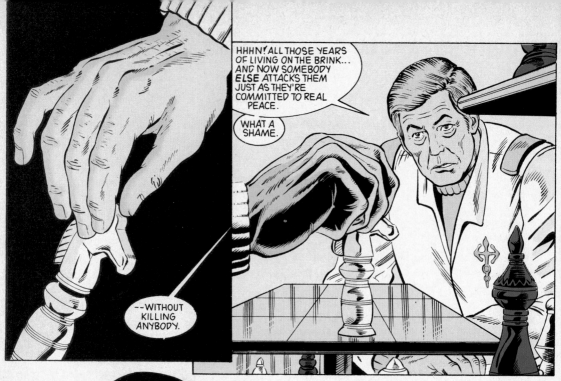

HHHN! ALL THOSE YEARS OF LIVING ON THE BRINK... AND NOW SOMEBODY *ELSE* ATTACKS THEM JUST AS THEY'RE COMMITTED TO REAL PEACE.

WHAT A SHAME.

--WITHOUT KILLING ANYBODY.

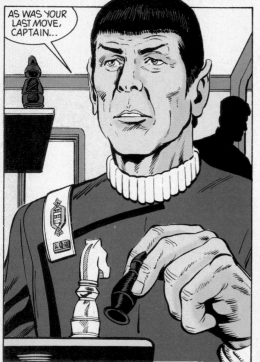

AS WAS YOUR LAST MOVE, CAPTAIN...

...CHECKMATE.

=SIGH= SPOCK...

...ARE YOU *ABSOLUTELY SURE*... IT'S IMPOSSIBLE... FOR VULCANS TO BE...SMUG?

QUITE CERTAIN, CAPTAIN.

WELL, THAT'S A RELIEF.

TOOWHEEOOO

BRIDGE TO CAPTAIN KIRK... WE'VE PICKED UP A MEDICAL DISTRESS CALL FROM A COLONY ON *EPSILON KITAJ*.

14

THE MESSAGE WAS URGENT, AND IT DOES REPEAT...BUT THERE'S NO RESPONSE TO OUR RETURN SIGNAL.

JIM, IT'S A MEDICAL EMERGENCY. WE CAN'T JUST IGNORE IT.

I KNOW THAT, BONES...

WE COULD SPLIT UP, CAPTAIN. EPSILON KITAJ ISN'T MUCH OF A DETOUR--ENTERPRISE CAN CHECK OUT THE SITUATION THERE WHILE EXCELSIOR CONTINUES ON TO TABUK.

I'M NOT SURE I LIKE THE IDEA OF SPLITTING UP, CAPTAIN SULU.

EXCELSIOR CAN KEEP THINGS UNDER CONTROL UNTIL YOU REJOIN US.

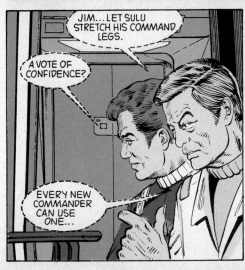

JIM...LET SULU STRETCH HIS COMMAND LEGS.

A VOTE OF CONFIDENCE?

EVERY NEW COMMANDER CAN USE ONE...

ALL RIGHT, CAPTAIN. WE'LL TRY TO KEEP OUR DIVERSION A SHORT ONE. BUT IF THE SITUATION AT TABUK WARRANTS BACK-UP BEFORE WE GET THERE, CALL US.

ACKNOWLEDGED, CAPTAIN KIRK. EXCELSIOR OUT.

15

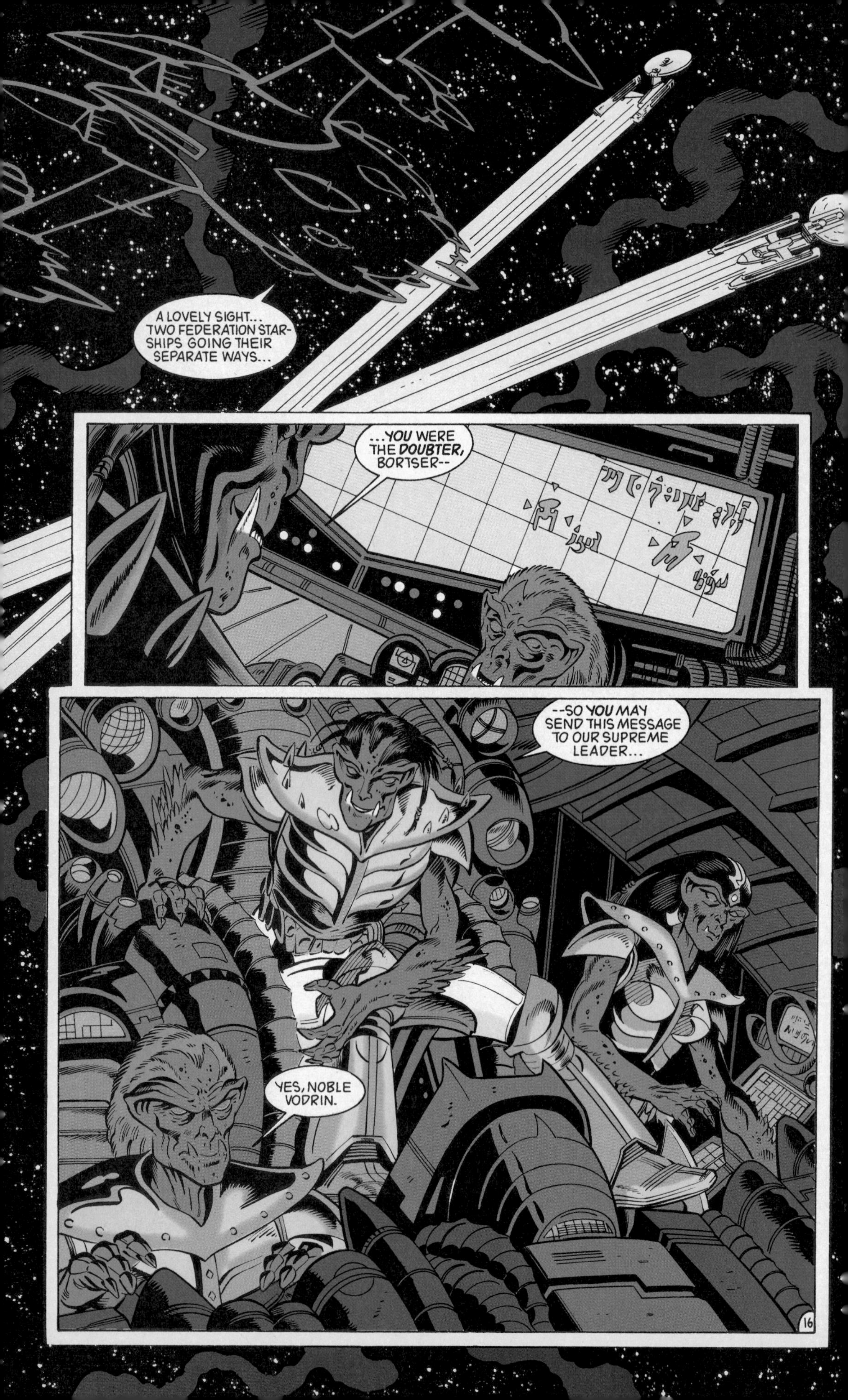
A LOVELY SIGHT... TWO FEDERATION STAR-SHIPS GOING THEIR SEPARATE WAYS...
...YOU WERE THE DOUBTER, BORTSER--
--SO YOU MAY SEND THIS MESSAGE TO OUR SUPREME LEADER...
YES, NOBLE VODRIN.
16

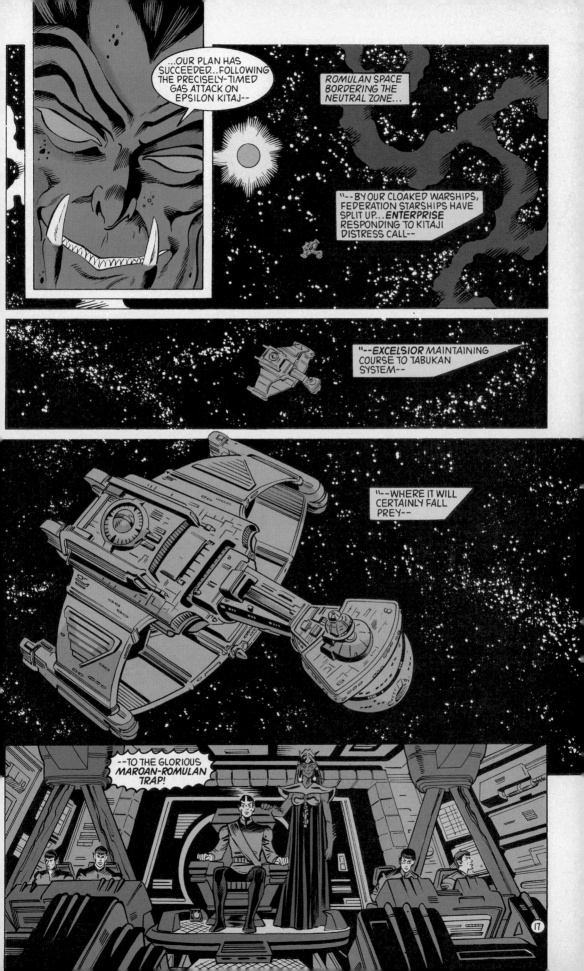

...OUR PLAN HAS SUCCEEDED...FOLLOWING THE PRECISELY-TIMED GAS ATTACK ON EPSILON KITAJ--

ROMULAN SPACE BORDERING THE NEUTRAL ZONE...

"--BY OUR CLOAKED WARSHIPS, FEDERATION STARSHIPS HAVE SPLIT UP...*ENTERPRISE* RESPONDING TO KITAJI DISTRESS CALL--

"--*EXCELSIOR* MAINTAINING COURSE TO TABUKAN SYSTEM--

"--WHERE IT WILL CERTAINLY FALL PREY--

--TO THE GLORIOUS *MAROAN-ROMULAN* TRAP!

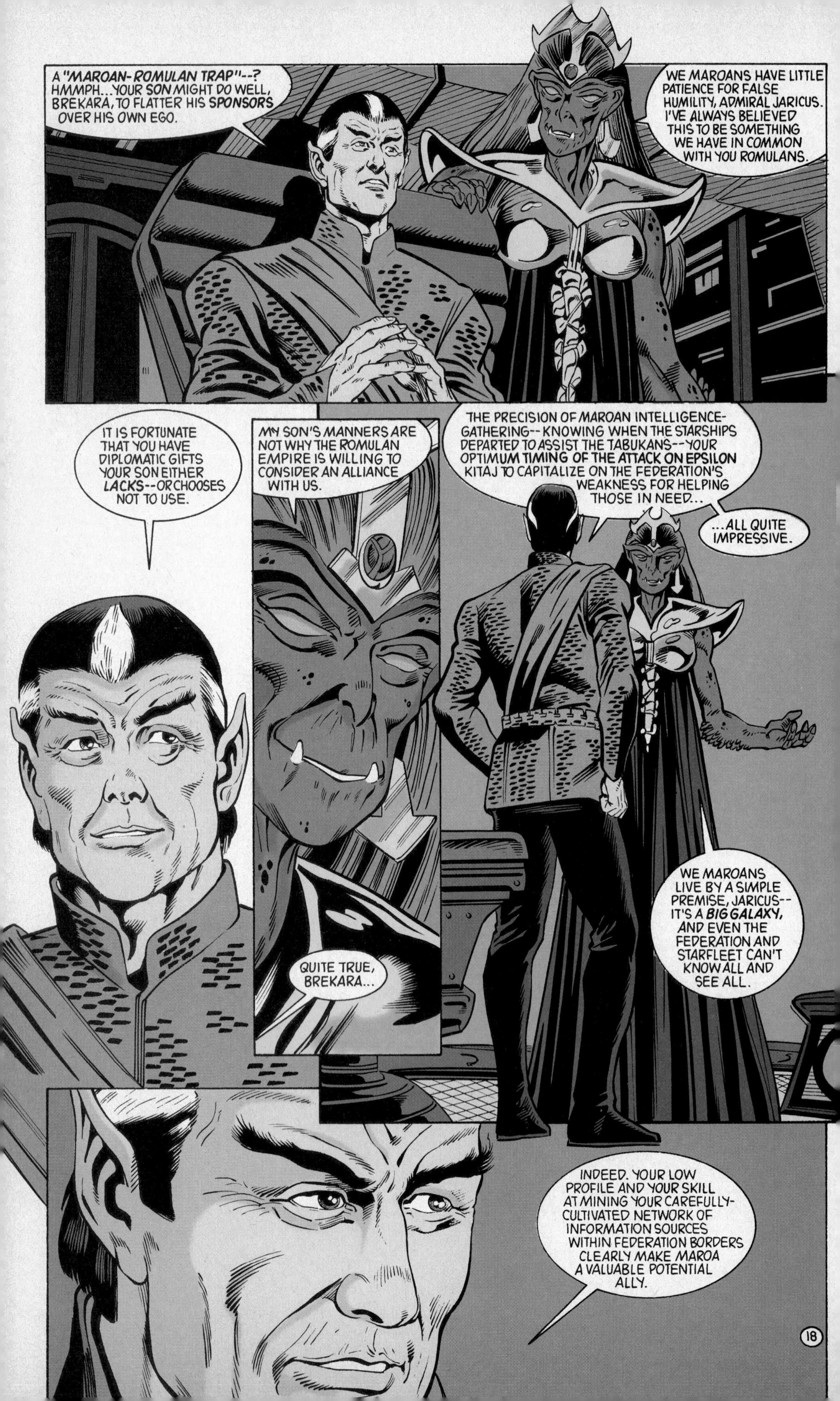
A "MAROAN-ROMULAN TRAP"--? HMMPH... YOUR SON MIGHT DO WELL, BREKARA, TO FLATTER HIS SPONSORS OVER HIS OWN EGO.
WE MAROANS HAVE LITTLE PATIENCE FOR FALSE HUMILITY, ADMIRAL JARICUS. I'VE ALWAYS BELIEVED THIS TO BE SOMETHING WE HAVE IN COMMON WITH YOU ROMULANS.
IT IS FORTUNATE THAT YOU HAVE DIPLOMATIC GIFTS YOUR SON EITHER LACKS--OR CHOOSES NOT TO USE.
MY SON'S MANNERS ARE NOT WHY THE ROMULAN EMPIRE IS WILLING TO CONSIDER AN ALLIANCE WITH US.
QUITE TRUE, BREKARA...
THE PRECISION OF MAROAN INTELLIGENCE-GATHERING--KNOWING WHEN THE STARSHIPS DEPARTED TO ASSIST THE TABUKANS--YOUR OPTIMUM TIMING OF THE ATTACK ON EPSILON KITAJ TO CAPITALIZE ON THE FEDERATION'S WEAKNESS FOR HELPING THOSE IN NEED...
...ALL QUITE IMPRESSIVE.
WE MAROANS LIVE BY A SIMPLE PREMISE, JARICUS--IT'S A BIG GALAXY, AND EVEN THE FEDERATION AND STARFLEET CAN'T KNOW ALL AND SEE ALL.
INDEED. YOUR LOW PROFILE AND YOUR SKILL AT MINING YOUR CAREFULLY-CULTIVATED NETWORK OF INFORMATION SOURCES WITHIN FEDERATION BORDERS CLEARLY MAKE MAROA A VALUABLE POTENTIAL ALLY.

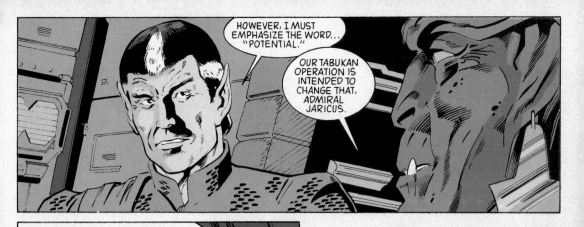

HOWEVER, I MUST EMPHASIZE THE WORD... "POTENTIAL."

OUR TABUKAN OPERATION IS INTENDED TO CHANGE THAT, ADMIRAL JARICUS.

WE SHALL SEE. IF YOU SUCCESSFULLY STEAL THESE TABUKAN WEAPONS--WHILE KEEPING YOUR IDENTITY SECRET--YOU'LL HAVE SHOWN AN ABILITY TO PLAN *AND* CARRY OUT A MAJOR COVERT OPERATION--

--RIGHT UNDER THE FEDERATION'S NOSE. WILL THAT CONVINCE THE ROMULAN IMPERIAL COUNCIL OF OUR WORTH?

QUITE LIKELY...QUITE LIKELY.

A TOAST, THEN.

TO OUR COURTSHIP--

--AND A LONG AND *FRUITFUL* RELATIONSHIP.

19

BUT NOBLE VODRIN--! YOUR MOTHER ORDERED US TO RETURN TO THE TABUKAN SYSTEM AT ONCE!

AND THOSE ORDERS ARE SUBJECT TO MY INTERPRETATION AND JUDGMENT--ARE THEY NOT, SUB-MARSHAL TRIN?

YES, SIR. BUT--

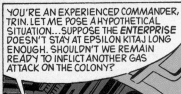

YOU'RE AN EXPERIENCED COMMANDER, TRIN. LET ME POSE A HYPOTHETICAL SITUATION...SUPPOSE THE ENTERPRISE DOESN'T STAY AT EPSILON KITAJ LONG ENOUGH. SHOULDN'T WE REMAIN READY TO INFLICT ANOTHER GAS ATTACK ON THE COLONY?

BUT OUR FOUR SMALL SHIPS CAN'T BATTLE A STARSHIP, NOBLE VODRIN--!

WE WON'T HAVE TO. WE HAVE THE CLOAKING FIELD, AND THE ELEMENT OF SURPRISE. HERE IS WHERE WE MAY BE MOST NEEDED...

20

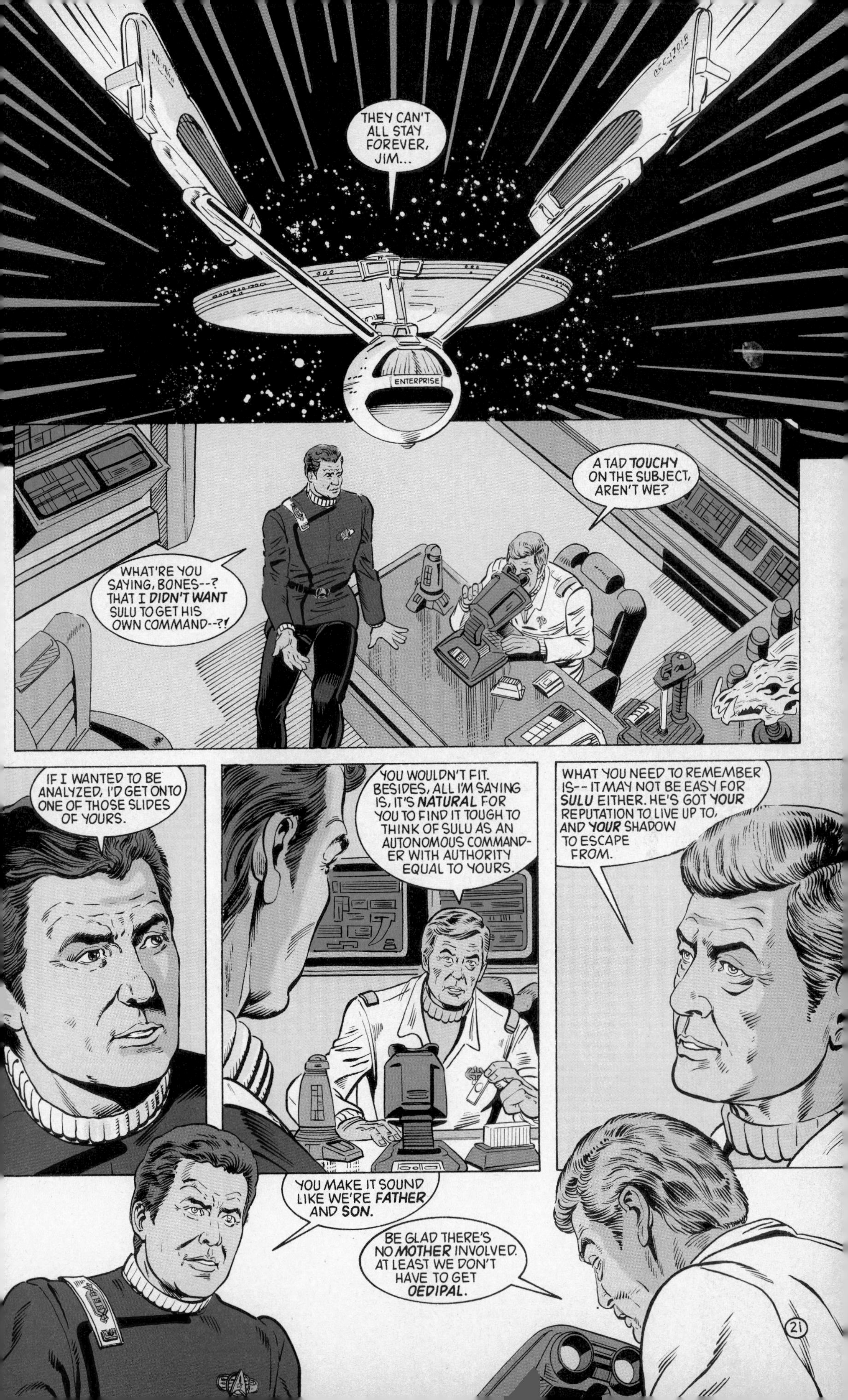
THEY CAN'T ALL STAY FOREVER, JIM...
ENTERPRISE
A TAD TOUCHY ON THE SUBJECT, AREN'T WE?
WHAT'RE YOU SAYING, BONES--? THAT I DIDN'T WANT SULU TO GET HIS OWN COMMAND--?!
IF I WANTED TO BE ANALYZED, I'D GET ONTO ONE OF THOSE SLIDES OF YOURS.
YOU WOULDN'T FIT. BESIDES, ALL I'M SAYING IS, IT'S NATURAL FOR YOU TO FIND IT TOUGH TO THINK OF SULU AS AN AUTONOMOUS COMMANDER WITH AUTHORITY EQUAL TO YOURS.
WHAT YOU NEED TO REMEMBER IS-- IT MAY NOT BE EASY FOR SULU EITHER. HE'S GOT YOUR REPUTATION TO LIVE UP TO, AND YOUR SHADOW TO ESCAPE FROM.
YOU MAKE IT SOUND LIKE WE'RE FATHER AND SON.
BE GLAD THERE'S NO MOTHER INVOLVED. AT LEAST WE DON'T HAVE TO GET OEDIPAL.

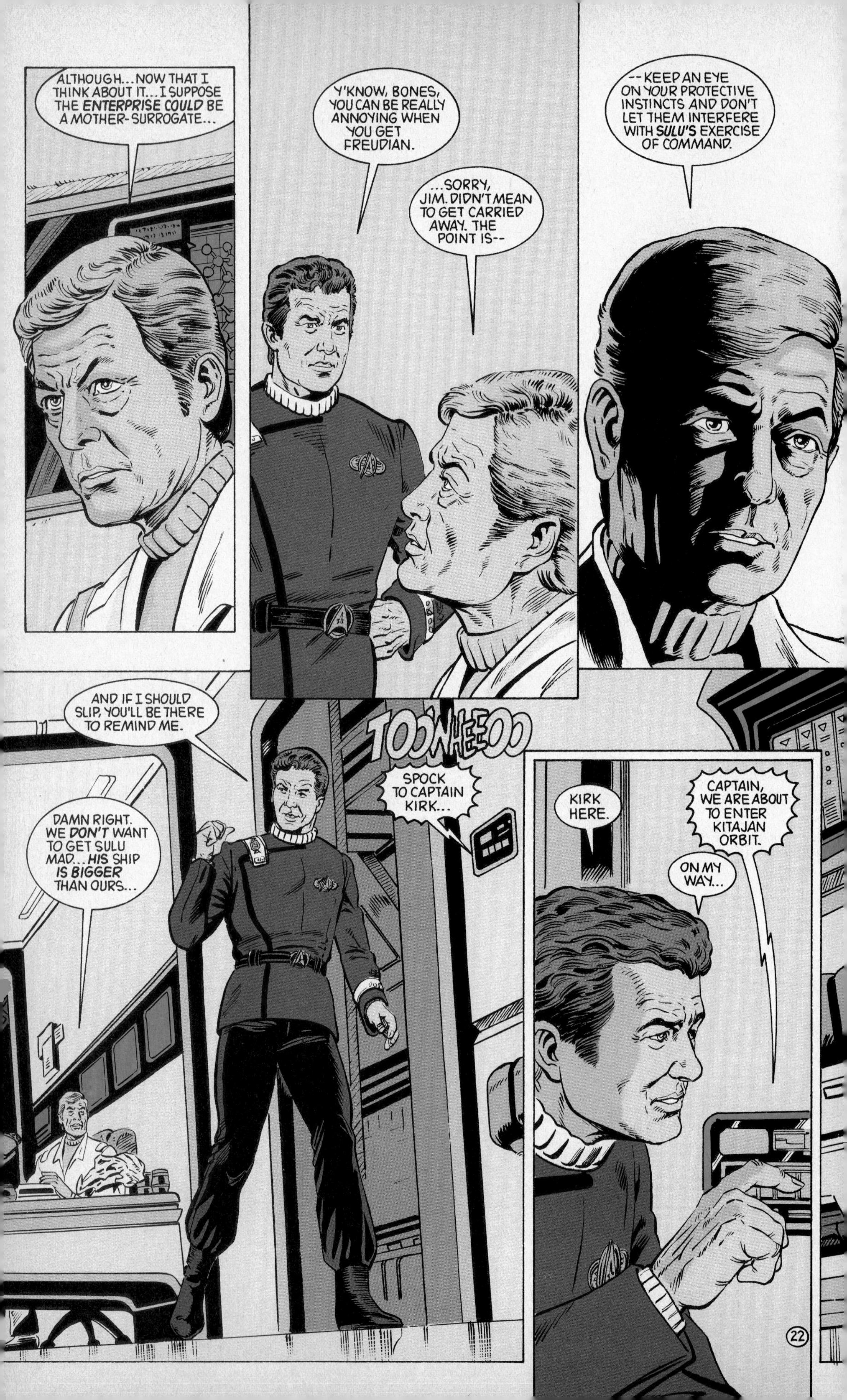
ALTHOUGH... NOW THAT I THINK ABOUT IT... I SUPPOSE THE ENTERPRISE COULD BE A MOTHER-SURROGATE...
Y'KNOW, BONES, YOU CAN BE REALLY ANNOYING WHEN YOU GET FREUDIAN.
...SORRY, JIM. DIDN'T MEAN TO GET CARRIED AWAY. THE POINT IS--
--KEEP AN EYE ON YOUR PROTECTIVE INSTINCTS AND DON'T LET THEM INTERFERE WITH SULU'S EXERCISE OF COMMAND.
AND IF I SHOULD SLIP, YOU'LL BE THERE TO REMIND ME.
DAMN RIGHT. WE DON'T WANT TO GET SULU MAD... HIS SHIP IS BIGGER THAN OURS...
TOONHEEOO
SPOCK TO CAPTAIN KIRK...
KIRK HERE.
CAPTAIN, WE ARE ABOUT TO ENTER KITAJAN ORBIT.
ON MY WAY...
22

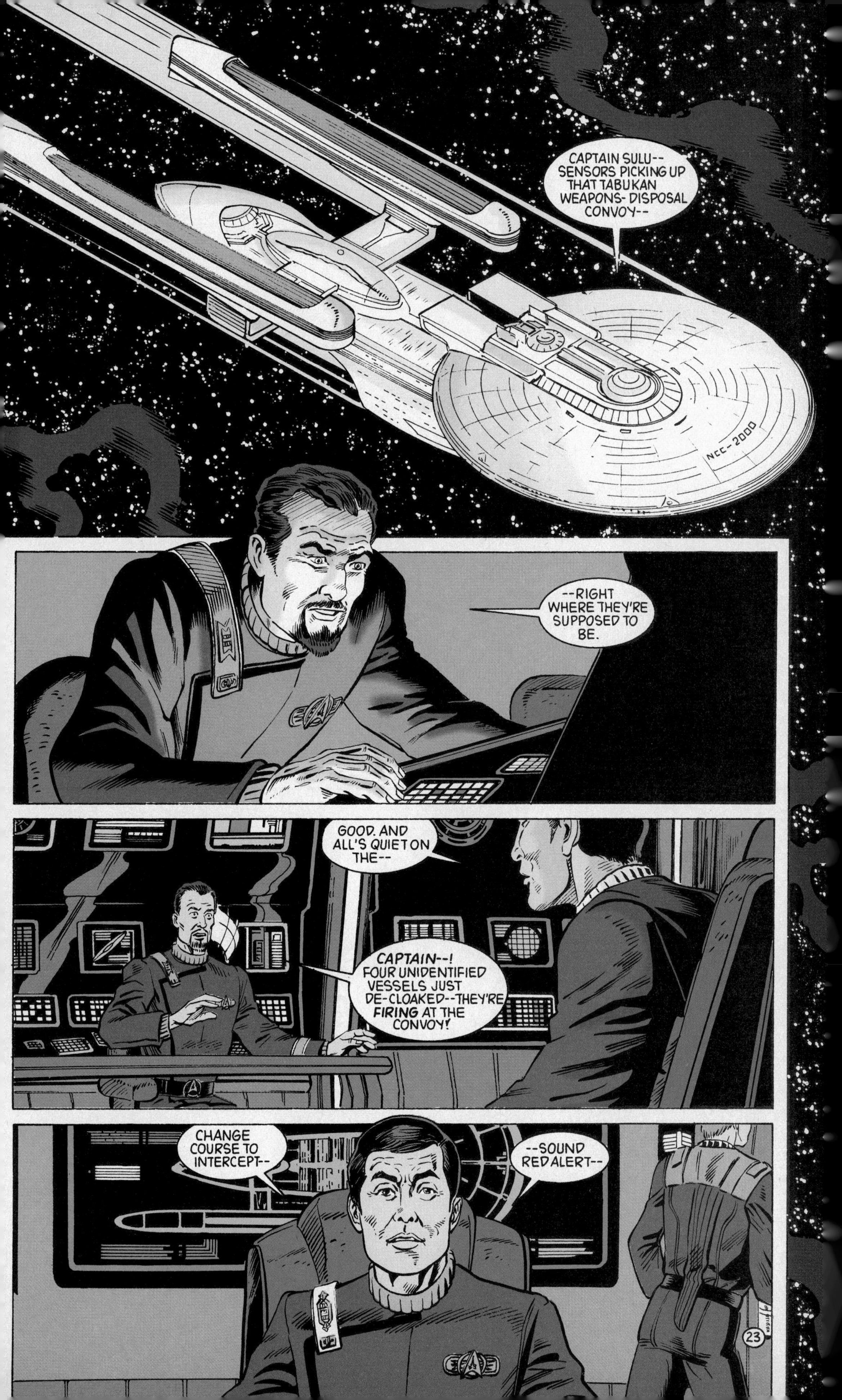
CAPTAIN SULU-- SENSORS PICKING UP THAT TABUKAN WEAPONS- DISPOSAL CONVOY--
NCC-2000
--RIGHT WHERE THEY'RE SUPPOSED TO BE.
GOOD. AND ALL'S QUIET ON THE--
CAPTAIN--! FOUR UNIDENTIFIED VESSELS JUST DE-CLOAKED--THEY'RE FIRING AT THE CONVOY!
CHANGE COURSE TO INTERCEPT--
--SOUND RED ALERT--
23

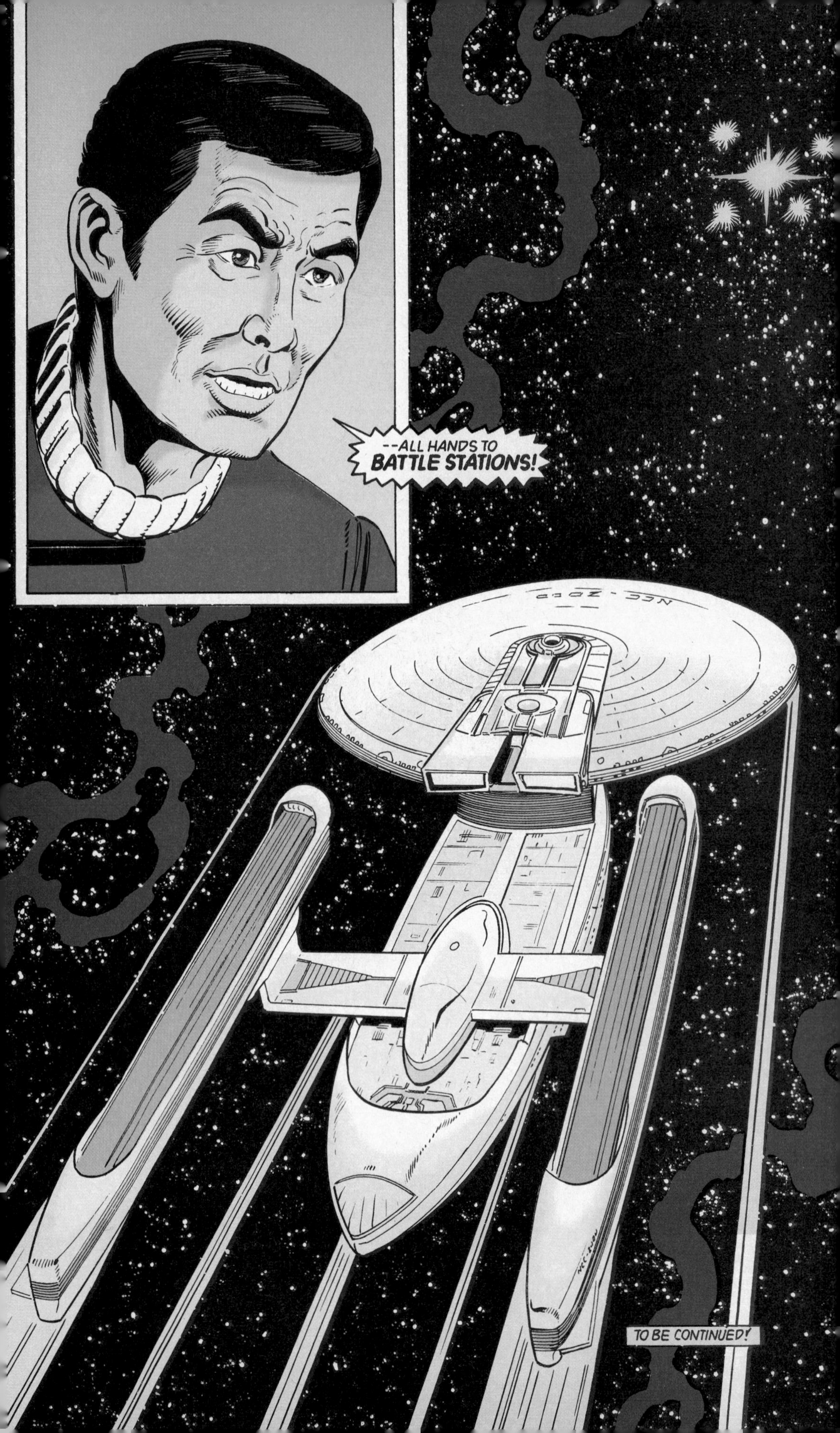
--ALL HANDS TO
BATTLE STATIONS!
TO BE CONTINUED!

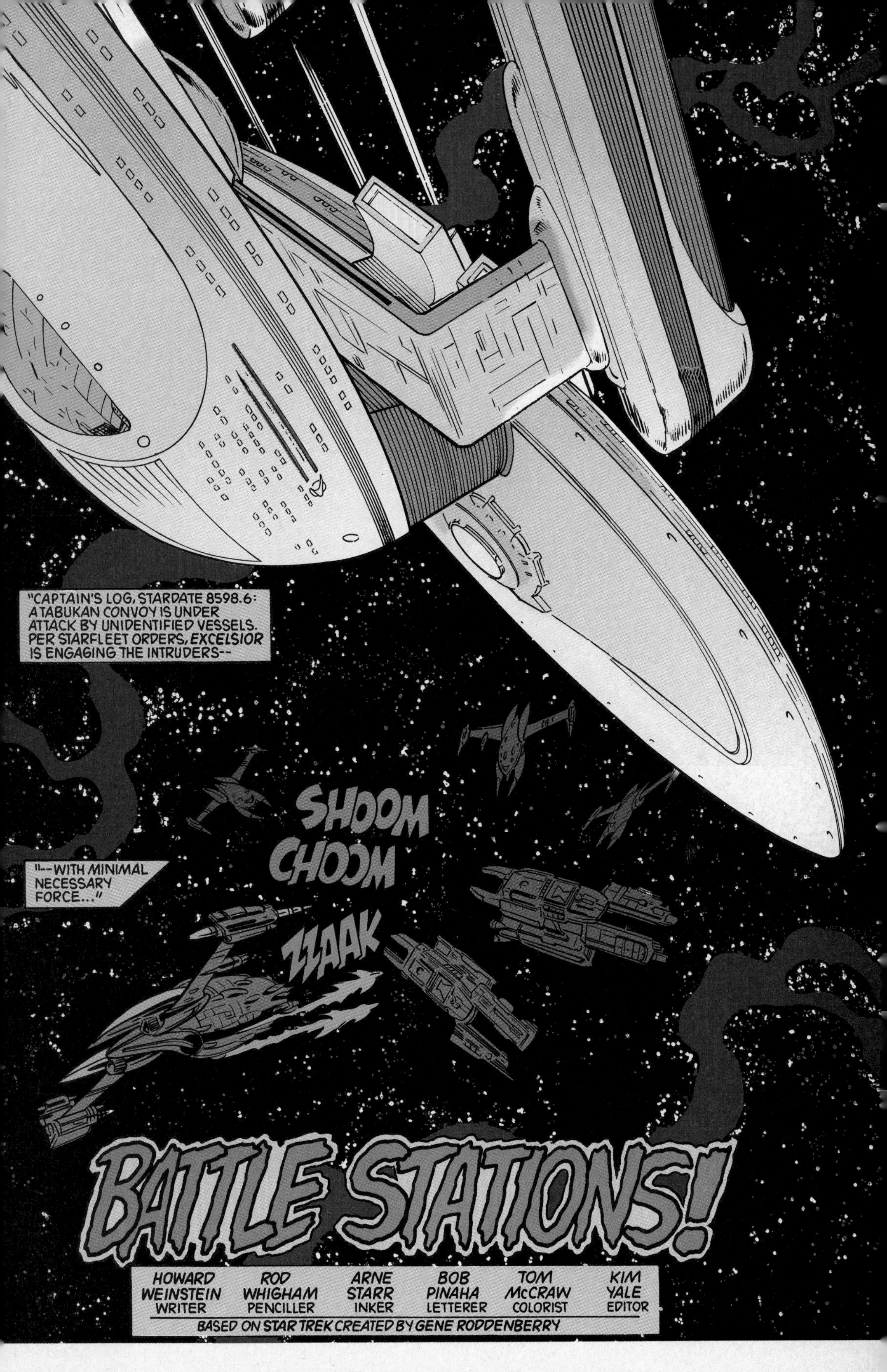
"CAPTAIN'S LOG, STARDATE 8598.6: ATABUKAN CONVOY IS UNDER ATTACK BY UNIDENTIFIED VESSELS. PER STARFLEET ORDERS, EXCELSIOR IS ENGAGING THE INTRUDERS--
"--WITH MINIMAL NECESSARY FORCE..."
SHOOM
CHOOM
ZZAAK
BATTLE STATIONS!
HOWARD WEINSTEIN WRITER
ROD WHIGHAM PENCILLER
ARNE STARR INKER
BOB PINAHA LETTERER
TOM McCRAW COLORIST
KIM YALE EDITOR
BASED ON STAR TREK CREATED BY GENE RODDENBERRY

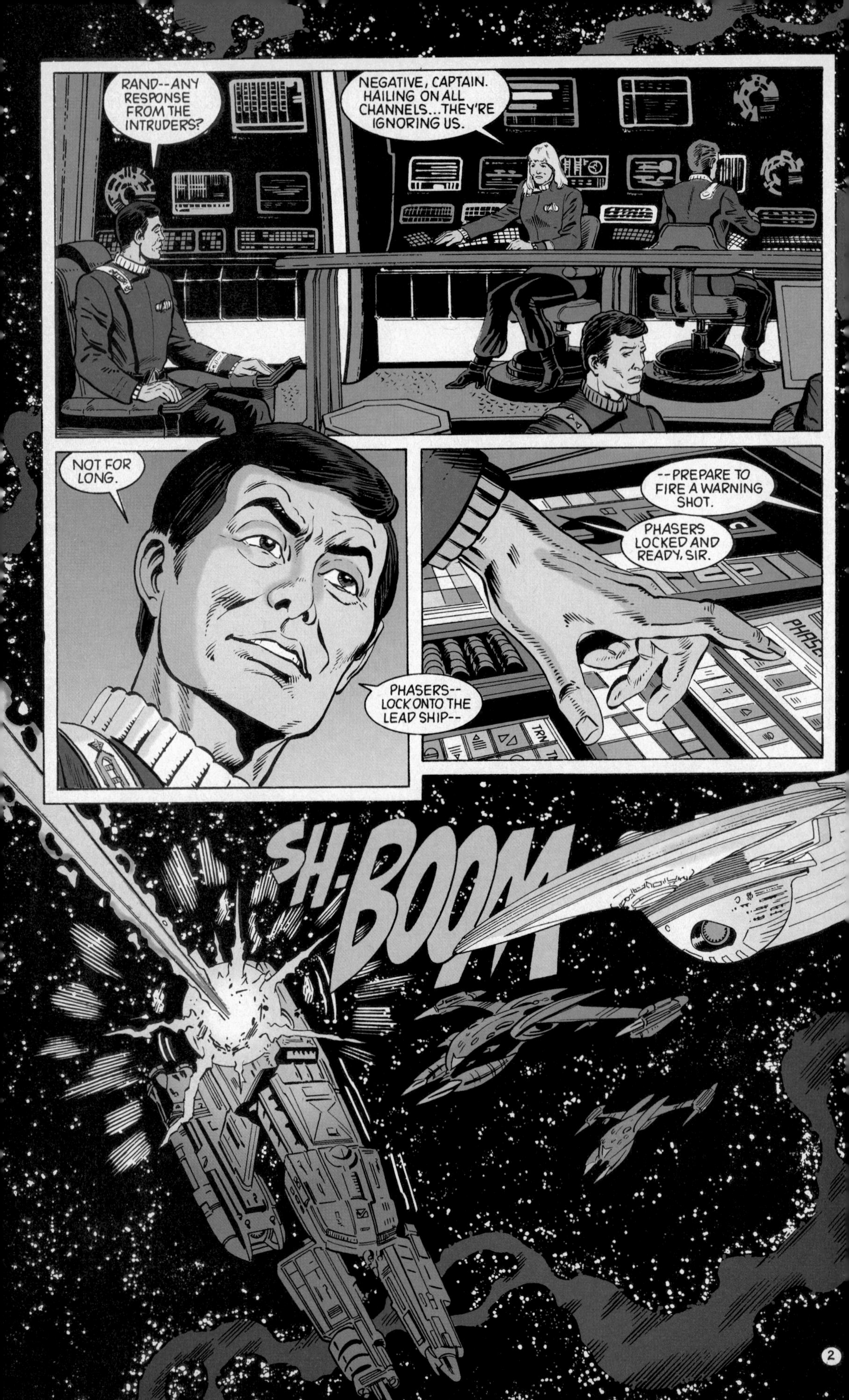
RAND--ANY RESPONSE FROM THE INTRUDERS?
NEGATIVE, CAPTAIN. HAILING ON ALL CHANNELS...THEY'RE IGNORING US.
NOT FOR LONG.
PHASERS-- LOCK ONTO THE LEAD SHIP--
--PREPARE TO FIRE A WARNING SHOT.
PHASERS LOCKED AND READY, SIR.
SH-BOOM

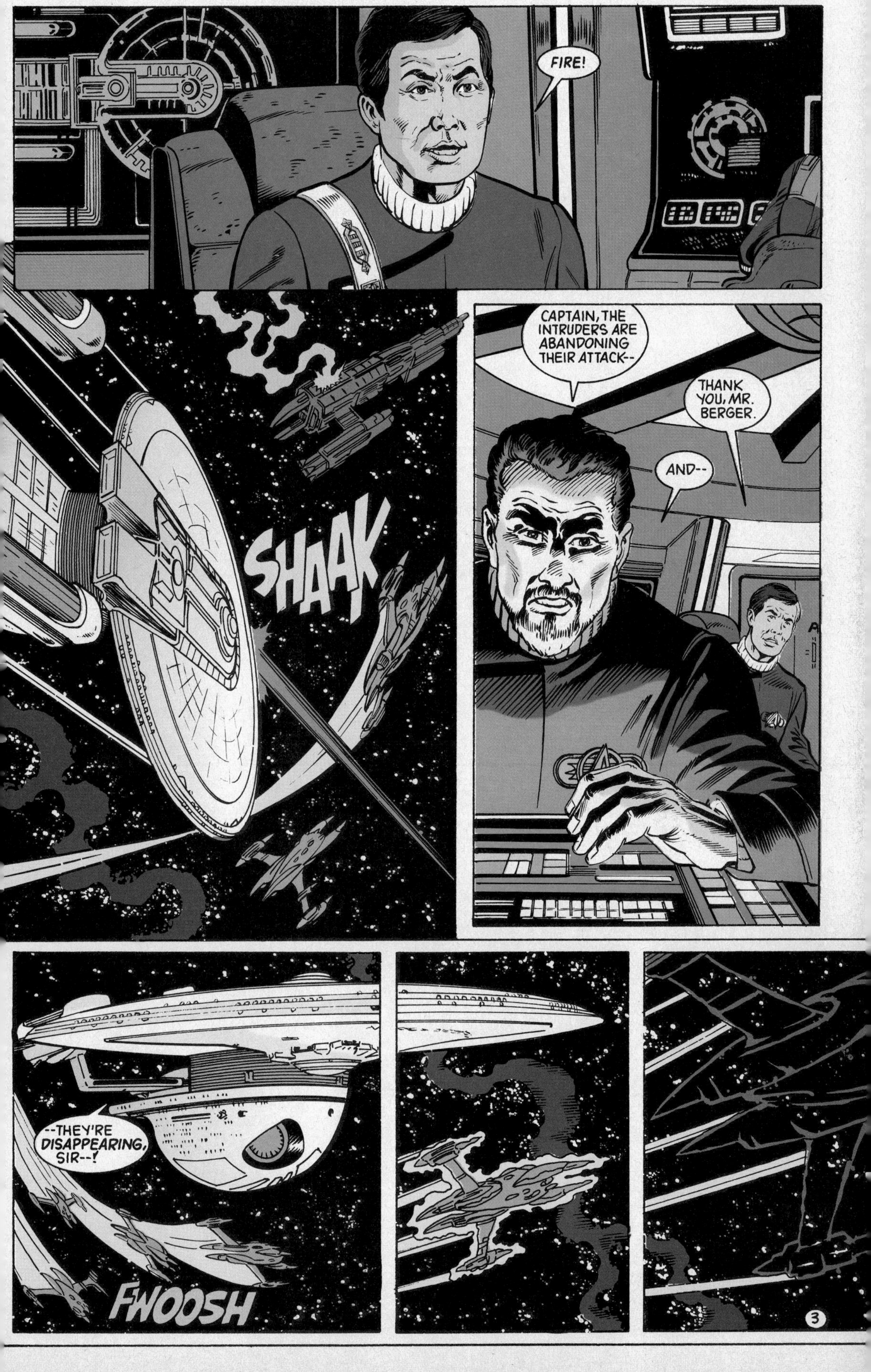
FIRE!
CAPTAIN, THE INTRUDERS ARE ABANDONING THEIR ATTACK--
THANK YOU, MR. BERGER.
AND--
SHAAK
--THEY'RE DISAPPEARING, SIR--!
FWOOSH

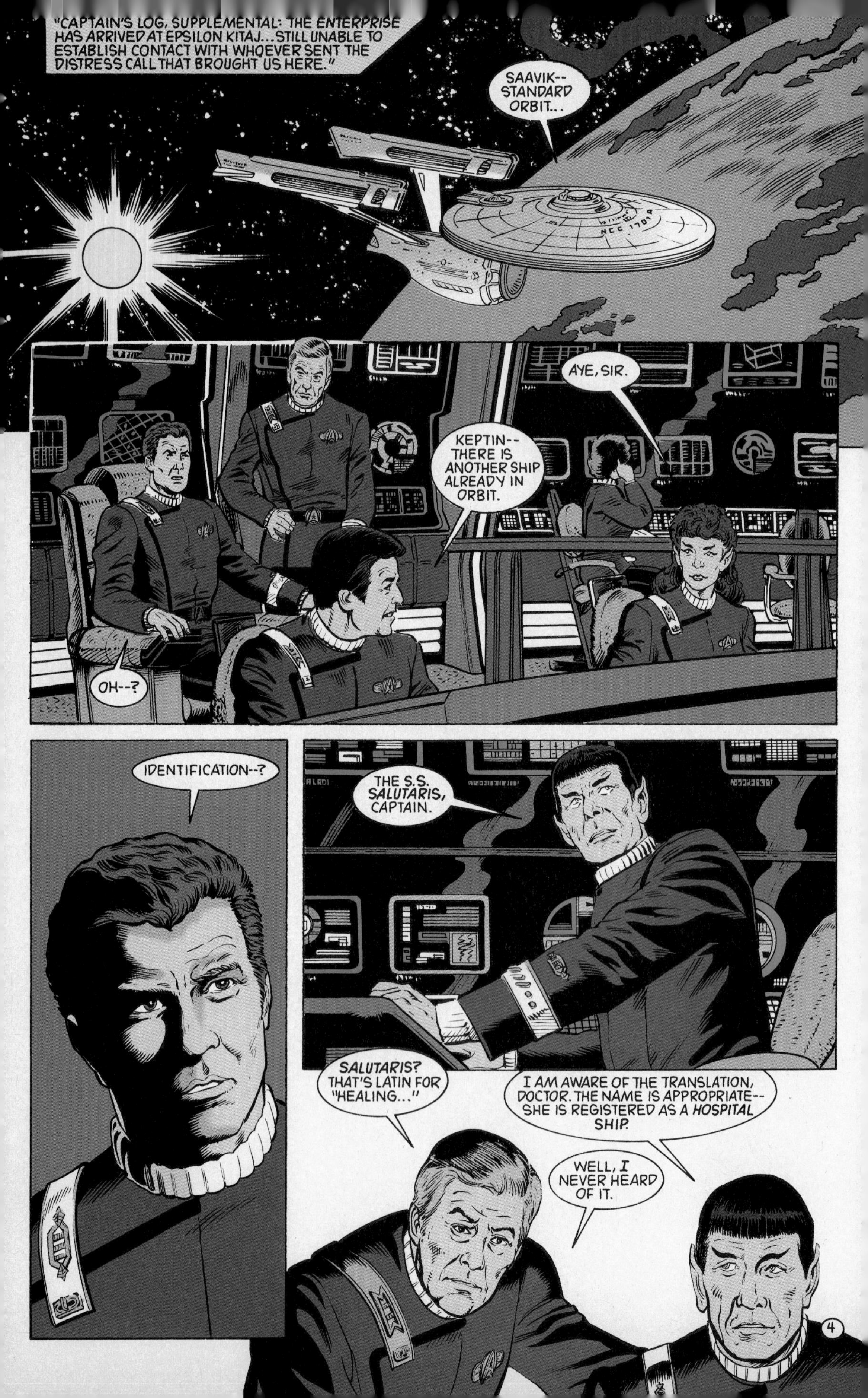
"CAPTAIN'S LOG, SUPPLEMENTAL: THE ENTERPRISE HAS ARRIVED AT EPSILON KITAJ... STILL UNABLE TO ESTABLISH CONTACT WITH WHOEVER SENT THE DISTRESS CALL THAT BROUGHT US HERE."
SAAVIK-- STANDARD ORBIT...
NCC-1701-A
AYE, SIR.
KEPTIN-- THERE IS ANOTHER SHIP ALREADY IN ORBIT.
OH--?
IDENTIFICATION--?
THE S.S. SALUTARIS, CAPTAIN.
SALUTARIS? THAT'S LATIN FOR "HEALING..."
I AM AWARE OF THE TRANSLATION, DOCTOR. THE NAME IS APPROPRIATE-- SHE IS REGISTERED AS A HOSPITAL SHIP.
WELL, I NEVER HEARD OF IT.
4

NEITHER HAVE I. WHAT DO WE KNOW ABOUT THIS *HOSPITAL* SHIP, SPOCK?

THE *SALUTARIS* IS A CONVERTED CLARKE CLASS SCIENCE-EXPLORATION VESSEL, FORMERLY REGISTERED AS THE *BENJAMIN FRANKLIN*...

...DECOMMISSIONED TEN YEARS AGO, THEN PURCHASED BY A GROUP OF PRIVATE INVESTORS SEVEN YEARS AGO...AND REFITTED AS A MEDICAL-SERVICES SHIP.

THEY MUST'VE HEARD THE SAME DISTRESS CALL WE DID.

THEN MAYBE HER CAPTAIN CAN FILL US IN ON WHAT'S GOING ON. WHO'S IN COMMAND?

MOST INTERESTING...

...THE LISTED *COMMANDING OFFICER* IS A *PHYSICIAN*--

--DR. *ABIGAIL WILSON.*

DID YOU SAY-- *ABBY WILSON*--?!

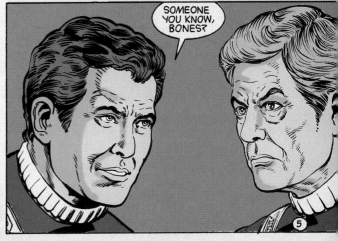

SOMEONE YOU KNOW, BONES?

5

EXCELLENT WORK, MR. BERGER.

IT WASN'T EASY TO SPOT, CAPTAIN--BUT IT *WAS* THERE--ONCE WE FIGURED OUT WHAT TO LOOK FOR.

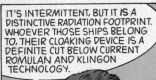

IT'S INTERMITTENT, BUT IT *IS* A DISTINCTIVE RADIATION FOOTPRINT. WHOEVER THOSE SHIPS BELONG TO, THEIR CLOAKING DEVICE IS A DEFINITE CUT BELOW CURRENT ROMULAN AND KLINGON TECHNOLOGY.

OUR GOOD NEWS FOR THE DAY.

NOT AS GOOD AS WE MIGHT LIKE, COMMANDER. THIS GIVES US A *POTENTIAL* TOOL FOR TRACKING THESE GUYS, BUT IT'S *FAR* FROM *FOOLPROOF*...

...AND WE STILL DON'T HAVE A CLUE ABOUT *WHO* THEY *ARE.*

BUT WE DO HAVE A CLUE AS TO WHO THEY *AREN'T.* WITH SECOND-RATE CLOAKING TECHNOLOGY--

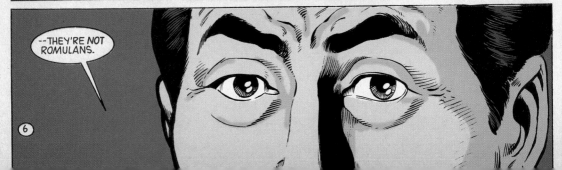

--THEY'RE NOT ROMULANS.

ROMULAN SURROGATES, THEN? THERE'S A LOT OF NON-ALIGNED SPACE AROUND THE TABUKAN SYSTEM--OUTSIDE THE NEUTRAL ZONE--

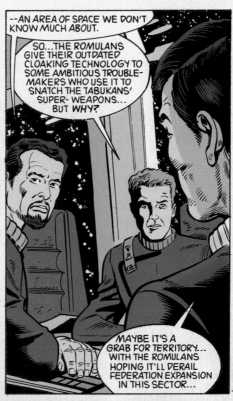

--AN AREA OF SPACE WE DON'T KNOW MUCH ABOUT.

SO...THE ROMULANS GIVE THEIR OUTDATED CLOAKING TECHNOLOGY TO SOME AMBITIOUS TROUBLE-MAKERS WHO USE IT TO SNATCH THE TABUKANS' SUPER- WEAPONS... BUT WHY?

MAYBE IT'S A GRAB FOR TERRITORY... WITH THE ROMULANS HOPING IT'LL DERAIL FEDERATION EXPANSION IN THIS SECTOR...

...AND ALL WITHOUT LEAVING ANY FINGER-PRINTS THAT POINT TO THE ROMULANS.

...AN INTERESTING THEORY...

...BUT WE NEED PROOF. LET'S HOPE WE CAN GET IT WITHOUT GETTING INTO A WAR.

TOO-WHEE-OOO

BRIDGE TO CAPTAIN SULU.

SULU HERE.

SIGNAL FROM THE TABUKANS, SIR... PRESIDENT SODRIDJ AND DEPUTY GEFION ARE READY TO TRANSPORT.

GOOD. HAVE THEM BEAMED ABOARD AND ESCORTED TO THE MAIN BRIEFING LOUNGE.

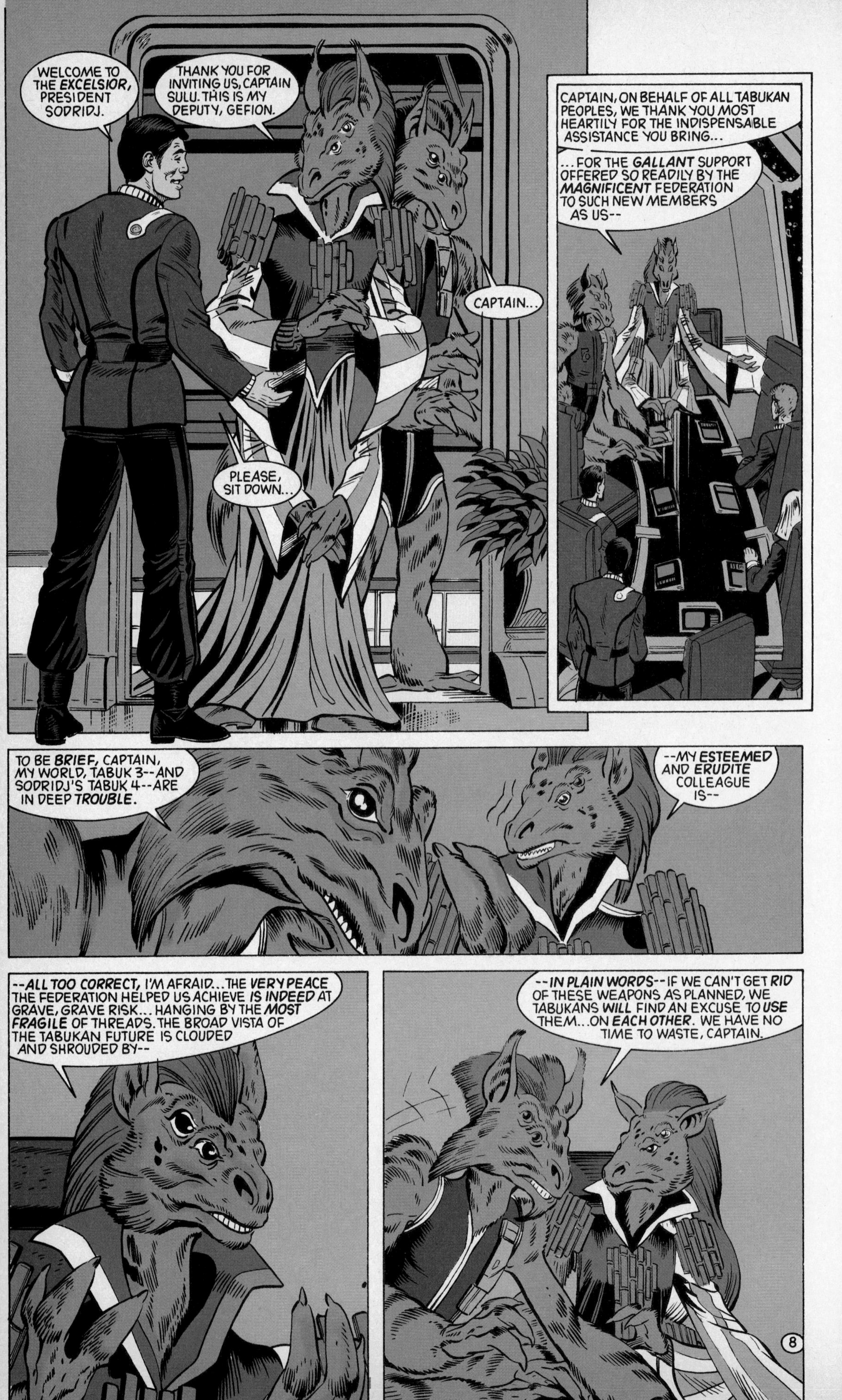
WELCOME TO THE *EXCELSIOR*, PRESIDENT SODRIDJ.
THANK YOU FOR INVITING US, CAPTAIN SULU. THIS IS MY DEPUTY, GEFION.
CAPTAIN...
PLEASE, SIT DOWN...
CAPTAIN, ON BEHALF OF ALL TABUKAN PEOPLES, WE THANK YOU MOST HEARTILY FOR THE INDISPENSABLE ASSISTANCE YOU BRING...
...FOR THE *GALLANT* SUPPORT OFFERED SO READILY BY THE *MAGNIFICENT* FEDERATION TO SUCH NEW MEMBERS AS US--
TO BE *BRIEF*, CAPTAIN, MY WORLD, TABUK 3--AND SODRIDJ'S TABUK 4--ARE IN DEEP *TROUBLE*.
--MY *ESTEEMED* AND *ERUDITE* COLLEAGUE IS--
--*ALL TOO CORRECT*, I'M AFRAID...THE *VERY PEACE* THE FEDERATION HELPED US ACHIEVE *IS INDEED* AT GRAVE, GRAVE RISK... HANGING BY THE *MOST FRAGILE* OF THREADS. THE BROAD VISTA OF THE TABUKAN FUTURE IS CLOUDED AND SHROUDED BY--
--*IN PLAIN WORDS*--IF WE CAN'T GET *RID* OF THESE WEAPONS AS PLANNED, WE TABUKANS *WILL* FIND AN EXCUSE TO *USE* THEM...ON *EACH OTHER*. WE HAVE NO TIME TO WASTE, CAPTAIN.

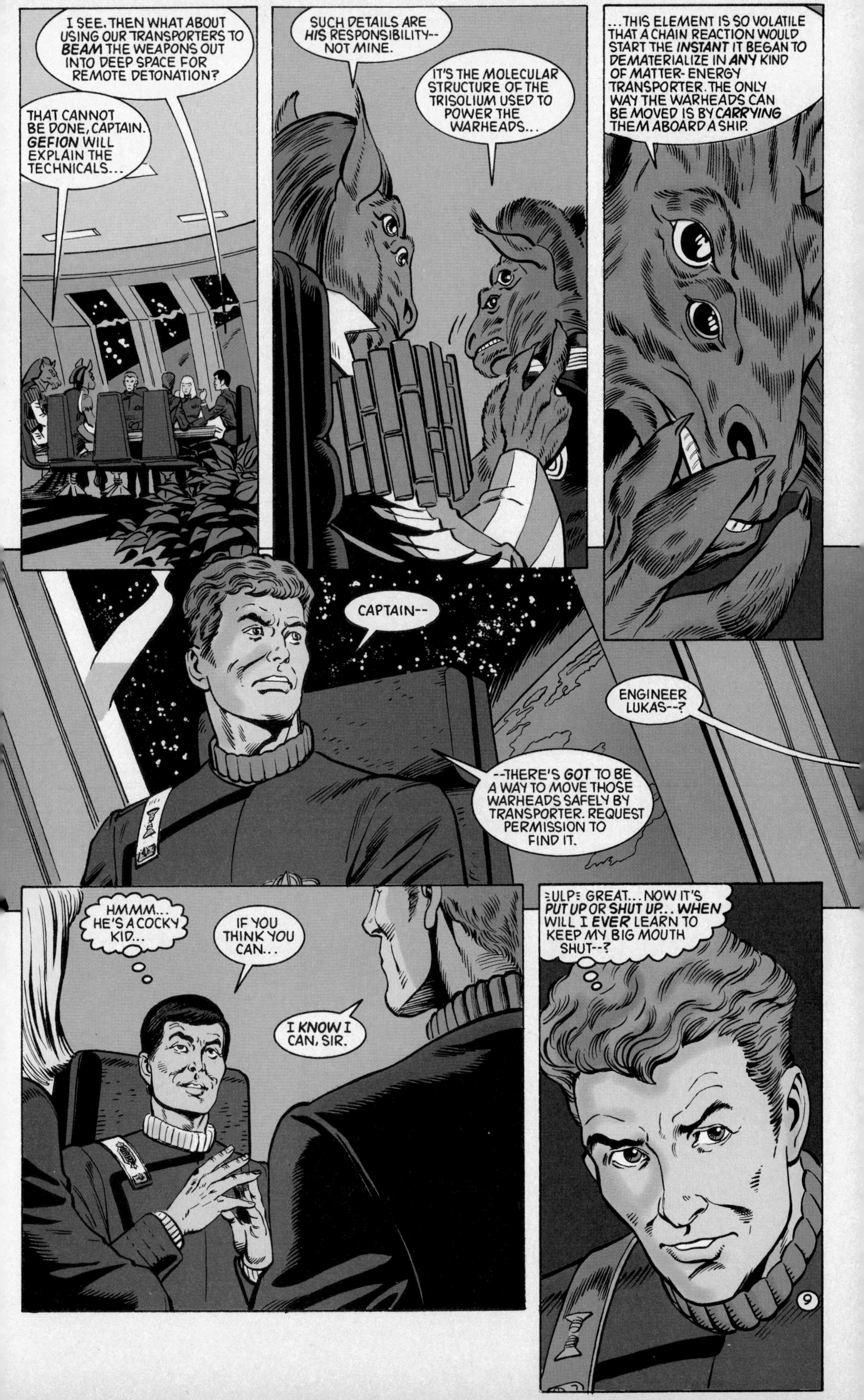
I SEE. THEN WHAT ABOUT USING OUR TRANSPORTERS TO BEAM THE WEAPONS OUT INTO DEEP SPACE FOR REMOTE DETONATION?
THAT CANNOT BE DONE, CAPTAIN. GEFION WILL EXPLAIN THE TECHNICALS...
SUCH DETAILS ARE HIS RESPONSIBILITY-- NOT MINE.
IT'S THE MOLECULAR STRUCTURE OF THE TRISOLIUM USED TO POWER THE WARHEADS...
...THIS ELEMENT IS SO VOLATILE THAT A CHAIN REACTION WOULD START THE INSTANT IT BEGAN TO DEMATERIALIZE IN ANY KIND OF MATTER-ENERGY TRANSPORTER. THE ONLY WAY THE WARHEADS CAN BE MOVED IS BY CARRYING THEM ABOARD A SHIP.
CAPTAIN--
ENGINEER LUKAS--?
--THERE'S GOT TO BE A WAY TO MOVE THOSE WARHEADS SAFELY BY TRANSPORTER. REQUEST PERMISSION TO FIND IT.
HMMM... HE'S A COCKY KID...
IF YOU THINK YOU CAN...
I KNOW I CAN, SIR.
=ULP= GREAT... NOW IT'S PUT UP OR SHUT UP... WHEN WILL I EVER LEARN TO KEEP MY BIG MOUTH SHUT--?
9

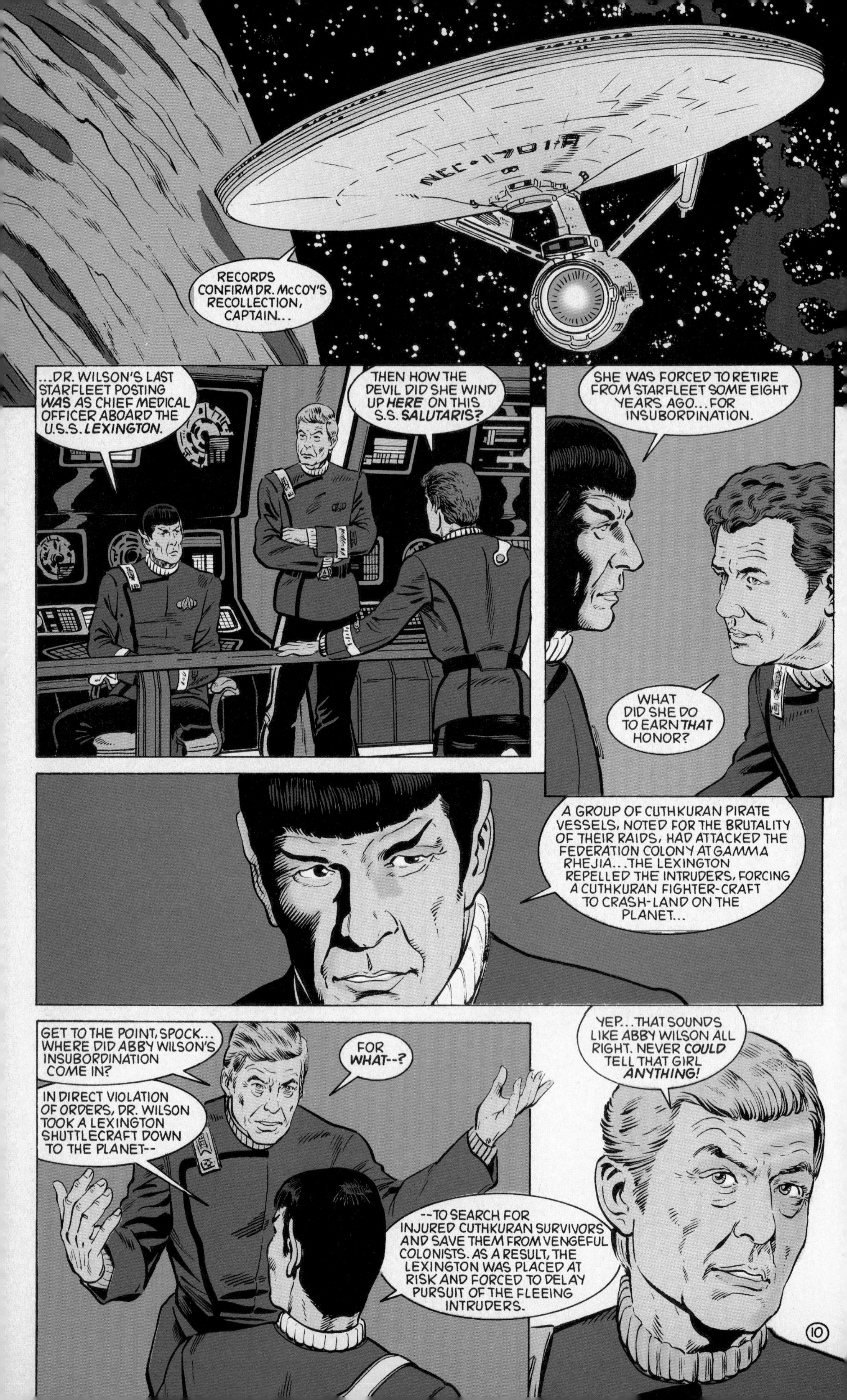

RECORDS CONFIRM DR. McCOY'S RECOLLECTION, CAPTAIN...
...DR. WILSON'S LAST STARFLEET POSTING WAS AS CHIEF MEDICAL OFFICER ABOARD THE U.S.S. LEXINGTON.
THEN HOW THE DEVIL DID SHE WIND UP HERE ON THIS S.S. SALUTARIS?
SHE WAS FORCED TO RETIRE FROM STARFLEET SOME EIGHT YEARS AGO... FOR INSUBORDINATION.
WHAT DID SHE DO TO EARN THAT HONOR?
A GROUP OF CUTHKURAN PIRATE VESSELS, NOTED FOR THE BRUTALITY OF THEIR RAIDS, HAD ATTACKED THE FEDERATION COLONY AT GAMMA RHEJIA... THE LEXINGTON REPELLED THE INTRUDERS, FORCING A CUTHKURAN FIGHTER-CRAFT TO CRASH-LAND ON THE PLANET...
GET TO THE POINT, SPOCK... WHERE DID ABBY WILSON'S INSUBORDINATION COME IN?
IN DIRECT VIOLATION OF ORDERS, DR. WILSON TOOK A LEXINGTON SHUTTLECRAFT DOWN TO THE PLANET--
FOR WHAT--?
--TO SEARCH FOR INJURED CUTHKURAN SURVIVORS AND SAVE THEM FROM VENGEFUL COLONISTS. AS A RESULT, THE LEXINGTON WAS PLACED AT RISK AND FORCED TO DELAY PURSUIT OF THE FLEEING INTRUDERS.
YEP... THAT SOUNDS LIKE ABBY WILSON ALL RIGHT. NEVER COULD TELL THAT GIRL ANYTHING!

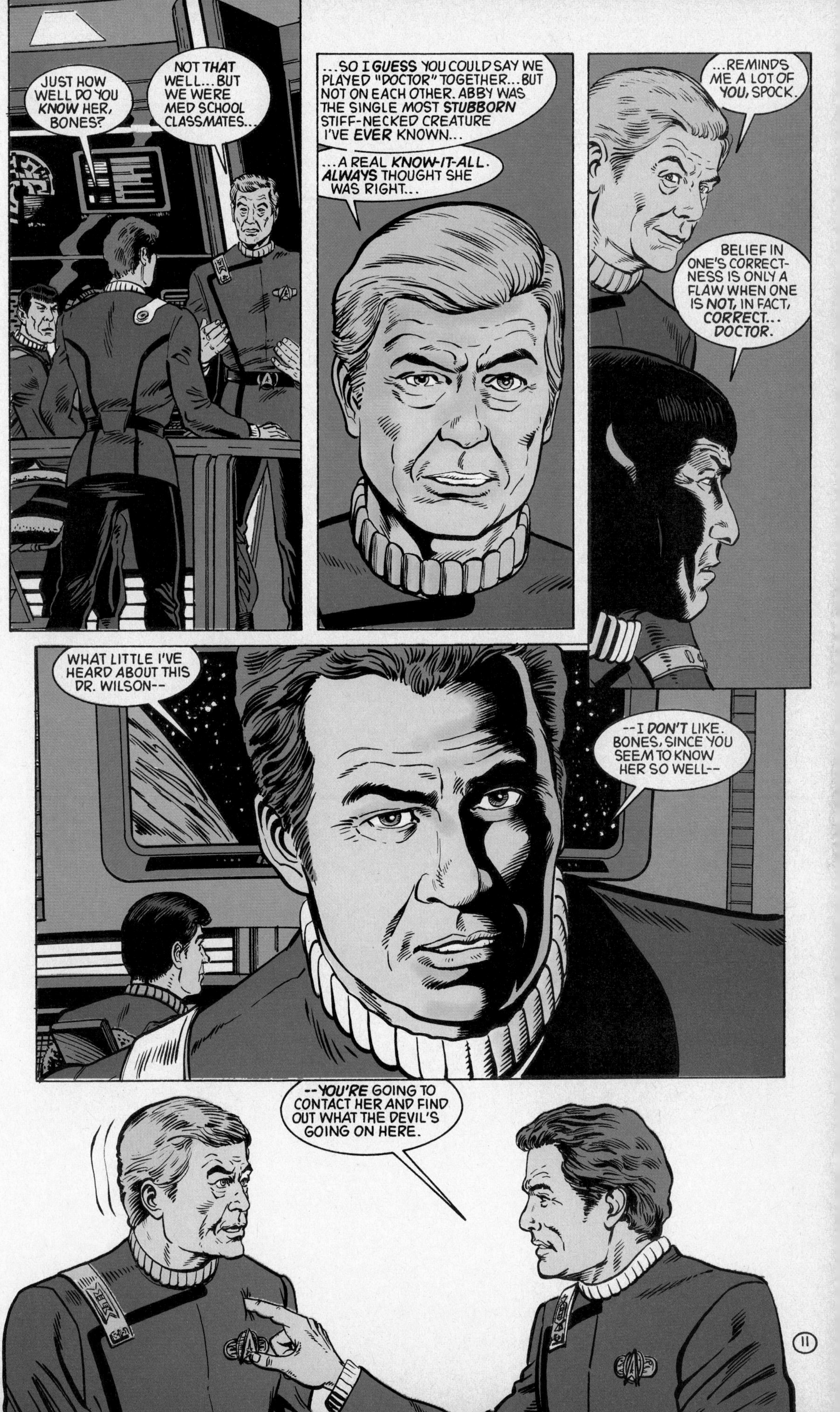
JUST HOW WELL DO YOU KNOW HER, BONES?
NOT THAT WELL... BUT WE WERE MED SCHOOL CLASSMATES...
...SO I GUESS YOU COULD SAY WE PLAYED "DOCTOR" TOGETHER... BUT NOT ON EACH OTHER. ABBY WAS THE SINGLE MOST STUBBORN STIFF-NECKED CREATURE I'VE EVER KNOWN...
...A REAL KNOW-IT-ALL. ALWAYS THOUGHT SHE WAS RIGHT...
...REMINDS ME A LOT OF YOU, SPOCK.
BELIEF IN ONE'S CORRECTNESS IS ONLY A FLAW WHEN ONE IS NOT, IN FACT, CORRECT... DOCTOR.
WHAT LITTLE I'VE HEARD ABOUT THIS DR. WILSON--
--I DON'T LIKE. BONES, SINCE YOU SEEM TO KNOW HER SO WELL--
--YOU'RE GOING TO CONTACT HER AND FIND OUT WHAT THE DEVIL'S GOING ON HERE.

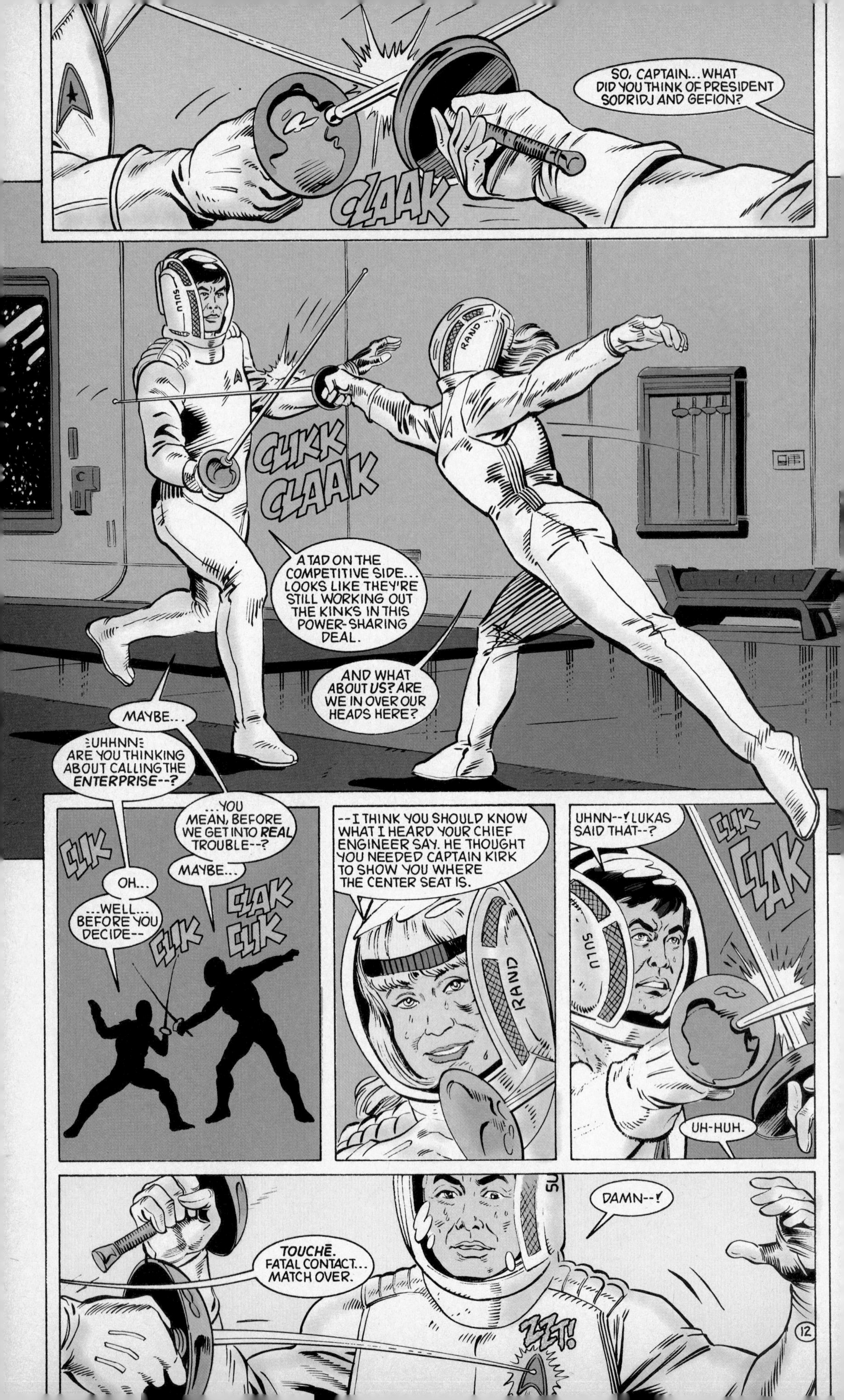

SO, CAPTAIN... WHAT DID YOU THINK OF PRESIDENT SODRIDJ AND GEFION?
CLAAK
SULU
RAND
CLIKK CLAAK
A TAD ON THE COMPETITIVE SIDE... LOOKS LIKE THEY'RE STILL WORKING OUT THE KINKS IN THIS POWER-SHARING DEAL.
AND WHAT ABOUT US? ARE WE IN OVER OUR HEADS HERE?
MAYBE...
UHHNN
ARE YOU THINKING ABOUT CALLING THE ENTERPRISE--?
...YOU MEAN, BEFORE WE GET INTO REAL TROUBLE--?
MAYBE...
CLIK
OH...
...WELL... BEFORE YOU DECIDE--
CLAK CLIK
CLIK
--I THINK YOU SHOULD KNOW WHAT I HEARD YOUR CHIEF ENGINEER SAY. HE THOUGHT YOU NEEDED CAPTAIN KIRK TO SHOW YOU WHERE THE CENTER SEAT IS.
RAND
UHNN--! LUKAS SAID THAT--?
CLIK CLAK
SULU
UH-HUH.
DAMN--!
TOUCHÉ. FATAL CONTACT... MATCH OVER.
ZZT!
12

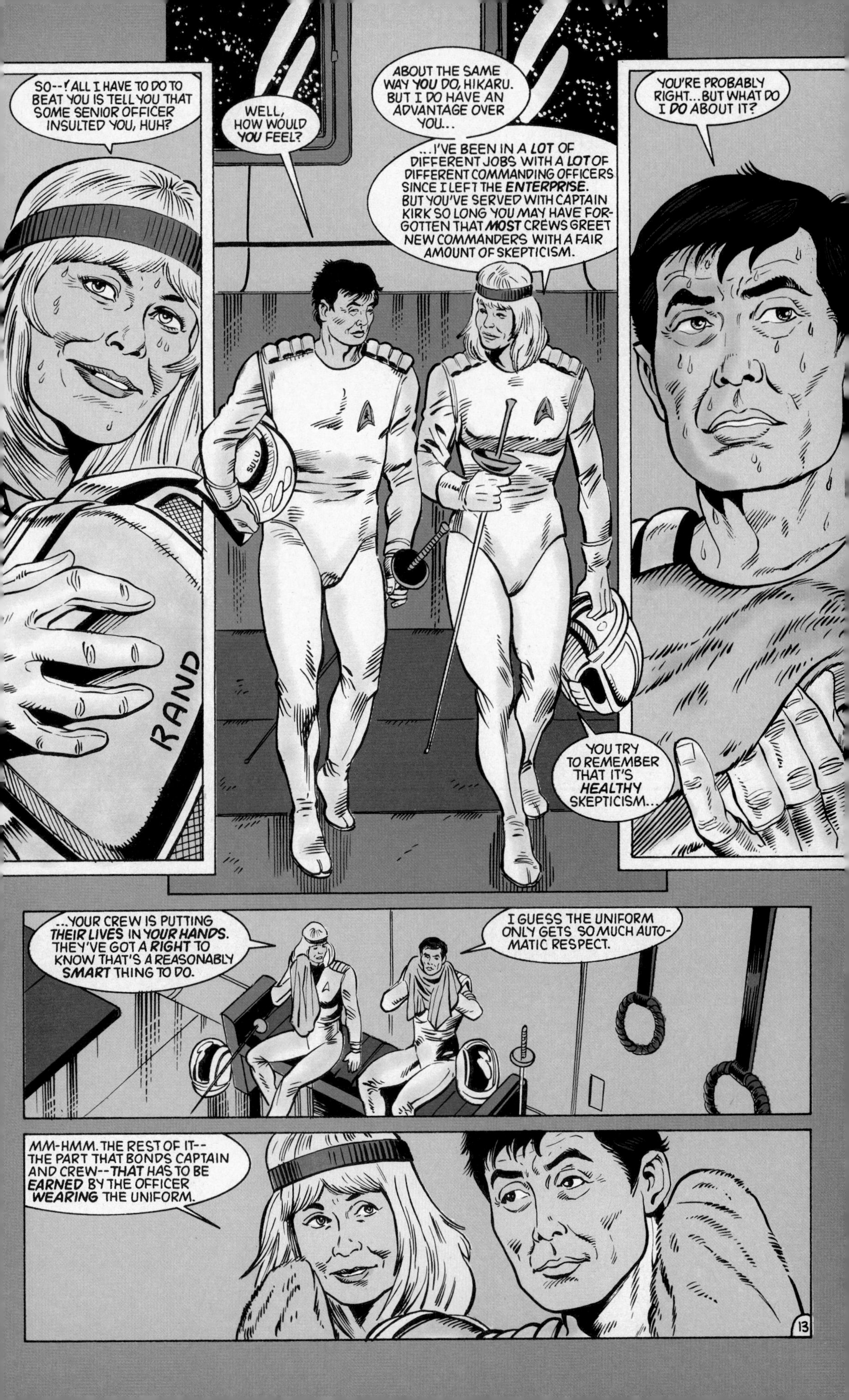

SO--! ALL I HAVE TO DO TO BEAT YOU IS TELL YOU THAT SOME SENIOR OFFICER INSULTED YOU, HUH?
WELL, HOW WOULD YOU FEEL?
ABOUT THE SAME WAY YOU DO, HIKARU. BUT I DO HAVE AN ADVANTAGE OVER YOU...
...I'VE BEEN IN A LOT OF DIFFERENT JOBS WITH A LOT OF DIFFERENT COMMANDING OFFICERS SINCE I LEFT THE ENTERPRISE. BUT YOU'VE SERVED WITH CAPTAIN KIRK SO LONG YOU MAY HAVE FORGOTTEN THAT MOST CREWS GREET NEW COMMANDERS WITH A FAIR AMOUNT OF SKEPTICISM.
YOU'RE PROBABLY RIGHT...BUT WHAT DO I DO ABOUT IT?
SULU
RAND
YOU TRY TO REMEMBER THAT IT'S HEALTHY SKEPTICISM...
...YOUR CREW IS PUTTING THEIR LIVES IN YOUR HANDS. THEY'VE GOT A RIGHT TO KNOW THAT'S A REASONABLY SMART THING TO DO.
I GUESS THE UNIFORM ONLY GETS SO MUCH AUTOMATIC RESPECT.
MM-HMM. THE REST OF IT-- THE PART THAT BONDS CAPTAIN AND CREW--THAT HAS TO BE EARNED BY THE OFFICER WEARING THE UNIFORM.

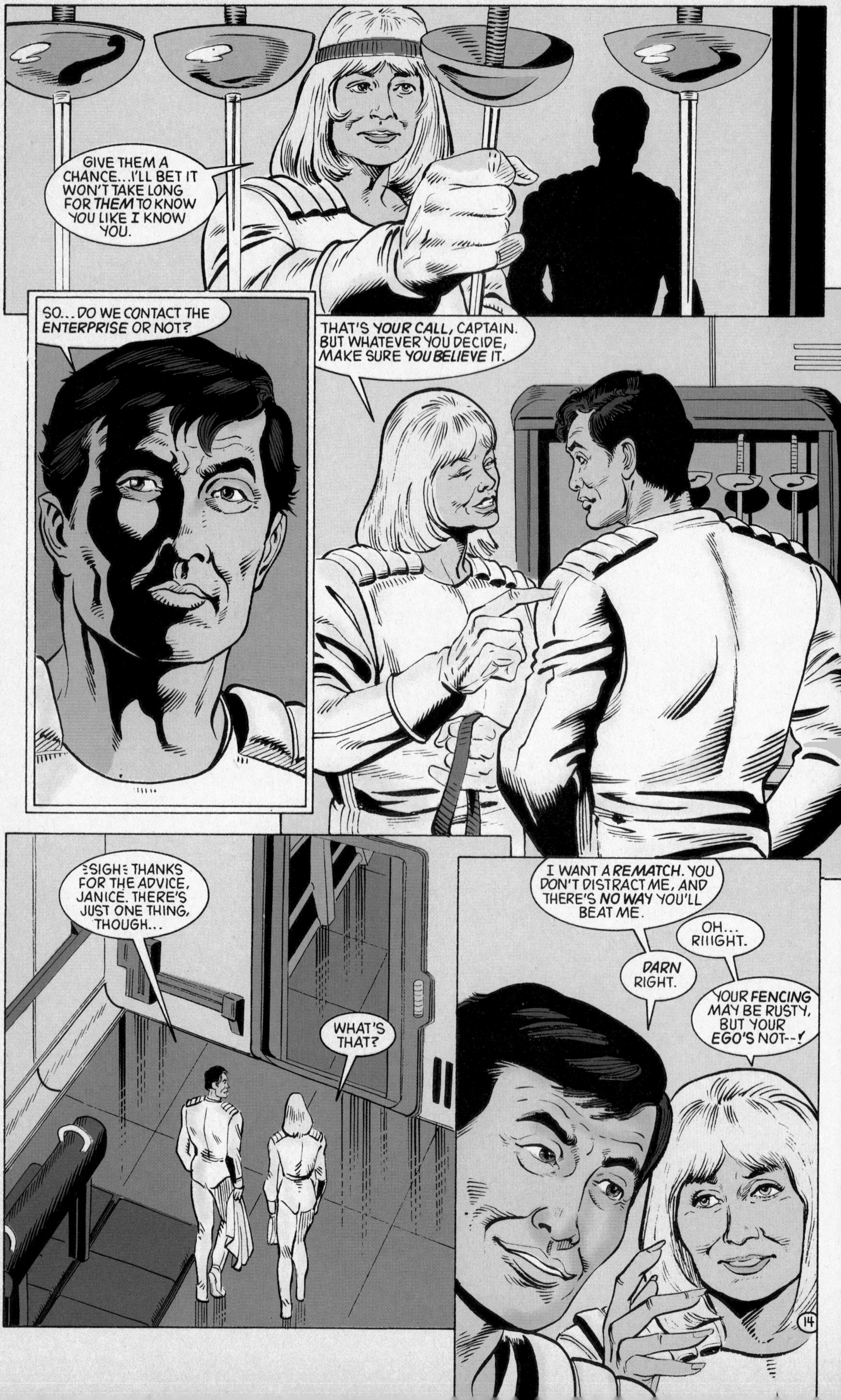
GIVE THEM A CHANCE...I'LL BET IT WON'T TAKE LONG FOR THEM TO KNOW YOU LIKE I KNOW YOU.
SO...DO WE CONTACT THE ENTERPRISE OR NOT?
THAT'S YOUR CALL, CAPTAIN. BUT WHATEVER YOU DECIDE, MAKE SURE YOU BELIEVE IT.
=SIGH= THANKS FOR THE ADVICE, JANICE. THERE'S JUST ONE THING, THOUGH...
WHAT'S THAT?
I WANT A REMATCH. YOU DON'T DISTRACT ME, AND THERE'S NO WAY YOU'LL BEAT ME.
OH... RIIIGHT.
DARN RIGHT.
YOUR FENCING MAY BE RUSTY, BUT YOUR EGO'S NOT--!
14

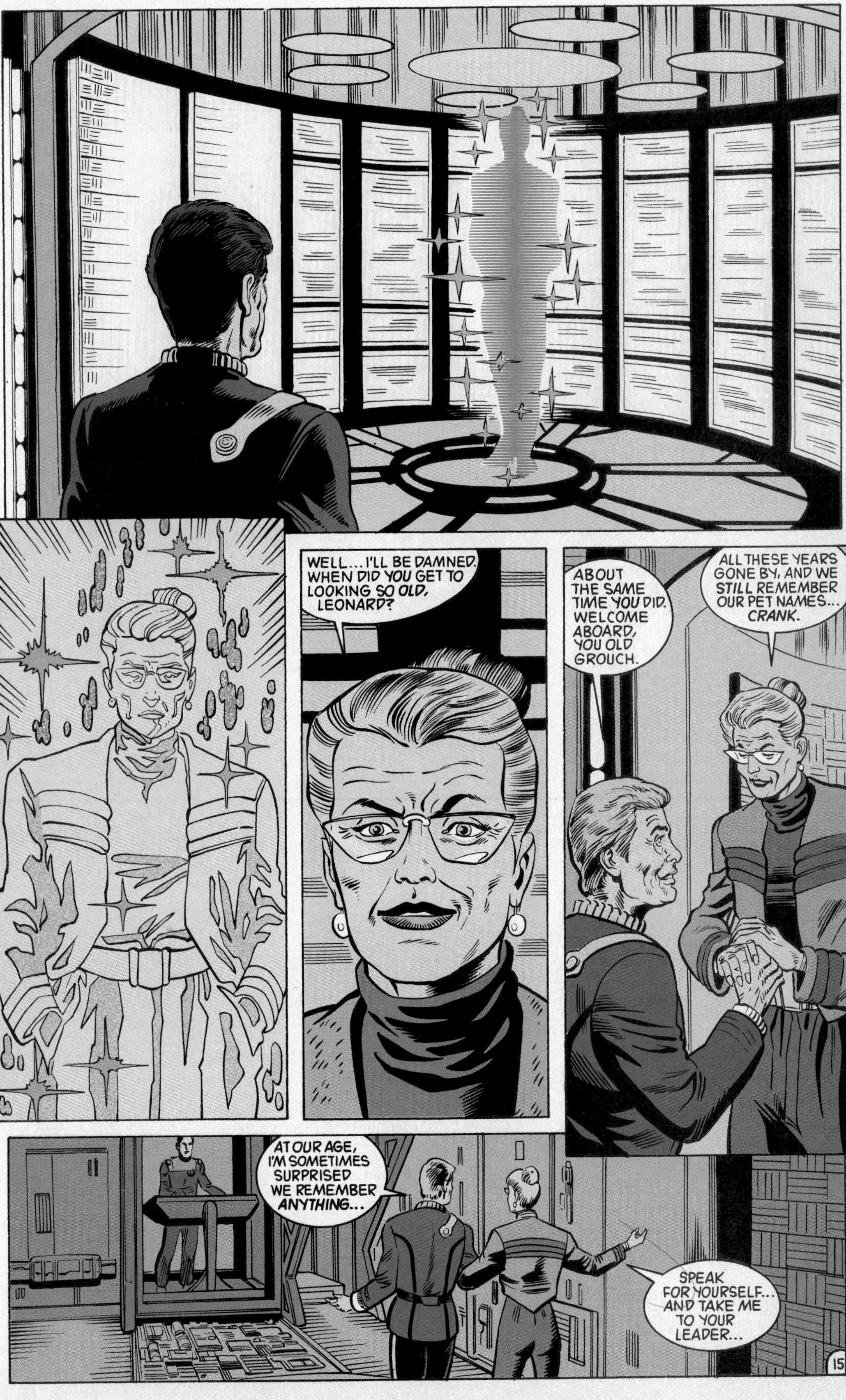
WELL... I'LL BE DAMNED. WHEN DID YOU GET TO LOOKING SO OLD, LEONARD?
ABOUT THE SAME TIME YOU DID. WELCOME ABOARD, YOU OLD GROUCH.
ALL THESE YEARS GONE BY, AND WE STILL REMEMBER OUR PET NAMES... CRANK.
AT OUR AGE, I'M SOMETIMES SURPRISED WE REMEMBER ANYTHING...
SPEAK FOR YOURSELF... AND TAKE ME TO YOUR LEADER...

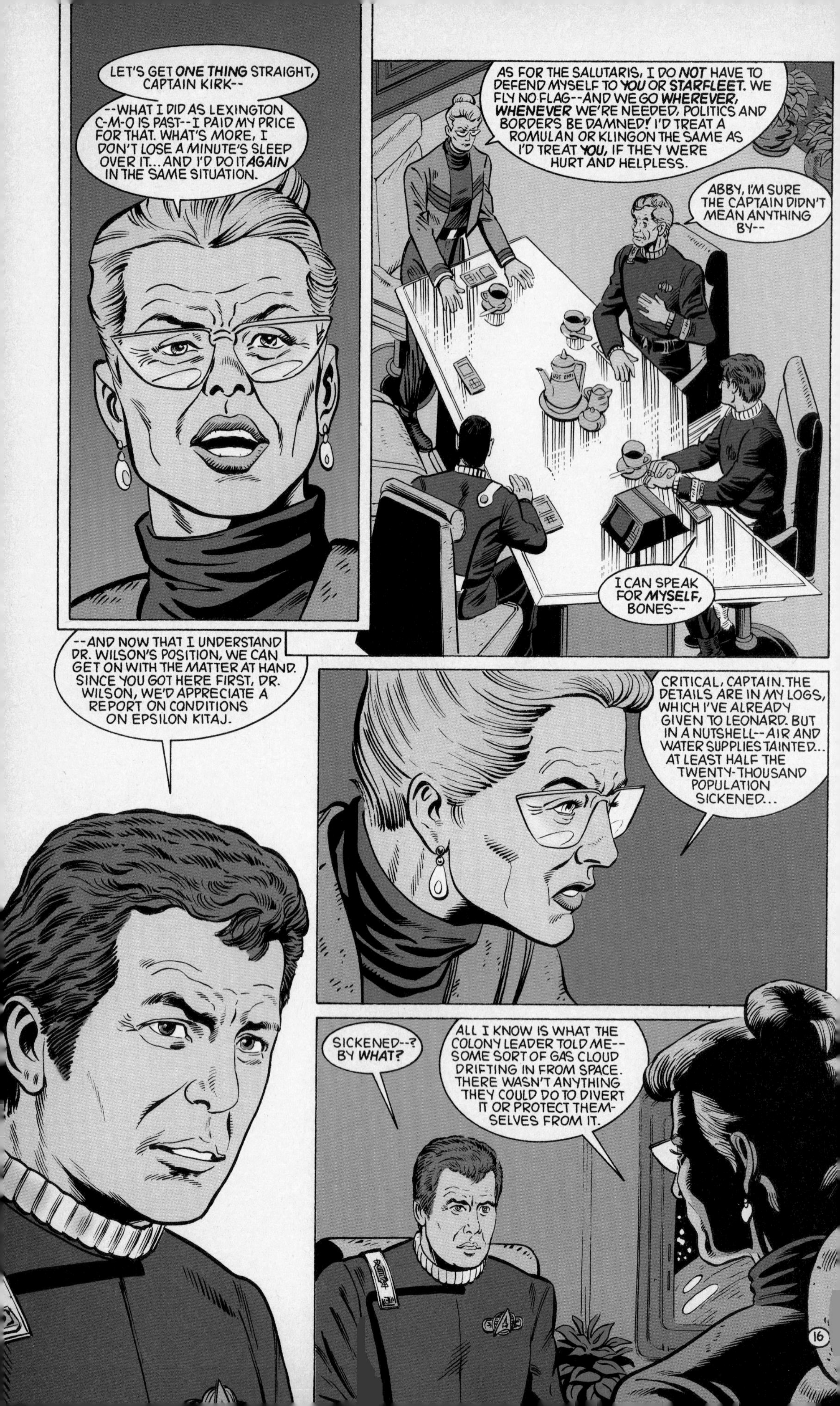
LET'S GET ONE THING STRAIGHT, CAPTAIN KIRK--
--WHAT I DID AS LEXINGTON C-M-O IS PAST--I PAID MY PRICE FOR THAT. WHAT'S MORE, I DON'T LOSE A MINUTE'S SLEEP OVER IT... AND I'D DO IT AGAIN IN THE SAME SITUATION.
AS FOR THE SALUTARIS, I DO NOT HAVE TO DEFEND MYSELF TO YOU OR STARFLEET. WE FLY NO FLAG--AND WE GO WHEREVER, WHENEVER WE'RE NEEDED, POLITICS AND BORDERS BE DAMNED! I'D TREAT A ROMULAN OR KLINGON THE SAME AS I'D TREAT YOU, IF THEY WERE HURT AND HELPLESS.
ABBY, I'M SURE THE CAPTAIN DIDN'T MEAN ANYTHING BY--
I CAN SPEAK FOR MYSELF, BONES--
--AND NOW THAT I UNDERSTAND DR. WILSON'S POSITION, WE CAN GET ON WITH THE MATTER AT HAND. SINCE YOU GOT HERE FIRST, DR. WILSON, WE'D APPRECIATE A REPORT ON CONDITIONS ON EPSILON KITAJ.
CRITICAL, CAPTAIN. THE DETAILS ARE IN MY LOGS, WHICH I'VE ALREADY GIVEN TO LEONARD. BUT IN A NUTSHELL--AIR AND WATER SUPPLIES TAINTED... AT LEAST HALF THE TWENTY-THOUSAND POPULATION SICKENED...
SICKENED--? BY WHAT?
ALL I KNOW IS WHAT THE COLONY LEADER TOLD ME--SOME SORT OF GAS CLOUD DRIFTING IN FROM SPACE. THERE WASN'T ANYTHING THEY COULD DO TO DIVERT IT OR PROTECT THEMSELVES FROM IT.
16

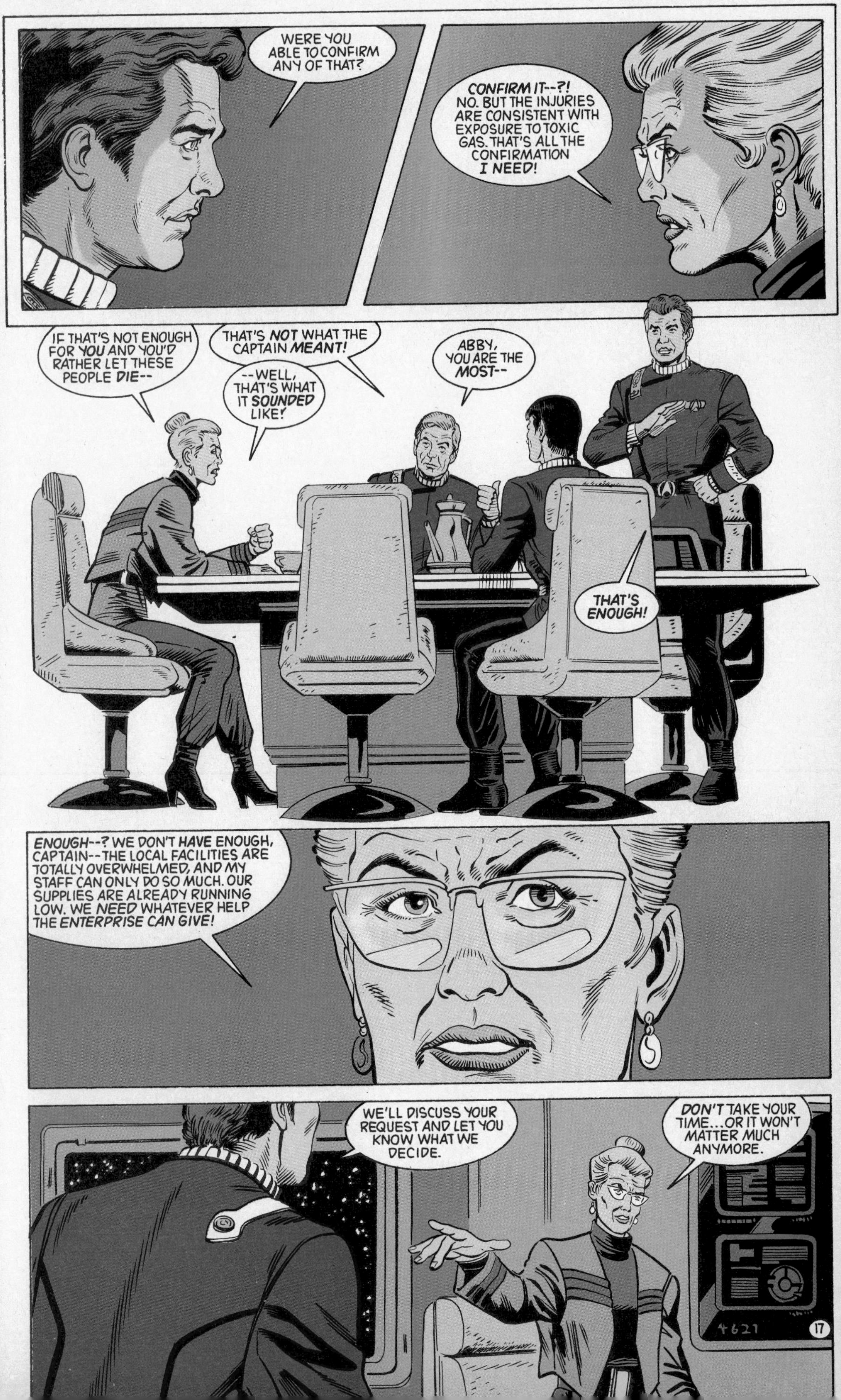
WERE YOU ABLE TO CONFIRM ANY OF THAT?
CONFIRM IT--?! NO. BUT THE INJURIES ARE CONSISTENT WITH EXPOSURE TO TOXIC GAS. THAT'S ALL THE CONFIRMATION I NEED!
IF THAT'S NOT ENOUGH FOR YOU AND YOU'D RATHER LET THESE PEOPLE DIE--
THAT'S NOT WHAT THE CAPTAIN MEANT!
--WELL, THAT'S WHAT IT SOUNDED LIKE!
ABBY, YOU ARE THE MOST--
THAT'S ENOUGH!
ENOUGH--? WE DON'T HAVE ENOUGH, CAPTAIN--THE LOCAL FACILITIES ARE TOTALLY OVERWHELMED, AND MY STAFF CAN ONLY DO SO MUCH. OUR SUPPLIES ARE ALREADY RUNNING LOW. WE NEED WHATEVER HELP THE ENTERPRISE CAN GIVE!
WE'LL DISCUSS YOUR REQUEST AND LET YOU KNOW WHAT WE DECIDE.
DON'T TAKE YOUR TIME...OR IT WON'T MATTER MUCH ANYMORE.
4621

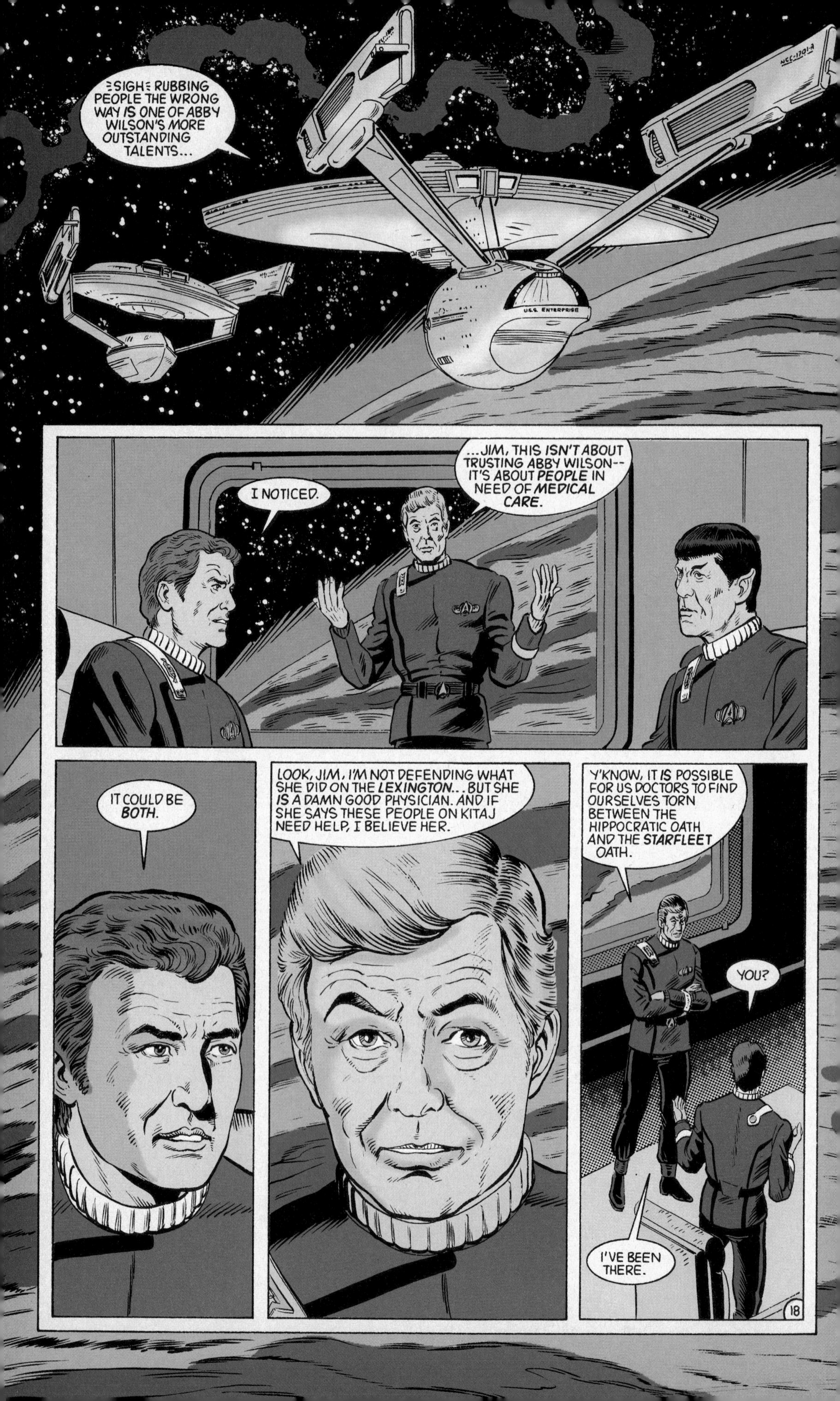

=SIGH= RUBBING PEOPLE THE WRONG WAY IS ONE OF ABBY WILSON'S MORE OUTSTANDING TALENTS...
NCC-1701-A
U.S.S. ENTERPRISE
...JIM, THIS ISN'T ABOUT TRUSTING ABBY WILSON-- IT'S ABOUT PEOPLE IN NEED OF MEDICAL CARE.
I NOTICED.
IT COULD BE BOTH.
LOOK, JIM, I'M NOT DEFENDING WHAT SHE DID ON THE LEXINGTON... BUT SHE IS A DAMN GOOD PHYSICIAN. AND IF SHE SAYS THESE PEOPLE ON KITAJ NEED HELP, I BELIEVE HER.
Y'KNOW, IT IS POSSIBLE FOR US DOCTORS TO FIND OURSELVES TORN BETWEEN THE HIPPOCRATIC OATH AND THE STARFLEET OATH.
YOU?
I'VE BEEN THERE.
18

YOU NEVER SAID ANYTHING.

EVERYBODY'S ENTITLED TO A PRIVATE WRESTLING MATCH NOW AND THEN.

THIS CONFLICT...WOULD YOU SOLVE IT WILSON'S WAY?

BY LEAVING STARFLEET? I HAVEN'T YET...

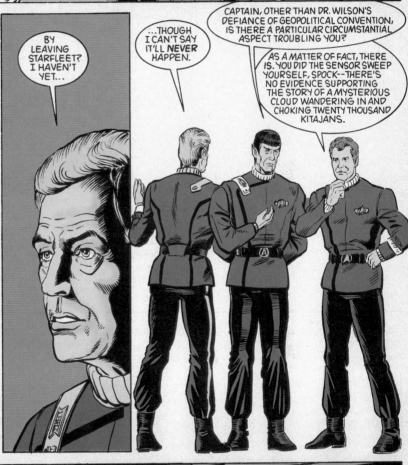

...THOUGH I CAN'T SAY IT'LL NEVER HAPPEN.

CAPTAIN, OTHER THAN DR. WILSON'S DEFIANCE OF GEOPOLITICAL CONVENTION, IS THERE A PARTICULAR CIRCUMSTANTIAL ASPECT TROUBLING YOU?

AS A MATTER OF FACT, THERE IS. YOU DID THE SENSOR SWEEP YOURSELF, SPOCK--THERE'S NO EVIDENCE SUPPORTING THE STORY OF A MYSTERIOUS CLOUD WANDERING IN AND CHOKING TWENTY THOUSAND KITAJANS.

THAT IS TRUE... BUT NEITHER IS THERE EVIDENCE TO REFUTE THE LOCAL ACCOUNT.

19

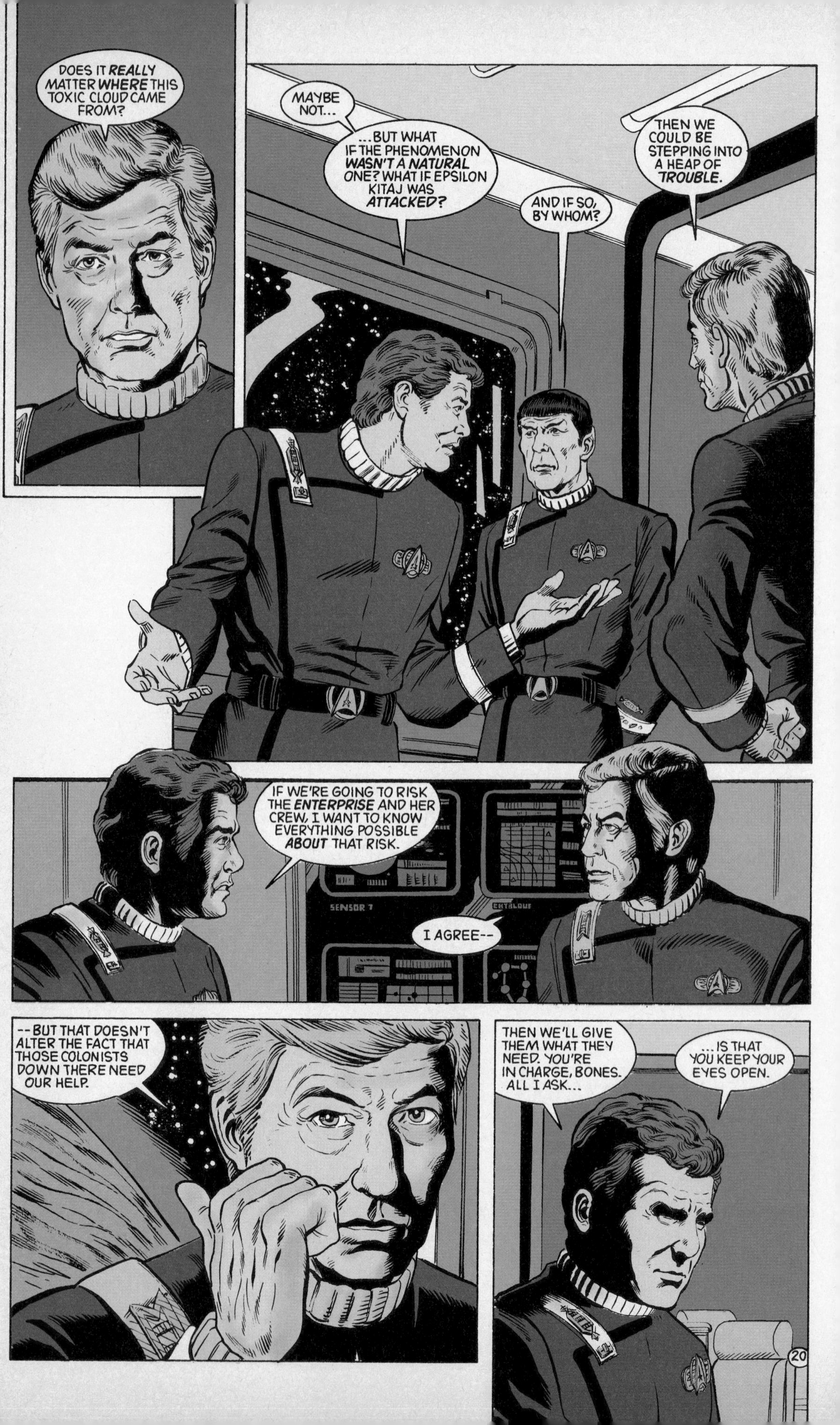
DOES IT REALLY MATTER WHERE THIS TOXIC CLOUD CAME FROM?
MAYBE NOT...
...BUT WHAT IF THE PHENOMENON WASN'T A NATURAL ONE? WHAT IF EPSILON KITAJ WAS ATTACKED?
AND IF SO, BY WHOM?
THEN WE COULD BE STEPPING INTO A HEAP OF TROUBLE.
IF WE'RE GOING TO RISK THE ENTERPRISE AND HER CREW, I WANT TO KNOW EVERYTHING POSSIBLE ABOUT THAT RISK.
SENSOR 7
I AGREE--
--BUT THAT DOESN'T ALTER THE FACT THAT THOSE COLONISTS DOWN THERE NEED OUR HELP.
THEN WE'LL GIVE THEM WHAT THEY NEED. YOU'RE IN CHARGE, BONES. ALL I ASK...
...IS THAT YOU KEEP YOUR EYES OPEN.
20

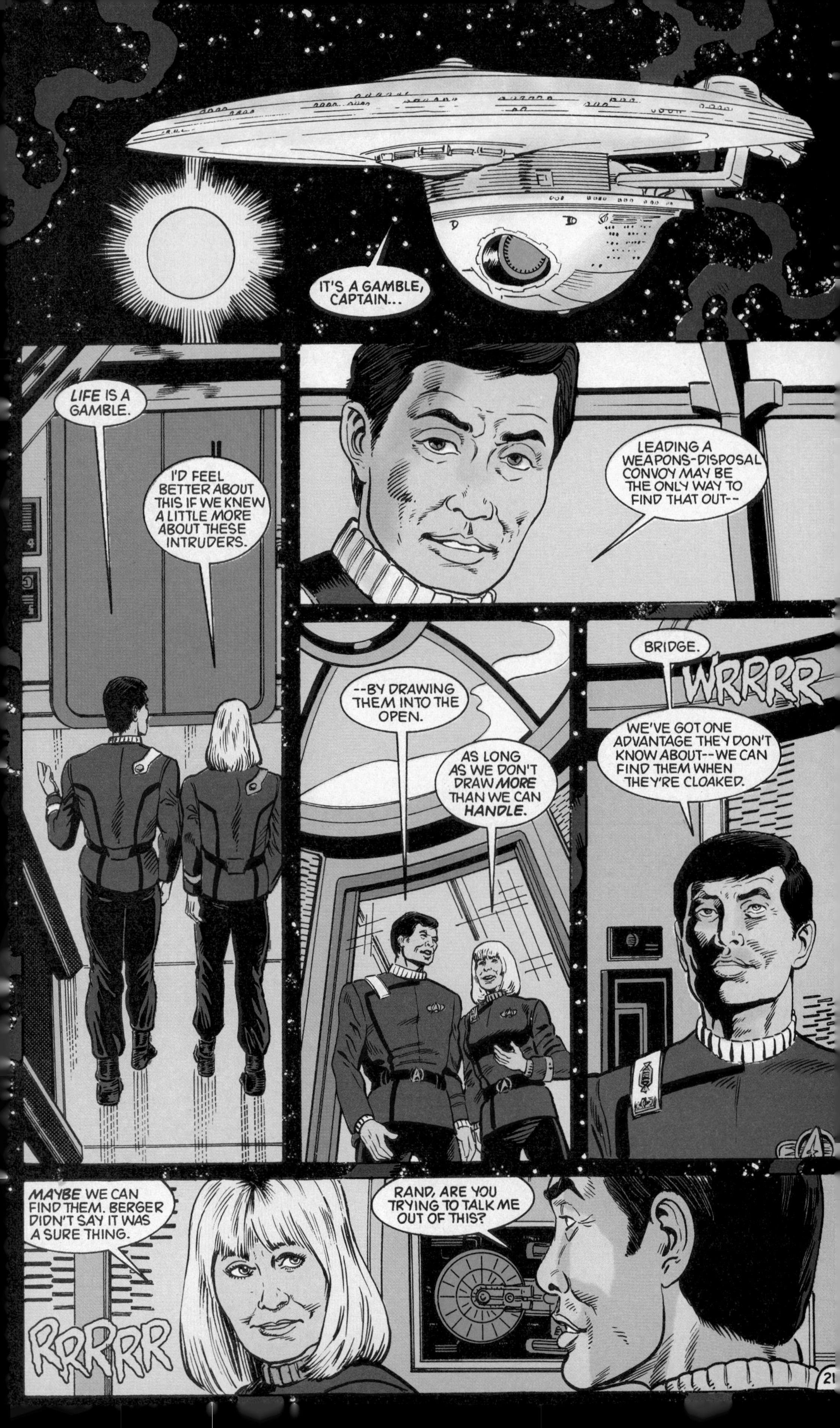
IT'S A GAMBLE, CAPTAIN...
LIFE IS A GAMBLE.
I'D FEEL BETTER ABOUT THIS IF WE KNEW A LITTLE MORE ABOUT THESE INTRUDERS.
LEADING A WEAPONS-DISPOSAL CONVOY MAY BE THE ONLY WAY TO FIND THAT OUT--
--BY DRAWING THEM INTO THE OPEN.
AS LONG AS WE DON'T DRAW MORE THAN WE CAN HANDLE.
BRIDGE.
WRRRR
WE'VE GOT ONE ADVANTAGE THEY DON'T KNOW ABOUT--WE CAN FIND THEM WHEN THEY'RE CLOAKED.
MAYBE WE CAN FIND THEM. BERGER DIDN'T SAY IT WAS A SURE THING.
RAND, ARE YOU TRYING TO TALK ME OUT OF THIS?
RRRRR

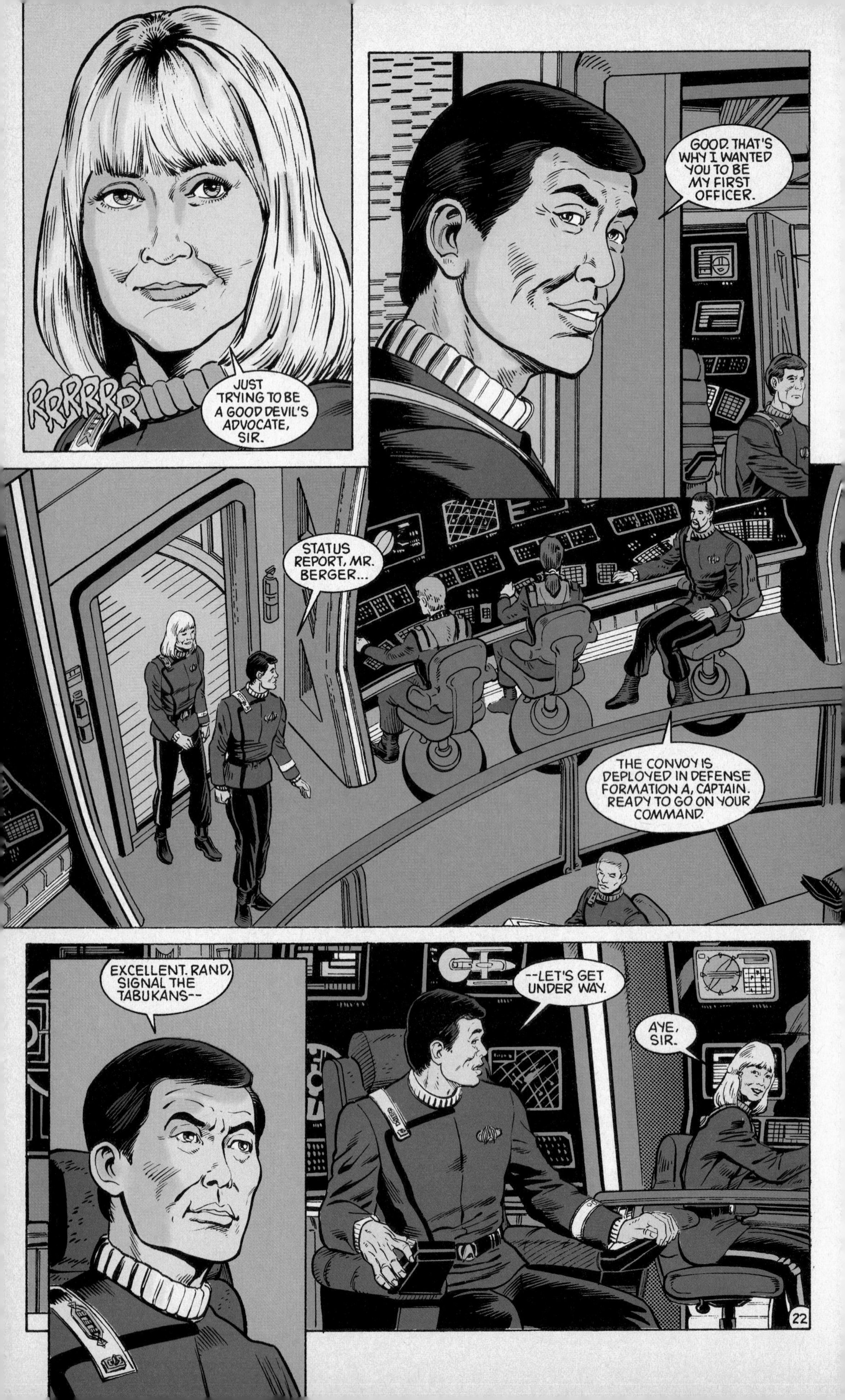
RRRRRR
JUST TRYING TO BE A GOOD DEVIL'S ADVOCATE, SIR.
GOOD. THAT'S WHY I WANTED YOU TO BE MY FIRST OFFICER.
STATUS REPORT, MR. BERGER...
THE CONVOY IS DEPLOYED IN DEFENSE FORMATION A, CAPTAIN. READY TO GO ON YOUR COMMAND.
EXCELLENT. RAND, SIGNAL THE TABUKANS--
--LET'S GET UNDER WAY.
AYE, SIR.
22

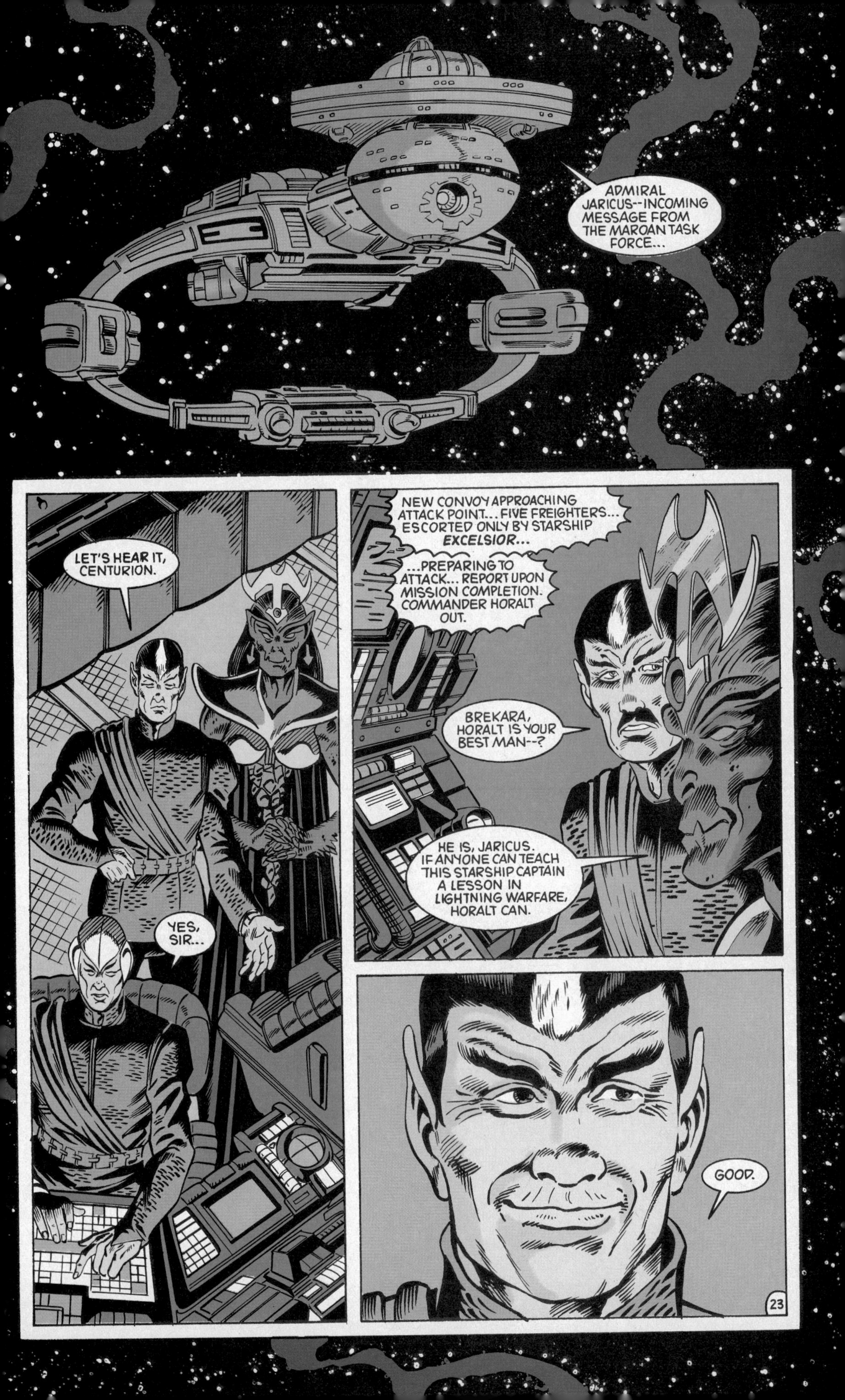
ADMIRAL JARICUS--INCOMING MESSAGE FROM THE MAROAN TASK FORCE...
LET'S HEAR IT, CENTURION.
YES, SIR...
NEW CONVOY APPROACHING ATTACK POINT... FIVE FREIGHTERS... ESCORTED ONLY BY STARSHIP EXCELSIOR...
...PREPARING TO ATTACK... REPORT UPON MISSION COMPLETION. COMMANDER HORALT OUT.
BREKARA, HORALT IS YOUR BEST MAN--?
HE IS, JARICUS. IF ANYONE CAN TEACH THIS STARSHIP CAPTAIN A LESSON IN LIGHTNING WARFARE, HORALT CAN.
GOOD.
23

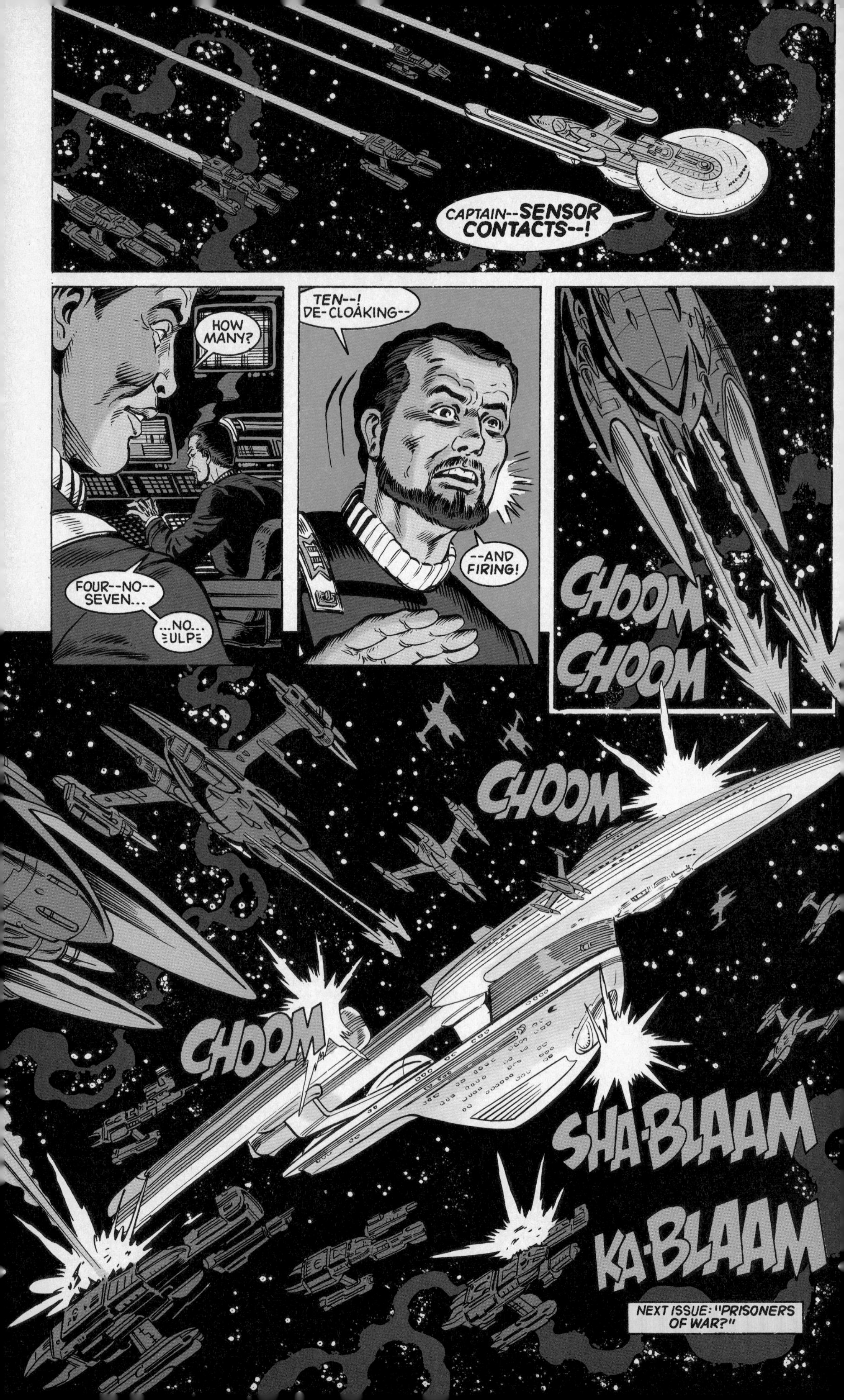
CAPTAIN--SENSOR CONTACTS--!
HOW MANY?
FOUR--NO--SEVEN...
...NO... ULP
TEN--! DE-CLOAKING--
--AND FIRING!
CHOOM CHOOM
CHOOM
CHOOM
SHA-BLAAM
KA-BLAAM
NEXT ISSUE: "PRISONERS OF WAR?"

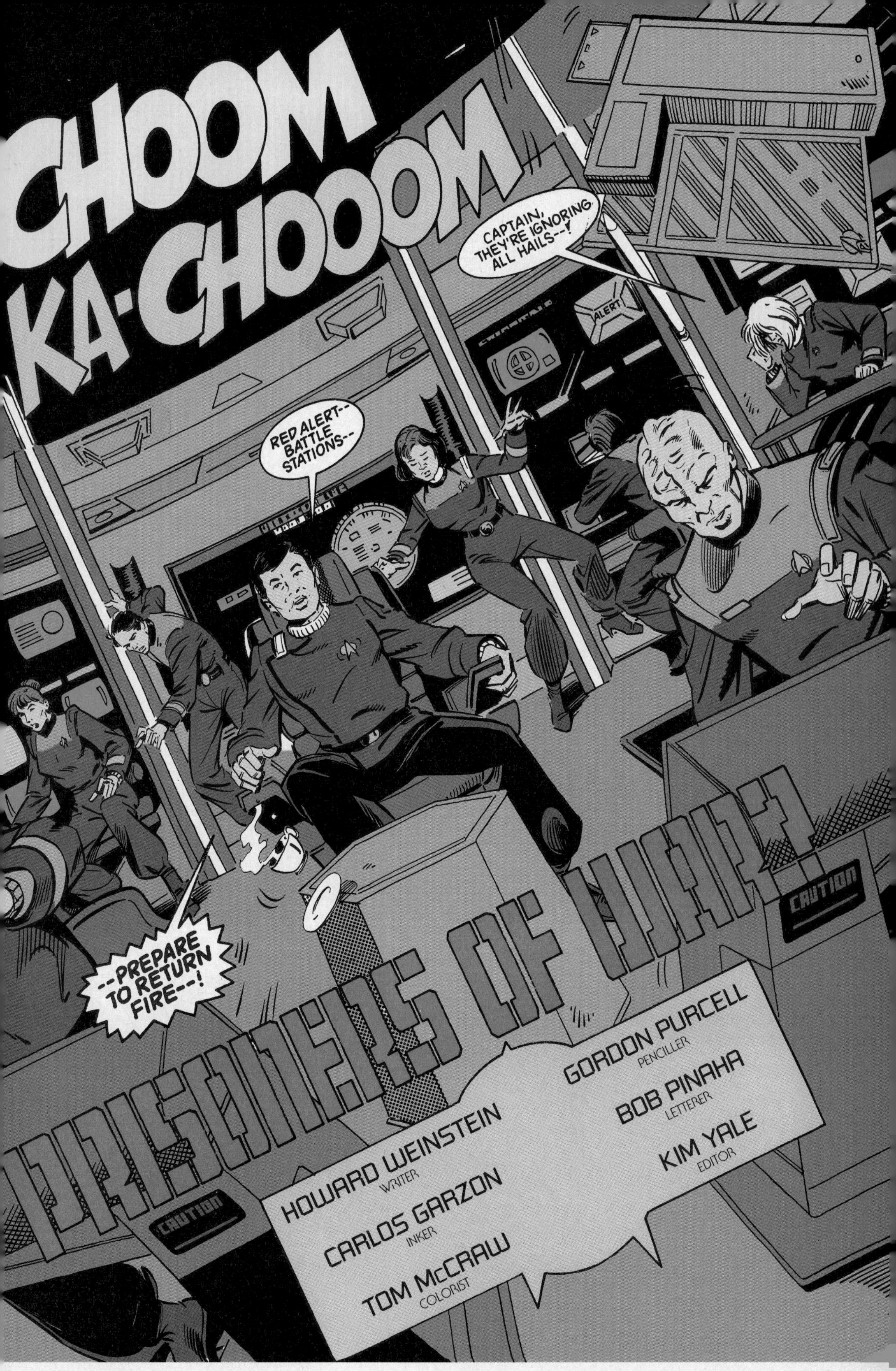
CHOOM
KA-CHOOOM
CAPTAIN, THEY'RE IGNORING ALL HAILS--!
RED ALERT-- BATTLE STATIONS--
--PREPARE TO RETURN FIRE--!
PRISONERS OF WAR
HOWARD WEINSTEIN
WRITER
CARLOS GARZON
INKER
TOM McCRAW
COLORIST
GORDON PURCELL
PENCILLER
BOB PINAHA
LETTERER
KIM YALE
EDITOR
CAUTION
CAUTION
ALERT

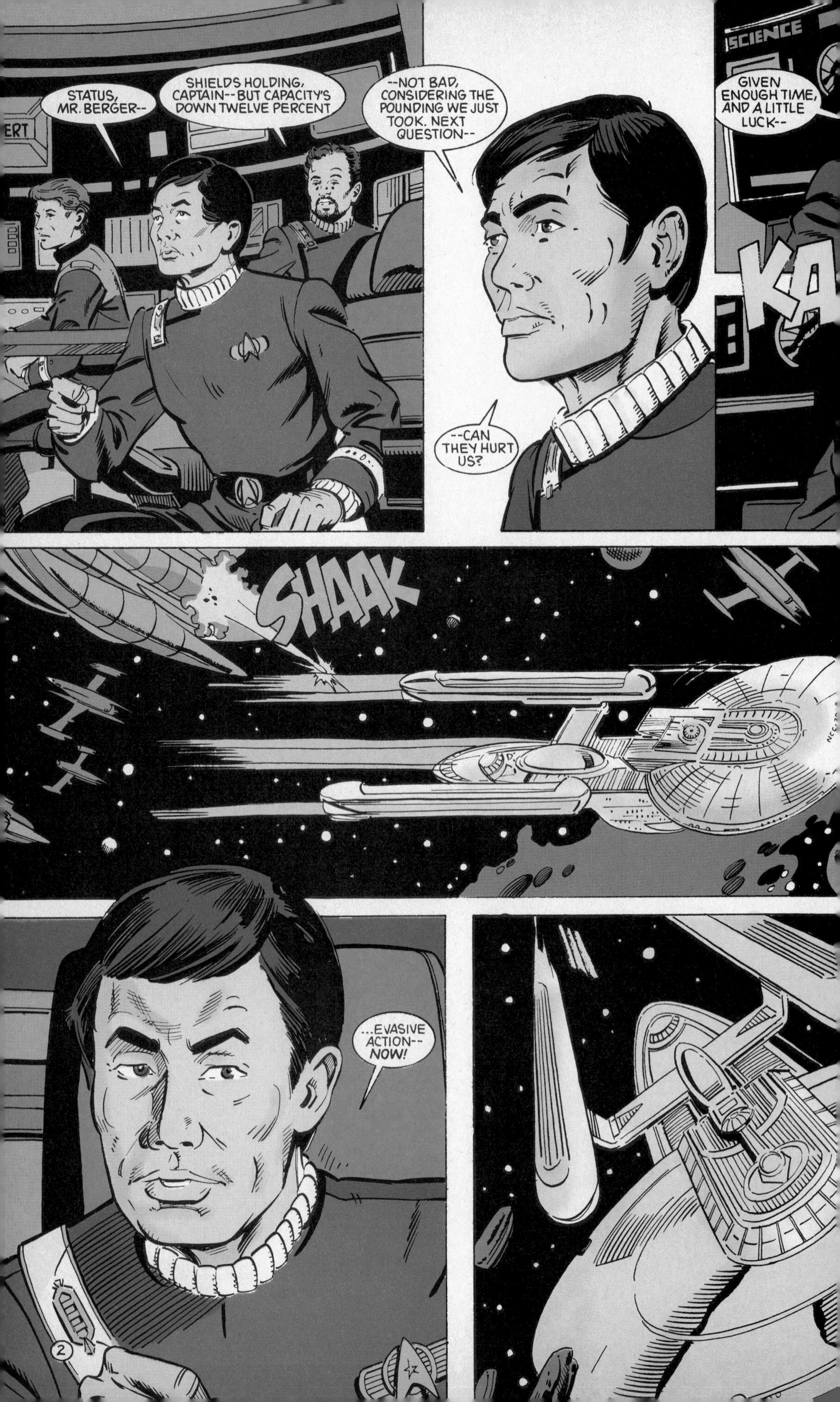
STATUS, MR. BERGER--
SHIELDS HOLDING, CAPTAIN-- BUT CAPACITY'S DOWN TWELVE PERCENT
--NOT BAD, CONSIDERING THE POUNDING WE JUST TOOK. NEXT QUESTION--
--CAN THEY HURT US?
SCIENCE
GIVEN ENOUGH TIME, AND A LITTLE LUCK--
KA
SHAAK
...EVASIVE ACTION-- NOW!
2

HHOOM!

--THEY COULD, SIR.

ALERT

CAPTAIN, THEY'RE REGROUPING...AND THEY APPEAR TO BE LEAVING THE FREIGHTER CONVOY ALONE.

ALE

GUNNING FOR US, EH? IT'S TIME THEY LEARNED WHAT A STARSHIP CAN DO. LOCK PHASERS AND TORPEDOES ON THEIR THREE LEADING SHIPS...

SHAAK

CAPTAIN-- THEY'RE FIRING--

SHAAK

KA-CHOOM

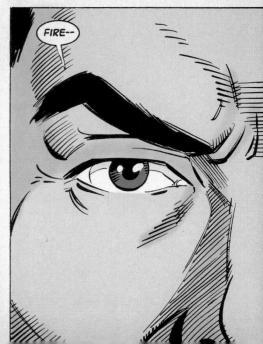

FIRE--

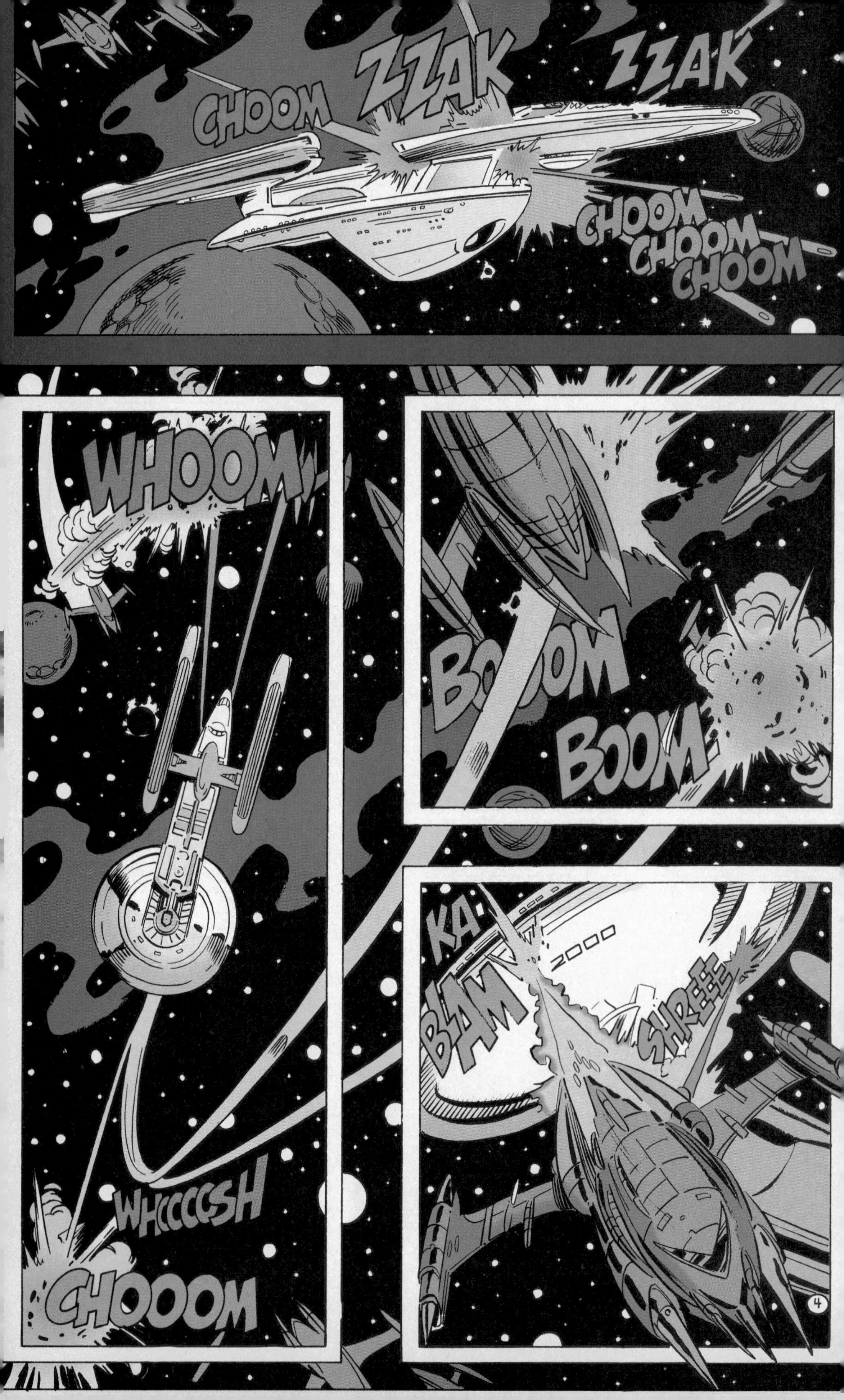
CHOOM
ZZAK
ZZAK
CHOOM
CHOOM
CHOOM
WHOOM
WHCCCCSH
CHOOOM
BOOM
BOOM
KA-
BLAM
SHREEE
2000
4

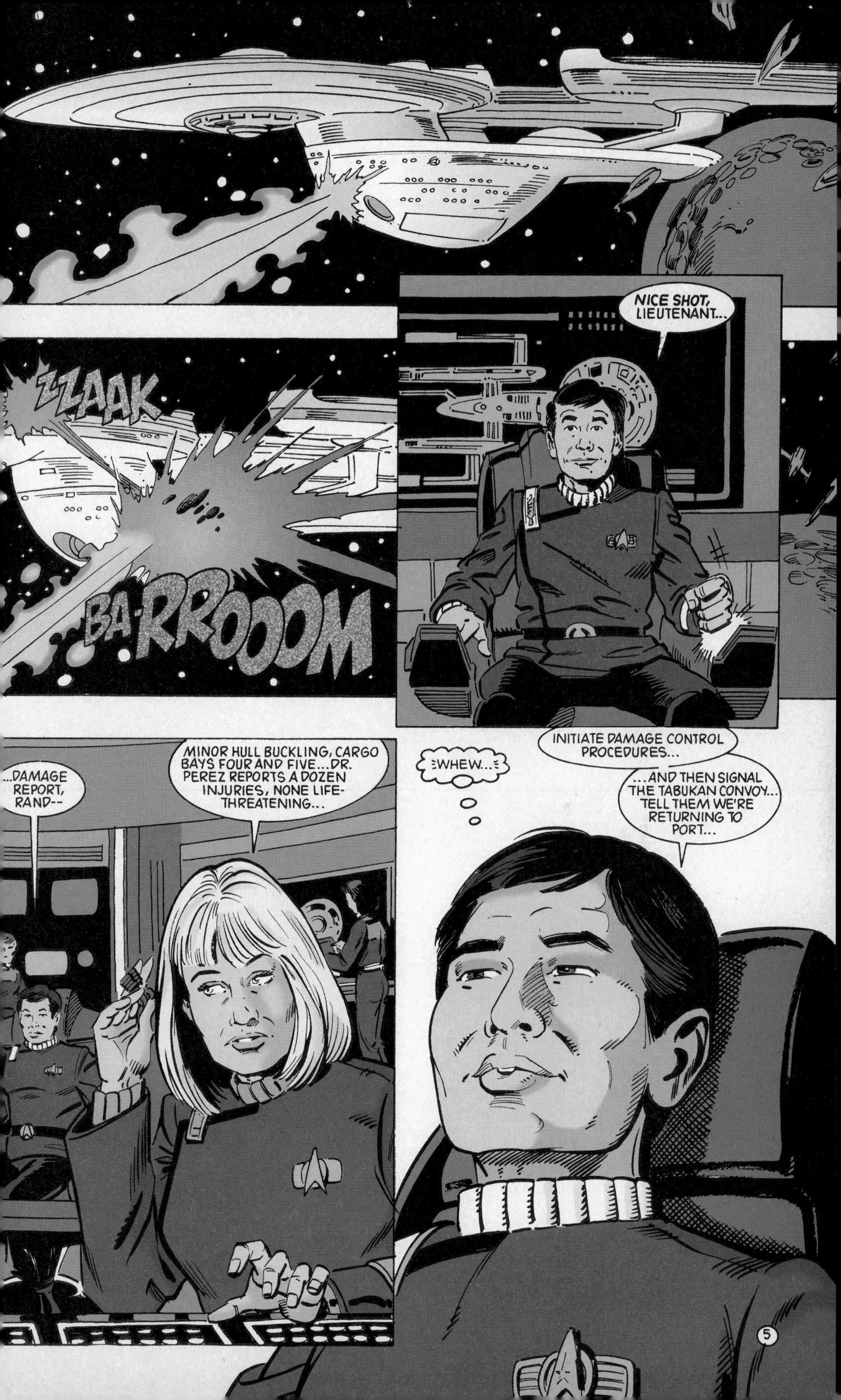
NICE SHOT, LIEUTENANT...
ZZAAK
BA-RROOOM
...DAMAGE REPORT, RAND--
MINOR HULL BUCKLING, CARGO BAYS FOUR AND FIVE...DR. PEREZ REPORTS A DOZEN INJURIES, NONE LIFE-THREATENING...
WHEW...
INITIATE DAMAGE CONTROL PROCEDURES...
...AND THEN SIGNAL THE TABUKAN CONVOY... TELL THEM WE'RE RETURNING TO PORT...
5

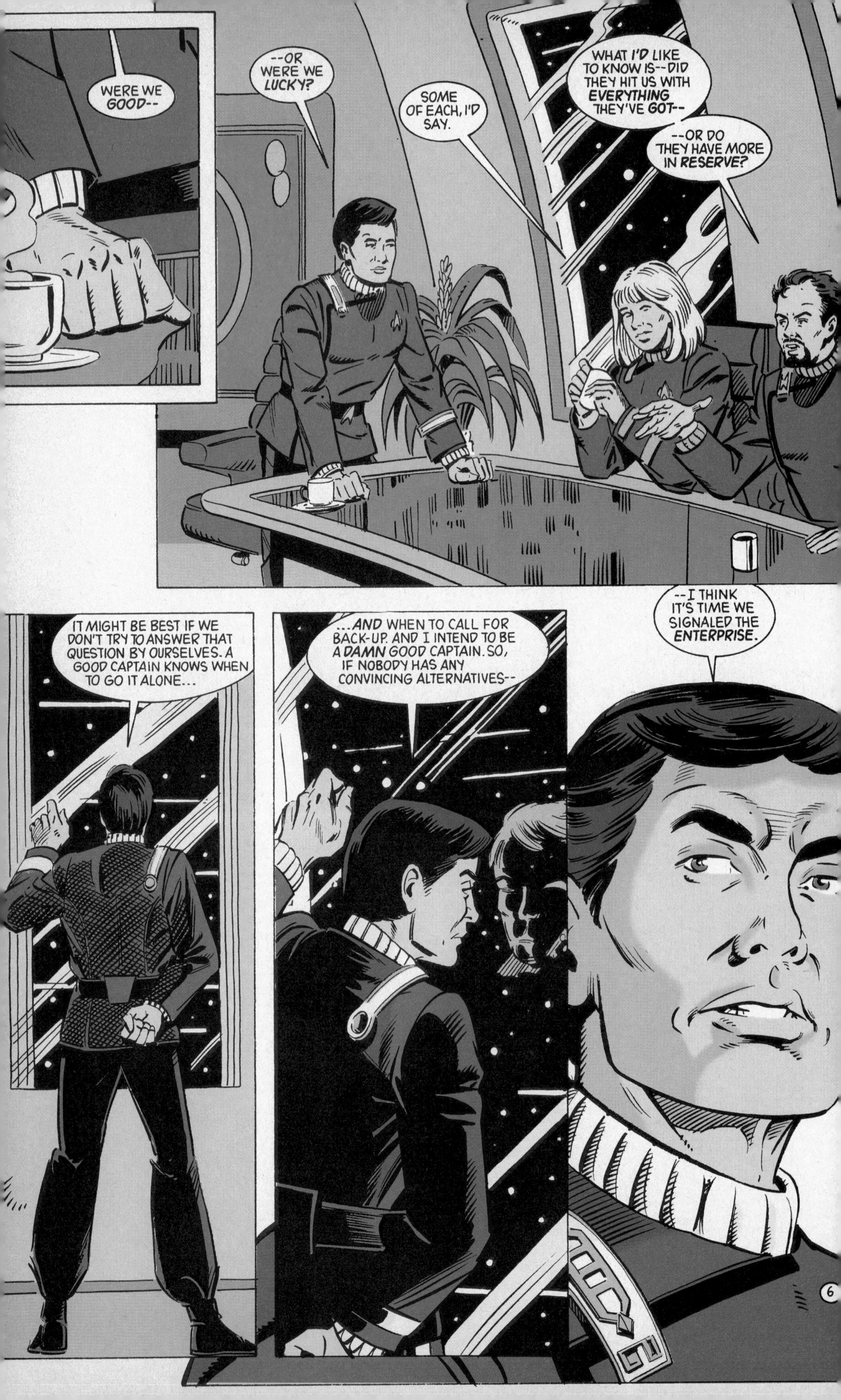
WERE WE GOOD--
--OR WERE WE LUCKY?
SOME OF EACH, I'D SAY.
WHAT I'D LIKE TO KNOW IS--DID THEY HIT US WITH EVERYTHING THEY'VE GOT--
--OR DO THEY HAVE MORE IN RESERVE?
IT MIGHT BE BEST IF WE DON'T TRY TO ANSWER THAT QUESTION BY OURSELVES. A GOOD CAPTAIN KNOWS WHEN TO GO IT ALONE...
...AND WHEN TO CALL FOR BACK-UP. AND I INTEND TO BE A DAMN GOOD CAPTAIN. SO, IF NOBODY HAS ANY CONVINCING ALTERNATIVES--
--I THINK IT'S TIME WE SIGNALED THE ENTERPRISE.

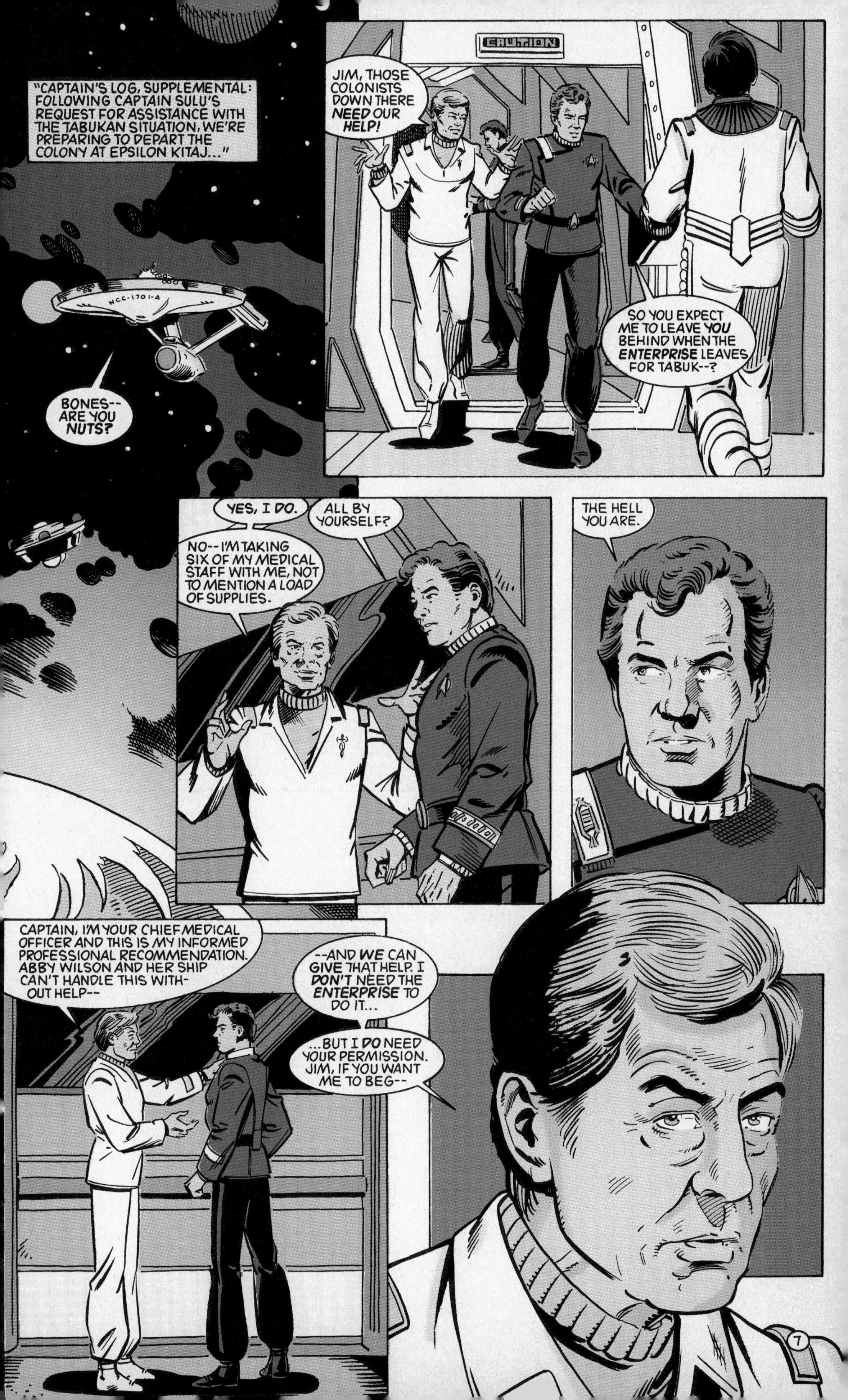
"CAPTAIN'S LOG, SUPPLEMENTAL: FOLLOWING CAPTAIN SULU'S REQUEST FOR ASSISTANCE WITH THE TABUKAN SITUATION, WE'RE PREPARING TO DEPART THE COLONY AT EPSILON KITAJ..."
NCC-1701-A
BONES-- ARE YOU NUTS?
CAUTION
JIM, THOSE COLONISTS DOWN THERE NEED OUR HELP!
SO YOU EXPECT ME TO LEAVE YOU BEHIND WHEN THE ENTERPRISE LEAVES FOR TABUK--?
YES, I DO.
ALL BY YOURSELF?
NO--I'M TAKING SIX OF MY MEDICAL STAFF WITH ME, NOT TO MENTION A LOAD OF SUPPLIES.
THE HELL YOU ARE.
CAPTAIN, I'M YOUR CHIEF MEDICAL OFFICER AND THIS IS MY INFORMED PROFESSIONAL RECOMMENDATION. ABBY WILSON AND HER SHIP CAN'T HANDLE THIS WITHOUT HELP--
--AND WE CAN GIVE THAT HELP. I DON'T NEED THE ENTERPRISE TO DO IT...
...BUT I DO NEED YOUR PERMISSION. JIM, IF YOU WANT ME TO BEG--

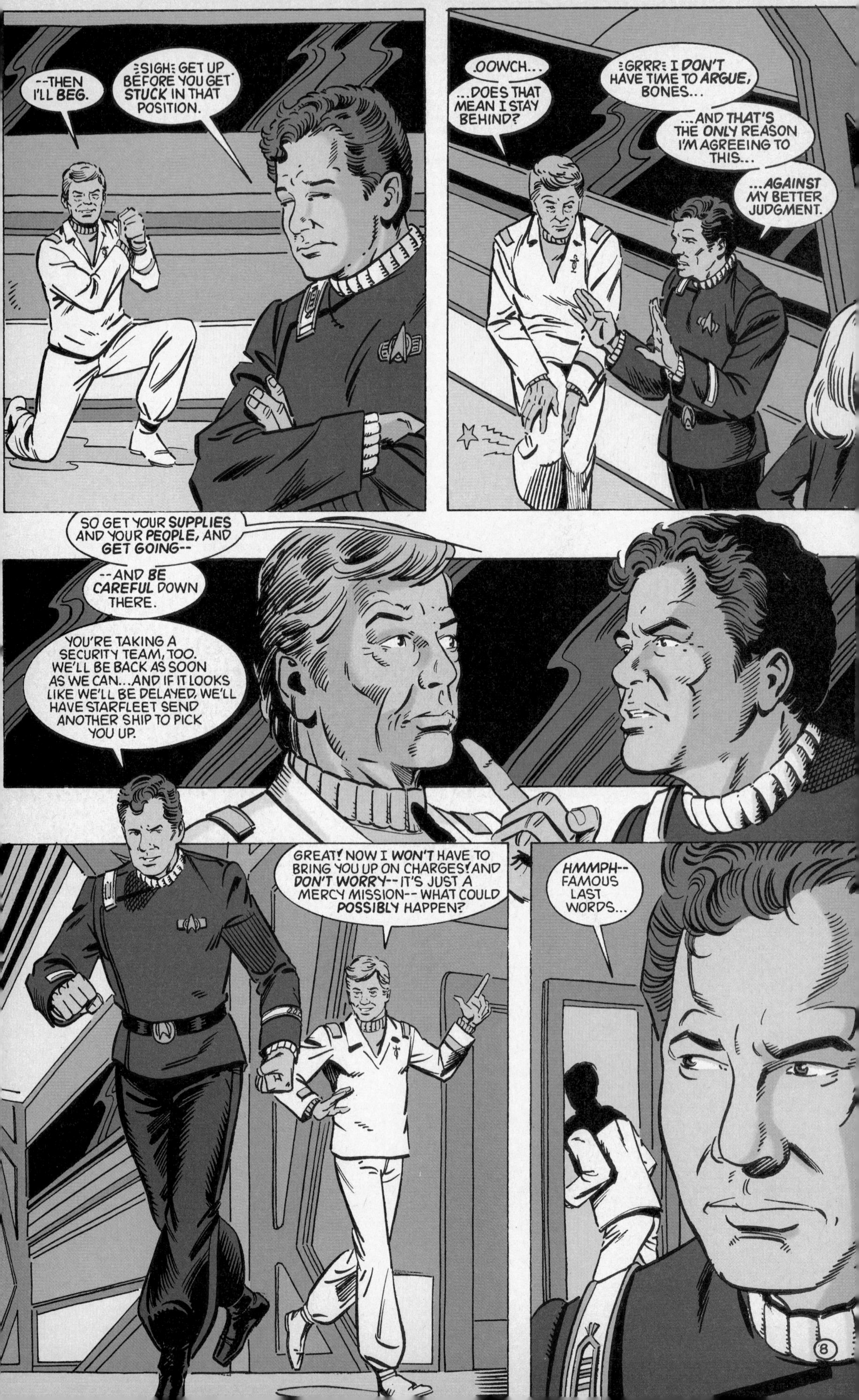
--THEN I'LL BEG.
=SIGH= GET UP BEFORE YOU GET STUCK IN THAT POSITION.
.OOWCH...
...DOES THAT MEAN I STAY BEHIND?
=GRRR= I DON'T HAVE TIME TO ARGUE, BONES...
...AND THAT'S THE ONLY REASON I'M AGREEING TO THIS...
...AGAINST MY BETTER JUDGMENT.
SO GET YOUR SUPPLIES AND YOUR PEOPLE, AND GET GOING--
--AND BE CAREFUL DOWN THERE.
YOU'RE TAKING A SECURITY TEAM, TOO. WE'LL BE BACK AS SOON AS WE CAN...AND IF IT LOOKS LIKE WE'LL BE DELAYED, WE'LL HAVE STARFLEET SEND ANOTHER SHIP TO PICK YOU UP.
GREAT! NOW I WON'T HAVE TO BRING YOU UP ON CHARGES! AND DON'T WORRY-- IT'S JUST A MERCY MISSION-- WHAT COULD POSSIBLY HAPPEN?
HMMPH-- FAMOUS LAST WORDS...
8

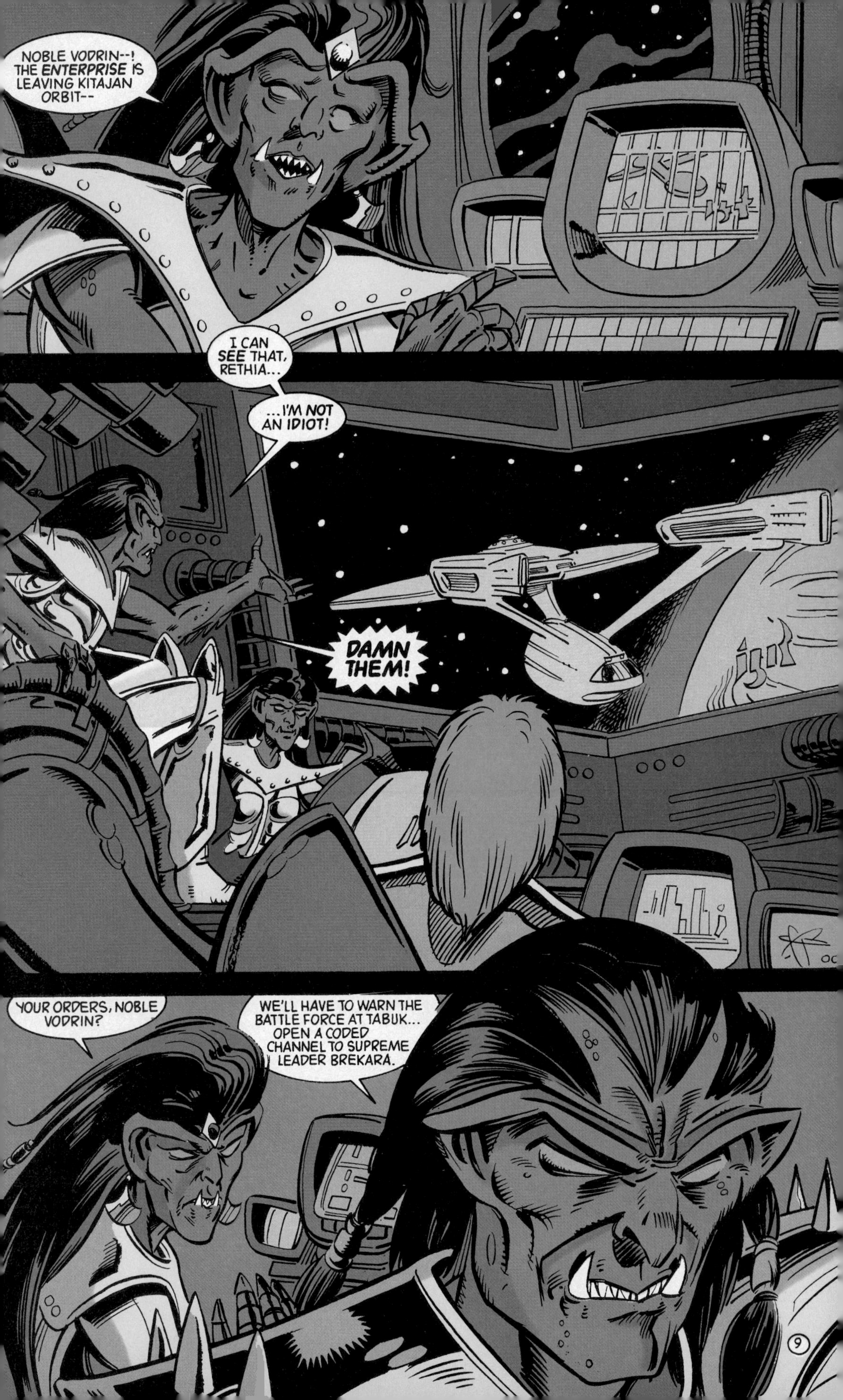
NOBLE VODRIN--! THE ENTERPRISE IS LEAVING KITAJAN ORBIT--
I CAN SEE THAT, RETHIA...
...I'M NOT AN IDIOT!
DAMN THEM!
YOUR ORDERS, NOBLE VODRIN?
WE'LL HAVE TO WARN THE BATTLE FORCE AT TABUK... OPEN A CODED CHANNEL TO SUPREME LEADER BREKARA.

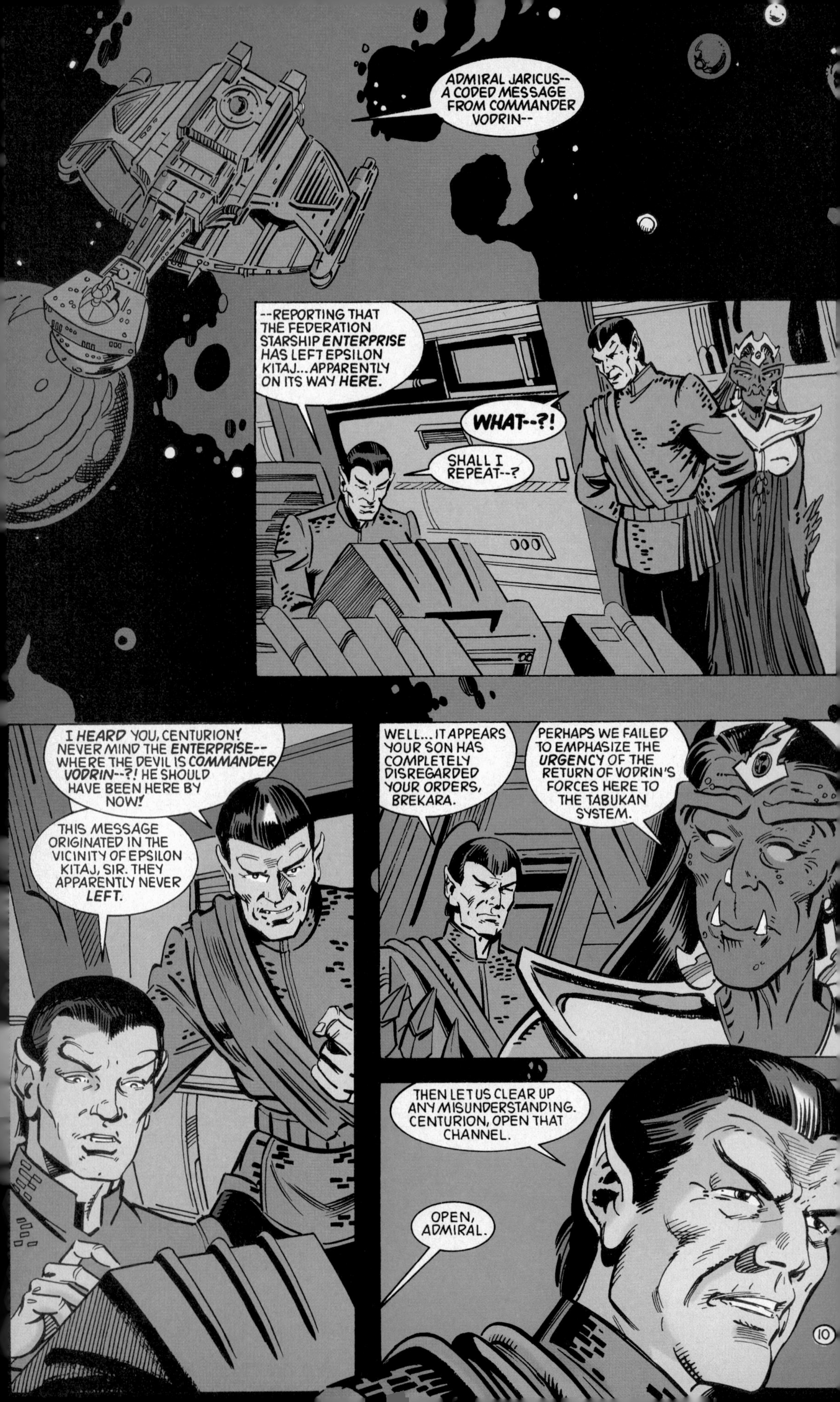
ADMIRAL JARICUS--A CODED MESSAGE FROM COMMANDER VODRIN--
--REPORTING THAT THE FEDERATION STARSHIP ENTERPRISE HAS LEFT EPSILON KITAJ... APPARENTLY ON ITS WAY HERE.
WHAT--?!
SHALL I REPEAT--?
I HEARD YOU, CENTURION! NEVER MIND THE ENTERPRISE--WHERE THE DEVIL IS COMMANDER VODRIN--?! HE SHOULD HAVE BEEN HERE BY NOW!
THIS MESSAGE ORIGINATED IN THE VICINITY OF EPSILON KITAJ, SIR. THEY APPARENTLY NEVER LEFT.
WELL... IT APPEARS YOUR SON HAS COMPLETELY DISREGARDED YOUR ORDERS, BREKARA.
PERHAPS WE FAILED TO EMPHASIZE THE URGENCY OF THE RETURN OF VODRIN'S FORCES HERE TO THE TABUKAN SYSTEM.
THEN LET US CLEAR UP ANY MISUNDERSTANDING. CENTURION, OPEN THAT CHANNEL.
OPEN, ADMIRAL.
10

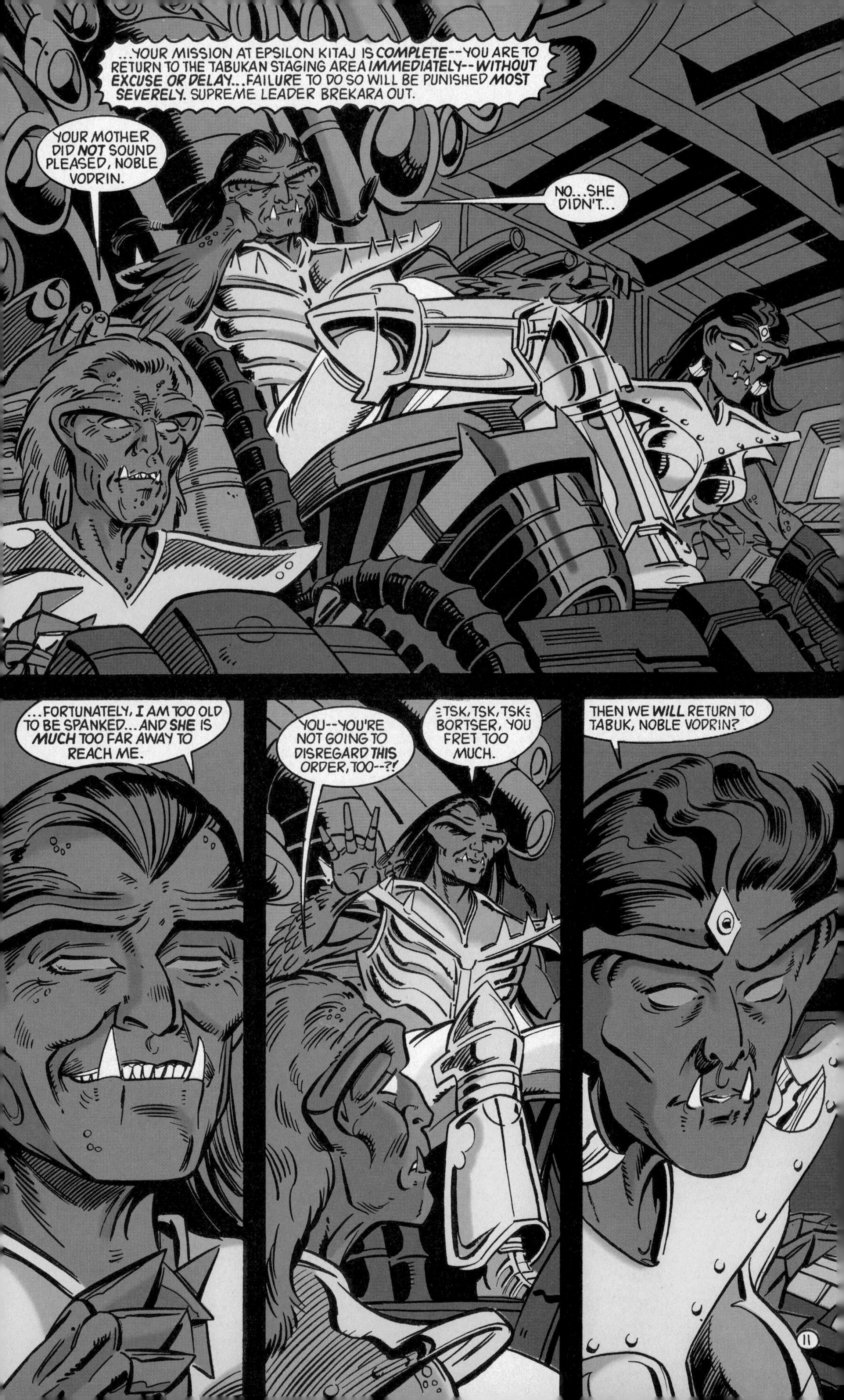
...YOUR MISSION AT EPSILON KITAJ IS COMPLETE--YOU ARE TO RETURN TO THE TABUKAN STAGING AREA IMMEDIATELY--WITHOUT EXCUSE OR DELAY...FAILURE TO DO SO WILL BE PUNISHED MOST SEVERELY. SUPREME LEADER BREKARA OUT.
YOUR MOTHER DID NOT SOUND PLEASED, NOBLE VODRIN.
NO...SHE DIDN'T...
...FORTUNATELY, I AM TOO OLD TO BE SPANKED...AND SHE IS MUCH TOO FAR AWAY TO REACH ME.
YOU--YOU'RE NOT GOING TO DISREGARD THIS ORDER, TOO--?!
=TSK, TSK, TSK= BORTSER, YOU FRET TOO MUCH.
THEN WE WILL RETURN TO TABUK, NOBLE VODRIN?
11

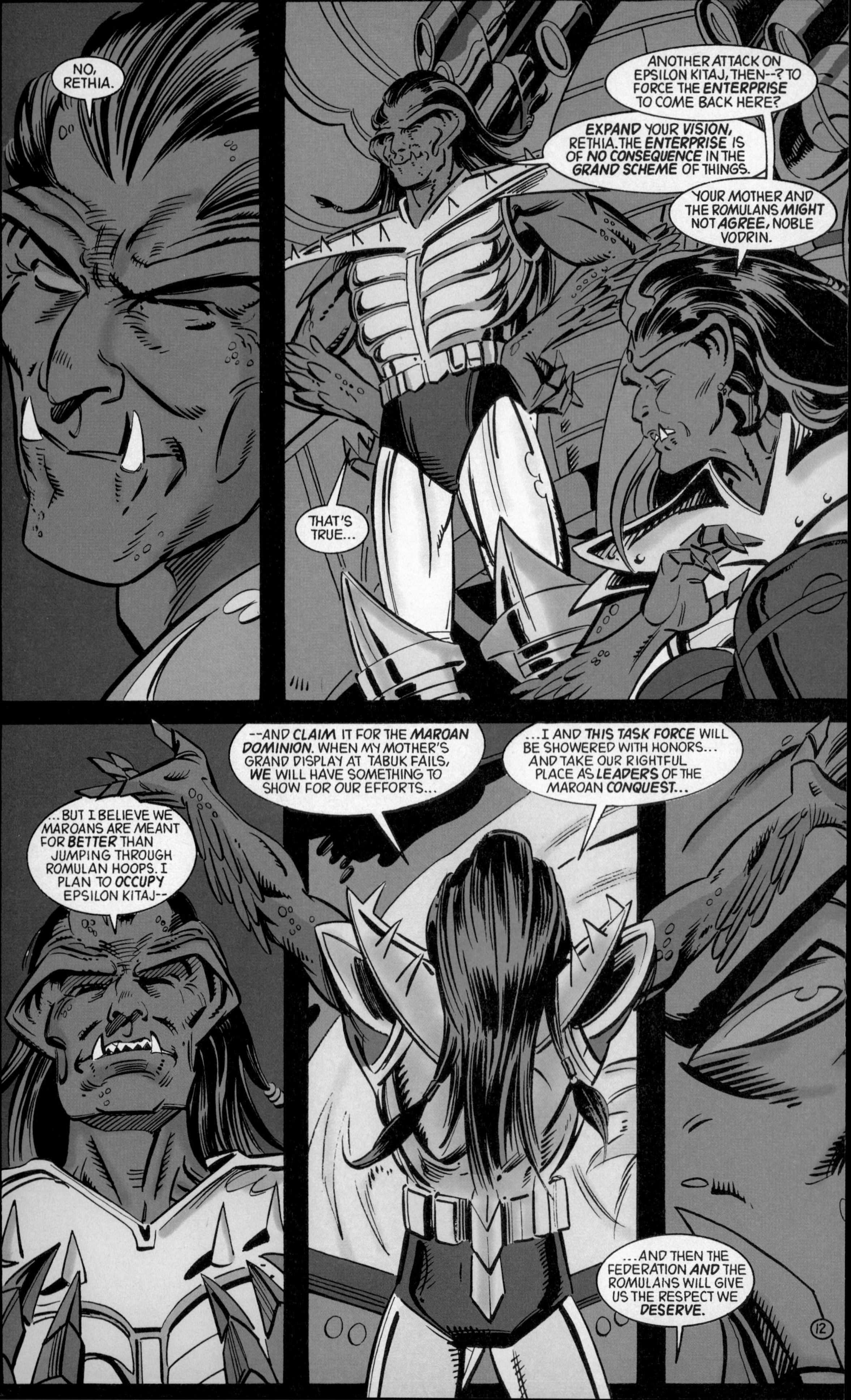
NO, RETHIA.
ANOTHER ATTACK ON EPSILON KITAJ, THEN--? TO FORCE THE ENTERPRISE TO COME BACK HERE?
EXPAND YOUR VISION, RETHIA. THE ENTERPRISE IS OF NO CONSEQUENCE IN THE GRAND SCHEME OF THINGS.
YOUR MOTHER AND THE ROMULANS MIGHT NOT AGREE, NOBLE VODRIN.
THAT'S TRUE...
...BUT I BELIEVE WE MAROANS ARE MEANT FOR BETTER THAN JUMPING THROUGH ROMULAN HOOPS. I PLAN TO OCCUPY EPSILON KITAJ--
--AND CLAIM IT FOR THE MAROAN DOMINION. WHEN MY MOTHER'S GRAND DISPLAY AT TABUK FAILS, WE WILL HAVE SOMETHING TO SHOW FOR OUR EFFORTS...
...I AND THIS TASK FORCE WILL BE SHOWERED WITH HONORS... AND TAKE OUR RIGHTFUL PLACE AS LEADERS OF THE MAROAN CONQUEST...
...AND THEN THE FEDERATION AND THE ROMULANS WILL GIVE US THE RESPECT WE DESERVE.
12

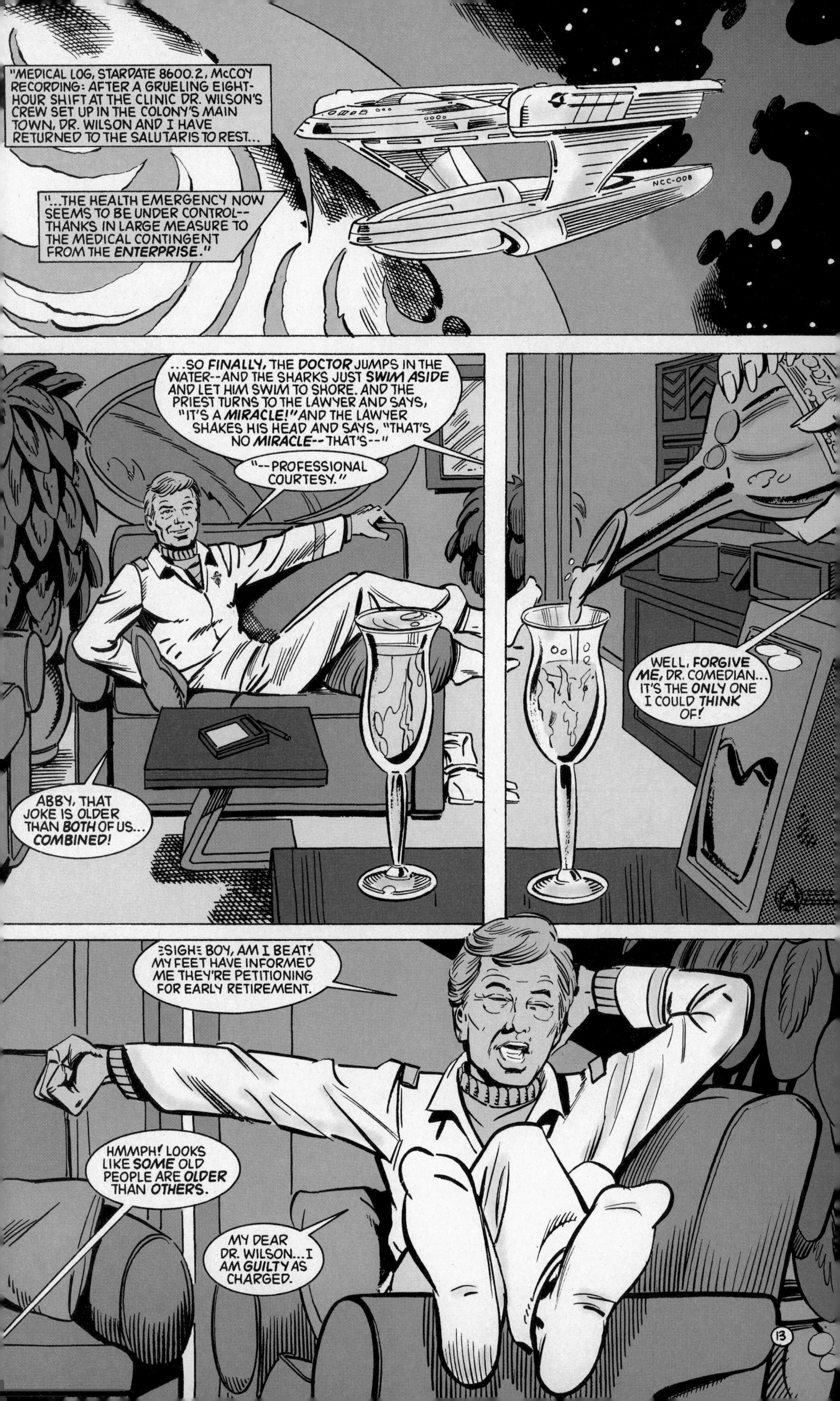
"MEDICAL LOG, STARDATE 8600.2, McCOY RECORDING: AFTER A GRUELING EIGHT-HOUR SHIFT AT THE CLINIC DR. WILSON'S CREW SET UP IN THE COLONY'S MAIN TOWN, DR. WILSON AND I HAVE RETURNED TO THE SALUTARIS TO REST...
NCC-008
"...THE HEALTH EMERGENCY NOW SEEMS TO BE UNDER CONTROL--THANKS IN LARGE MEASURE TO THE MEDICAL CONTINGENT FROM THE ENTERPRISE."
...SO FINALLY, THE DOCTOR JUMPS IN THE WATER--AND THE SHARKS JUST SWIM ASIDE AND LET HIM SWIM TO SHORE. AND THE PRIEST TURNS TO THE LAWYER AND SAYS, "IT'S A MIRACLE!" AND THE LAWYER SHAKES HIS HEAD AND SAYS, "THAT'S NO MIRACLE--THAT'S--"
"--PROFESSIONAL COURTESY."
ABBY, THAT JOKE IS OLDER THAN BOTH OF US... COMBINED!
WELL, FORGIVE ME, DR. COMEDIAN... IT'S THE ONLY ONE I COULD THINK OF!
=SIGH= BOY, AM I BEAT! MY FEET HAVE INFORMED ME THEY'RE PETITIONING FOR EARLY RETIREMENT.
HMMPH! LOOKS LIKE SOME OLD PEOPLE ARE OLDER THAN OTHERS.
MY DEAR DR. WILSON... I AM GUILTY AS CHARGED.

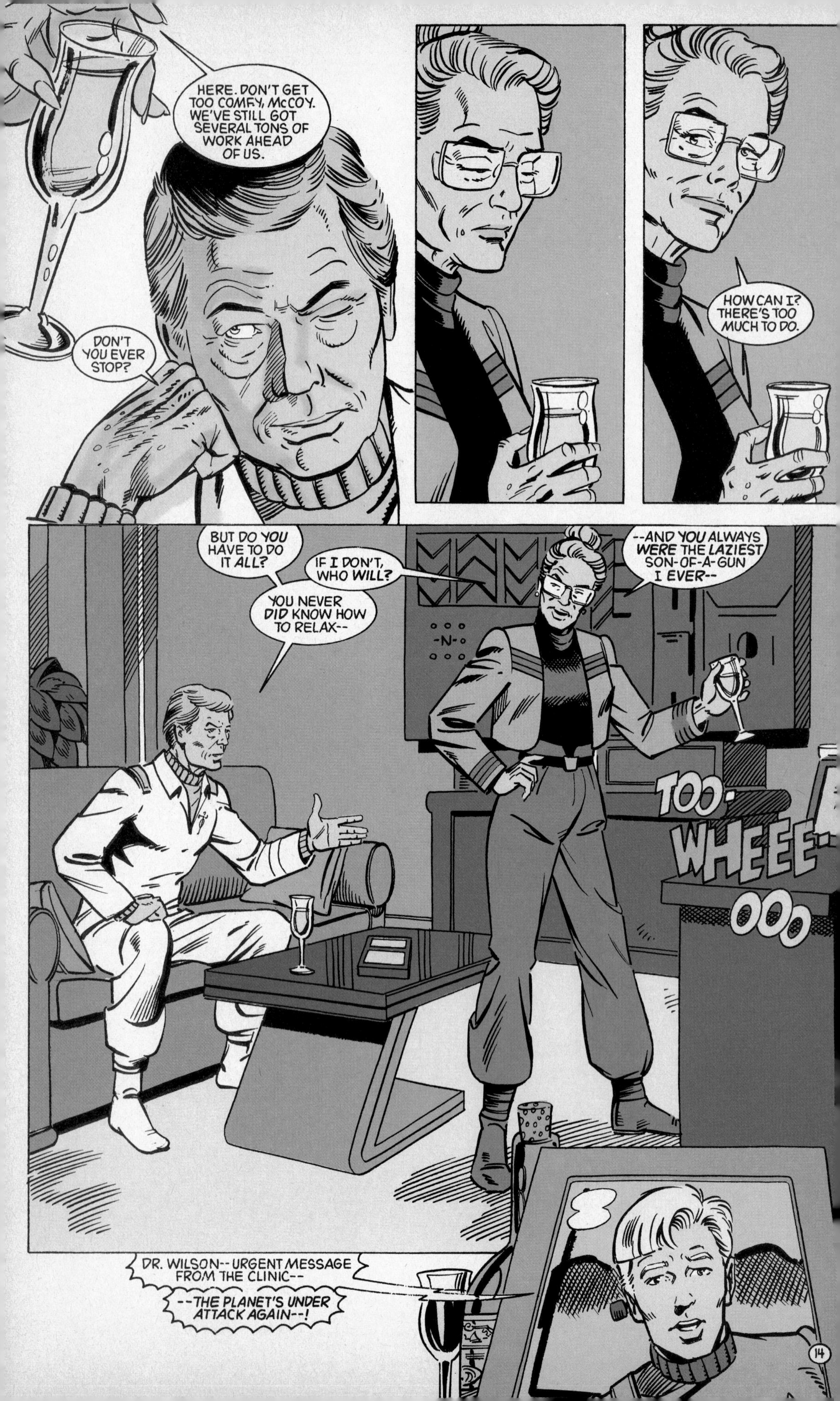

HERE. DON'T GET TOO COMFY, McCOY. WE'VE STILL GOT SEVERAL TONS OF WORK AHEAD OF US.
DON'T YOU EVER STOP?
HOW CAN I? THERE'S TOO MUCH TO DO.
BUT DO YOU HAVE TO DO IT ALL?
IF I DON'T, WHO WILL?
YOU NEVER DID KNOW HOW TO RELAX--
--AND YOU ALWAYS WERE THE LAZIEST SON-OF-A-GUN I EVER--
-N-
TOO-WHEEE-OOO
DR. WILSON--URGENT MESSAGE FROM THE CLINIC--
--THE PLANET'S UNDER ATTACK AGAIN--!

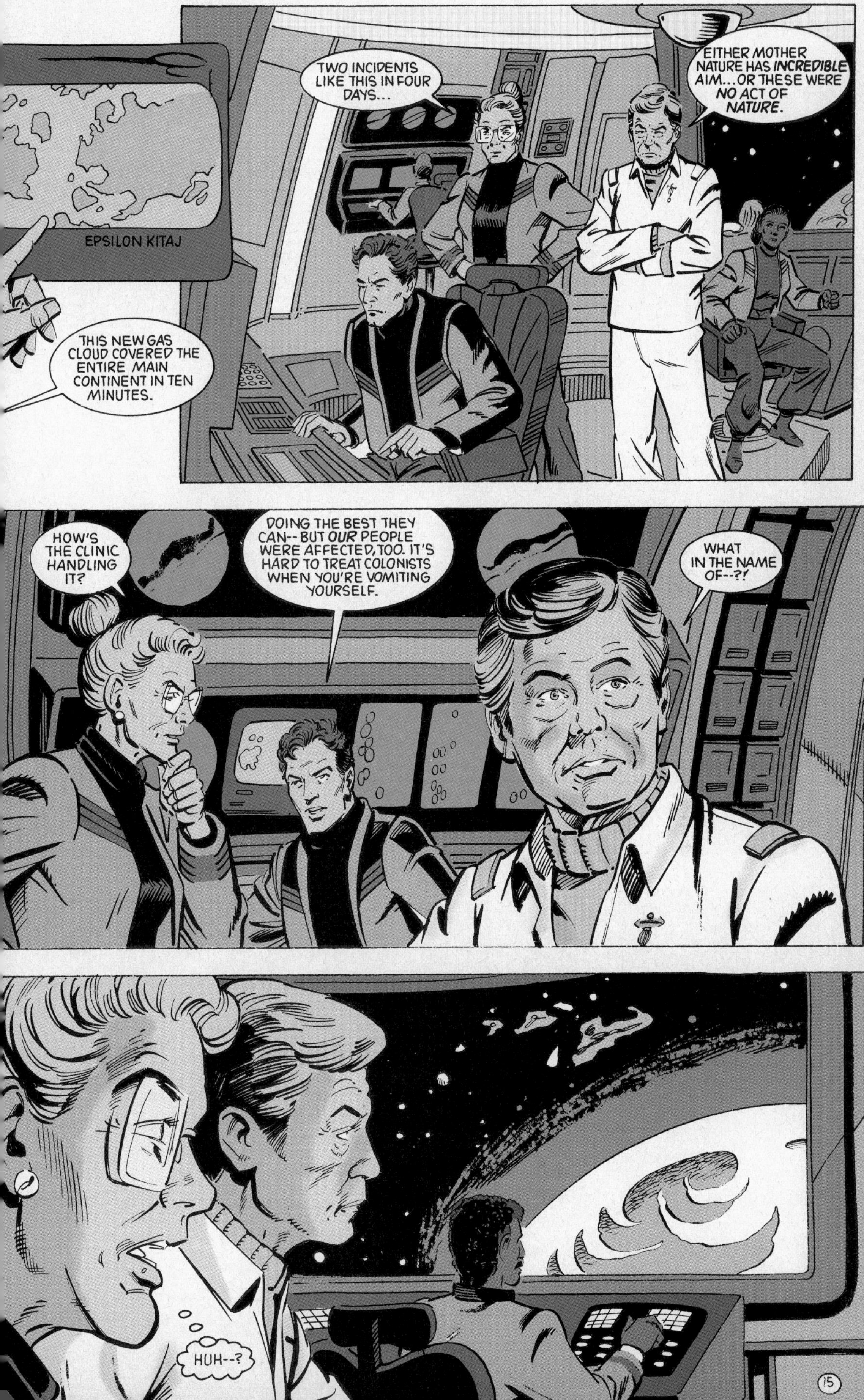
EPSILON KITAJ
THIS NEW GAS CLOUD COVERED THE ENTIRE MAIN CONTINENT IN TEN MINUTES.
TWO INCIDENTS LIKE THIS IN FOUR DAYS...
EITHER MOTHER NATURE HAS *INCREDIBLE* AIM...OR THESE WERE *NO ACT OF NATURE*.
HOW'S THE CLINIC HANDLING IT?
DOING THE BEST THEY CAN-- BUT *OUR* PEOPLE WERE AFFECTED, TOO. IT'S HARD TO TREAT COLONISTS WHEN YOU'RE VOMITING YOURSELF.
WHAT IN THE NAME OF--?!
HUH--?

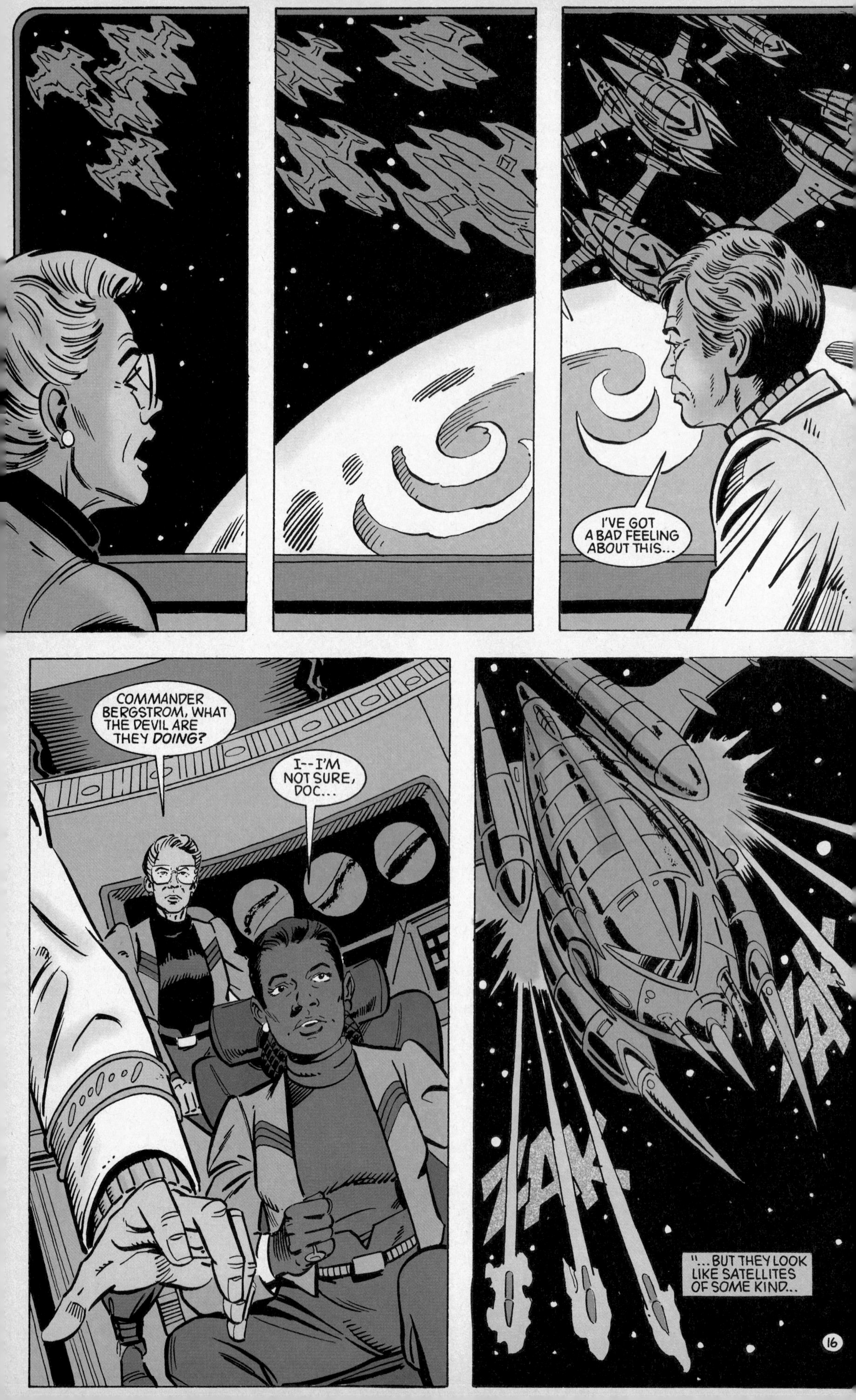
I'VE GOT A BAD FEELING ABOUT THIS...
COMMANDER BERGSTROM, WHAT THE DEVIL ARE THEY *DOING*?
I--I'M NOT SURE, DOC...
ZAK
ZAK
"...BUT THEY LOOK LIKE SATELLITES OF SOME KIND...

"...AND THEY'RE *ALL* LAUNCHING THEM..."

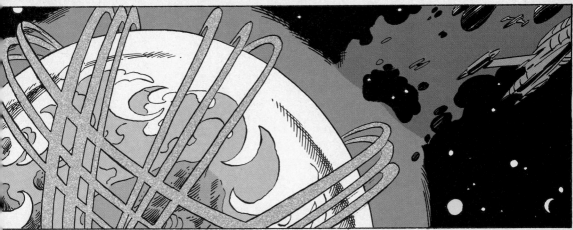

MY GOD... IT LOOKS LIKE THEY'RE SURROUNDING THE *WHOLE* PLANET!

EPSILON KITAJ

WHOEVER THEY ARE, THEY'RE SENDING A MESSAGE--TO THE PLANET AND ALL SHIPS IN THE VICINITY.

EULP'E LET'S HEAR IT.

17

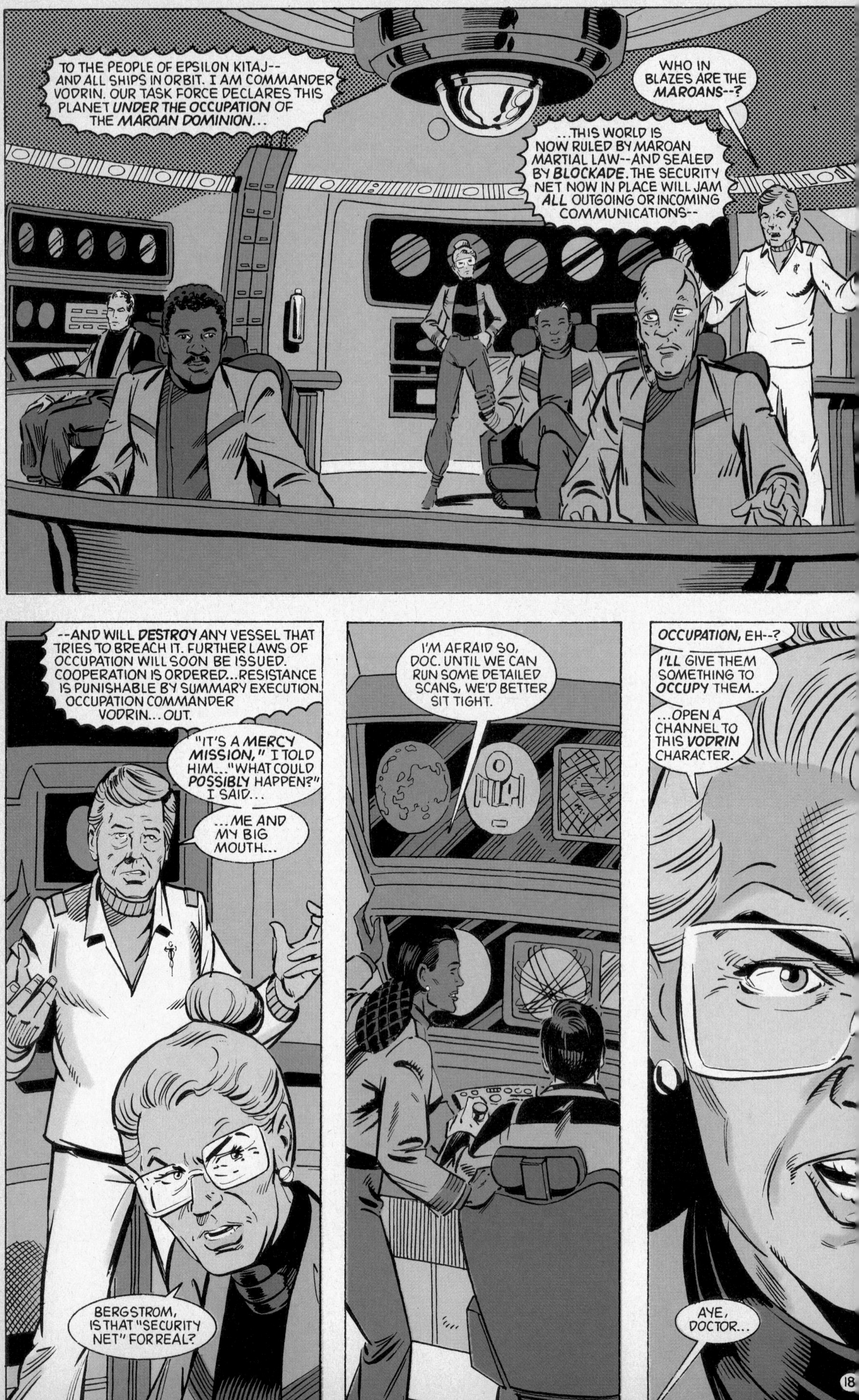
TO THE PEOPLE OF EPSILON KITAJ-- AND ALL SHIPS IN ORBIT. I AM COMMANDER VODRIN. OUR TASK FORCE DECLARES THIS PLANET UNDER THE OCCUPATION OF THE MAROAN DOMINION...
...THIS WORLD IS NOW RULED BY MAROAN MARTIAL LAW--AND SEALED BY BLOCKADE. THE SECURITY NET NOW IN PLACE WILL JAM ALL OUTGOING OR INCOMING COMMUNICATIONS--
WHO IN BLAZES ARE THE MAROANS--?
--AND WILL DESTROY ANY VESSEL THAT TRIES TO BREACH IT. FURTHER LAWS OF OCCUPATION WILL SOON BE ISSUED. COOPERATION IS ORDERED...RESISTANCE IS PUNISHABLE BY SUMMARY EXECUTION. OCCUPATION COMMANDER VODRIN... OUT.
"IT'S A MERCY MISSION," I TOLD HIM..."WHAT COULD POSSIBLY HAPPEN?" I SAID...
...ME AND MY BIG MOUTH...
BERGSTROM, IS THAT "SECURITY NET" FOR REAL?
I'M AFRAID SO, DOC. UNTIL WE CAN RUN SOME DETAILED SCANS, WE'D BETTER SIT TIGHT.
OCCUPATION, EH--?
I'LL GIVE THEM SOMETHING TO OCCUPY THEM...
...OPEN A CHANNEL TO THIS VODRIN CHARACTER.
AYE, DOCTOR...

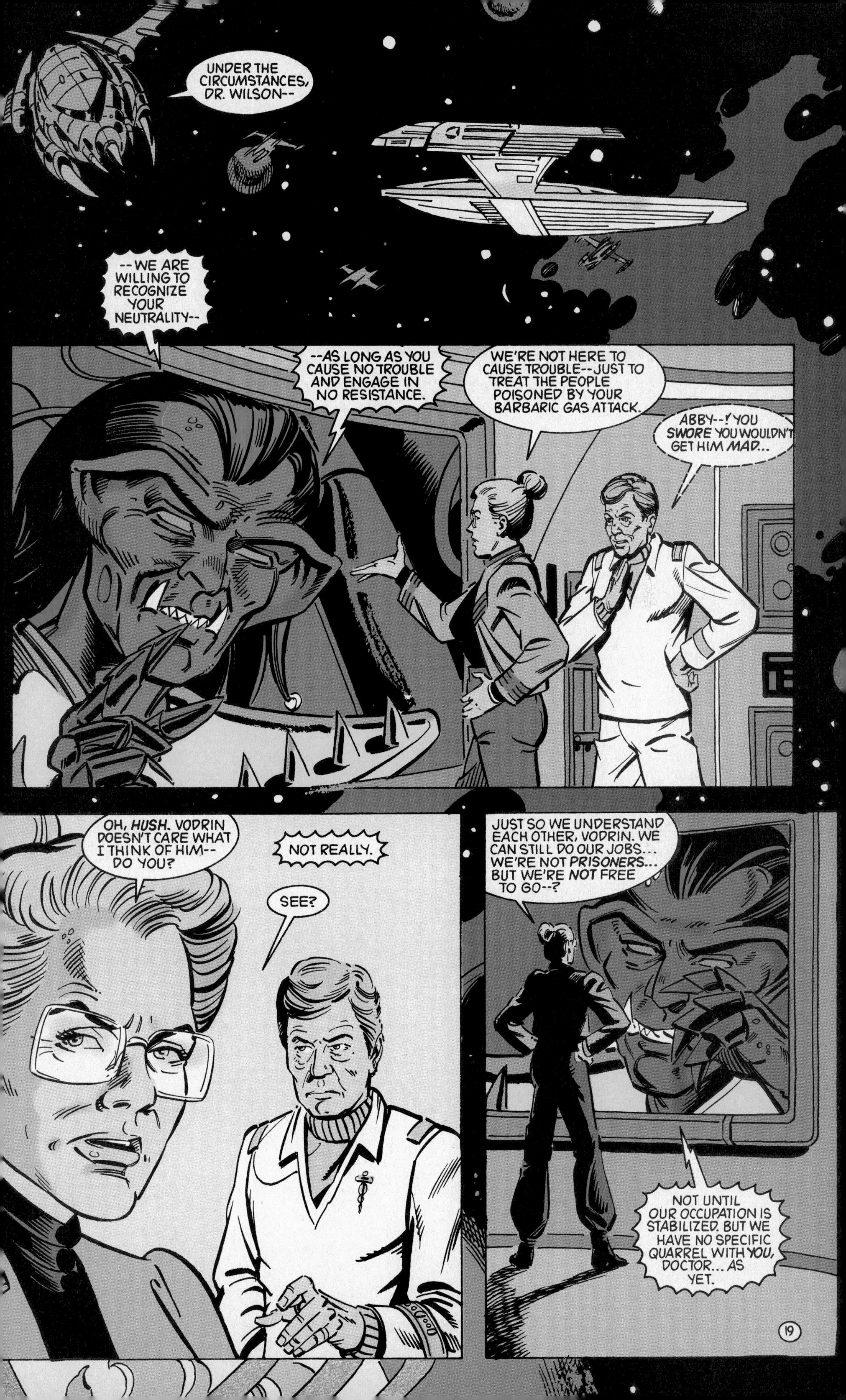

UNDER THE CIRCUMSTANCES, DR. WILSON--
--WE ARE WILLING TO RECOGNIZE YOUR NEUTRALITY--
--AS LONG AS YOU CAUSE NO TROUBLE AND ENGAGE IN NO RESISTANCE.
WE'RE NOT HERE TO CAUSE TROUBLE--JUST TO TREAT THE PEOPLE POISONED BY YOUR BARBARIC GAS ATTACK.
ABBY--! YOU SWORE YOU WOULDN'T GET HIM MAD...
OH, HUSH. VODRIN DOESN'T CARE WHAT I THINK OF HIM-- DO YOU?
NOT REALLY.
SEE?
JUST SO WE UNDERSTAND EACH OTHER, VODRIN. WE CAN STILL DO OUR JOBS... WE'RE NOT PRISONERS... BUT WE'RE NOT FREE TO GO--?
NOT UNTIL OUR OCCUPATION IS STABILIZED. BUT WE HAVE NO SPECIFIC QUARREL WITH YOU, DOCTOR... AS YET.

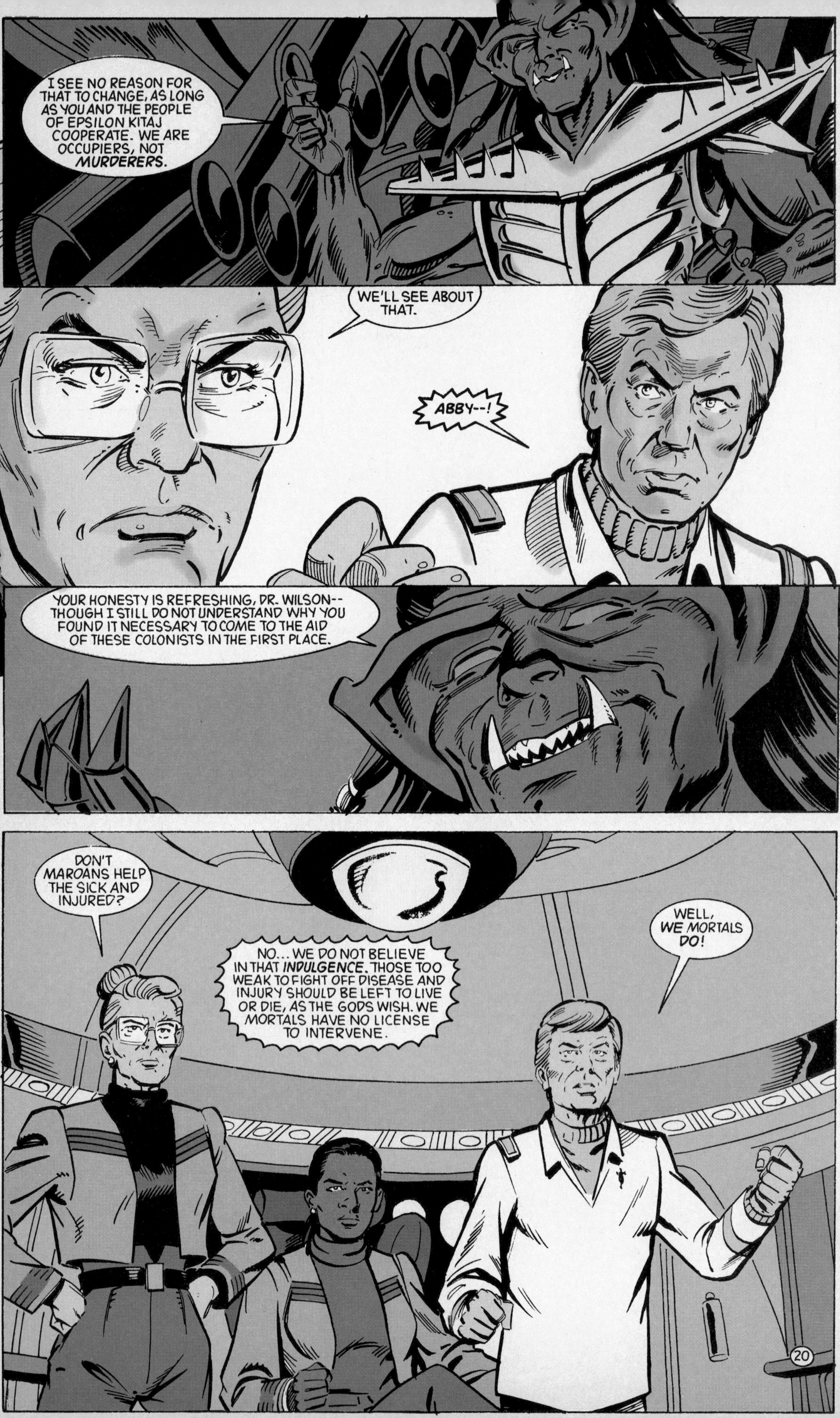
I SEE NO REASON FOR THAT TO CHANGE, AS LONG AS YOU AND THE PEOPLE OF EPSILON KITAJ COOPERATE. WE ARE OCCUPIERS, NOT *MURDERERS*.
WE'LL SEE ABOUT THAT.
ABBY--!
YOUR HONESTY IS REFRESHING, DR. WILSON-- THOUGH I STILL DO NOT UNDERSTAND WHY YOU FOUND IT NECESSARY TO COME TO THE AID OF THESE COLONISTS IN THE FIRST PLACE.
DON'T MAROANS HELP THE SICK AND INJURED?
NO... WE DO NOT BELIEVE IN THAT *INDULGENCE*. THOSE TOO WEAK TO FIGHT OFF DISEASE AND INJURY SHOULD BE LEFT TO LIVE OR DIE, AS THE GODS WISH. WE MORTALS HAVE NO LICENSE TO INTERVENE.
WELL, *WE MORTALS DO*!
20

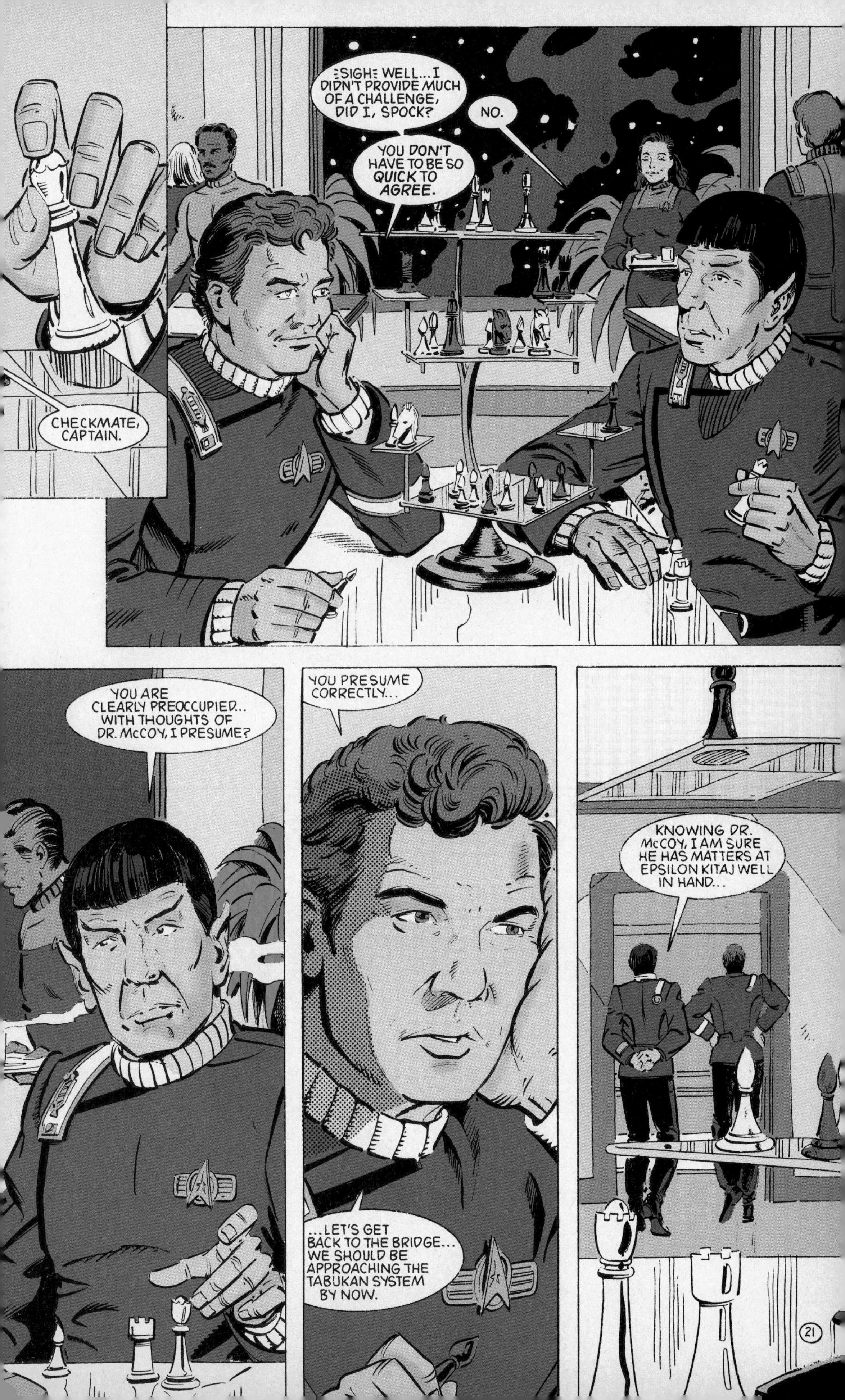

CHECKMATE, CAPTAIN.
≡SIGH≡ WELL...I DIDN'T PROVIDE MUCH OF A CHALLENGE, DID I, SPOCK?
NO.
YOU DON'T HAVE TO BE SO QUICK TO AGREE.
YOU ARE CLEARLY PREOCCUPIED... WITH THOUGHTS OF DR. McCOY, I PRESUME?
YOU PRESUME CORRECTLY...
...LET'S GET BACK TO THE BRIDGE... WE SHOULD BE APPROACHING THE TABUKAN SYSTEM BY NOW.
KNOWING DR. McCOY, I AM SURE HE HAS MATTERS AT EPSILON KITAJ WELL IN HAND...
21

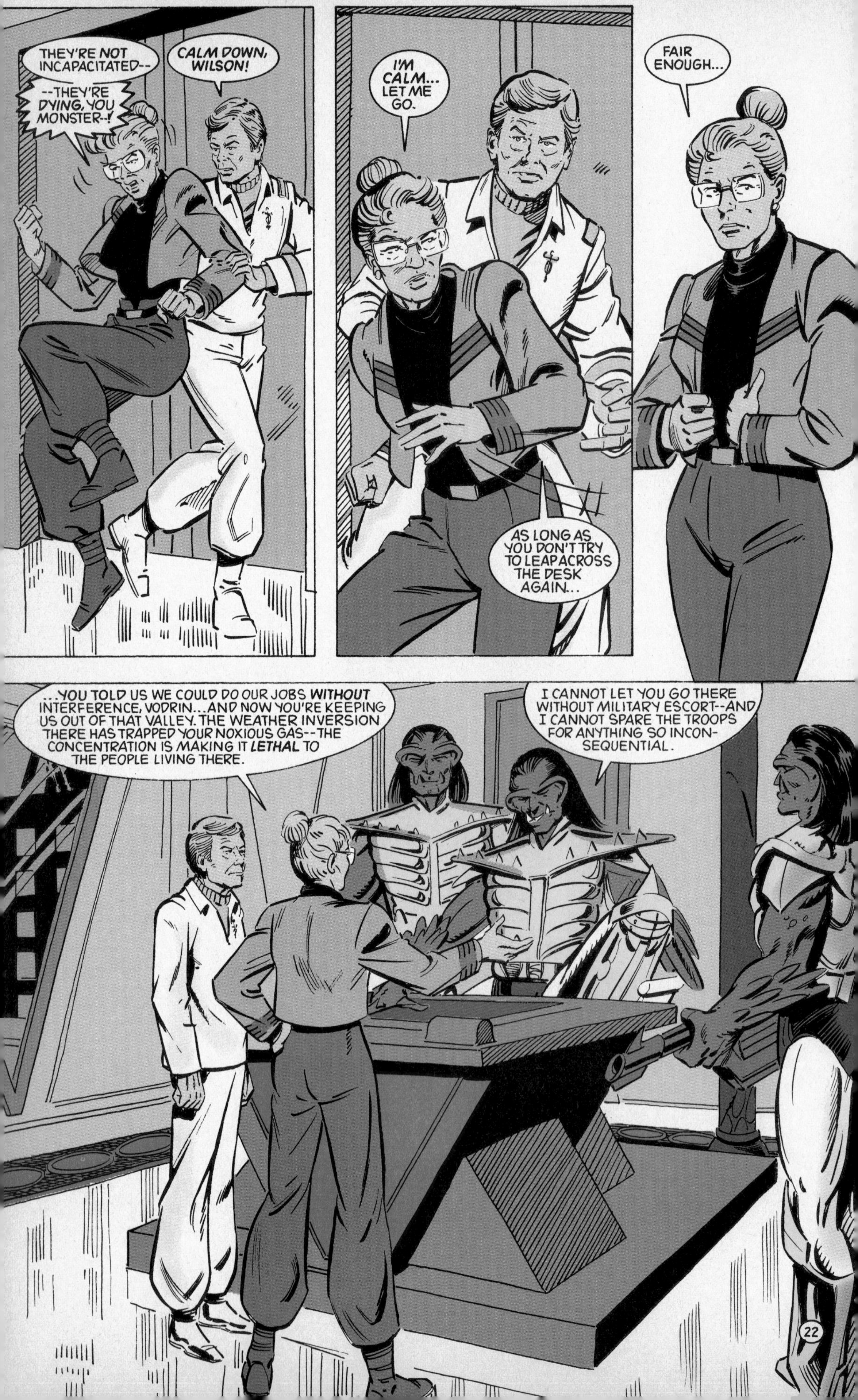
THEY'RE NOT INCAPACITATED--
--THEY'RE DYING, YOU MONSTER--!
CALM DOWN, WILSON!
I'M CALM... LET ME GO.
FAIR ENOUGH...
AS LONG AS YOU DON'T TRY TO LEAP ACROSS THE DESK AGAIN...
...YOU TOLD US WE COULD DO OUR JOBS WITHOUT INTERFERENCE, VODRIN...AND NOW YOU'RE KEEPING US OUT OF THAT VALLEY. THE WEATHER INVERSION THERE HAS TRAPPED YOUR NOXIOUS GAS--THE CONCENTRATION IS MAKING IT LETHAL TO THE PEOPLE LIVING THERE.
I CANNOT LET YOU GO THERE WITHOUT MILITARY ESCORT--AND I CANNOT SPARE THE TROOPS FOR ANYTHING SO INCON-SEQUENTIAL.
22

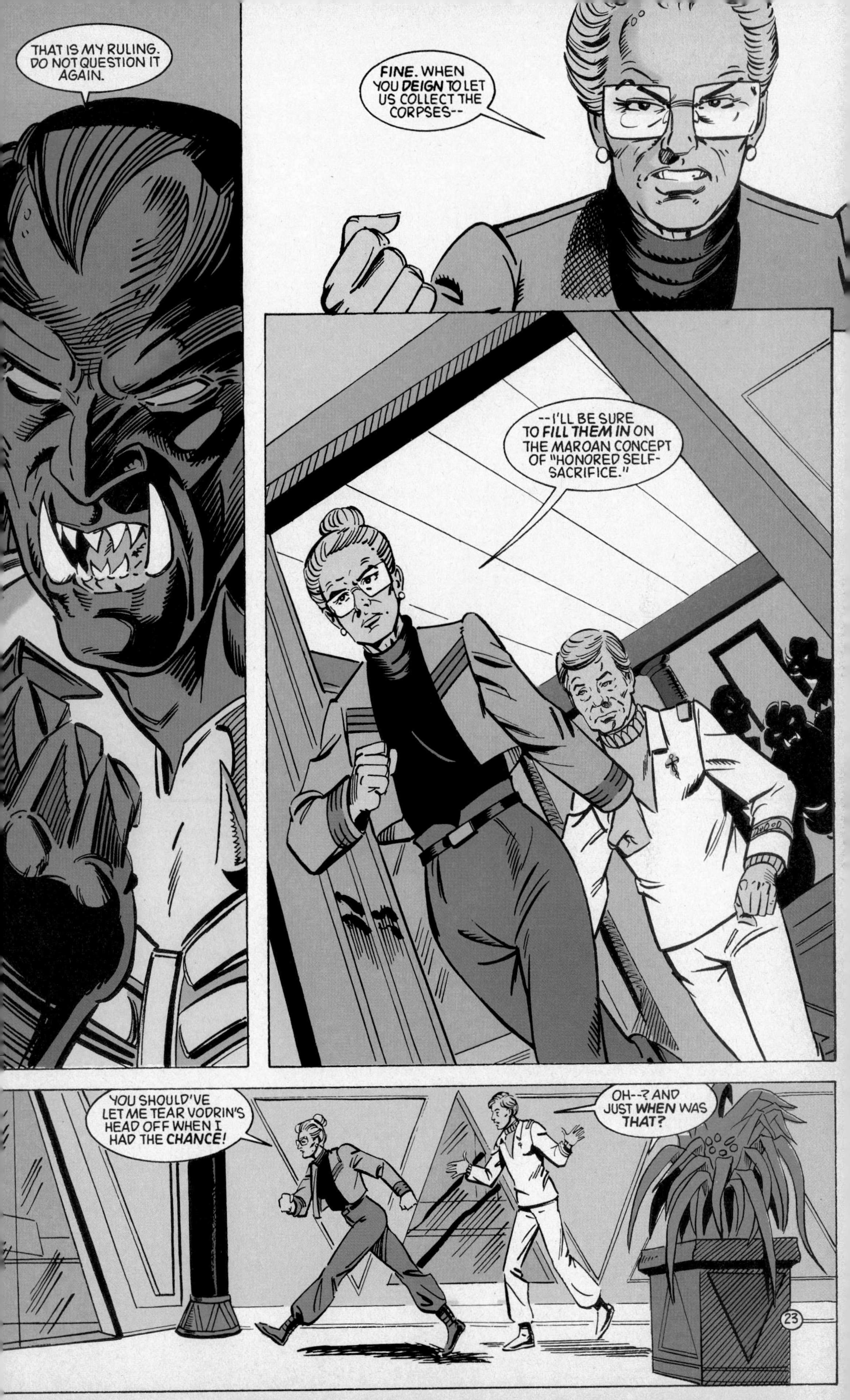
THAT IS MY RULING. DO NOT QUESTION IT AGAIN.
FINE. WHEN YOU DEIGN TO LET US COLLECT THE CORPSES--
--I'LL BE SURE TO FILL THEM IN ON THE MAROAN CONCEPT OF "HONORED SELF-SACRIFICE."
YOU SHOULD'VE LET ME TEAR VODRIN'S HEAD OFF WHEN I HAD THE CHANCE!
OH--? AND JUST WHEN WAS THAT?
23

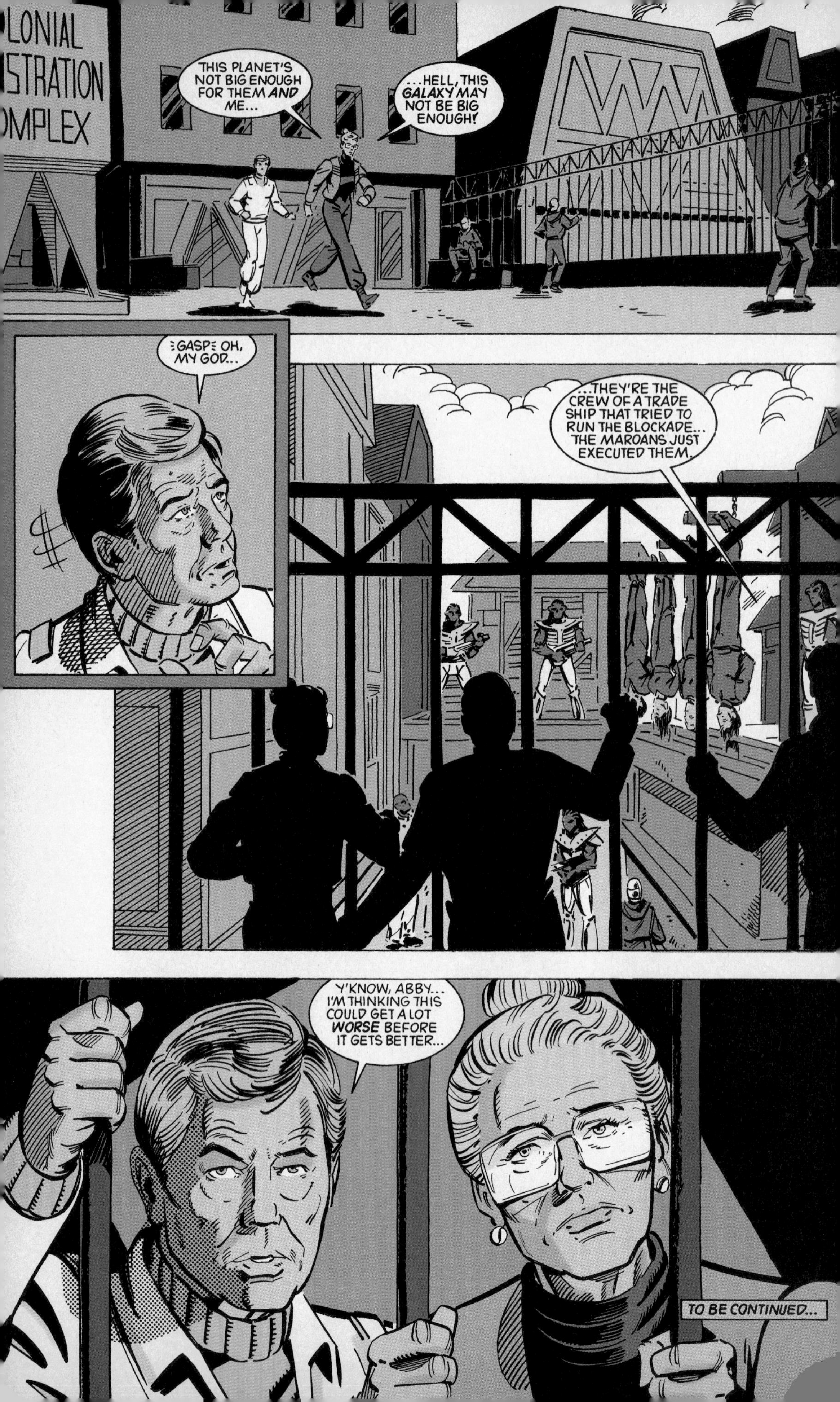
LONIAL
STRATION
MPLEX
THIS PLANET'S NOT BIG ENOUGH FOR THEM AND ME...
...HELL, THIS GALAXY MAY NOT BE BIG ENOUGH!
GASP OH, MY GOD...
...THEY'RE THE CREW OF A TRADE SHIP THAT TRIED TO RUN THE BLOCKADE... THE MAROANS JUST EXECUTED THEM.
Y'KNOW, ABBY... I'M THINKING THIS COULD GET A LOT WORSE BEFORE IT GETS BETTER...
TO BE CONTINUED...

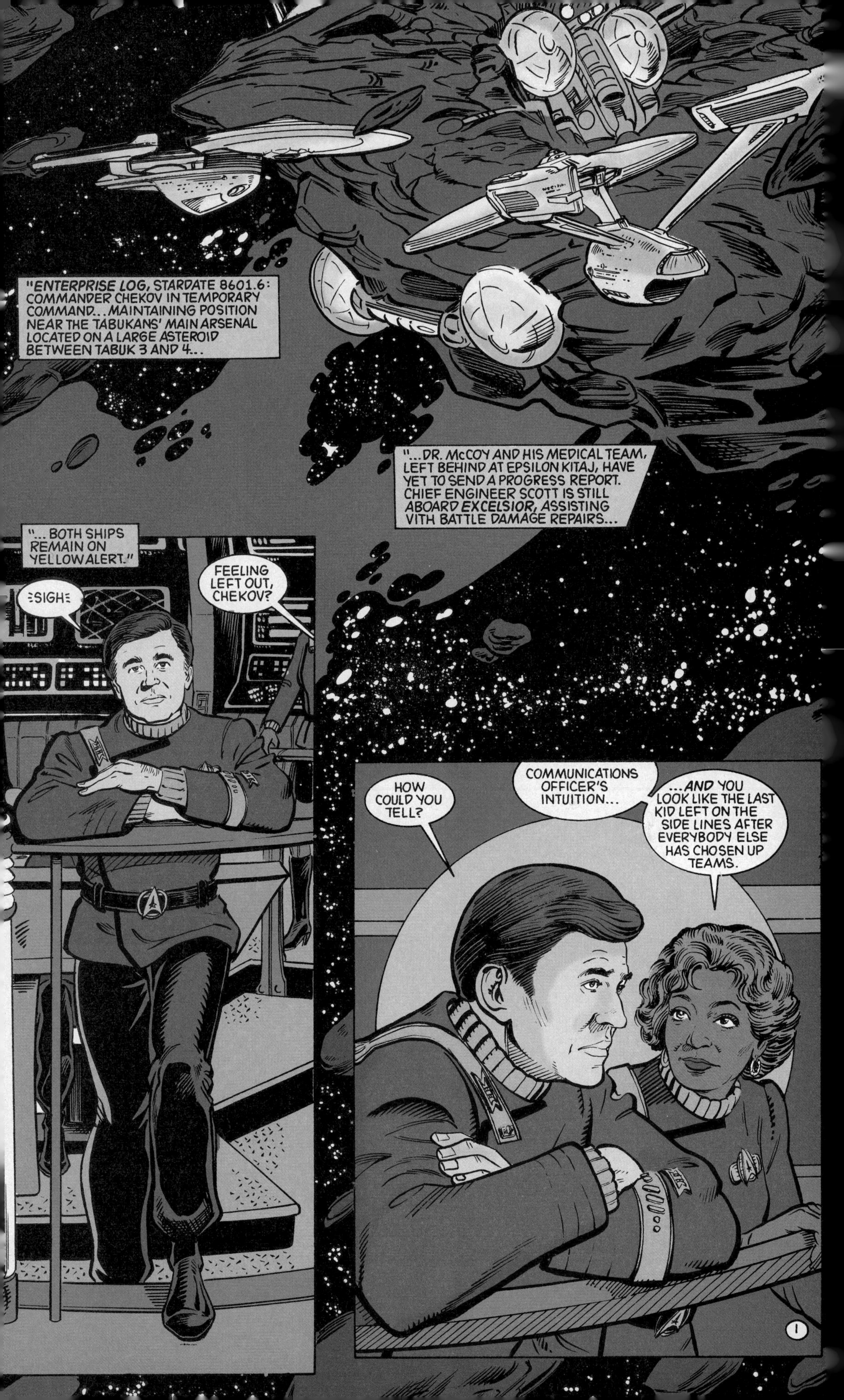
"ENTERPRISE LOG, STARDATE 8601.6: COMMANDER CHEKOV IN TEMPORARY COMMAND... MAINTAINING POSITION NEAR THE TABUKANS' MAIN ARSENAL LOCATED ON A LARGE ASTEROID BETWEEN TABUK 3 AND 4...
"...DR. McCOY AND HIS MEDICAL TEAM, LEFT BEHIND AT EPSILON KITAJ, HAVE YET TO SEND A PROGRESS REPORT. CHIEF ENGINEER SCOTT IS STILL ABOARD EXCELSIOR, ASSISTING VITH BATTLE DAMAGE REPAIRS...
"... BOTH SHIPS REMAIN ON YELLOW ALERT."
SIGH
FEELING LEFT OUT, CHEKOV?
HOW COULD YOU TELL?
COMMUNICATIONS OFFICER'S INTUITION...
...AND YOU LOOK LIKE THE LAST KID LEFT ON THE SIDE LINES AFTER EVERYBODY ELSE HAS CHOSEN UP TEAMS.
1

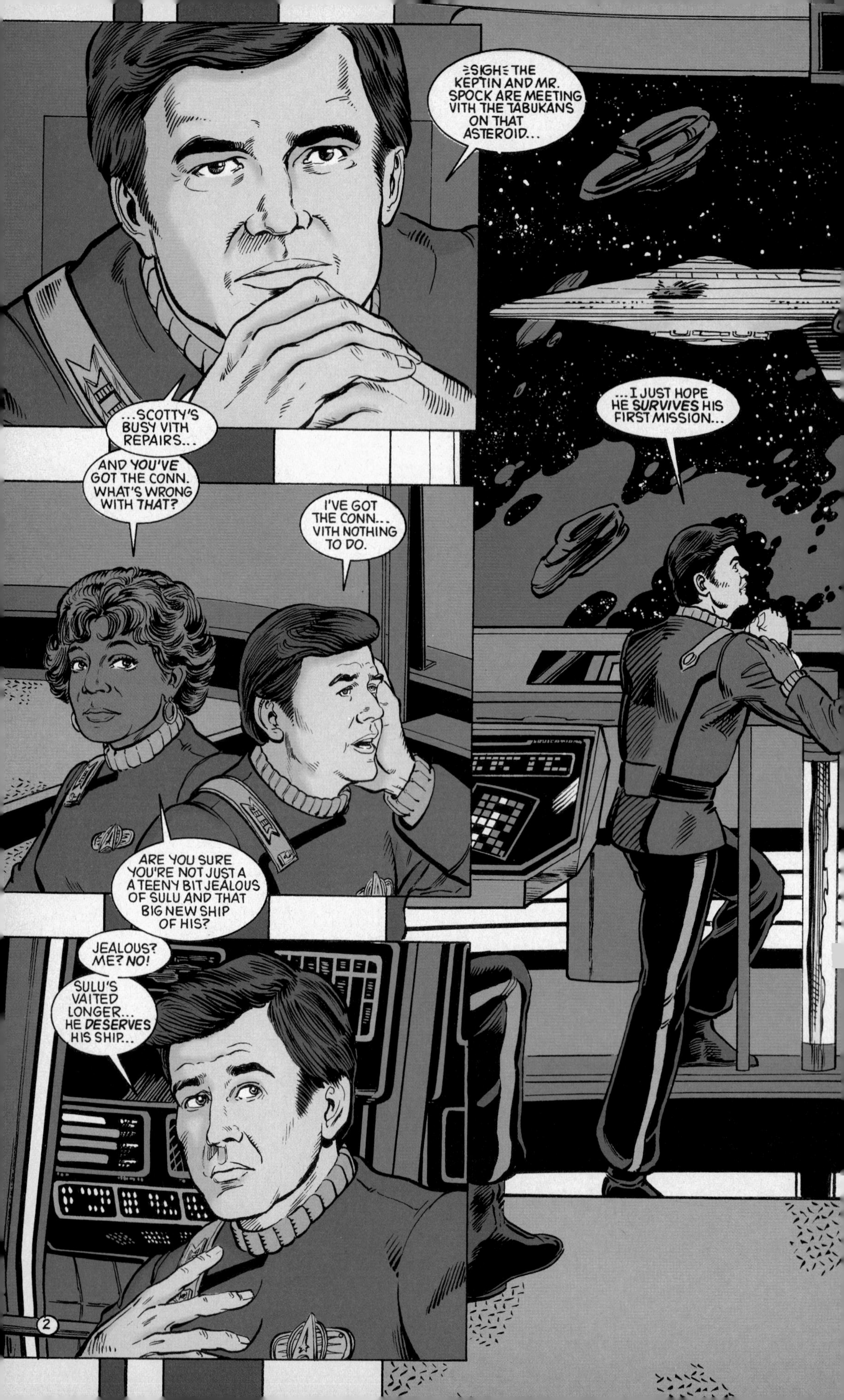

≥SIGH≤ THE KEP'TIN AND MR. SPOCK ARE MEETING VITH THE TABUKANS ON THAT ASTEROID...
...SCOTTY'S BUSY VITH REPAIRS...
AND YOU'VE GOT THE CONN. WHAT'S WRONG WITH THAT?
I'VE GOT THE CONN... VITH NOTHING TO DO.
ARE YOU SURE YOU'RE NOT JUST A A TEENY BIT JEALOUS OF SULU AND THAT BIG NEW SHIP OF HIS?
JEALOUS? ME? NO!
SULU'S VAITED LONGER... HE DESERVES HIS SHIP...
...I JUST HOPE HE SURVIVES HIS FIRST MISSION...

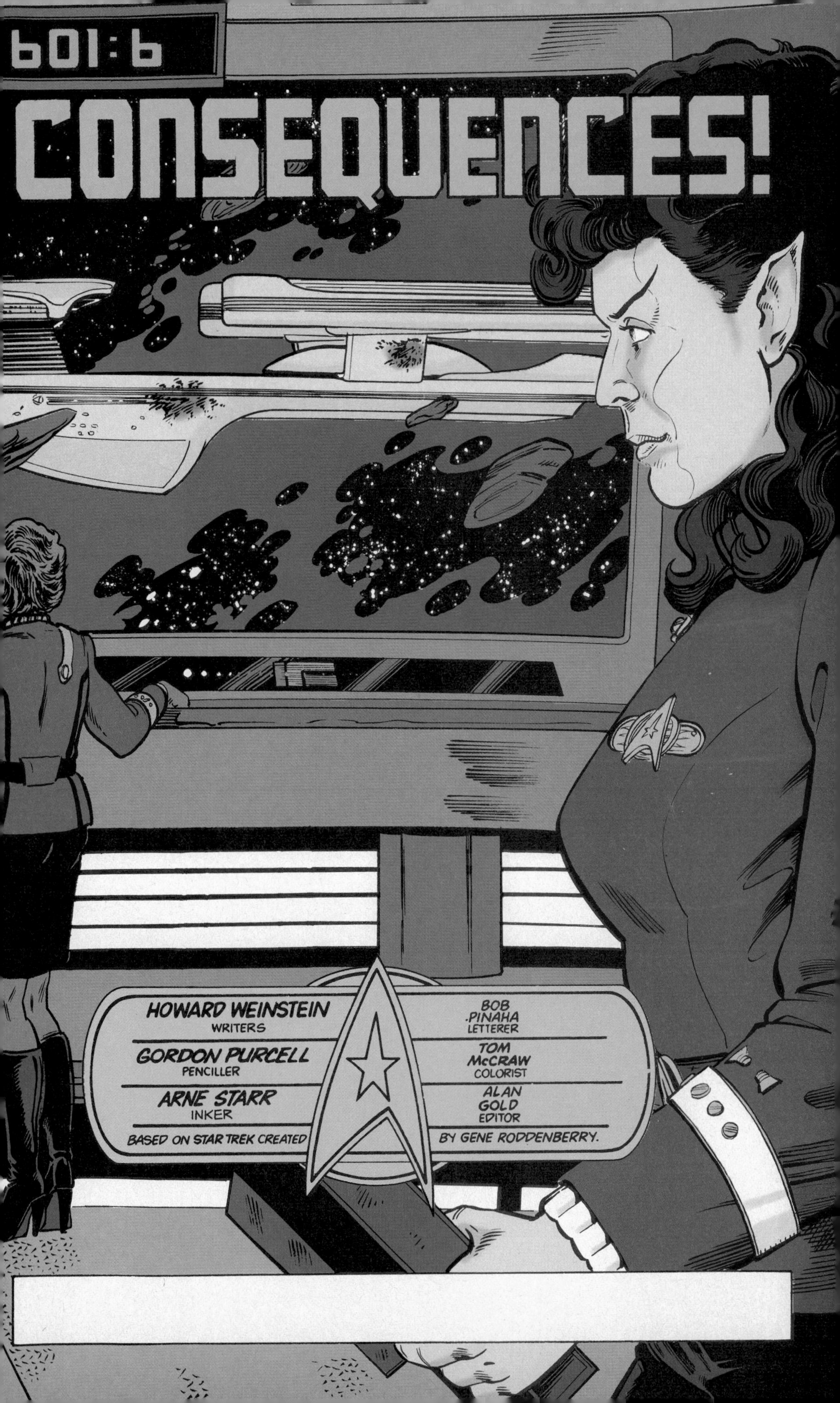
601:6
CONSEQUENCES!
HOWARD WEINSTEIN
WRITERS
GORDON PURCELL
PENCILLER
ARNE STARR
INKER
BOB PINAHA
LETTERER
TOM McCRAW
COLORIST
ALAN GOLD
EDITOR
BASED ON STAR TREK CREATED BY GENE RODDENBERRY.

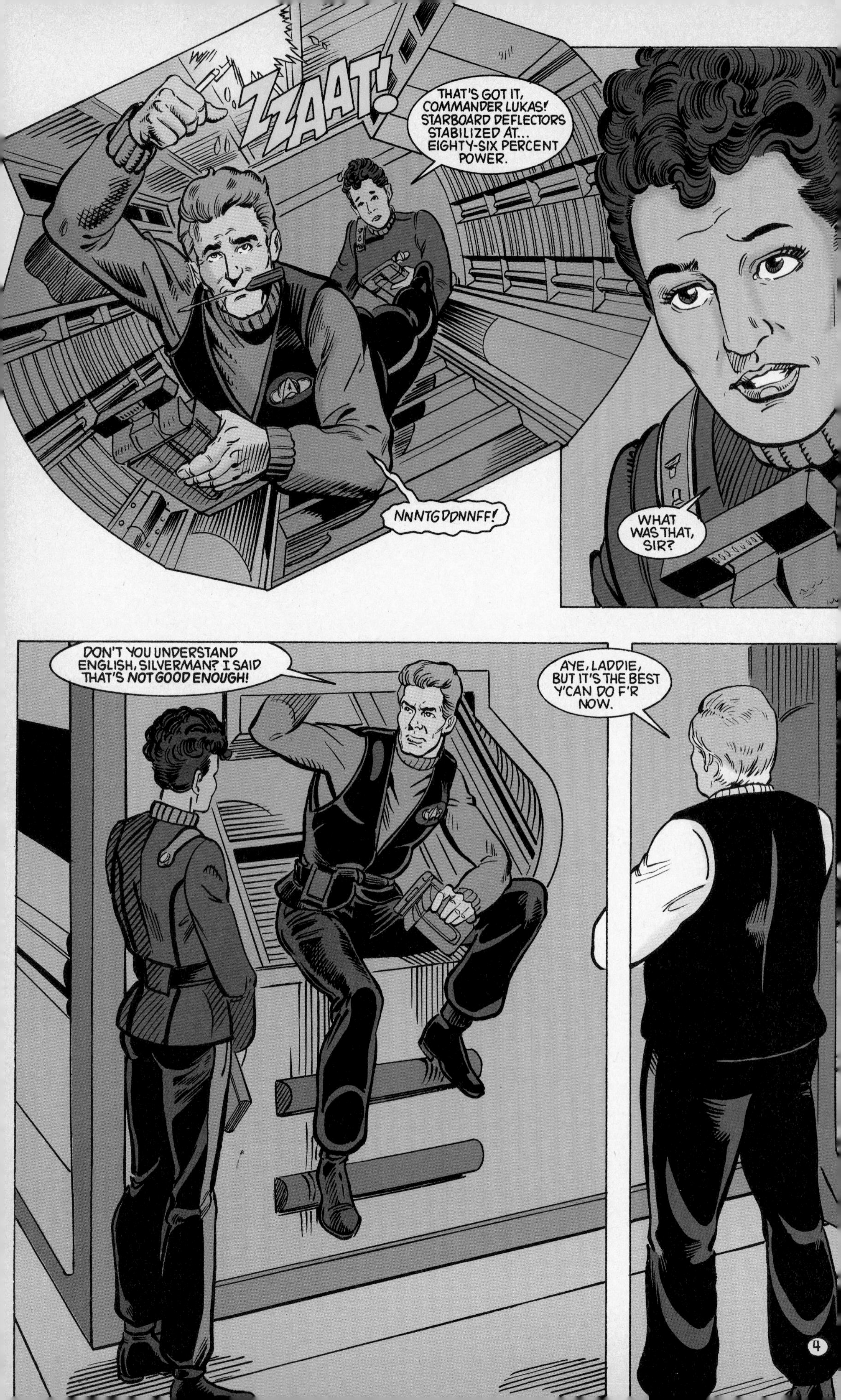
ZZAAT!
THAT'S GOT IT, COMMANDER LUKAS! STARBOARD DEFLECTORS STABILIZED AT... EIGHTY-SIX PERCENT POWER.
NNNTGDDNNFF!
WHAT WAS THAT, SIR?
DON'T YOU UNDERSTAND ENGLISH, SILVERMAN? I SAID THAT'S NOT GOOD ENOUGH!
AYE, LADDIE, BUT IT'S THE BEST Y'CAN DO F'R NOW.
4

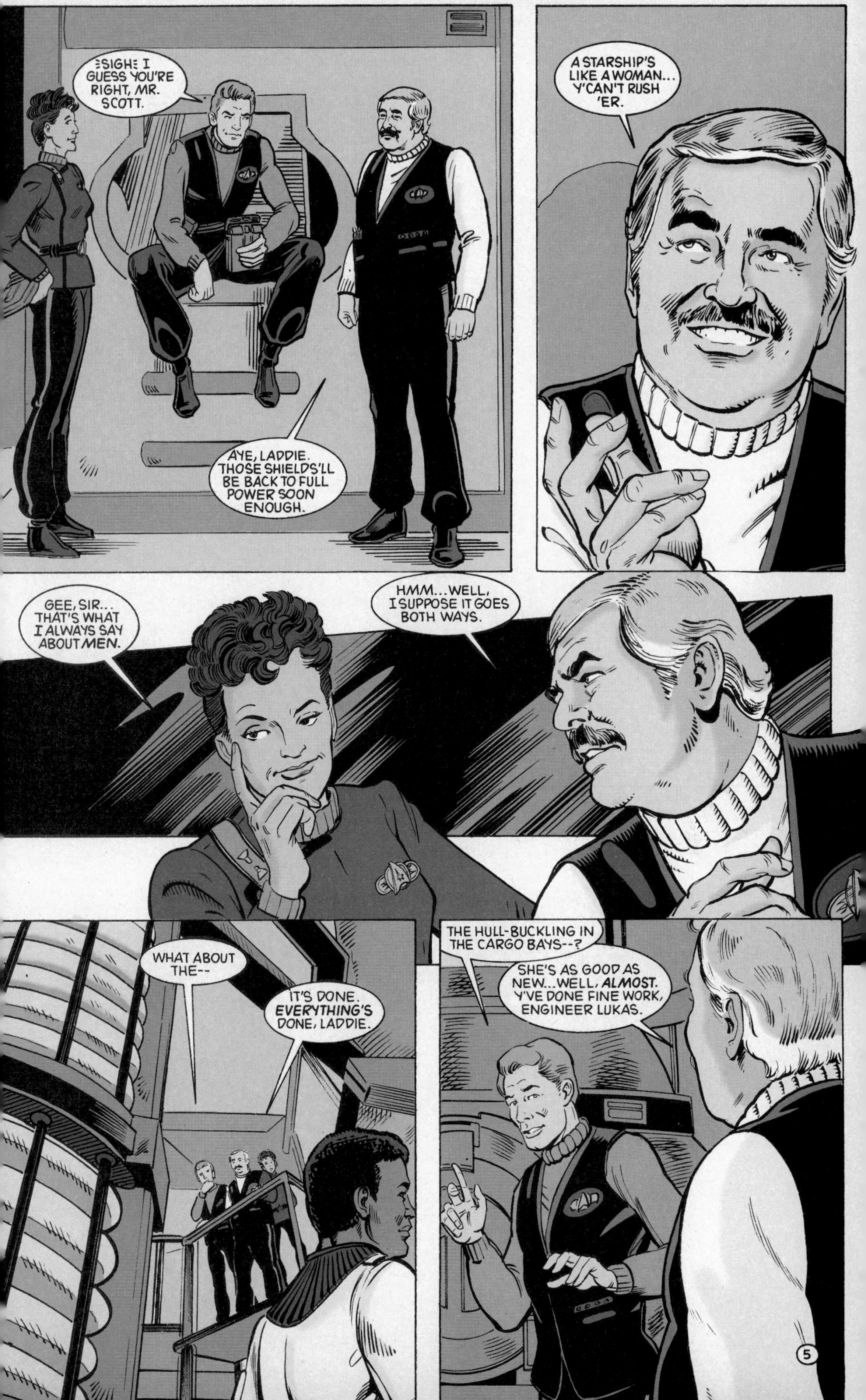

=SIGH= I GUESS YOU'RE RIGHT, MR. SCOTT.
AYE, LADDIE. THOSE SHIELDS'LL BE BACK TO FULL POWER SOON ENOUGH.
A STARSHIP'S LIKE A WOMAN... Y'CAN'T RUSH 'ER.
GEE, SIR... THAT'S WHAT I ALWAYS SAY ABOUT *MEN*.
HMM... WELL, I SUPPOSE IT GOES BOTH WAYS.
WHAT ABOUT THE--
IT'S DONE. *EVERYTHING'S* DONE, LADDIE.
THE HULL-BUCKLING IN THE CARGO BAYS--?
SHE'S AS GOOD AS NEW... WELL, *ALMOST*. Y'VE DONE FINE WORK, ENGINEER LUKAS.

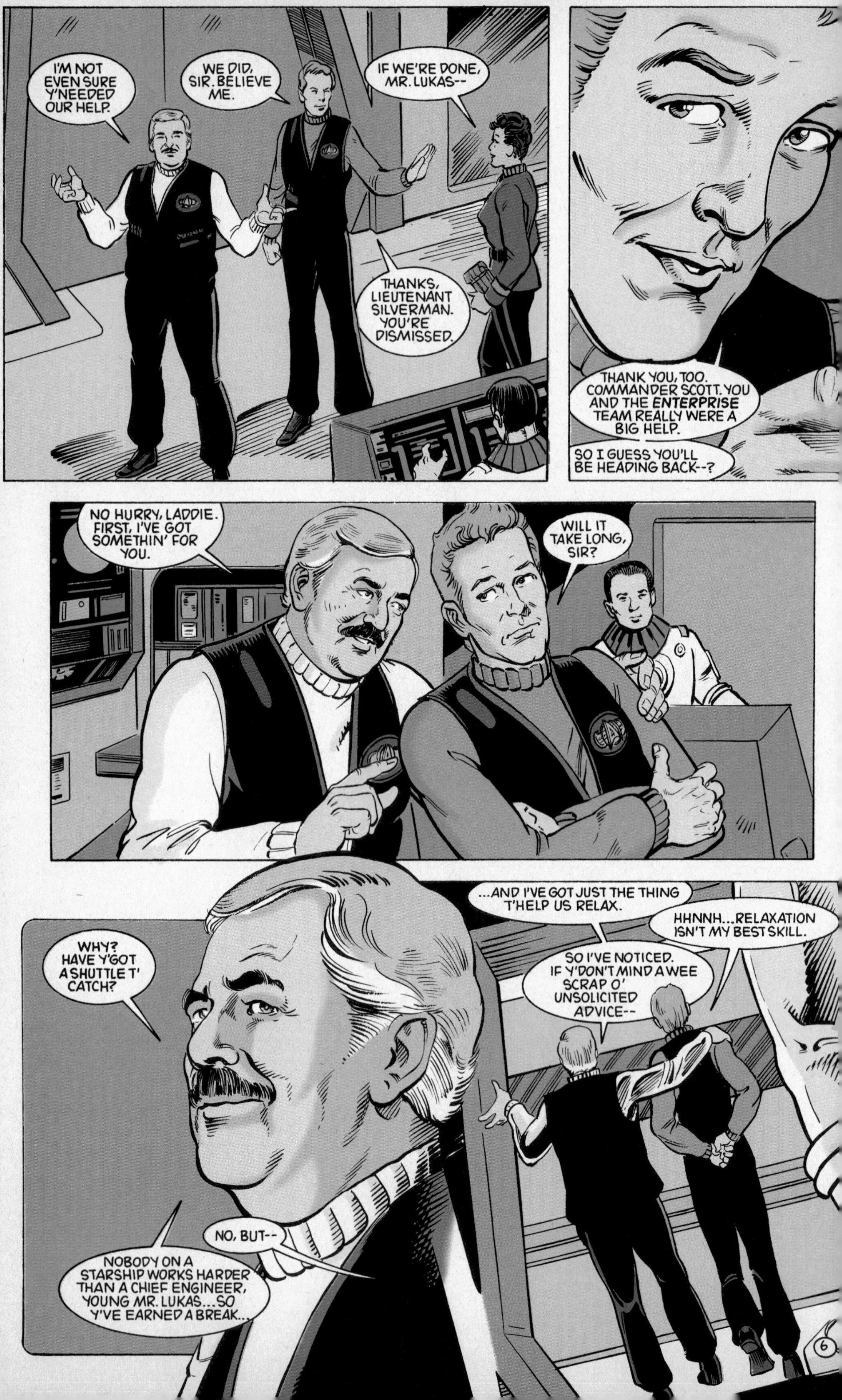
I'M NOT EVEN SURE Y'NEEDED OUR HELP.
WE DID, SIR. BELIEVE ME.
IF WE'RE DONE, MR. LUKAS--
THANKS, LIEUTENANT SILVERMAN. YOU'RE DISMISSED.
THANK YOU, TOO. COMMANDER SCOTT. YOU AND THE ENTERPRISE TEAM REALLY WERE A BIG HELP.
SO I GUESS YOU'LL BE HEADING BACK--?
NO HURRY, LADDIE. FIRST, I'VE GOT SOMETHIN' FOR YOU.
WILL IT TAKE LONG, SIR?
WHY? HAVE Y'GOT A SHUTTLE T' CATCH?
NO, BUT--
NOBODY ON A STARSHIP WORKS HARDER THAN A CHIEF ENGINEER, YOUNG MR. LUKAS... SO Y'VE EARNED A BREAK...
...AND I'VE GOT JUST THE THING T'HELP US RELAX.
HHNNH... RELAXATION ISN'T MY BEST SKILL.
SO I'VE NOTICED. IF Y'DON'T MIND A WEE SCRAP O' UNSOLICITED ADVICE--
6

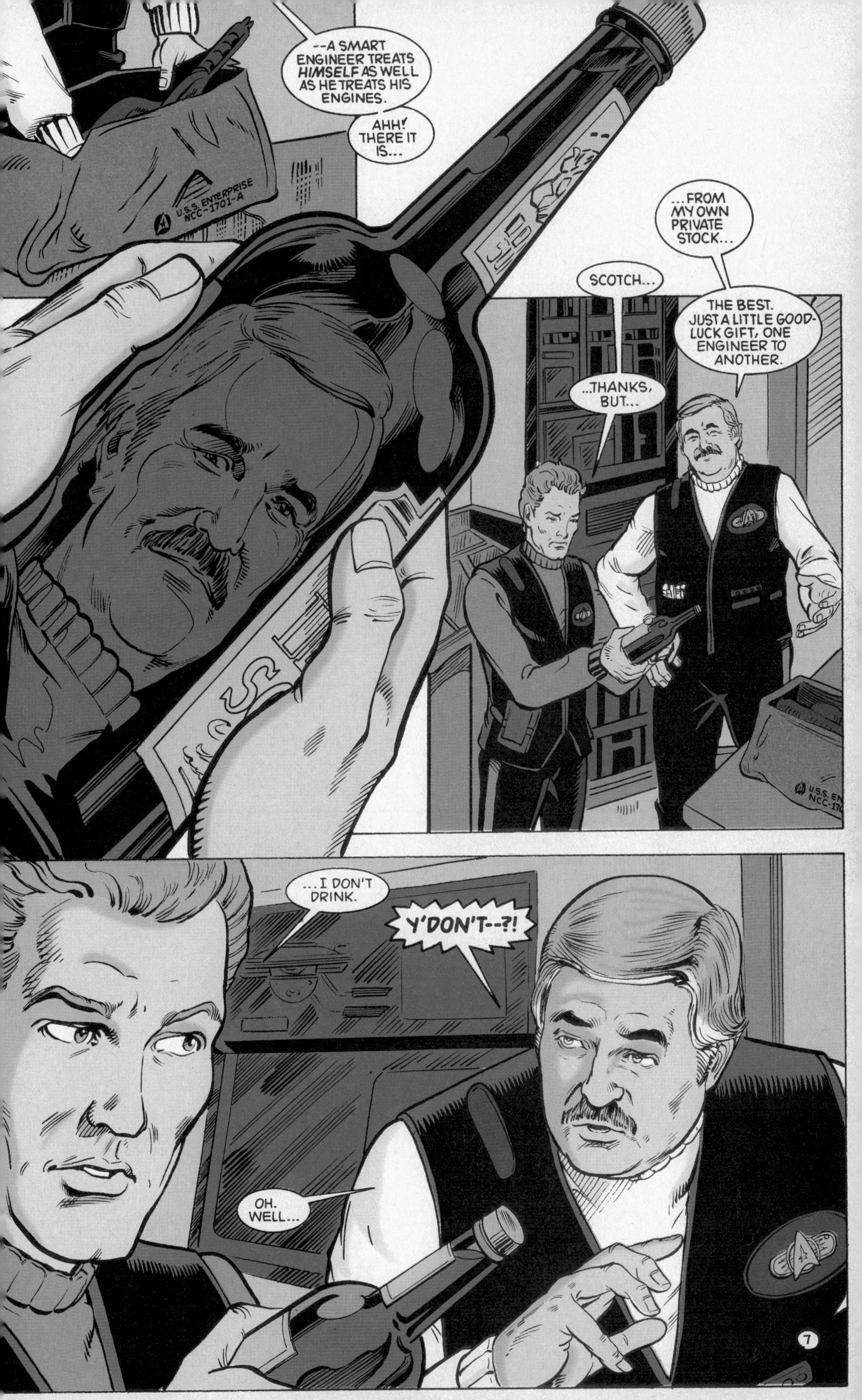

--A SMART ENGINEER TREATS *HIMSELF* AS WELL AS HE TREATS HIS ENGINES.
AHH! THERE IT IS...
U.S.S. ENTERPRISE NCC-1701-A
...FROM MY OWN PRIVATE STOCK...
SCOTCH...
THE BEST. JUST A LITTLE GOOD-LUCK GIFT, ONE ENGINEER TO ANOTHER.
...THANKS, BUT...
...I DON'T DRINK.
Y'DON'T--?!
OH. WELL...

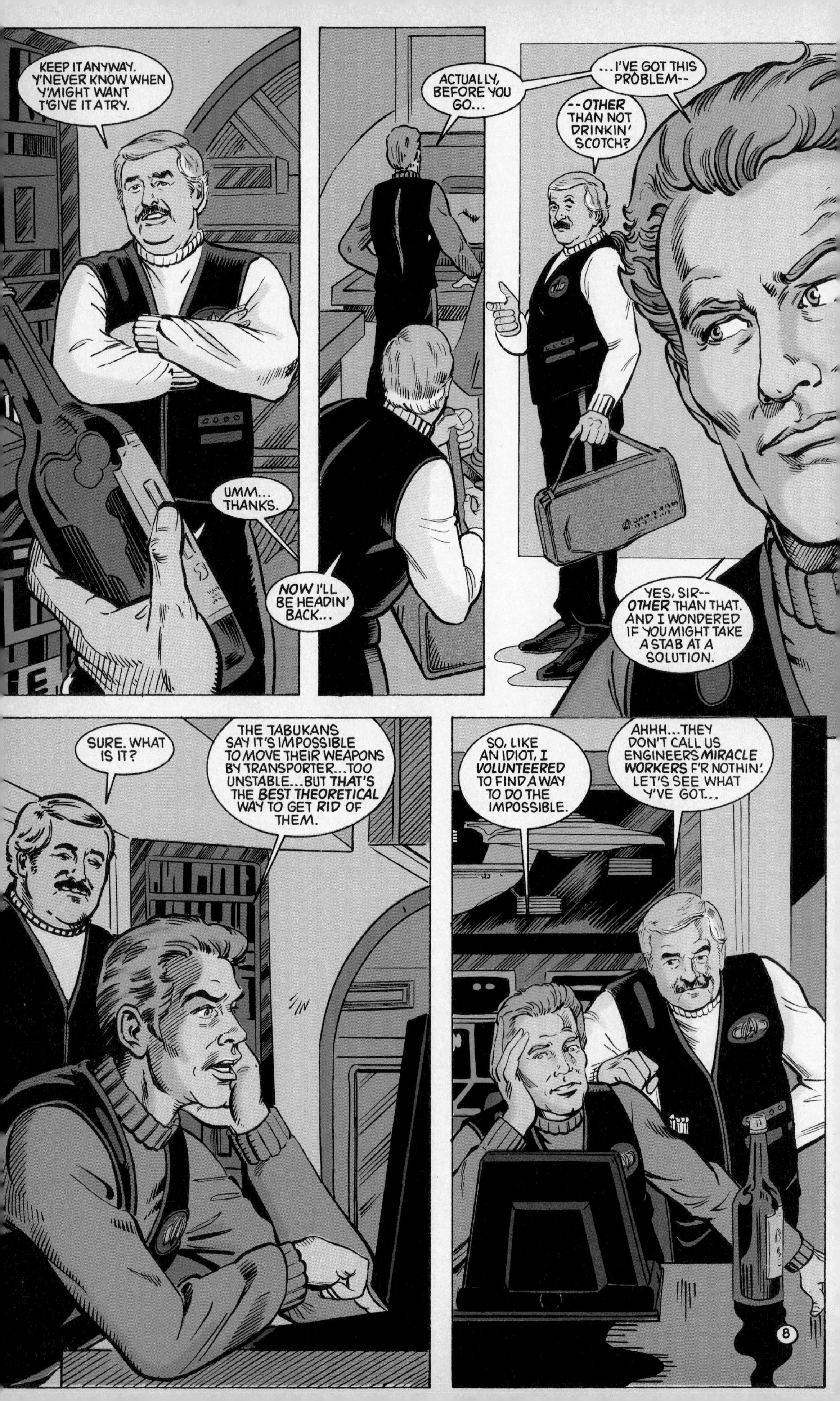
KEEP IT ANYWAY. Y'NEVER KNOW WHEN Y'MIGHT WANT T'GIVE IT A TRY.
UMM... THANKS.
NOW I'LL BE HEADIN' BACK...
ACTUALLY, BEFORE YOU GO...
...I'VE GOT THIS PROBLEM--
--OTHER THAN NOT DRINKIN' SCOTCH?
YES, SIR-- OTHER THAN THAT. AND I WONDERED IF YOU MIGHT TAKE A STAB AT A SOLUTION.
SURE. WHAT IS IT?
THE TABUKANS SAY IT'S IMPOSSIBLE TO MOVE THEIR WEAPONS BY TRANSPORTER...TOO UNSTABLE...BUT THAT'S THE BEST THEORETICAL WAY TO GET RID OF THEM.
SO, LIKE AN IDIOT, I VOLUNTEERED TO FIND A WAY TO DO THE IMPOSSIBLE.
AHHH...THEY DON'T CALL US ENGINEERS MIRACLE WORKERS F'R NOTHIN'. LET'S SEE WHAT Y'VE GOT...
8

WHAT WE'VE GOT, CAPTAIN KIRK, ARE THE MAKINGS OF *DISASTER*--OF *TRAGEDY*--

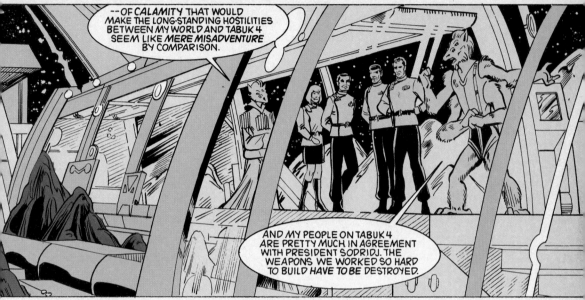

--OF *CALAMITY* THAT WOULD MAKE THE LONG-STANDING HOSTILITIES BETWEEN MY WORLD AND TABUK 4 SEEM LIKE *MERE MISADVENTURE* BY COMPARISON.

AND MY PEOPLE ON TABUK 4 ARE PRETTY MUCH IN AGREEMENT WITH PRESIDENT SODRIDJ. THE WEAPONS WE WORKED SO HARD TO BUILD *HAVE TO BE DESTROYED.*

THAT IS WHY WE'RE HERE, DEPUTY GEFION. WHOEVER IS RESPONSIBLE FOR THESE ATTACKS ON YOUR CONVOYS, THE PRESENCE OF BOTH THE *ENTERPRISE* AND THE *EXCELSIOR* SHOULD MAKE THEM THINK TWICE ABOUT FURTHER INTERFERENCE.

THAT'S RIGHT. WE *ARE* COMMITTED TO THIS MISSION.

HIGH SECURITY FACILITY — AUTHORIZED PERSONNEL ONLY

CLEARANCE-- VERIFIED.

THIS WAY, PLEASE...

9

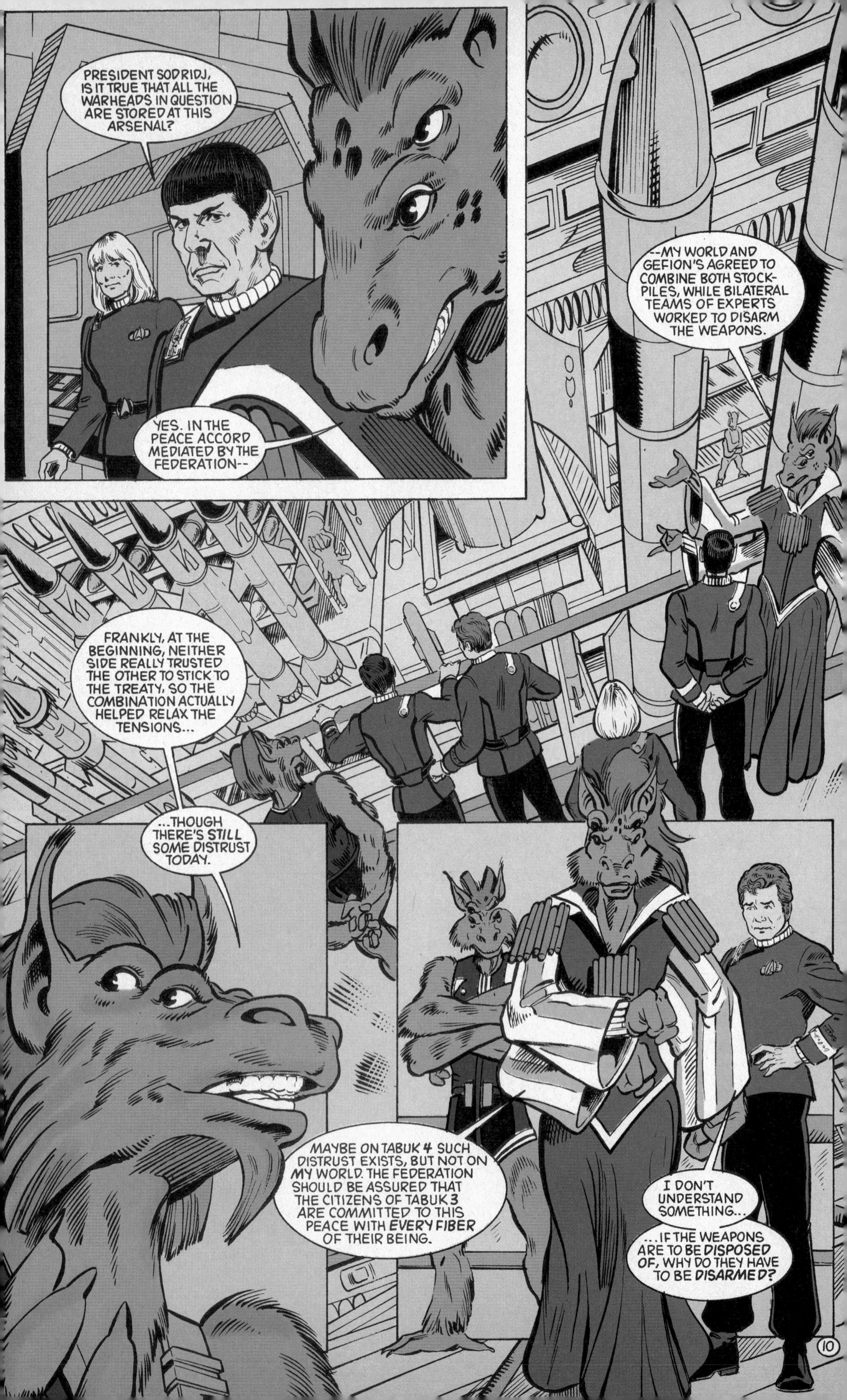

PRESIDENT SODRIDJ, IS IT TRUE THAT ALL THE WARHEADS IN QUESTION ARE STORED AT THIS ARSENAL?
YES. IN THE PEACE ACCORD MEDIATED BY THE FEDERATION--
--MY WORLD AND GEFION'S AGREED TO COMBINE BOTH STOCK-PILES, WHILE BILATERAL TEAMS OF EXPERTS WORKED TO DISARM THE WEAPONS.
FRANKLY, AT THE BEGINNING, NEITHER SIDE REALLY TRUSTED THE OTHER TO STICK TO THE TREATY, SO THE COMBINATION ACTUALLY HELPED RELAX THE TENSIONS...
...THOUGH THERE'S STILL SOME DISTRUST TODAY.
MAYBE ON TABUK 4 SUCH DISTRUST EXISTS, BUT NOT ON MY WORLD. THE FEDERATION SHOULD BE ASSURED THAT THE CITIZENS OF TABUK 3 ARE COMMITTED TO THIS PEACE WITH EVERY FIBER OF THEIR BEING.
I DON'T UNDERSTAND SOMETHING...
...IF THE WEAPONS ARE TO BE DISPOSED OF, WHY DO THEY HAVE TO BE DISARMED?

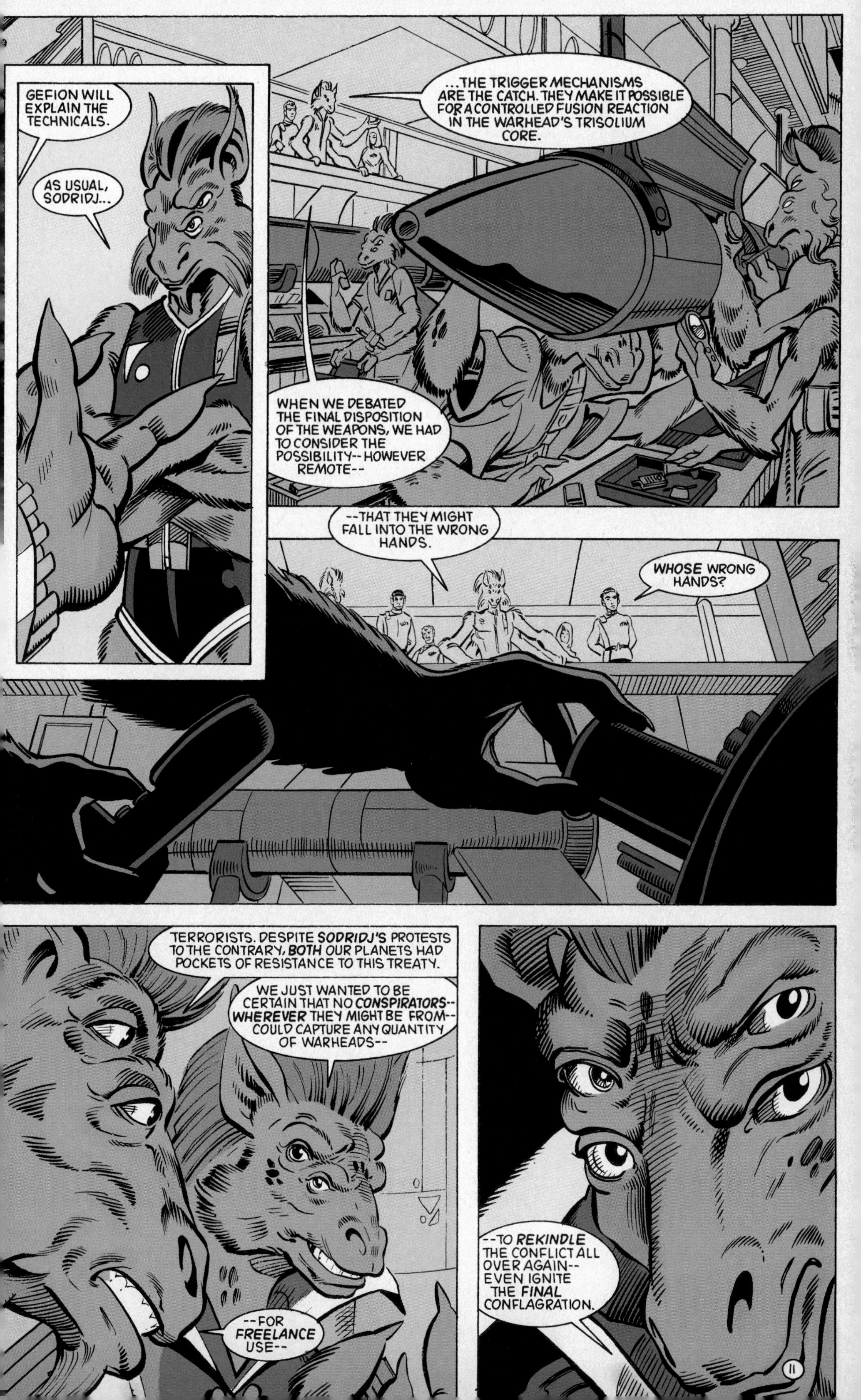
GEFION WILL EXPLAIN THE TECHNICALS.
AS USUAL, SODRIDJ...
...THE TRIGGER MECHANISMS ARE THE CATCH. THEY MAKE IT POSSIBLE FOR A CONTROLLED FUSION REACTION IN THE WARHEAD'S TRISOLIUM CORE.
WHEN WE DEBATED THE FINAL DISPOSITION OF THE WEAPONS, WE HAD TO CONSIDER THE POSSIBILITY-- HOWEVER REMOTE--
--THAT THEY MIGHT FALL INTO THE WRONG HANDS.
WHOSE WRONG HANDS?
TERRORISTS. DESPITE SODRIDJ'S PROTESTS TO THE CONTRARY, BOTH OUR PLANETS HAD POCKETS OF RESISTANCE TO THIS TREATY.
WE JUST WANTED TO BE CERTAIN THAT NO CONSPIRATORS-- WHEREVER THEY MIGHT BE FROM-- COULD CAPTURE ANY QUANTITY OF WARHEADS--
--FOR FREELANCE USE--
--TO REKINDLE THE CONFLICT ALL OVER AGAIN-- EVEN IGNITE THE FINAL CONFLAGRATION.

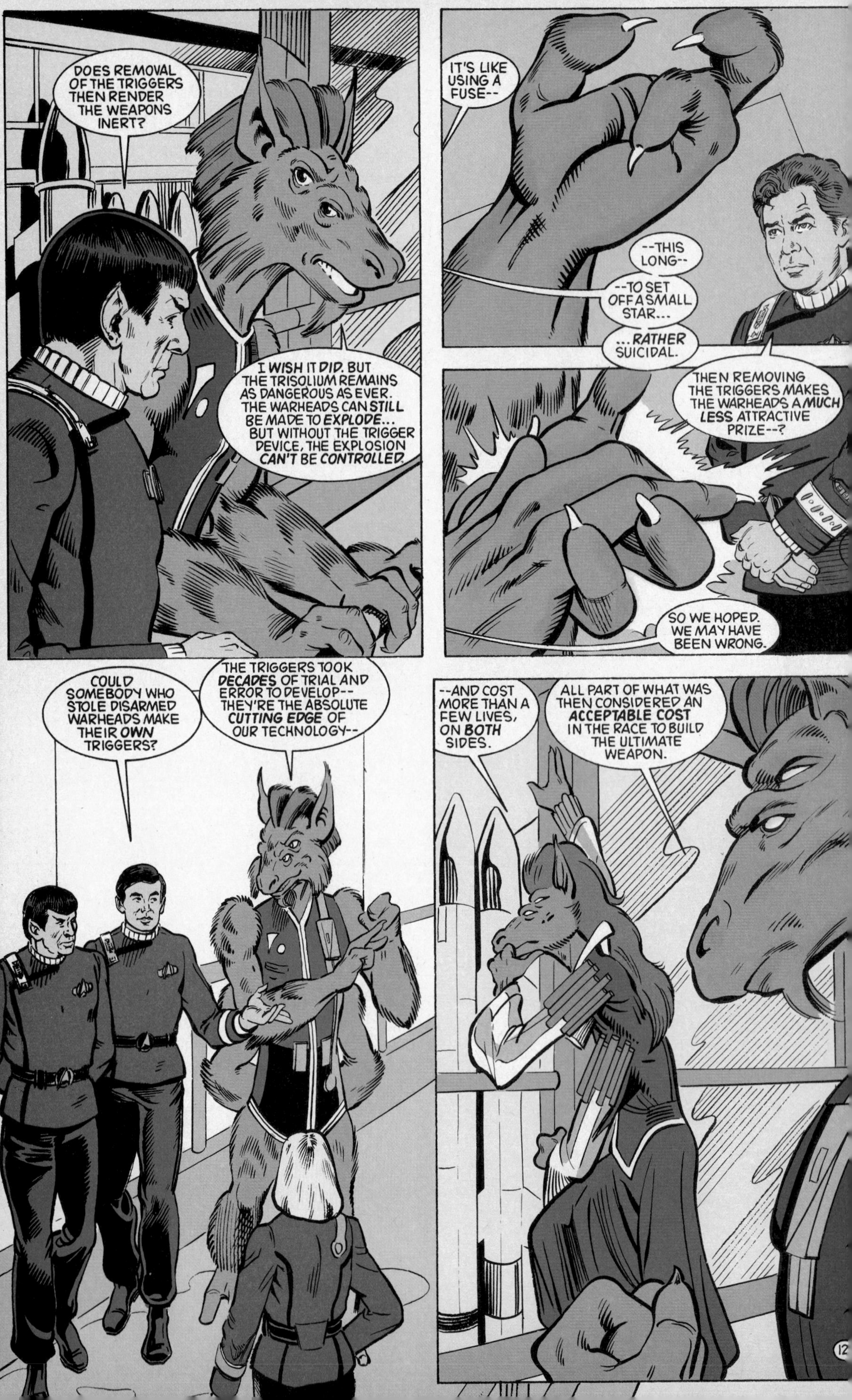
DOES REMOVAL OF THE TRIGGERS THEN RENDER THE WEAPONS INERT?
I WISH IT DID. BUT THE TRISOLIUM REMAINS AS DANGEROUS AS EVER. THE WARHEADS CAN STILL BE MADE TO EXPLODE... BUT WITHOUT THE TRIGGER DEVICE, THE EXPLOSION CAN'T BE CONTROLLED.
IT'S LIKE USING A FUSE--
--THIS LONG--
--TO SET OFF A SMALL STAR...
...RATHER SUICIDAL.
THEN REMOVING THE TRIGGERS MAKES THE WARHEADS A MUCH LESS ATTRACTIVE PRIZE--?
SO WE HOPED. WE MAY HAVE BEEN WRONG.
COULD SOMEBODY WHO STOLE DISARMED WARHEADS MAKE THEIR OWN TRIGGERS?
THE TRIGGERS TOOK DECADES OF TRIAL AND ERROR TO DEVELOP-- THEY'RE THE ABSOLUTE CUTTING EDGE OF OUR TECHNOLOGY--
--AND COST MORE THAN A FEW LIVES, ON BOTH SIDES.
ALL PART OF WHAT WAS THEN CONSIDERED AN ACCEPTABLE COST IN THE RACE TO BUILD THE ULTIMATE WEAPON.
12

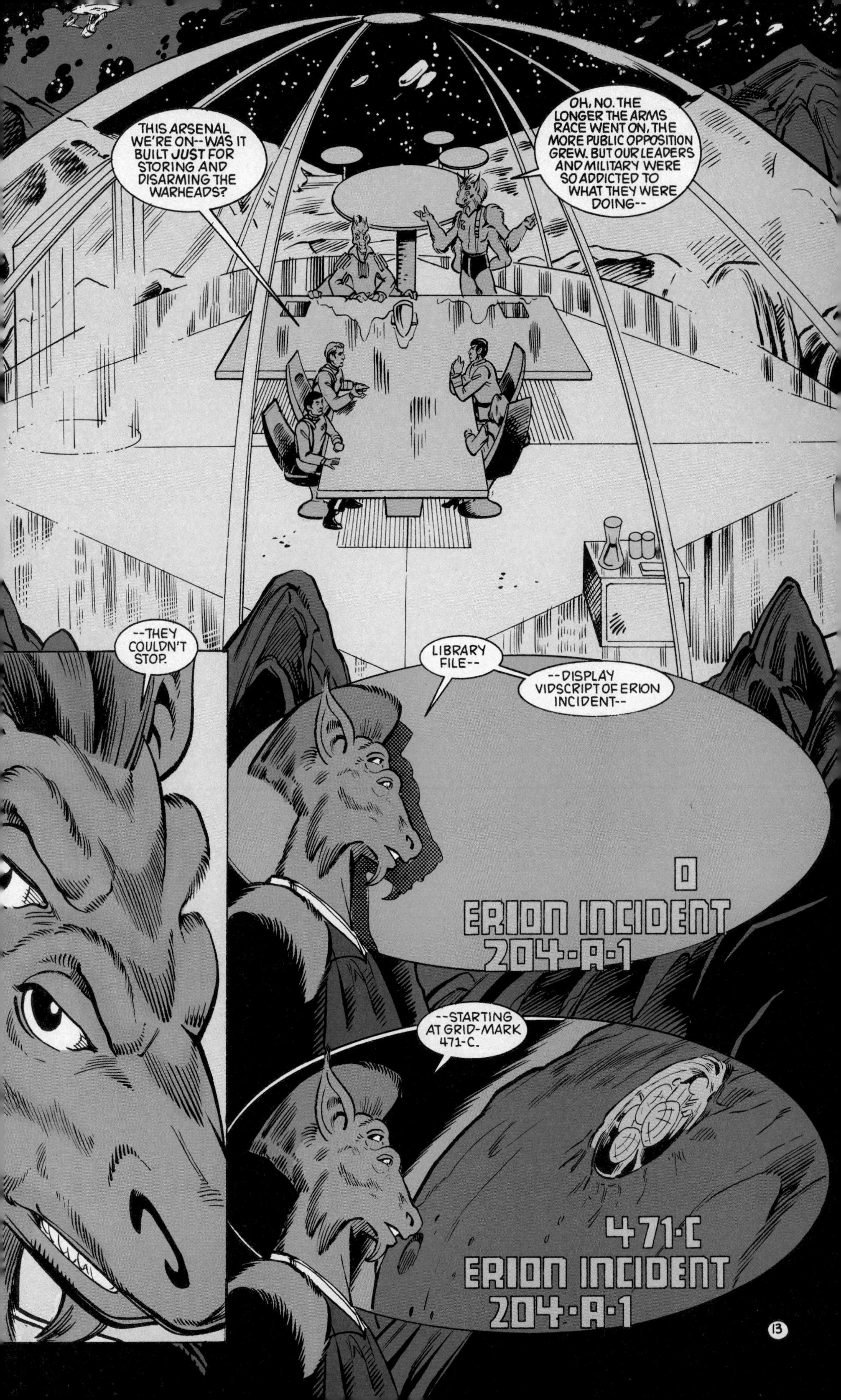
THIS ARSENAL WE'RE ON--WAS IT BUILT JUST FOR STORING AND DISARMING THE WARHEADS?
OH, NO. THE LONGER THE ARMS RACE WENT ON, THE MORE PUBLIC OPPOSITION GREW. BUT OUR LEADERS AND MILITARY WERE SO ADDICTED TO WHAT THEY WERE DOING--
--THEY COULDN'T STOP.
LIBRARY FILE--
--DISPLAY VIDSCRIPT OF ERION INCIDENT--
0
ERION INCIDENT
204-A-1
--STARTING AT GRID-MARK 471-C.
471-C
ERION INCIDENT
204-A-1

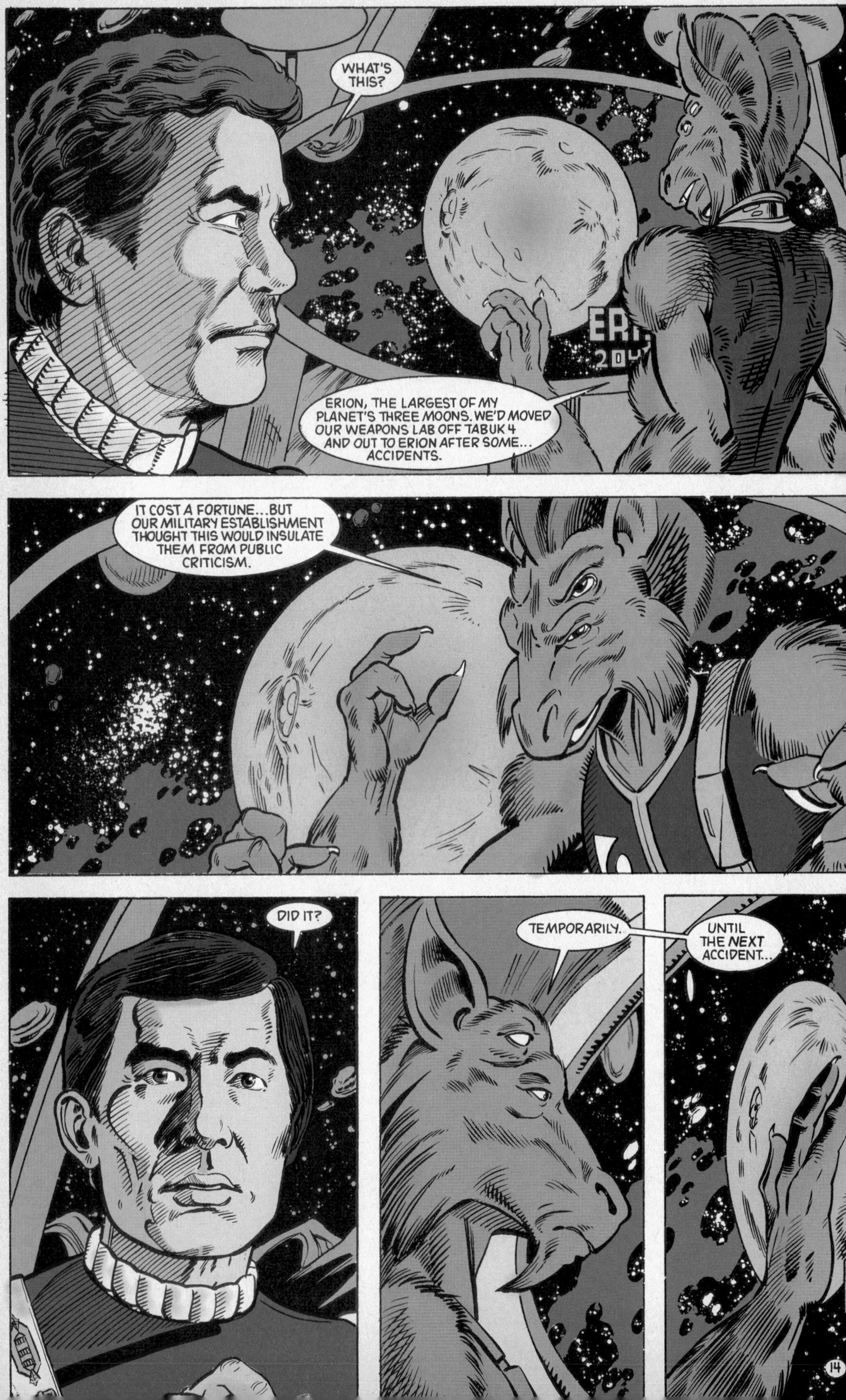
WHAT'S THIS?
ERION, THE LARGEST OF MY PLANET'S THREE MOONS. WE'D MOVED OUR WEAPONS LAB OFF TABUK 4 AND OUT TO ERION AFTER SOME... ACCIDENTS.
IT COST A FORTUNE...BUT OUR MILITARY ESTABLISHMENT THOUGHT THIS WOULD INSULATE THEM FROM PUBLIC CRITICISM.
DID IT?
TEMPORARILY.
UNTIL THE NEXT ACCIDENT...

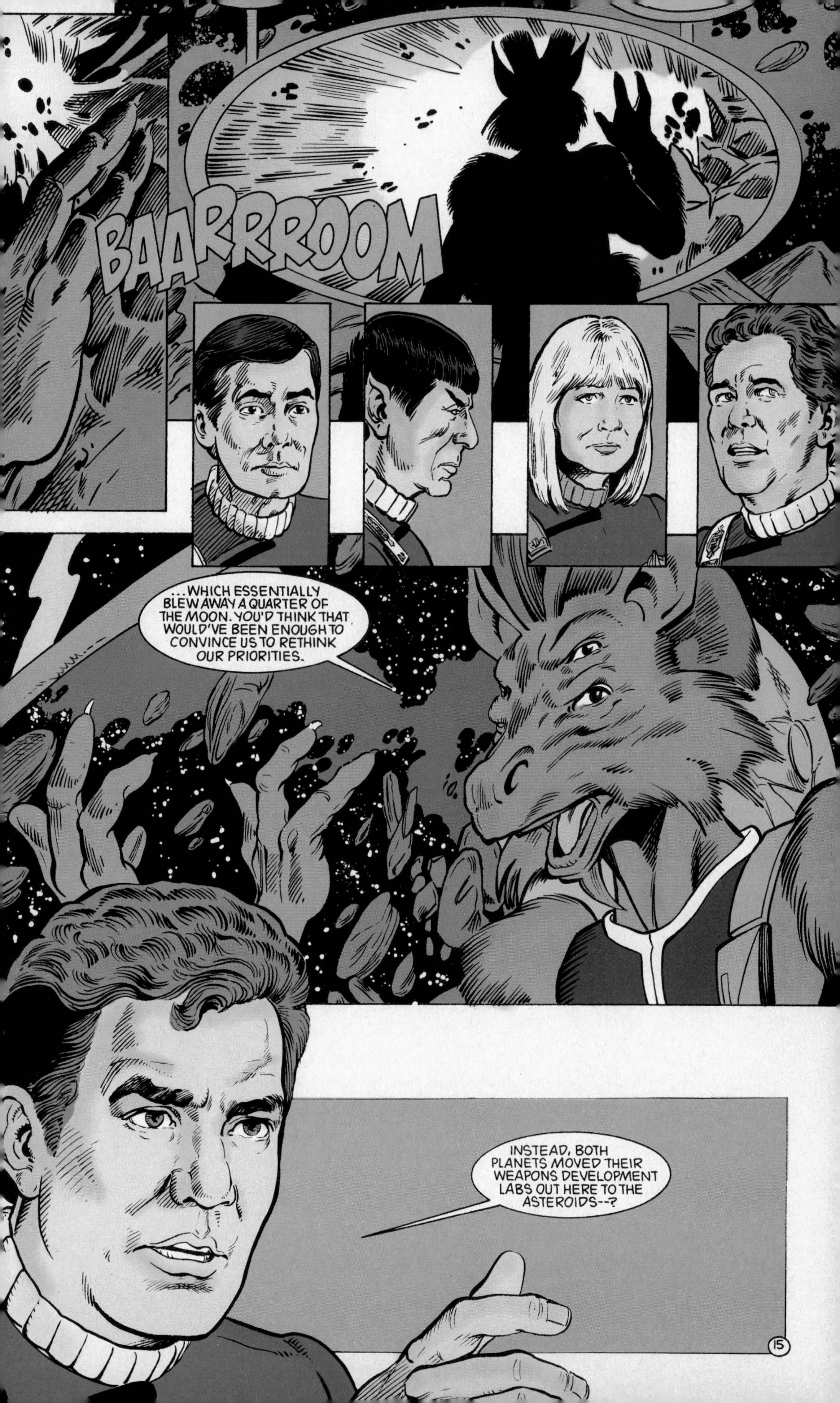
BAARRROOM
...WHICH ESSENTIALLY BLEW AWAY A QUARTER OF THE MOON. YOU'D THINK THAT WOULD'VE BEEN ENOUGH TO CONVINCE US TO RETHINK OUR PRIORITIES.
INSTEAD, BOTH PLANETS MOVED THEIR WEAPONS DEVELOPMENT LABS OUT HERE TO THE ASTEROIDS--?
15

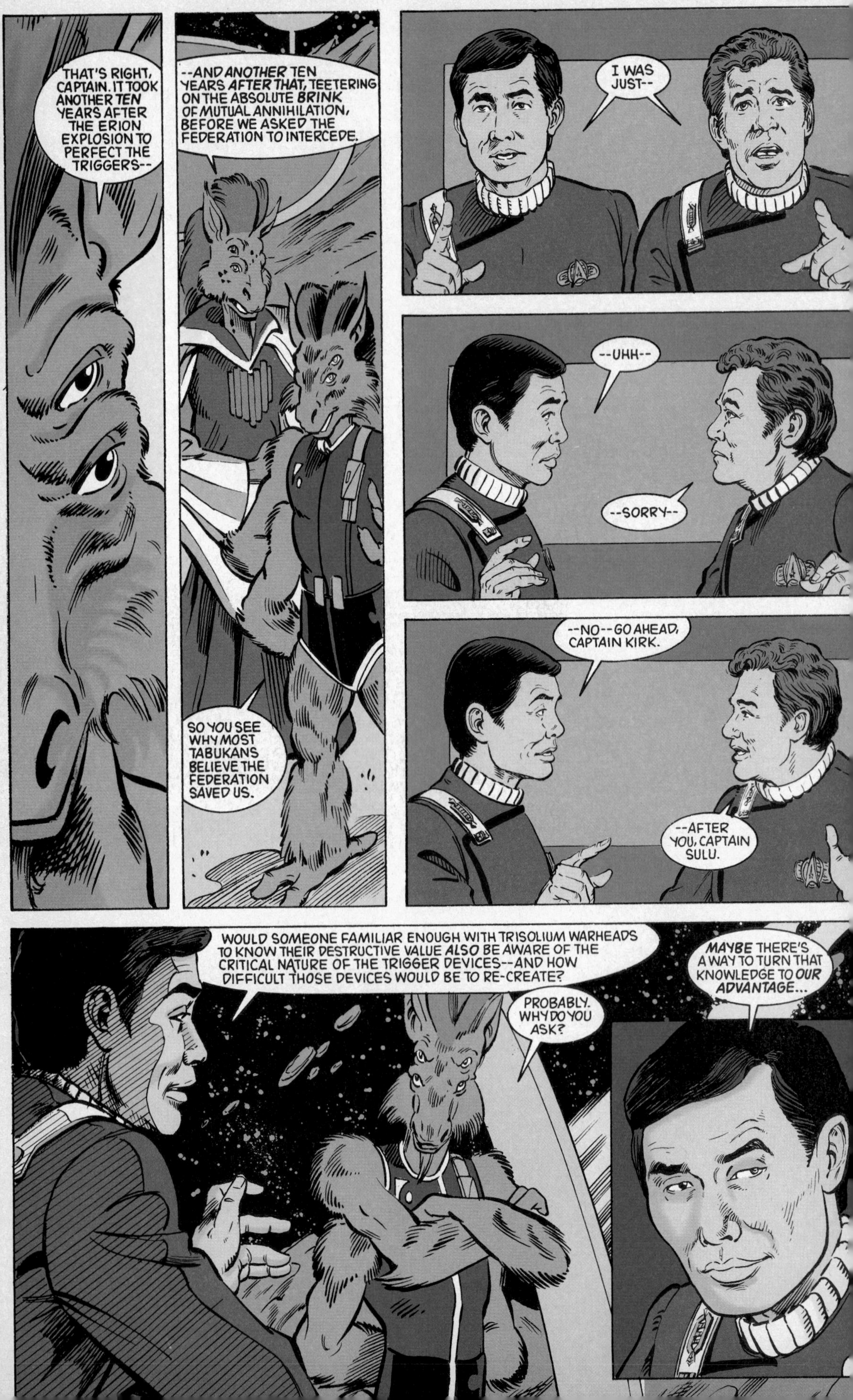
THAT'S RIGHT, CAPTAIN. IT TOOK ANOTHER TEN YEARS AFTER THE ERION EXPLOSION TO PERFECT THE TRIGGERS--
--AND ANOTHER TEN YEARS AFTER THAT, TEETERING ON THE ABSOLUTE BRINK OF MUTUAL ANNIHILATION, BEFORE WE ASKED THE FEDERATION TO INTERCEDE.
SO YOU SEE WHY MOST TABUKANS BELIEVE THE FEDERATION SAVED US.
I WAS JUST--
--UHH--
--SORRY--
--NO--GO AHEAD, CAPTAIN KIRK.
--AFTER YOU, CAPTAIN SULU.
WOULD SOMEONE FAMILIAR ENOUGH WITH TRISOLIUM WARHEADS TO KNOW THEIR DESTRUCTIVE VALUE ALSO BE AWARE OF THE CRITICAL NATURE OF THE TRIGGER DEVICES--AND HOW DIFFICULT THOSE DEVICES WOULD BE TO RE-CREATE?
PROBABLY. WHY DO YOU ASK?
MAYBE THERE'S A WAY TO TURN THAT KNOWLEDGE TO OUR ADVANTAGE...

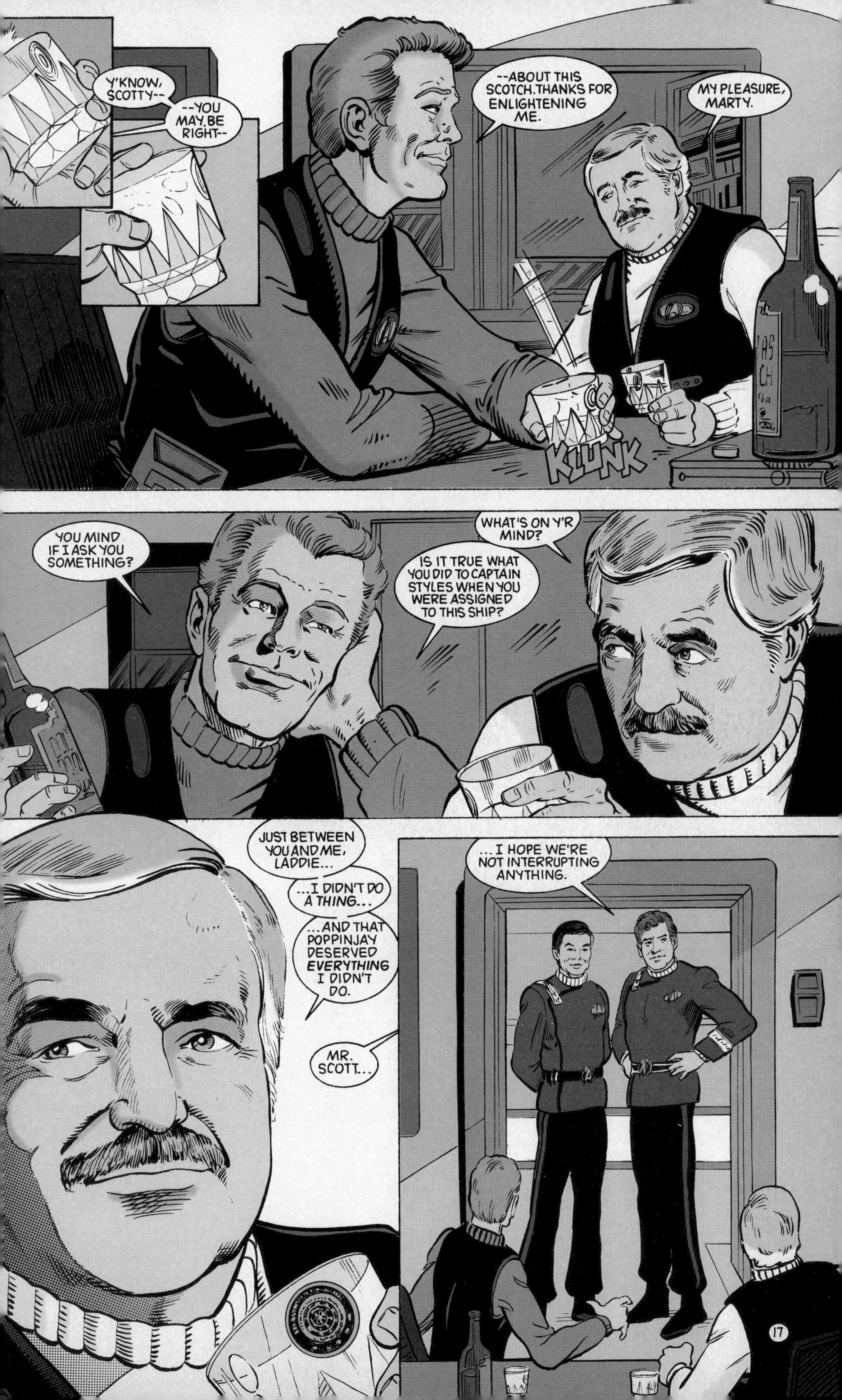
Y'KNOW, SCOTTY--
--YOU MAY BE RIGHT--
--ABOUT THIS SCOTCH. THANKS FOR ENLIGHTENING ME.
MY PLEASURE, MARTY.
KLUNK
YOU MIND IF I ASK YOU SOMETHING?
WHAT'S ON Y'R MIND?
IS IT TRUE WHAT YOU DID TO CAPTAIN STYLES WHEN YOU WERE ASSIGNED TO THIS SHIP?
JUST BETWEEN YOU AND ME, LADDIE...
...I DIDN'T DO A THING...
...AND THAT POPPINJAY DESERVED EVERYTHING I DIDN'T DO.
MR. SCOTT...
...I HOPE WE'RE NOT INTERRUPTING ANYTHING.

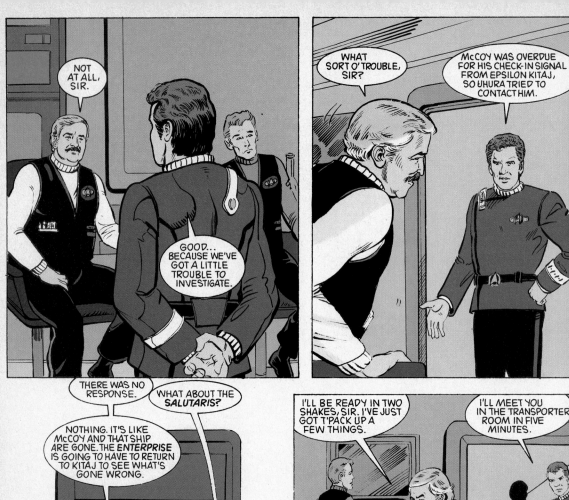

NOT AT ALL, SIR.

GOOD... BECAUSE WE'VE GOT A LITTLE TROUBLE TO INVESTIGATE.

WHAT SORT O' TROUBLE, SIR?

McCOY WAS OVERDUE FOR HIS CHECK-IN SIGNAL FROM EPSILON KITAJ, SO UHURA TRIED TO CONTACT HIM.

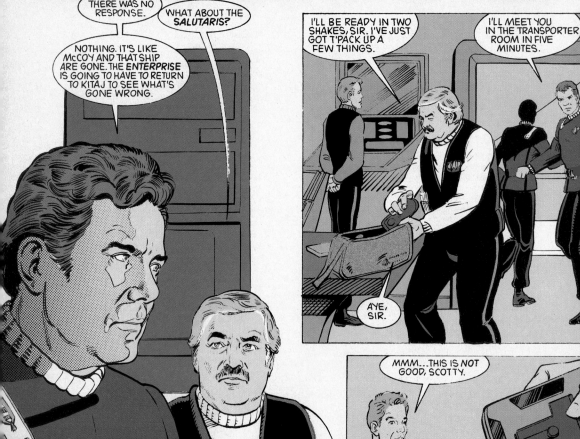

THERE WAS NO RESPONSE.

WHAT ABOUT THE *SALUTARIS?*

NOTHING. IT'S LIKE McCOY AND THAT SHIP ARE GONE. THE *ENTERPRISE* IS GOING TO HAVE TO RETURN TO KITAJ TO SEE WHAT'S GONE WRONG.

I'LL BE READY IN TWO SHAKES, SIR. I'VE JUST GOT T'PACK UP A FEW THINGS.

I'LL MEET YOU IN THE TRANSPORTER ROOM IN FIVE MINUTES.

AYE, SIR.

MMM...THIS IS *NOT* GOOD, SCOTTY.

IT'S PROBABLY NOTHIN' SERIOUS...

18

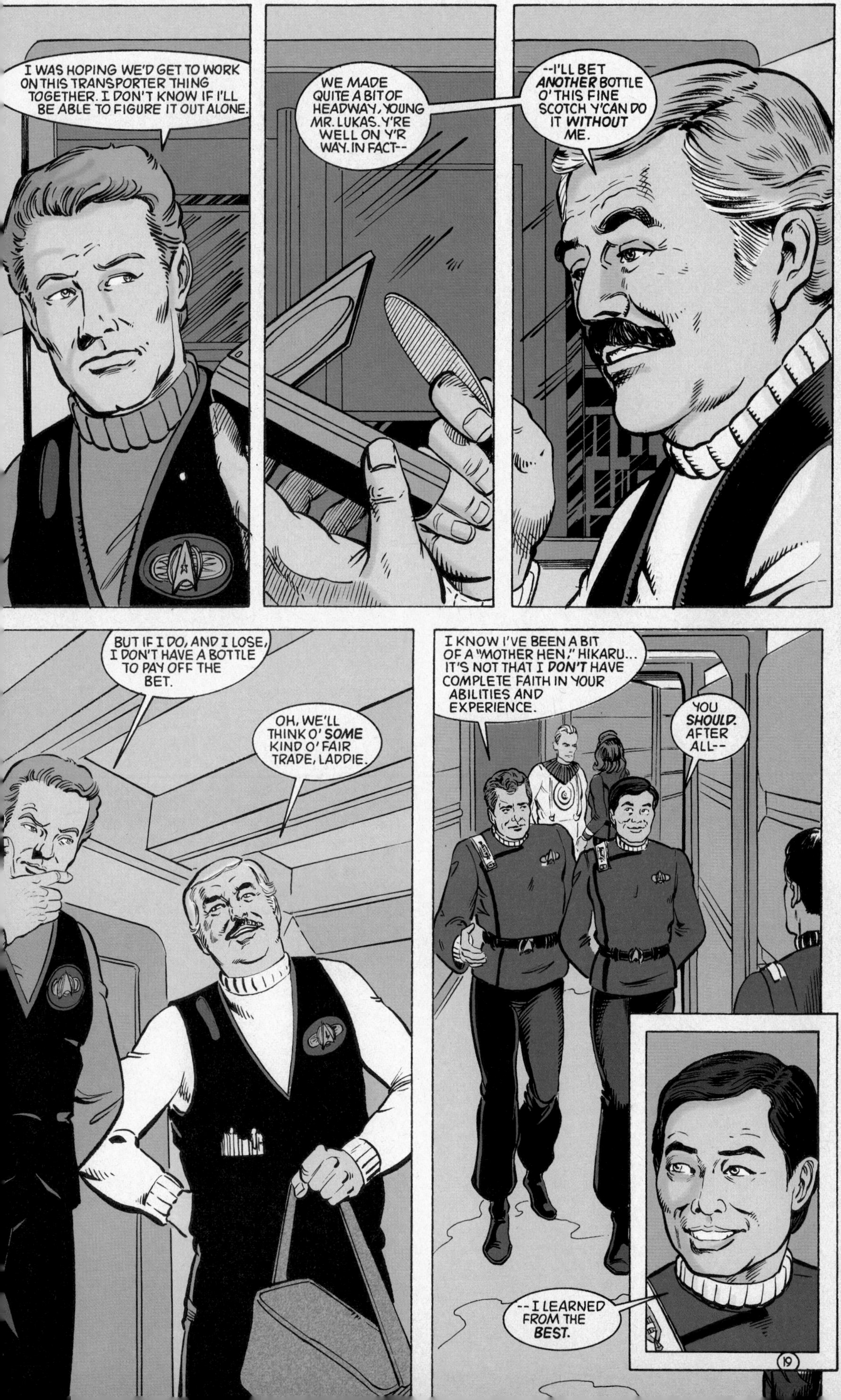
I WAS HOPING WE'D GET TO WORK ON THIS TRANSPORTER THING TOGETHER. I DON'T KNOW IF I'LL BE ABLE TO FIGURE IT OUT ALONE.
WE MADE QUITE A BIT OF HEADWAY, YOUNG MR. LUKAS. Y'RE WELL ON Y'R WAY. IN FACT--
--I'LL BET ANOTHER BOTTLE O' THIS FINE SCOTCH Y'CAN DO IT WITHOUT ME.
BUT IF I DO, AND I LOSE, I DON'T HAVE A BOTTLE TO PAY OFF THE BET.
OH, WE'LL THINK O' SOME KIND O' FAIR TRADE, LADDIE.
I KNOW I'VE BEEN A BIT OF A "MOTHER HEN," HIKARU... IT'S NOT THAT I DON'T HAVE COMPLETE FAITH IN YOUR ABILITIES AND EXPERIENCE.
YOU SHOULD. AFTER ALL--
--I LEARNED FROM THE BEST.
19

FROM MY MISTAKES AS WELL AS MY SUCCESSES, I HOPE.

MISTAKES? WHAT MISTAKES?

THERE'S NO NEED TO APOLOGIZE, JIM. I APPRECIATE THE CONCERN... AND I UNDERSTAND. I DON'T MIND CONFESSING TO HAVING A FEW BUTTERFLIES...

...BUT YOU REALLY *DID* TEACH ME WELL. AND I PLAN TO COMMAND THIS SHIP FOR A LONG, *LONG* TIME...

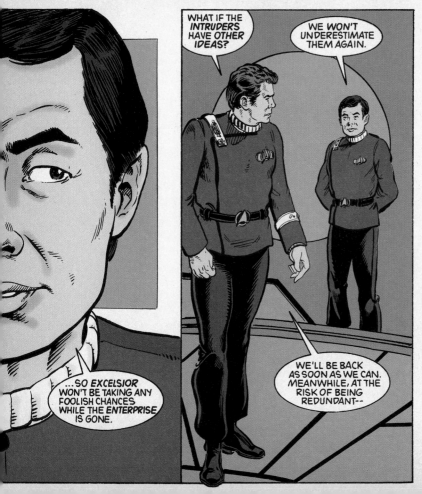

WHAT IF THE *INTRUDERS* HAVE OTHER IDEAS?

WE WON'T UNDERESTIMATE THEM AGAIN.

...SO *EXCELSIOR* WON'T BE TAKING ANY FOOLISH CHANCES WHILE THE *ENTERPRISE* IS GONE.

WE'LL BE BACK AS SOON AS WE CAN. MEANWHILE, AT THE RISK OF BEING REDUNDANT--

--BE CAREFUL.

20

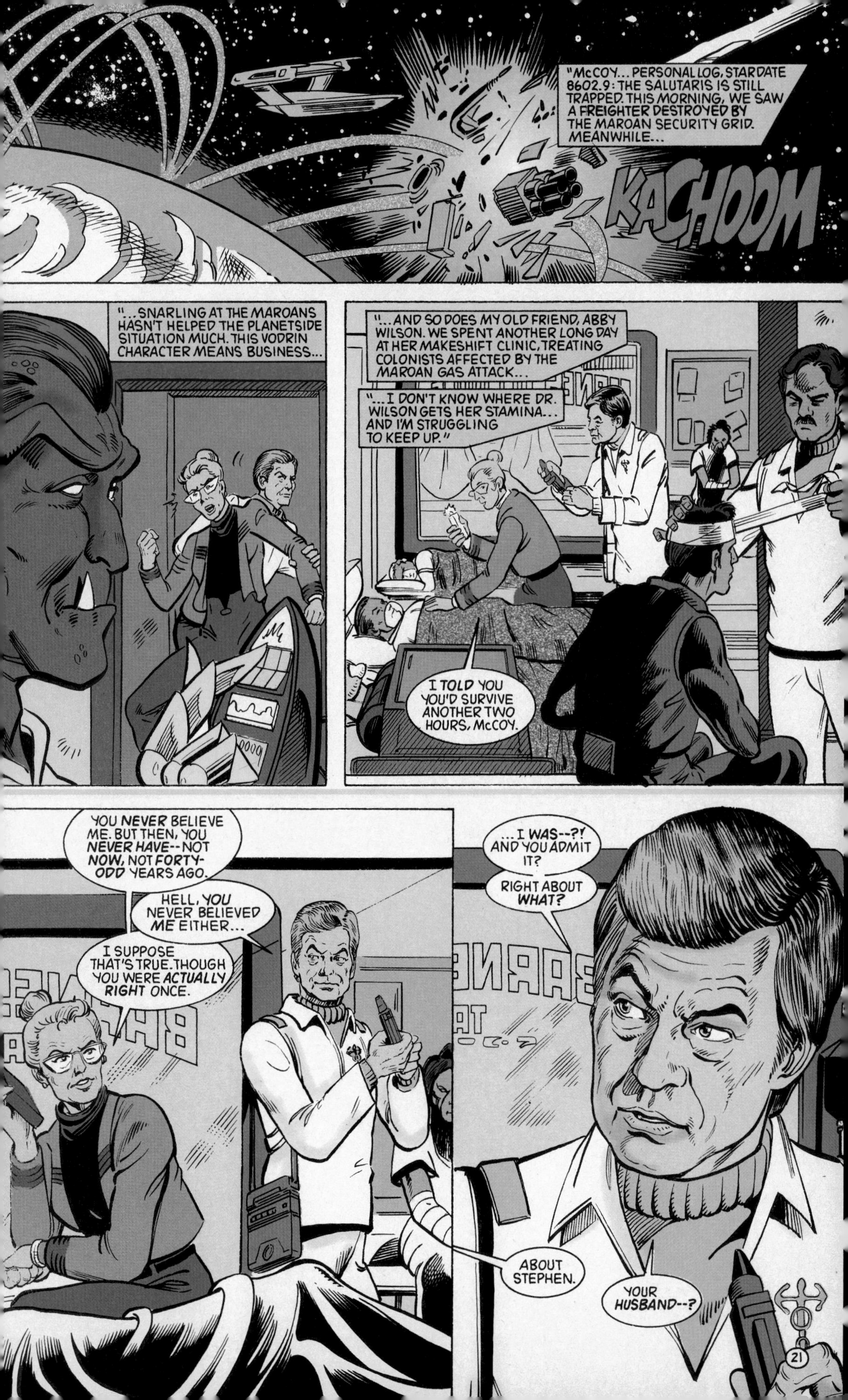
"McCOY... PERSONAL LOG, STARDATE 8602.9: THE SALUTARIS IS STILL TRAPPED. THIS MORNING, WE SAW A FREIGHTER DESTROYED BY THE MAROAN SECURITY GRID. MEANWHILE...
KACHOOM
"...SNARLING AT THE MAROANS HASN'T HELPED THE PLANETSIDE SITUATION MUCH. THIS VODRIN CHARACTER MEANS BUSINESS...
"...AND SO DOES MY OLD FRIEND, ABBY WILSON. WE SPENT ANOTHER LONG DAY AT HER MAKESHIFT CLINIC, TREATING COLONISTS AFFECTED BY THE MAROAN GAS ATTACK...
"...I DON'T KNOW WHERE DR. WILSON GETS HER STAMINA... AND I'M STRUGGLING TO KEEP UP."
I TOLD YOU YOU'D SURVIVE ANOTHER TWO HOURS, McCOY.
YOU NEVER BELIEVE ME. BUT THEN, YOU NEVER HAVE--NOT NOW, NOT FORTY-ODD YEARS AGO.
HELL, YOU NEVER BELIEVED ME EITHER...
I SUPPOSE THAT'S TRUE. THOUGH YOU WERE ACTUALLY RIGHT ONCE.
...I WAS--?! AND YOU ADMIT IT?
RIGHT ABOUT WHAT?
ABOUT STEPHEN.
YOUR HUSBAND--?

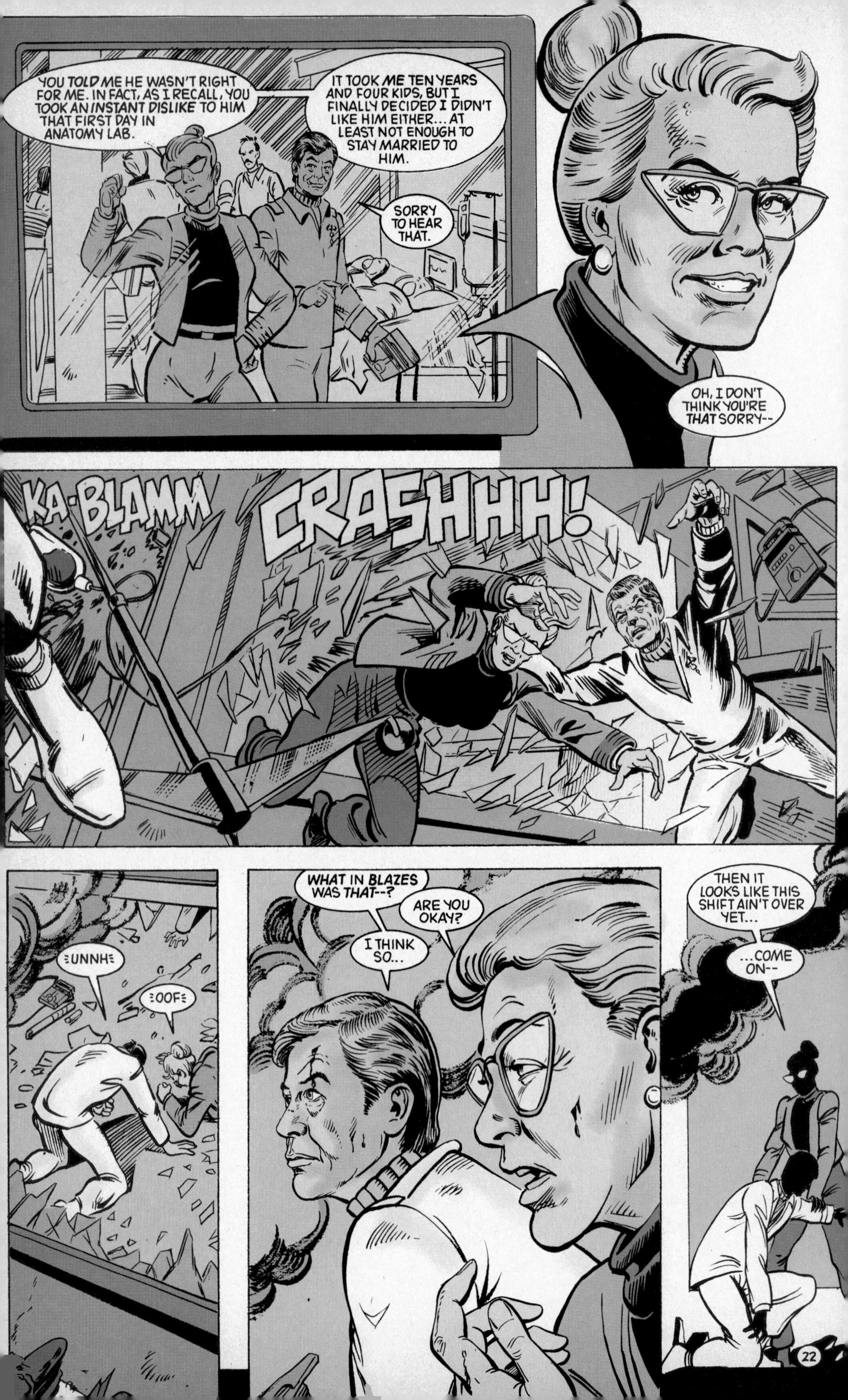
YOU TOLD ME HE WASN'T RIGHT FOR ME. IN FACT, AS I RECALL, YOU TOOK AN INSTANT DISLIKE TO HIM THAT FIRST DAY IN ANATOMY LAB.
IT TOOK ME TEN YEARS AND FOUR KIDS, BUT I FINALLY DECIDED I DIDN'T LIKE HIM EITHER... AT LEAST NOT ENOUGH TO STAY MARRIED TO HIM.
SORRY TO HEAR THAT.
OH, I DON'T THINK YOU'RE THAT SORRY--
KA-BLAMM
CRASHHH!
UNNH
OOF
WHAT IN BLAZES WAS THAT--?
ARE YOU OKAY?
I THINK SO...
THEN IT LOOKS LIKE THIS SHIFT AIN'T OVER YET...
...COME ON--
22

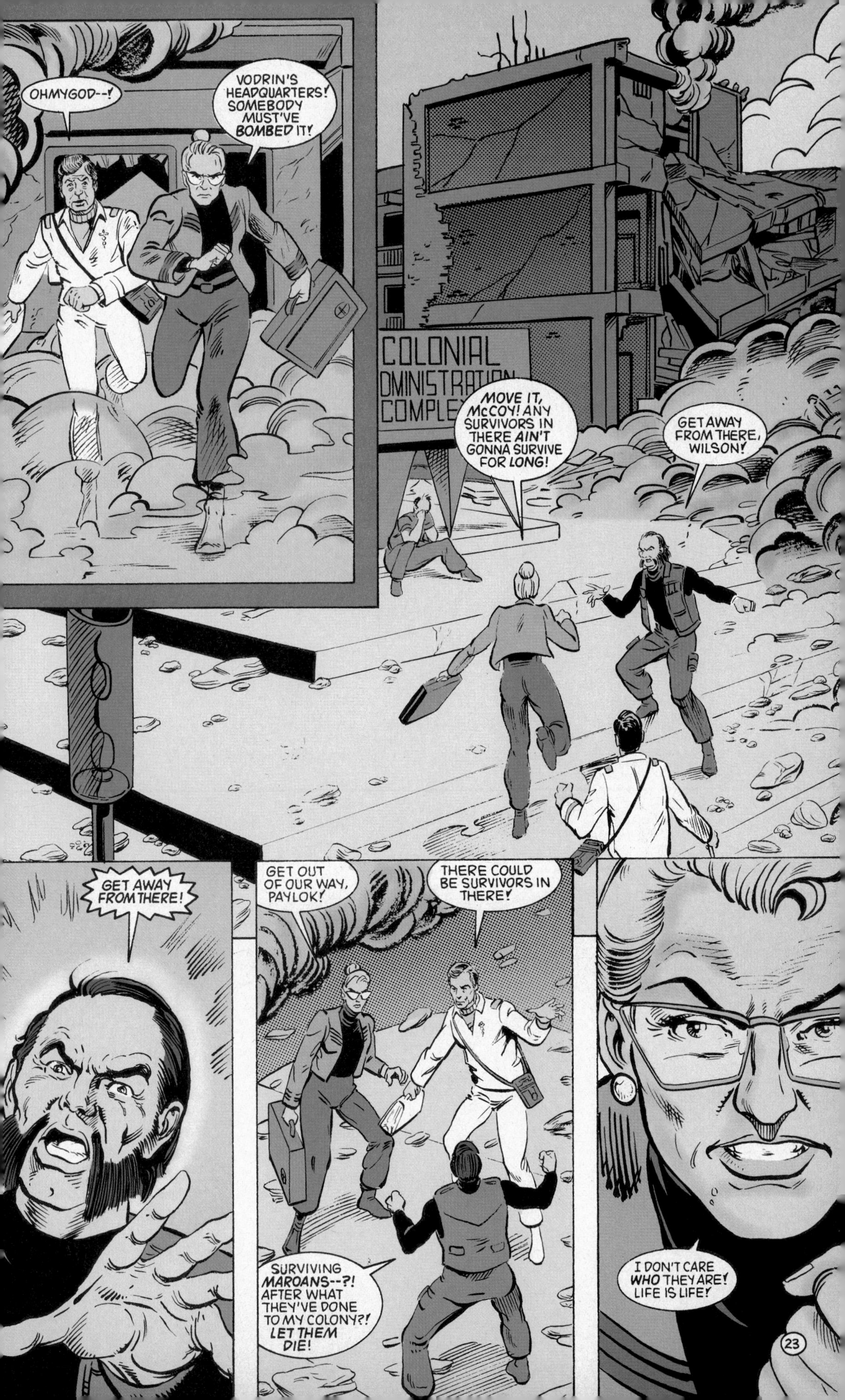
OHMYGOD--!
VODRIN'S HEADQUARTERS! SOMEBODY MUST'VE BOMBED IT!
COLONIAL
OMINISTRATION
COMPLE
MOVE IT, McCOY! ANY SURVIVORS IN THERE AIN'T GONNA SURVIVE FOR LONG!
GET AWAY FROM THERE, WILSON!
GET AWAY FROM THERE!
GET OUT OF OUR WAY, PAYLOK!
THERE COULD BE SURVIVORS IN THERE!
SURVIVING MAROANS--?! AFTER WHAT THEY'VE DONE TO MY COLONY?! LET THEM DIE!
I DON'T CARE WHO THEY ARE! LIFE IS LIFE!

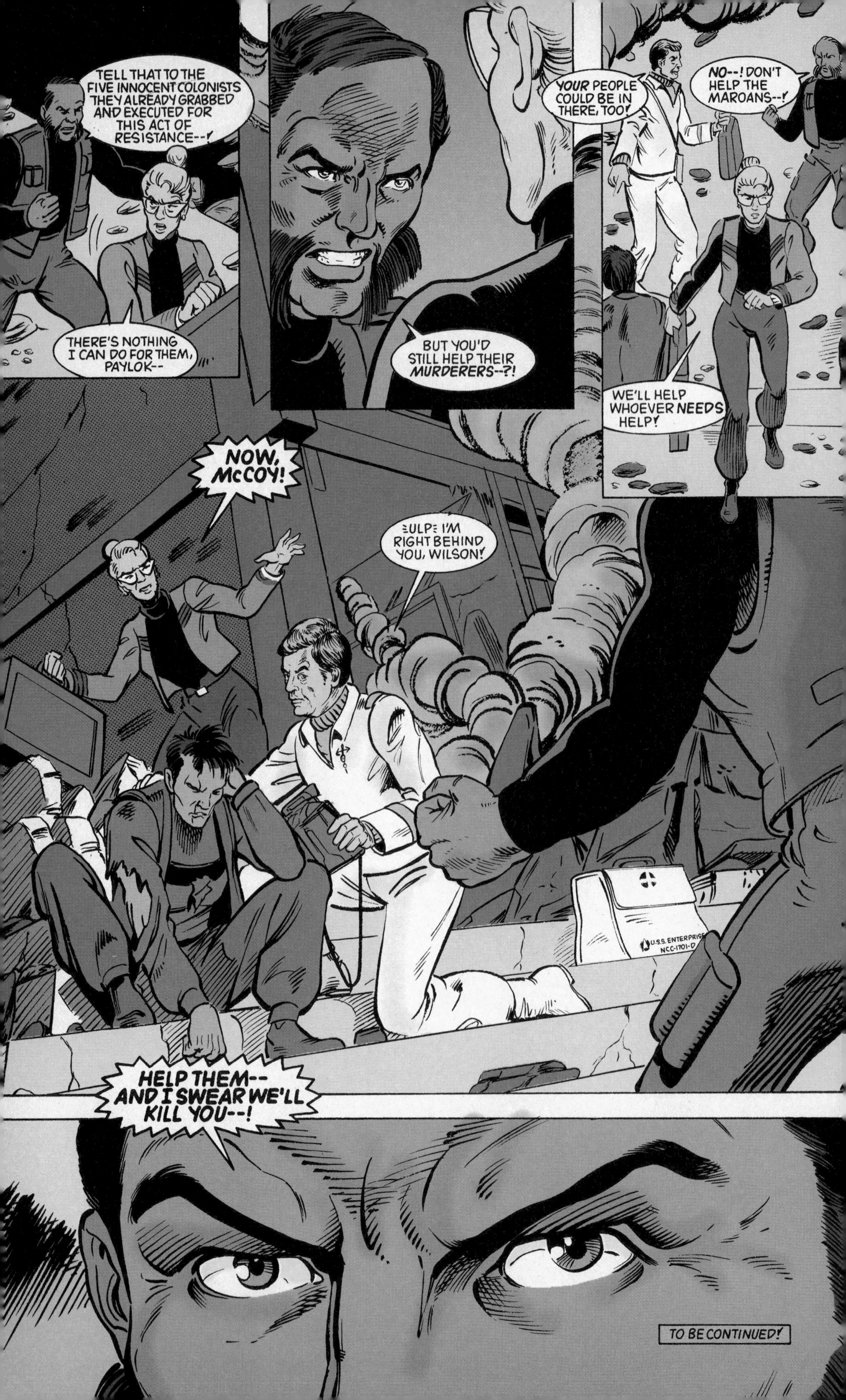
TELL THAT TO THE FIVE INNOCENT COLONISTS THEY ALREADY GRABBED AND EXECUTED FOR THIS ACT OF RESISTANCE--!
THERE'S NOTHING I CAN DO FOR THEM, PAYLOK--
BUT YOU'D STILL HELP THEIR MURDERERS--?!
YOUR PEOPLE COULD BE IN THERE, TOO!
NO--! DON'T HELP THE MAROANS--!
WE'LL HELP WHOEVER NEEDS HELP!
NOW, McCOY!
GULP! I'M RIGHT BEHIND YOU, WILSON!
U.S.S. ENTERPRISE NCC-1701-D
HELP THEM-- AND I SWEAR WE'LL KILL YOU--!
TO BE CONTINUED!

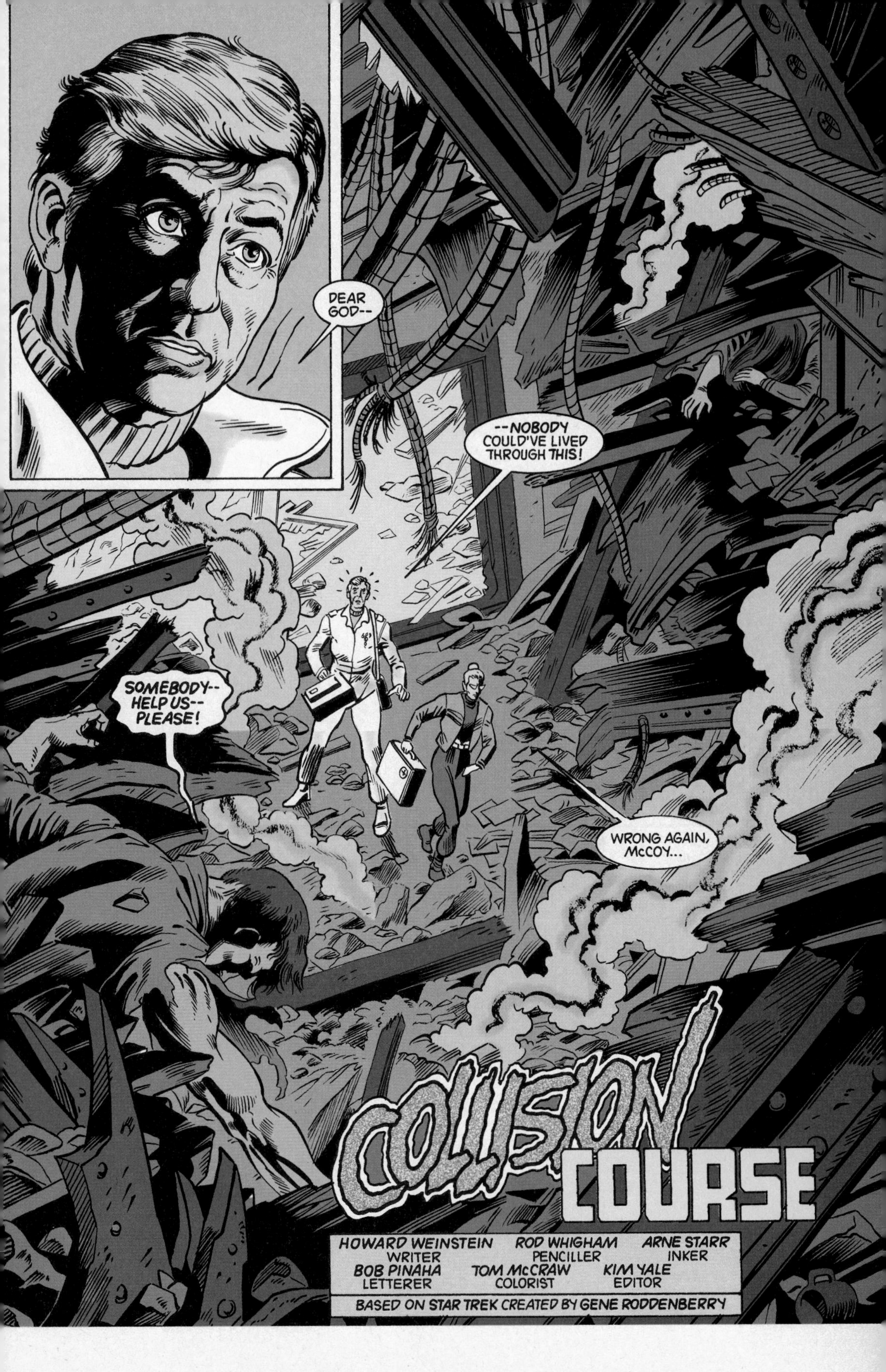

DEAR GOD--
--NOBODY COULD'VE LIVED THROUGH THIS!
SOMEBODY-- HELP US-- PLEASE!
WRONG AGAIN, McCOY...
COLLISION COURSE
HOWARD WEINSTEIN WRITER
ROD WHIGHAM PENCILLER
ARNE STARR INKER
BOB PINAHA LETTERER
TOM McCRAW COLORIST
KIM YALE EDITOR
BASED ON STAR TREK CREATED BY GENE RODDENBERRY

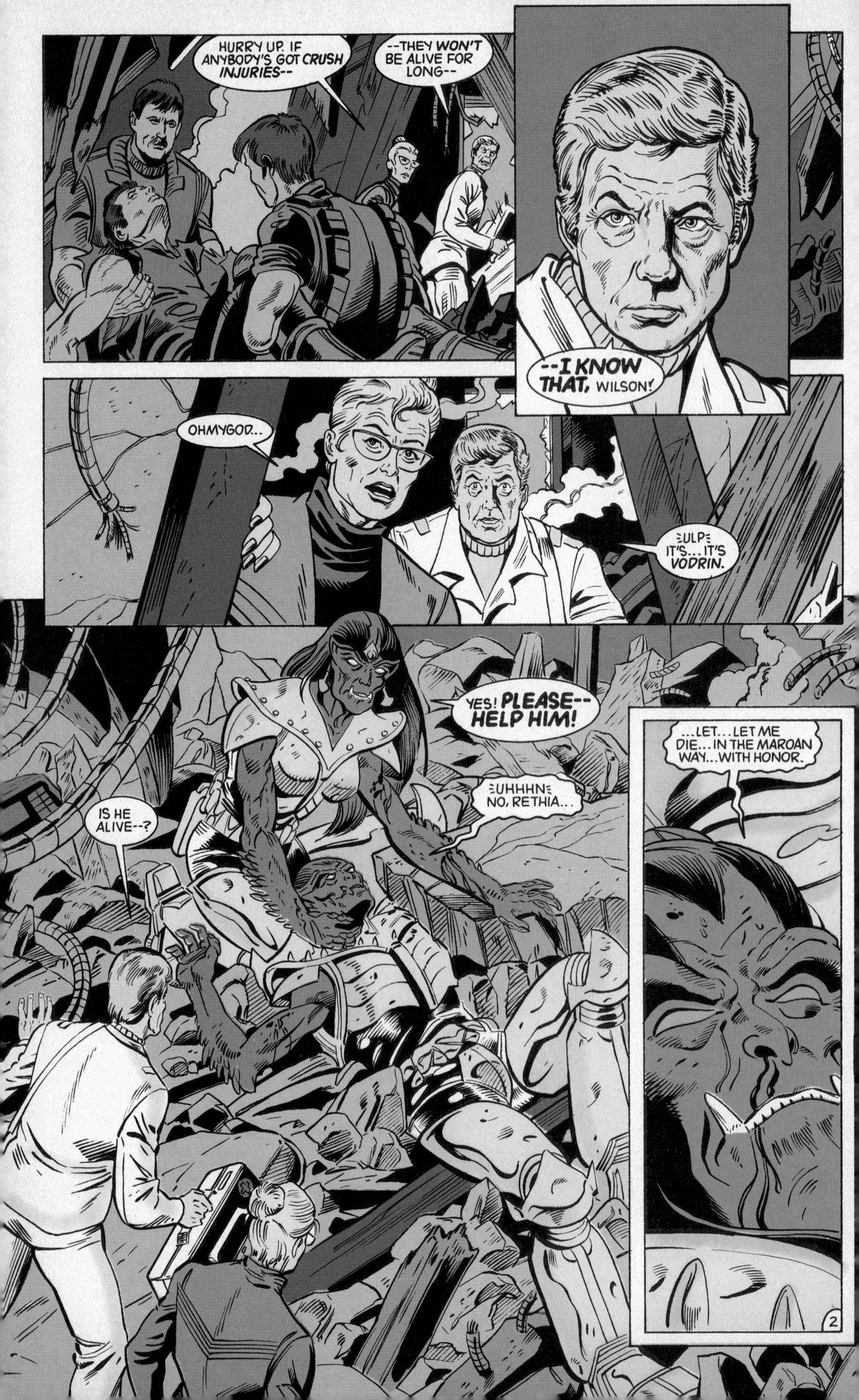
HURRY UP. IF ANYBODY'S GOT CRUSH INJURIES--
--THEY WON'T BE ALIVE FOR LONG--
--I KNOW THAT, WILSON!
OHMYGOD...
ULP IT'S... IT'S VODRIN.
YES! PLEASE-- HELP HIM!
IS HE ALIVE--?
UHHHN NO, RETHIA...
...LET...LET ME DIE...IN THE MAROAN WAY...WITH HONOR.
2

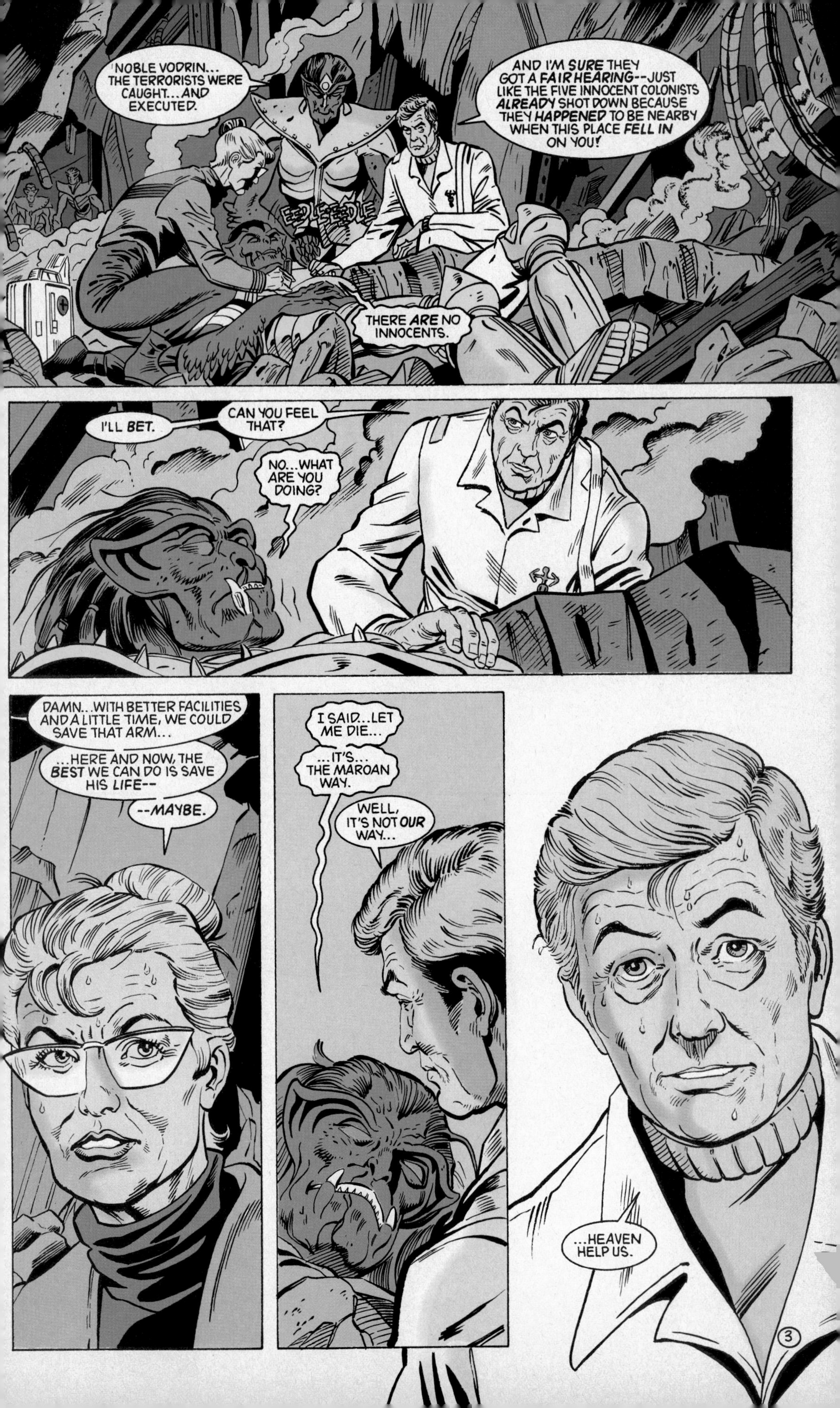
NOBLE VODRIN... THE TERRORISTS WERE CAUGHT... AND EXECUTED.
AND I'M SURE THEY GOT A FAIR HEARING--JUST LIKE THE FIVE INNOCENT COLONISTS ALREADY SHOT DOWN BECAUSE THEY HAPPENED TO BE NEARBY WHEN THIS PLACE FELL IN ON YOU!
EEDLEEEDLE
THERE ARE NO INNOCENTS.
I'LL BET.
CAN YOU FEEL THAT?
NO...WHAT ARE YOU DOING?
DAMN...WITH BETTER FACILITIES AND A LITTLE TIME, WE COULD SAVE THAT ARM...
...HERE AND NOW, THE BEST WE CAN DO IS SAVE HIS LIFE--
--MAYBE.
I SAID...LET ME DIE...
...IT'S... THE MAROAN WAY.
WELL, IT'S NOT OUR WAY...
...HEAVEN HELP US.

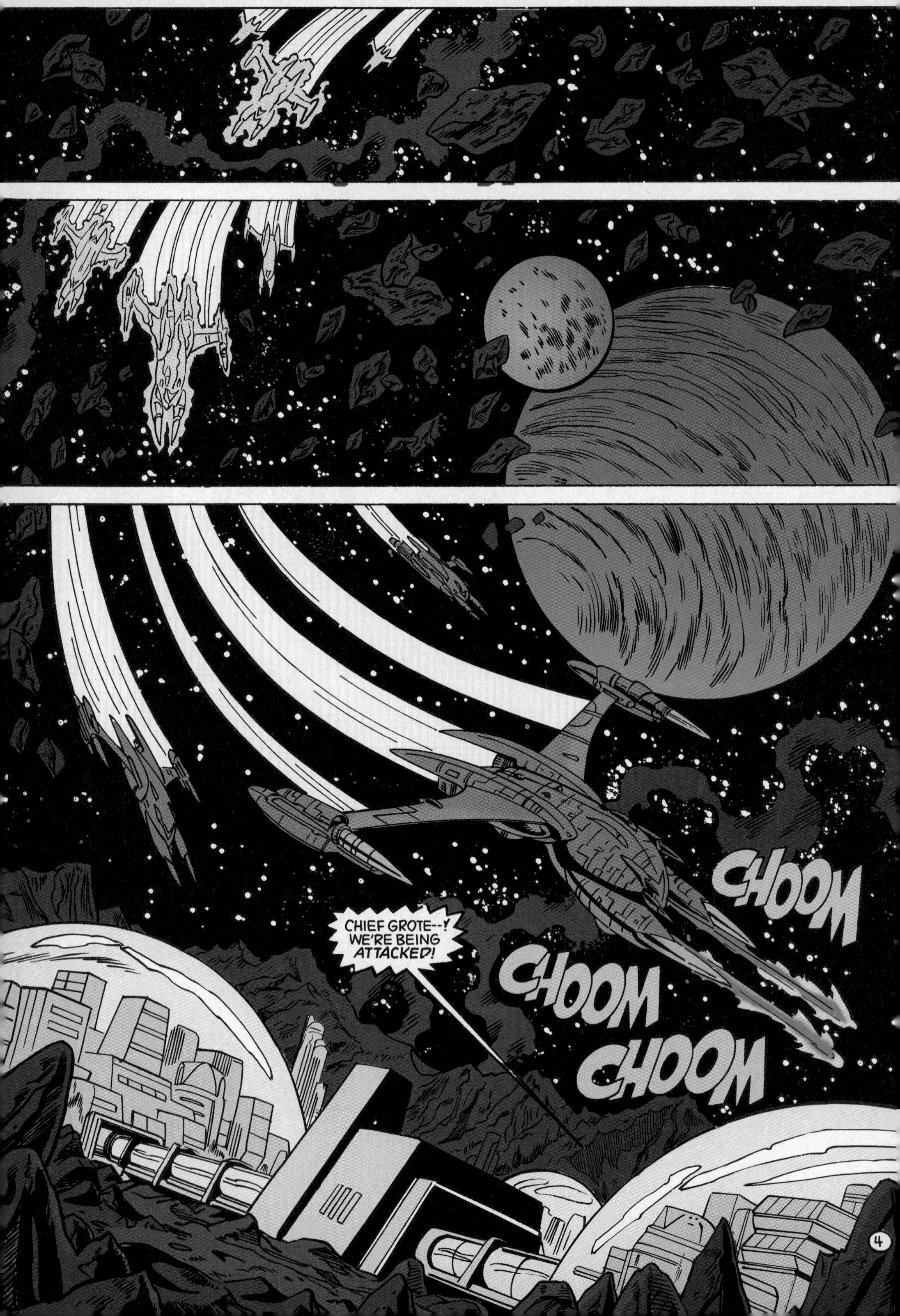
CHIEF GROTE--! WE'RE BEING ATTACKED!
CHOOM
CHOOM
CHOOM

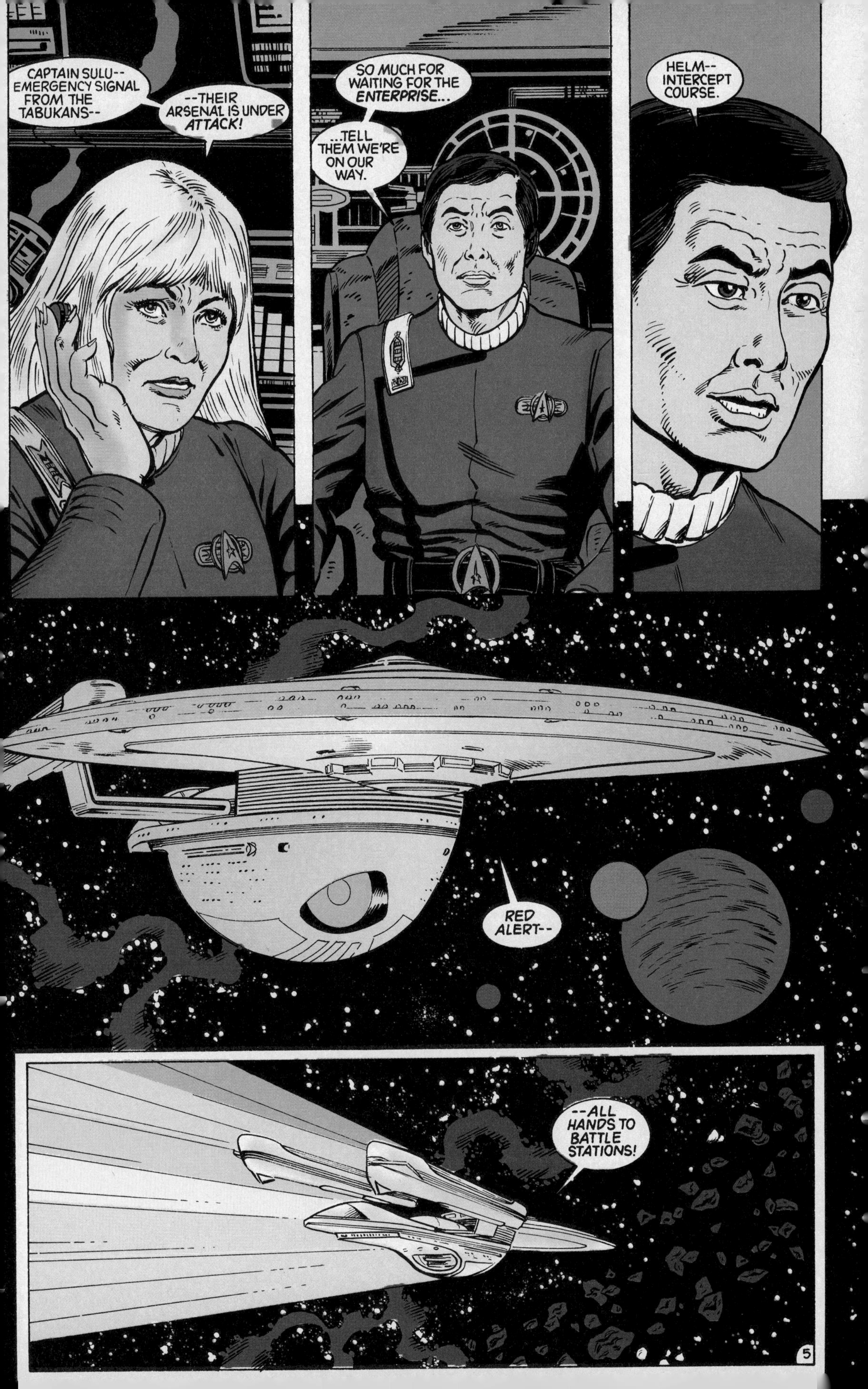
CAPTAIN SULU-- EMERGENCY SIGNAL FROM THE TABUKANS--
--THEIR ARSENAL IS UNDER ATTACK!
SO MUCH FOR WAITING FOR THE ENTERPRISE...
..TELL THEM WE'RE ON OUR WAY.
HELM-- INTERCEPT COURSE.
RED ALERT--
--ALL HANDS TO BATTLE STATIONS!
5

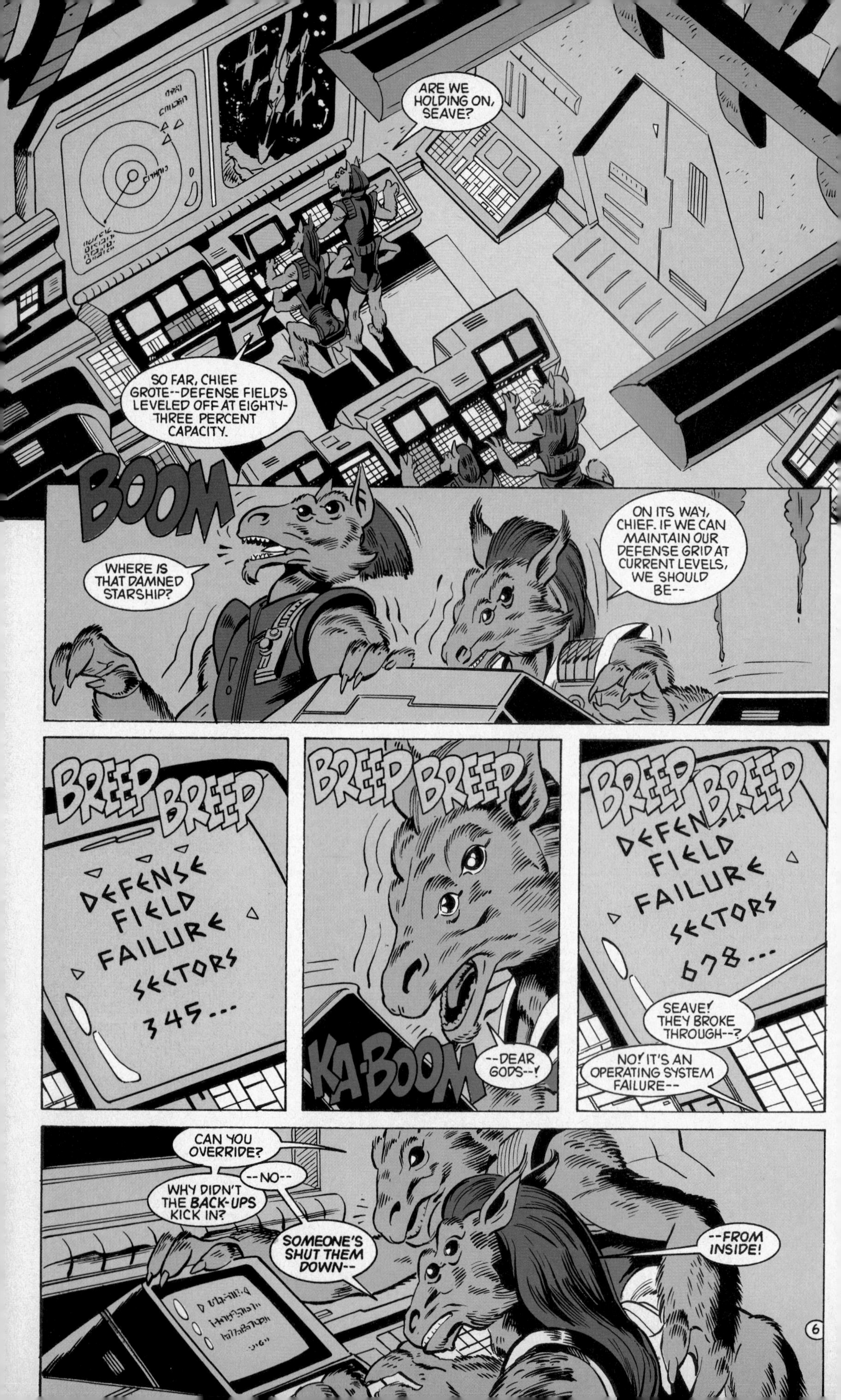
ARE WE HOLDING ON, SEAVE?
SO FAR, CHIEF GROTE--DEFENSE FIELDS LEVELED OFF AT EIGHTY-THREE PERCENT CAPACITY.
BOOM
WHERE IS THAT DAMNED STARSHIP?
ON ITS WAY, CHIEF. IF WE CAN MAINTAIN OUR DEFENSE GRID AT CURRENT LEVELS, WE SHOULD BE--
BREEP BREEP
DEFENSE FIELD FAILURE SECTORS 345...
BREEP BREEP
KA-BOOM
--DEAR GODS--!
BREEP BREEP
DEFENSE FIELD FAILURE SECTORS 678...
SEAVE! THEY BROKE THROUGH--?
NO! IT'S AN OPERATING SYSTEM FAILURE--
CAN YOU OVERRIDE?
--NO--
WHY DIDN'T THE BACK-UPS KICK IN?
SOMEONE'S SHUT THEM DOWN--
--FROM INSIDE!

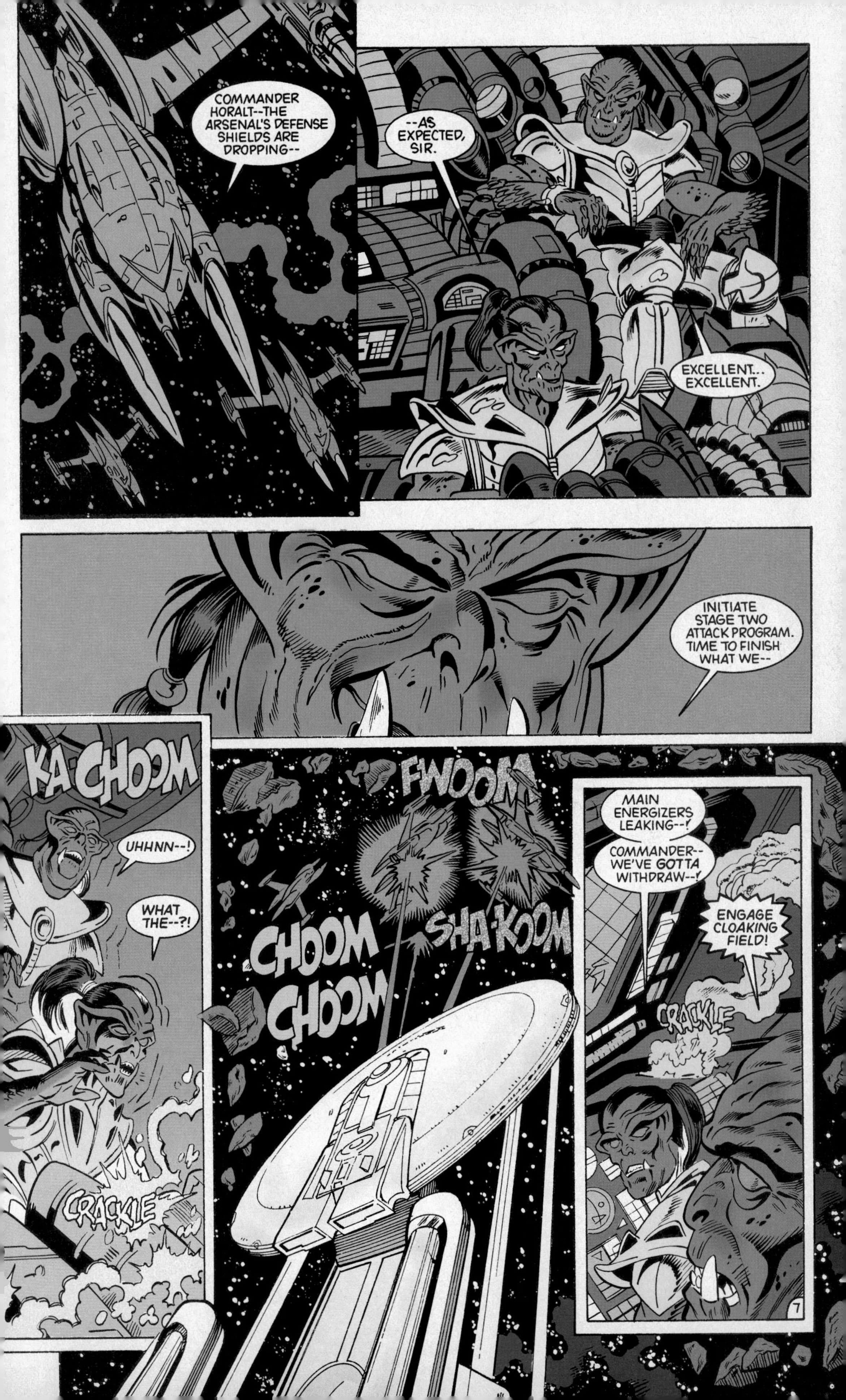
COMMANDER HORALT--THE ARSENAL'S DEFENSE SHIELDS ARE DROPPING--
--AS EXPECTED, SIR.
EXCELLENT... EXCELLENT.
INITIATE STAGE TWO ATTACK PROGRAM. TIME TO FINISH WHAT WE--
KA-CHOOM
UHHNN--!
WHAT THE--?!
CRACKLE
FWOOM
CHOOM CHOOM
SHA-KOOM
MAIN ENERGIZERS LEAKING--!
COMMANDER-- WE'VE GOTTA WITHDRAW--!
ENGAGE CLOAKING FIELD!
CRACKLE
7

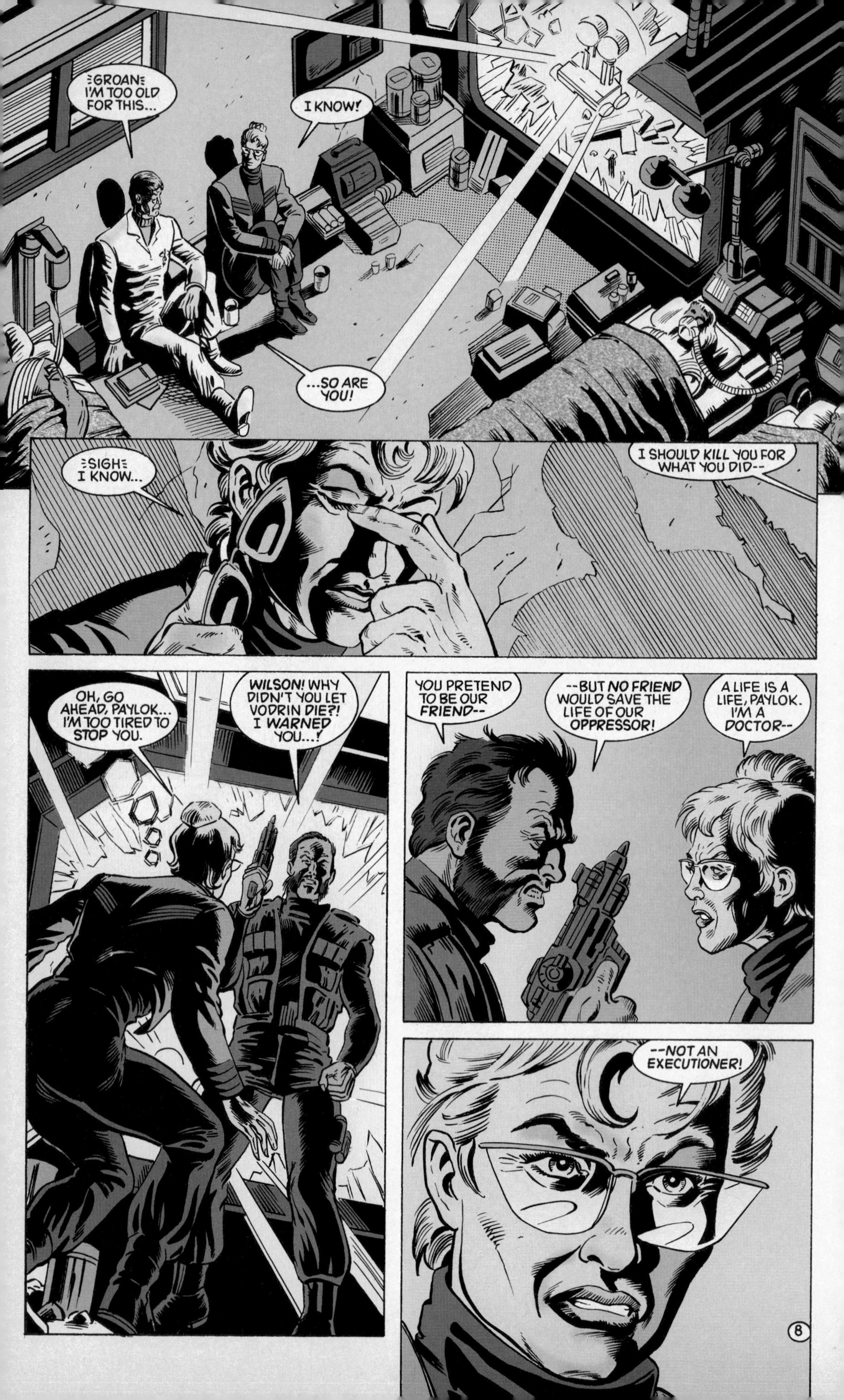

=GROAN= I'M TOO OLD FOR THIS...
I KNOW!
...SO ARE YOU!
=SIGH= I KNOW...
I SHOULD KILL YOU FOR WHAT YOU DID--
OH, GO AHEAD, PAYLOK... I'M TOO TIRED TO STOP YOU.
WILSON! WHY DIDN'T YOU LET VODRIN DIE?! I WARNED YOU...!
YOU PRETEND TO BE OUR FRIEND--
--BUT NO FRIEND WOULD SAVE THE LIFE OF OUR OPPRESSOR!
A LIFE IS A LIFE, PAYLOK. I'M A DOCTOR--
--NOT AN EXECUTIONER!

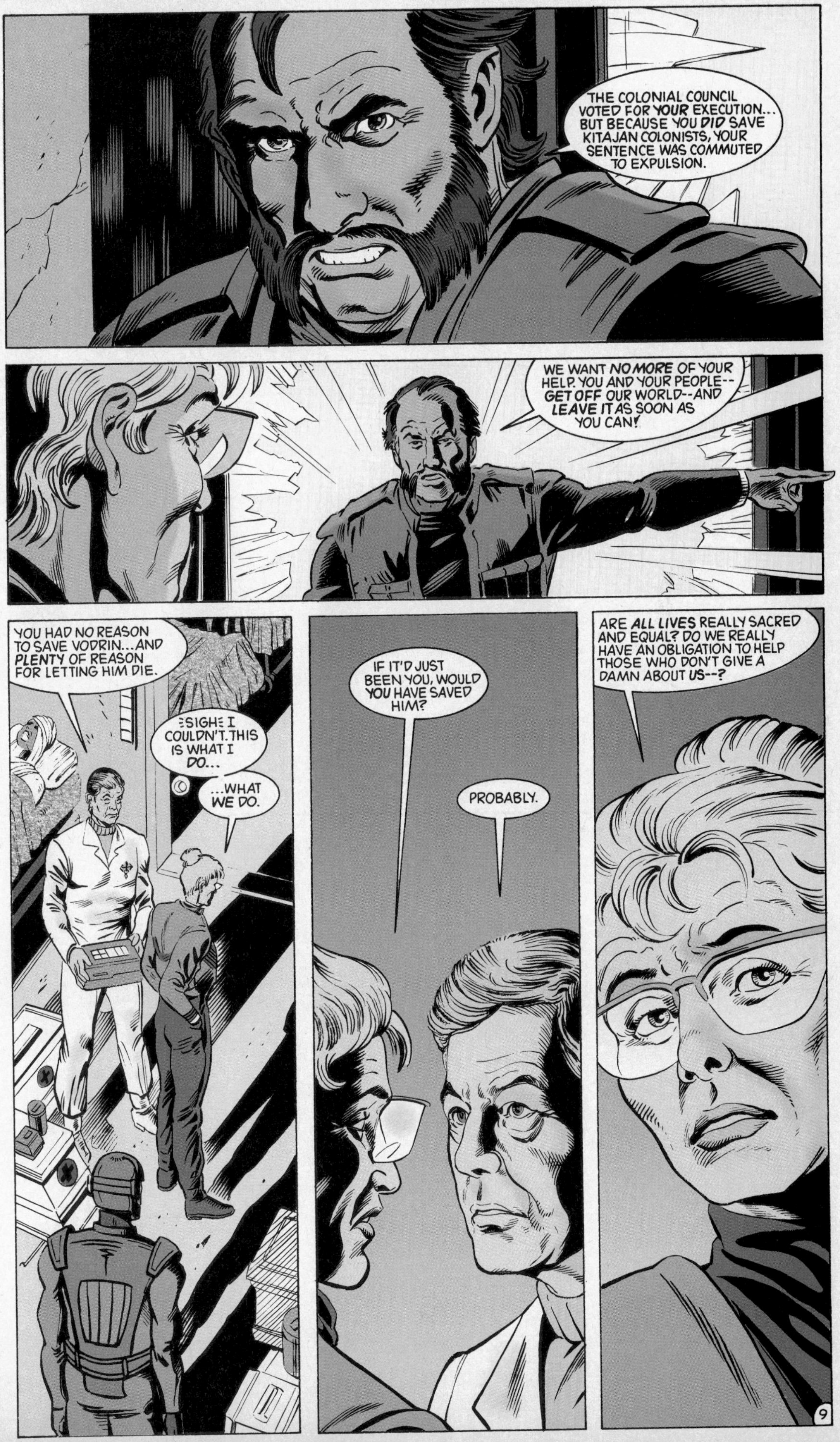
THE COLONIAL COUNCIL VOTED FOR YOUR EXECUTION... BUT BECAUSE YOU DID SAVE KITAJAN COLONISTS, YOUR SENTENCE WAS COMMUTED TO EXPULSION.
WE WANT NO MORE OF YOUR HELP. YOU AND YOUR PEOPLE-- GET OFF OUR WORLD--AND LEAVE IT AS SOON AS YOU CAN!
YOU HAD NO REASON TO SAVE VODRIN...AND PLENTY OF REASON FOR LETTING HIM DIE.
SIGH I COULDN'T. THIS IS WHAT I DO...
...WHAT WE DO.
IF IT'D JUST BEEN YOU, WOULD YOU HAVE SAVED HIM?
PROBABLY.
ARE ALL LIVES REALLY SACRED AND EQUAL? DO WE REALLY HAVE AN OBLIGATION TO HELP THOSE WHO DON'T GIVE A DAMN ABOUT US--?
9

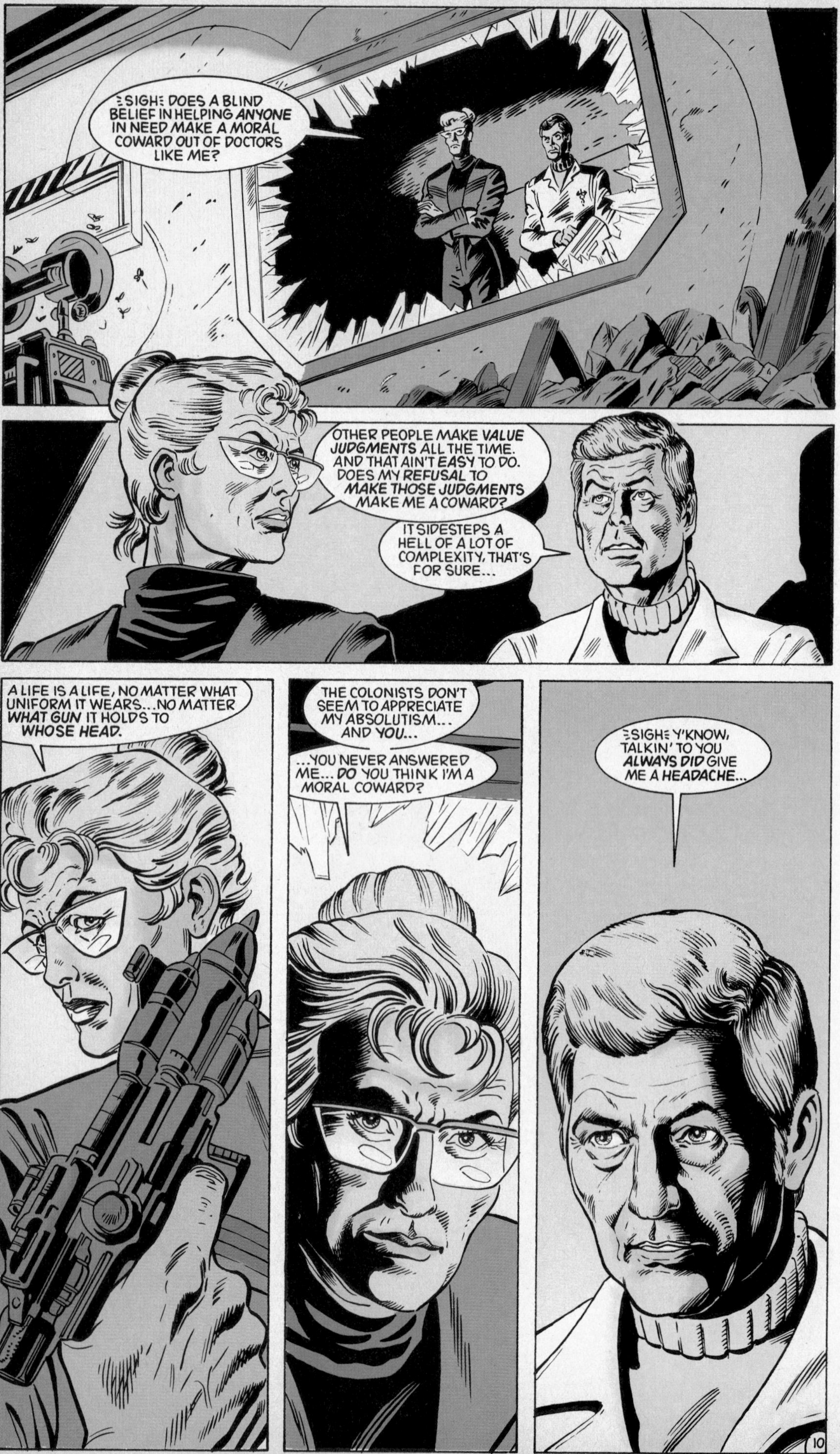

≡SIGH≡ DOES A BLIND BELIEF IN HELPING ANYONE IN NEED MAKE A MORAL COWARD OUT OF DOCTORS LIKE ME?
OTHER PEOPLE MAKE VALUE JUDGMENTS ALL THE TIME. AND THAT AIN'T EASY TO DO. DOES MY REFUSAL TO MAKE THOSE JUDGMENTS MAKE ME A COWARD?
IT SIDESTEPS A HELL OF A LOT OF COMPLEXITY, THAT'S FOR SURE...
A LIFE IS A LIFE, NO MATTER WHAT UNIFORM IT WEARS... NO MATTER WHAT GUN IT HOLDS TO WHOSE HEAD.
THE COLONISTS DON'T SEEM TO APPRECIATE MY ABSOLUTISM... AND YOU...
...YOU NEVER ANSWERED ME... DO YOU THINK I'M A MORAL COWARD?
≡SIGH≡ Y'KNOW, TALKIN' TO YOU ALWAYS DID GIVE ME A HEADACHE...

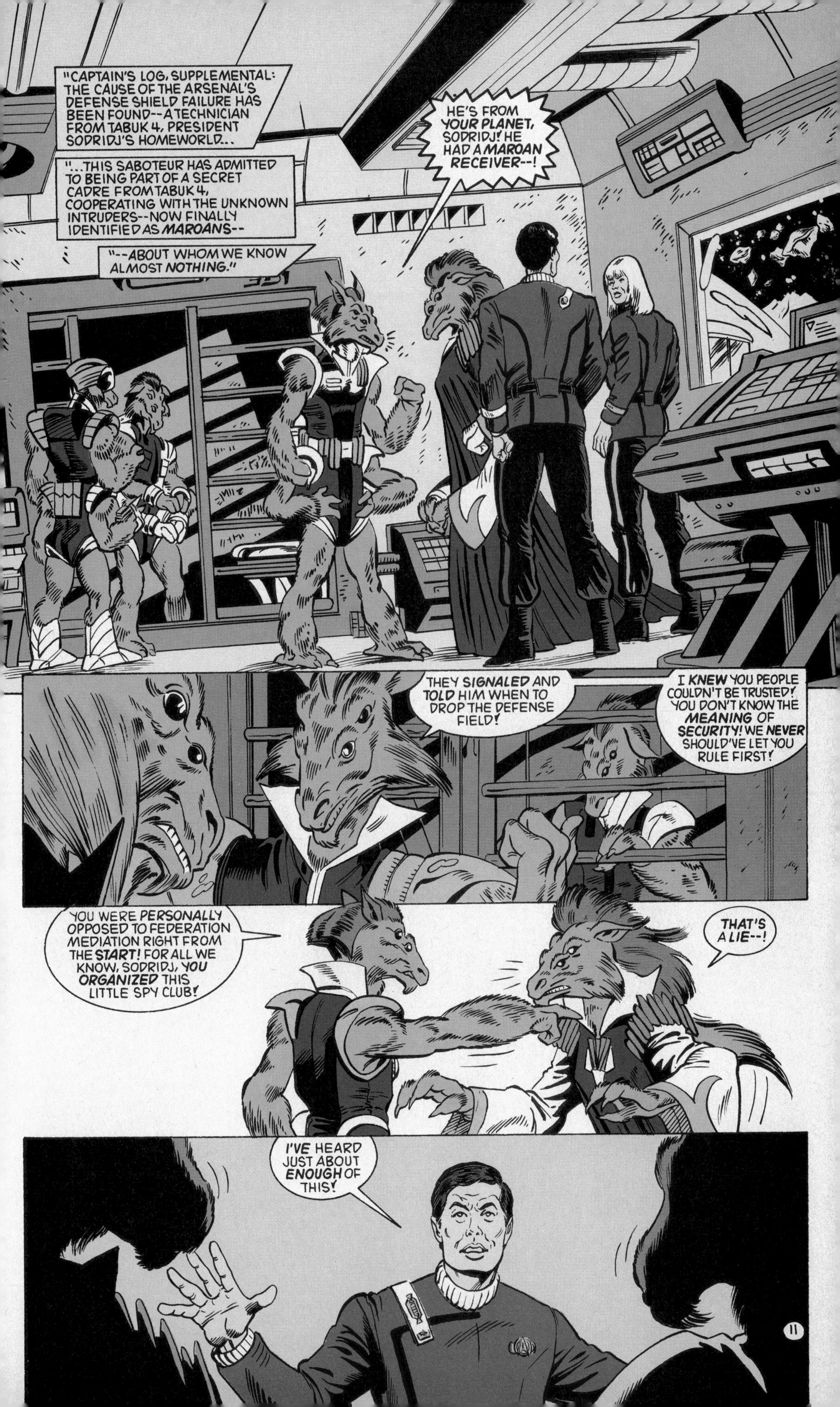
"CAPTAIN'S LOG, SUPPLEMENTAL: THE CAUSE OF THE ARSENAL'S DEFENSE SHIELD FAILURE HAS BEEN FOUND--A TECHNICIAN FROM TABUK 4, PRESIDENT SODRIDJ'S HOMEWORLD...
"...THIS SABOTEUR HAS ADMITTED TO BEING PART OF A SECRET CADRE FROM TABUK 4, COOPERATING WITH THE UNKNOWN INTRUDERS--NOW FINALLY IDENTIFIED AS MAROANS--
"--ABOUT WHOM WE KNOW ALMOST NOTHING."
HE'S FROM YOUR PLANET, SODRIDJ! HE HAD A MAROAN RECEIVER--!
THEY SIGNALED AND TOLD HIM WHEN TO DROP THE DEFENSE FIELD!
I KNEW YOU PEOPLE COULDN'T BE TRUSTED! YOU DON'T KNOW THE MEANING OF SECURITY! WE NEVER SHOULD'VE LET YOU RULE FIRST!
YOU WERE PERSONALLY OPPOSED TO FEDERATION MEDIATION RIGHT FROM THE START! FOR ALL WE KNOW, SODRIDJ, YOU ORGANIZED THIS LITTLE SPY CLUB!
THAT'S A LIE--!
I'VE HEARD JUST ABOUT ENOUGH OF THIS!
11

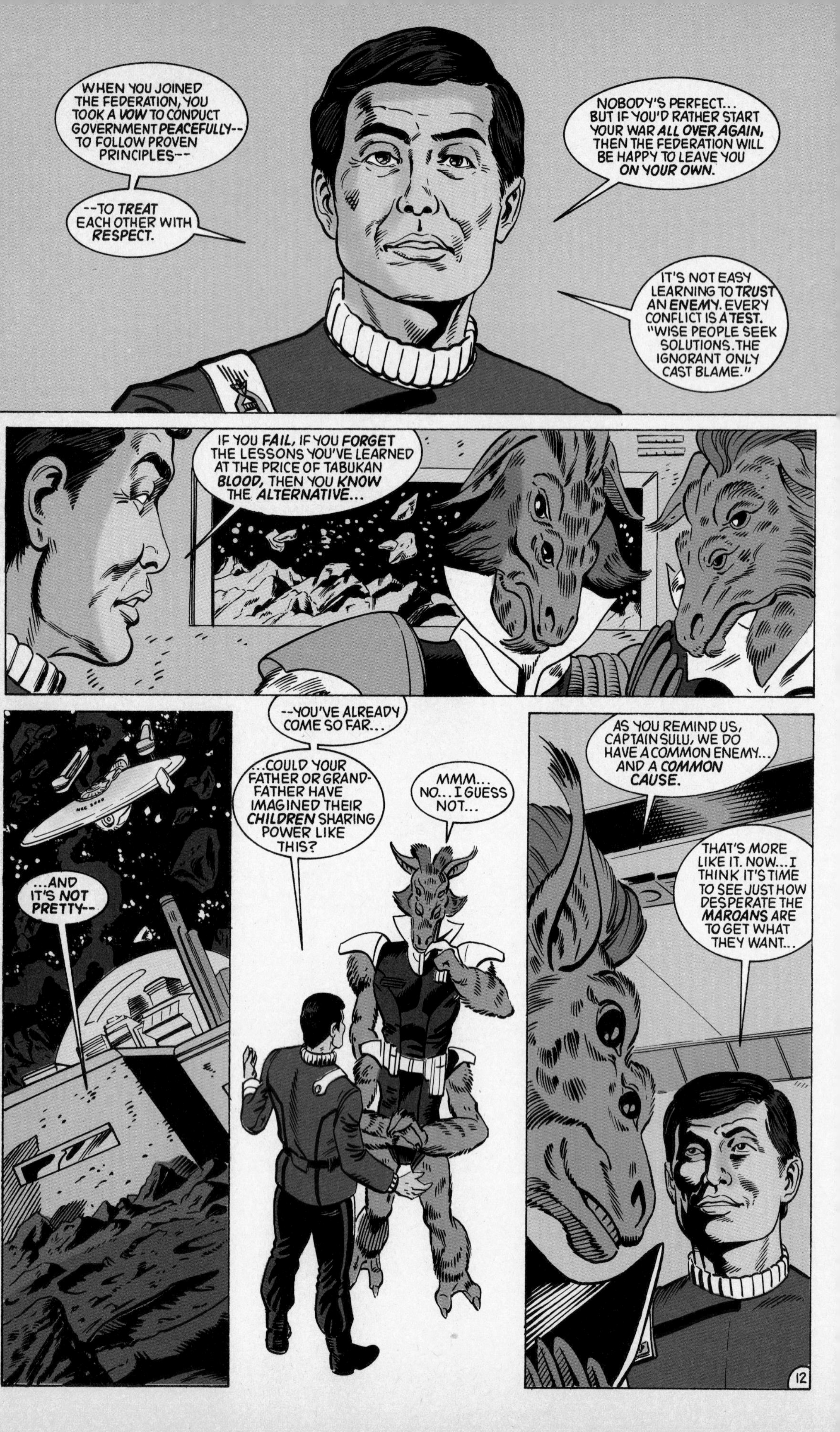
WHEN YOU JOINED THE FEDERATION, YOU TOOK A VOW TO CONDUCT GOVERNMENT PEACEFULLY-- TO FOLLOW PROVEN PRINCIPLES--
--TO TREAT EACH OTHER WITH RESPECT.
NOBODY'S PERFECT... BUT IF YOU'D RATHER START YOUR WAR ALL OVER AGAIN, THEN THE FEDERATION WILL BE HAPPY TO LEAVE YOU ON YOUR OWN.
IT'S NOT EASY LEARNING TO TRUST AN ENEMY. EVERY CONFLICT IS A TEST. "WISE PEOPLE SEEK SOLUTIONS. THE IGNORANT ONLY CAST BLAME."
IF YOU FAIL, IF YOU FORGET THE LESSONS YOU'VE LEARNED AT THE PRICE OF TABUKAN BLOOD, THEN YOU KNOW THE ALTERNATIVE...
...AND IT'S NOT PRETTY--
--YOU'VE ALREADY COME SO FAR...
...COULD YOUR FATHER OR GRAND-FATHER HAVE IMAGINED THEIR CHILDREN SHARING POWER LIKE THIS?
MMM... NO... I GUESS NOT...
AS YOU REMIND US, CAPTAIN SULU, WE DO HAVE A COMMON ENEMY... AND A COMMON CAUSE.
THAT'S MORE LIKE IT. NOW... I THINK IT'S TIME TO SEE JUST HOW DESPERATE THE MAROANS ARE TO GET WHAT THEY WANT...
12

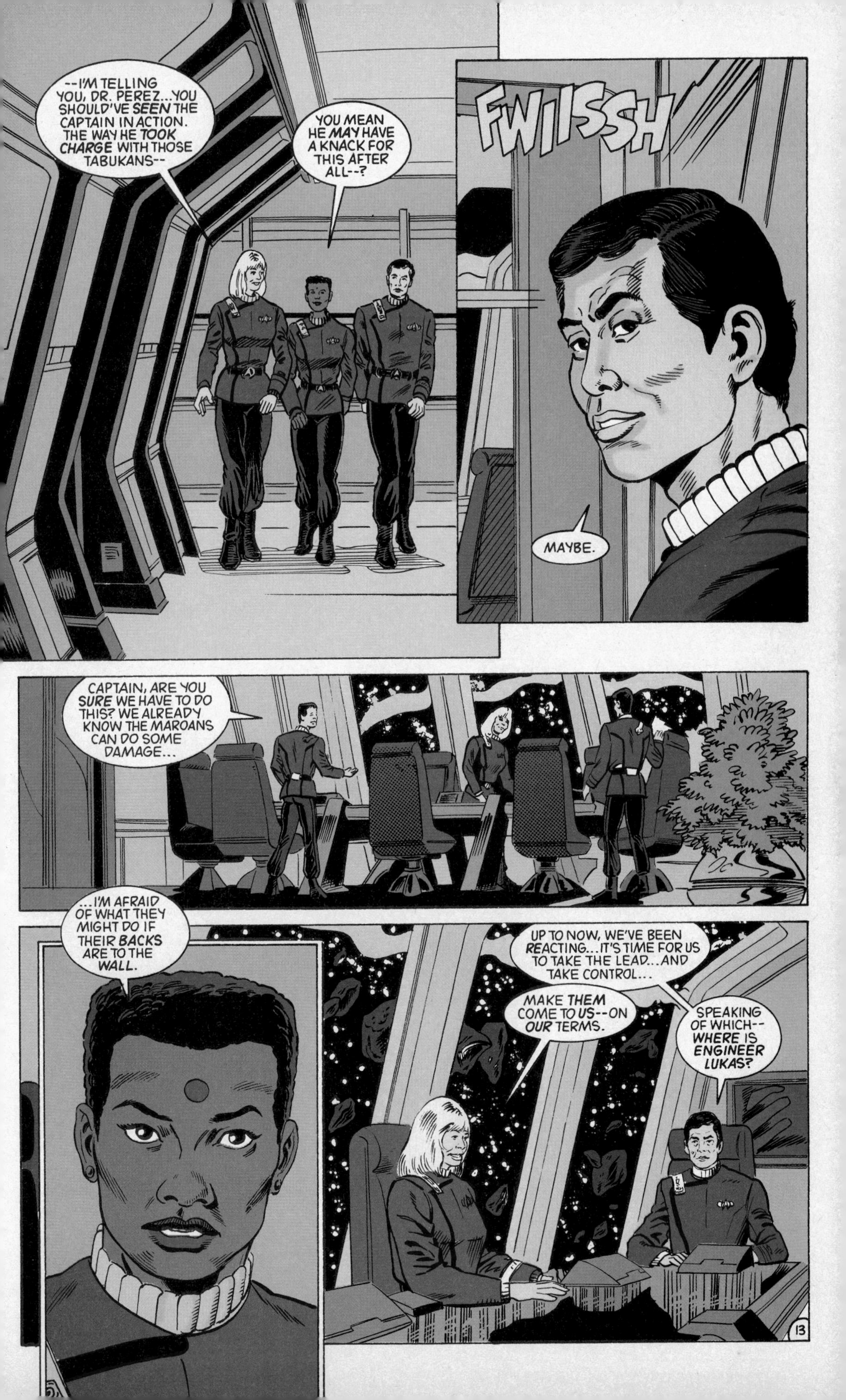
--I'M TELLING YOU, DR. PEREZ...YOU SHOULD'VE SEEN THE CAPTAIN IN ACTION. THE WAY HE TOOK CHARGE WITH THOSE TABUKANS--
YOU MEAN HE MAY HAVE A KNACK FOR THIS AFTER ALL--?
FWIISSH
MAYBE.
CAPTAIN, ARE YOU SURE WE HAVE TO DO THIS? WE ALREADY KNOW THE MAROANS CAN DO SOME DAMAGE...
...I'M AFRAID OF WHAT THEY MIGHT DO IF THEIR BACKS ARE TO THE WALL.
UP TO NOW, WE'VE BEEN REACTING...IT'S TIME FOR US TO TAKE THE LEAD...AND TAKE CONTROL...
MAKE THEM COME TO US--ON OUR TERMS.
SPEAKING OF WHICH--WHERE IS ENGINEER LUKAS?
13

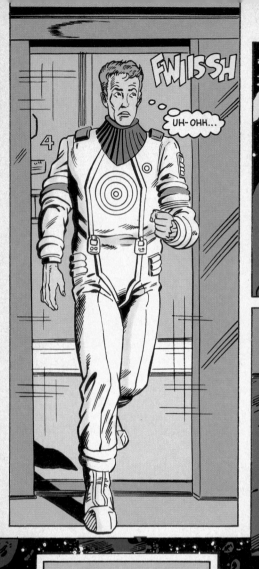

FWIISSH

UH-OHH...

YOU'RE LATE, MR. LUKAS.

I KNOW, SIR. I'M SORRY.

WHEN I CALL A BRIEFING, I EXPECT YOU TO BE THERE. IF YOU'RE NOT, YOU'D BETTER HAVE A GOOD EXCUSE.

I DO, SIR.

I'VE GOT SOME GOOD NEWS FOR YOU, SIR...VERY GOOD NEWS...

U.S.S. EXCELSIOR

OH? LET'S HEAR IT, THEN.

14

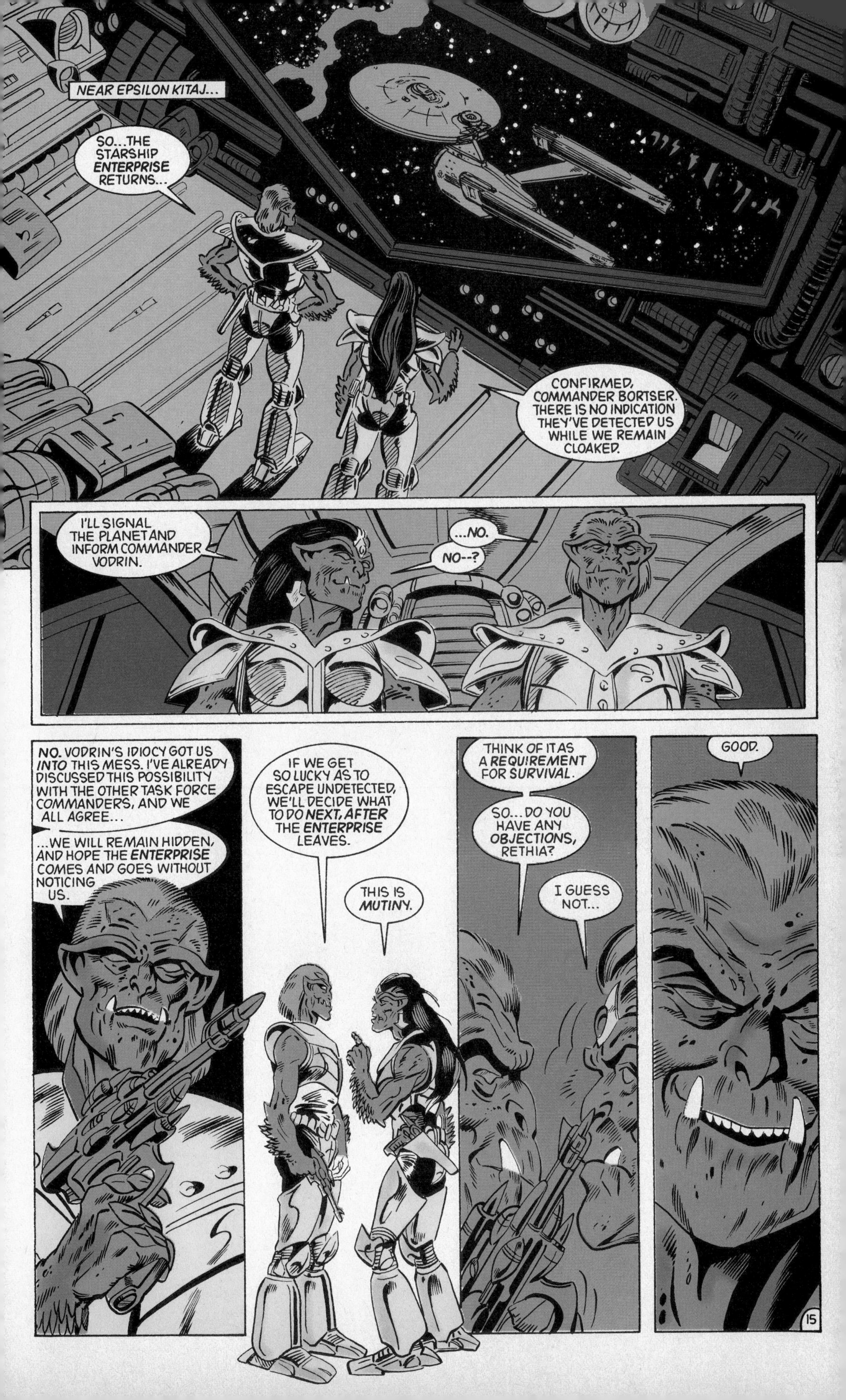

NEAR EPSILON KITAJ...
SO...THE STARSHIP ENTERPRISE RETURNS...
CONFIRMED, COMMANDER BORTSER. THERE IS NO INDICATION THEY'VE DETECTED US WHILE WE REMAIN CLOAKED.
I'LL SIGNAL THE PLANET AND INFORM COMMANDER VODRIN.
...NO.
NO--?
NO. VODRIN'S IDIOCY GOT US INTO THIS MESS. I'VE ALREADY DISCUSSED THIS POSSIBILITY WITH THE OTHER TASK FORCE COMMANDERS, AND WE ALL AGREE...
...WE WILL REMAIN HIDDEN, AND HOPE THE ENTERPRISE COMES AND GOES WITHOUT NOTICING US.
IF WE GET SO LUCKY AS TO ESCAPE UNDETECTED, WE'LL DECIDE WHAT TO DO NEXT, AFTER THE ENTERPRISE LEAVES.
THIS IS MUTINY.
THINK OF IT AS A REQUIREMENT FOR SURVIVAL.
SO... DO YOU HAVE ANY OBJECTIONS, RETHIA?
I GUESS NOT...
GOOD.
15

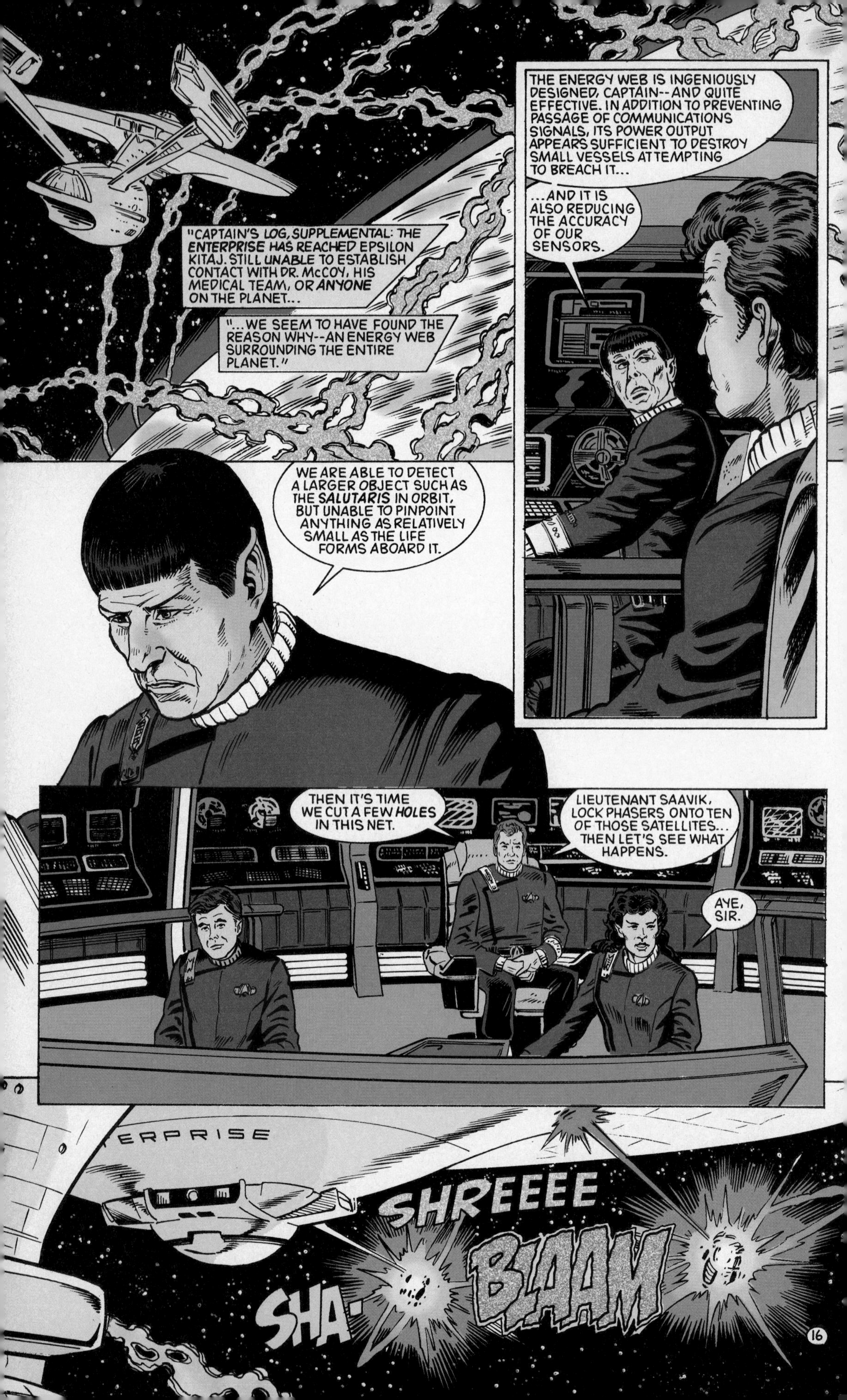
"CAPTAIN'S LOG, SUPPLEMENTAL: THE ENTERPRISE HAS REACHED EPSILON KITAJ. STILL UNABLE TO ESTABLISH CONTACT WITH DR. McCOY, HIS MEDICAL TEAM, OR ANYONE ON THE PLANET...
"...WE SEEM TO HAVE FOUND THE REASON WHY--AN ENERGY WEB SURROUNDING THE ENTIRE PLANET."
THE ENERGY WEB IS INGENIOUSLY DESIGNED, CAPTAIN--AND QUITE EFFECTIVE. IN ADDITION TO PREVENTING PASSAGE OF COMMUNICATIONS SIGNALS, ITS POWER OUTPUT APPEARS SUFFICIENT TO DESTROY SMALL VESSELS ATTEMPTING TO BREACH IT...
...AND IT IS ALSO REDUCING THE ACCURACY OF OUR SENSORS.
WE ARE ABLE TO DETECT A LARGER OBJECT SUCH AS THE SALUTARIS IN ORBIT, BUT UNABLE TO PINPOINT ANYTHING AS RELATIVELY SMALL AS THE LIFE FORMS ABOARD IT.
THEN IT'S TIME WE CUT A FEW HOLES IN THIS NET.
LIEUTENANT SAAVIK, LOCK PHASERS ONTO TEN OF THOSE SATELLITES... THEN LET'S SEE WHAT HAPPENS.
AYE, SIR.
ERPRISE
SHREEEE
SHA-
BLAAM

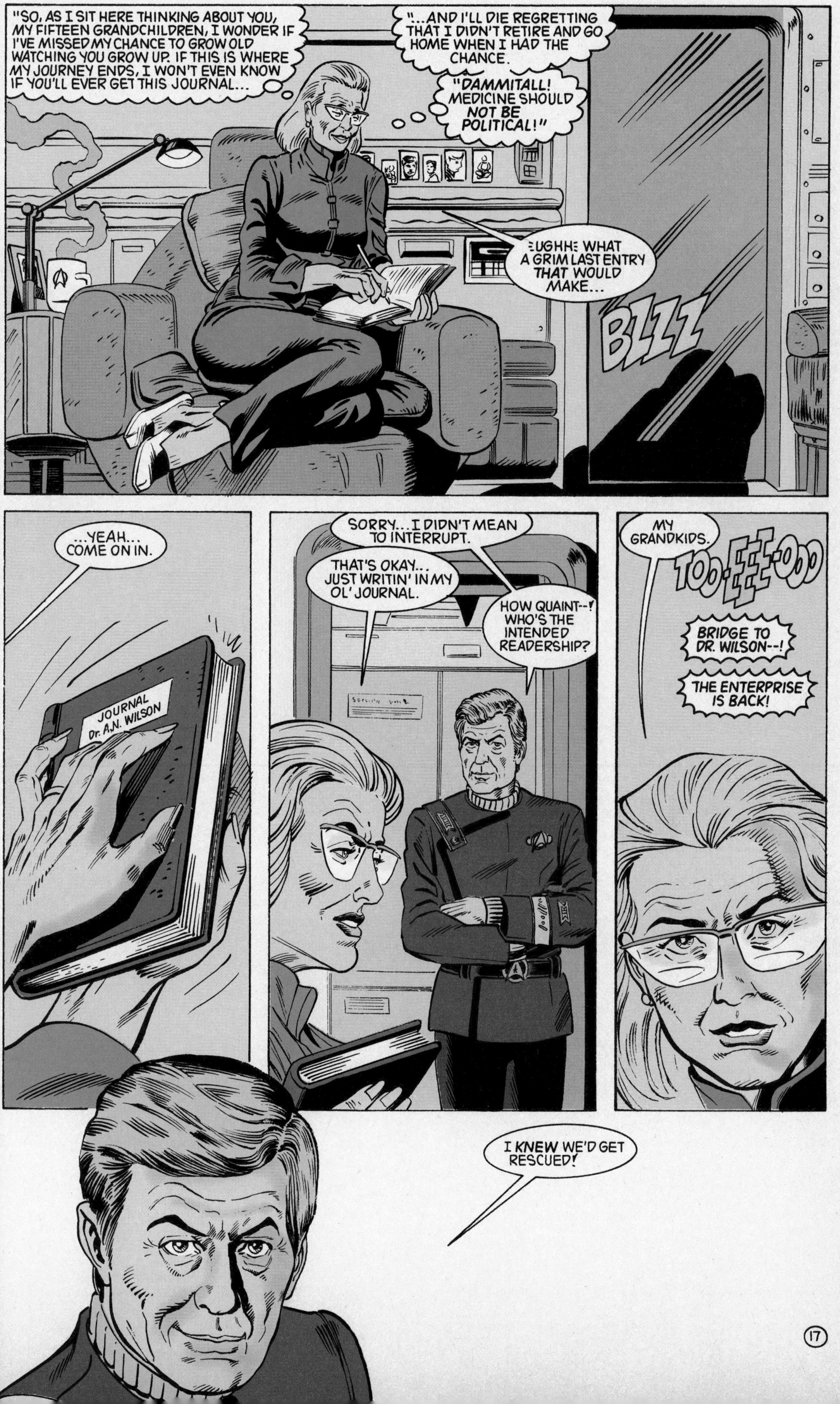
"SO, AS I SIT HERE THINKING ABOUT YOU, MY FIFTEEN GRANDCHILDREN, I WONDER IF I'VE MISSED MY CHANCE TO GROW OLD WATCHING YOU GROW UP. IF THIS IS WHERE MY JOURNEY ENDS, I WON'T EVEN KNOW IF YOU'LL EVER GET THIS JOURNAL...
"...AND I'LL DIE REGRETTING THAT I DIDN'T RETIRE AND GO HOME WHEN I HAD THE CHANCE.
"DAMMITALL! MEDICINE SHOULD NOT BE POLITICAL!"
EUGHH! WHAT A GRIM LAST ENTRY THAT WOULD MAKE...
BZZZ
...YEAH... COME ON IN.
JOURNAL Dr. A.N. WILSON
SORRY... I DIDN'T MEAN TO INTERRUPT.
THAT'S OKAY... JUST WRITIN' IN MY OL' JOURNAL.
HOW QUAINT--! WHO'S THE INTENDED READERSHIP?
MY GRANDKIDS.
TOO-EEE-OOO
BRIDGE TO DR. WILSON--!
THE ENTERPRISE IS BACK!
I KNEW WE'D GET RESCUED!

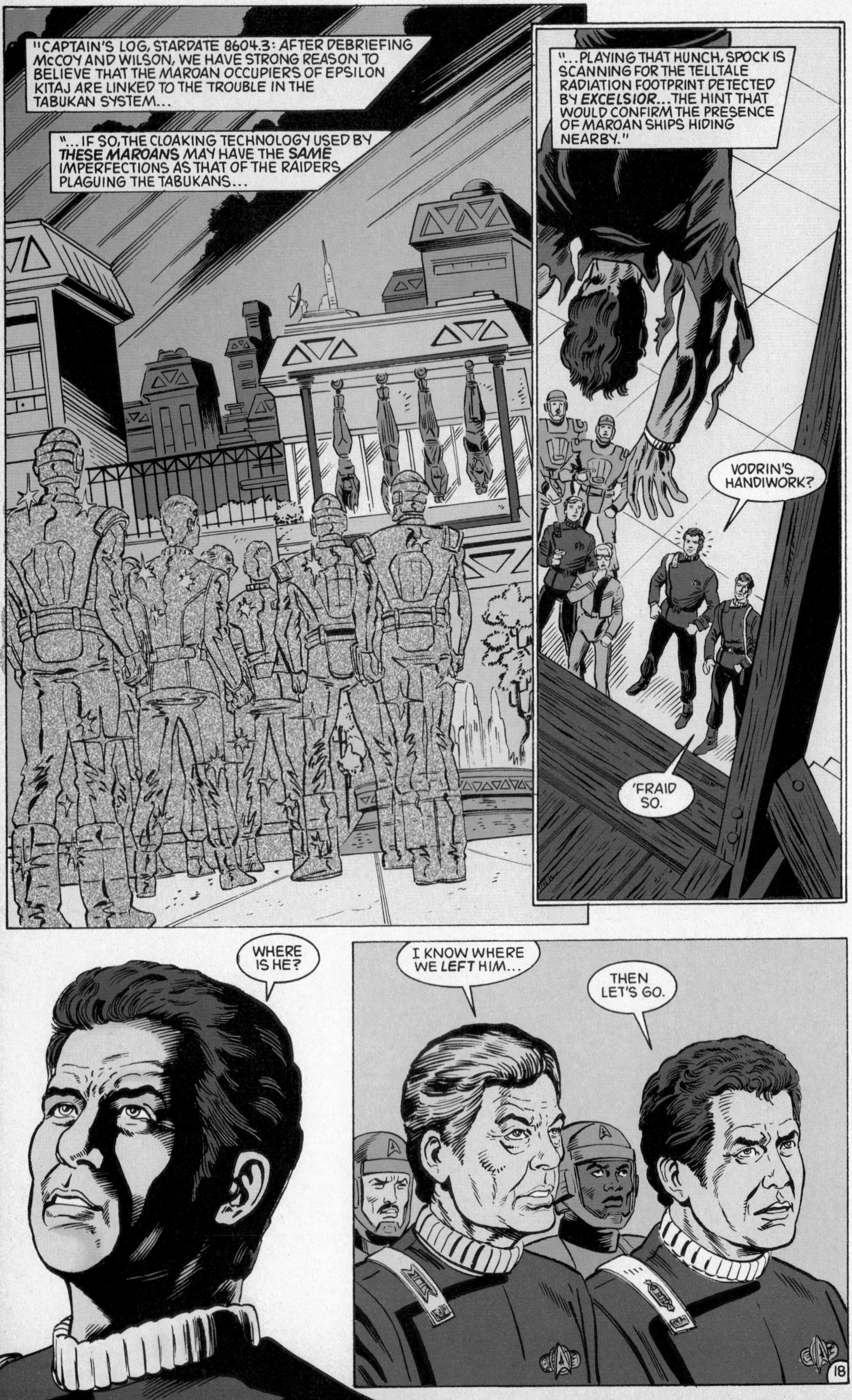
"CAPTAIN'S LOG, STARDATE 8604.3: AFTER DEBRIEFING McCOY AND WILSON, WE HAVE STRONG REASON TO BELIEVE THAT THE MAROAN OCCUPIERS OF EPSILON KITAJ ARE LINKED TO THE TROUBLE IN THE TABUKAN SYSTEM...
"...IF SO, THE CLOAKING TECHNOLOGY USED BY THESE MAROANS MAY HAVE THE SAME IMPERFECTIONS AS THAT OF THE RAIDERS PLAGUING THE TABUKANS...
"...PLAYING THAT HUNCH, SPOCK IS SCANNING FOR THE TELLTALE RADIATION FOOTPRINT DETECTED BY EXCELSIOR...THE HINT THAT WOULD CONFIRM THE PRESENCE OF MAROAN SHIPS HIDING NEARBY."
VODRIN'S HANDIWORK?
'FRAID SO.
WHERE IS HE?
I KNOW WHERE WE LEFT HIM...
THEN LET'S GO.
18

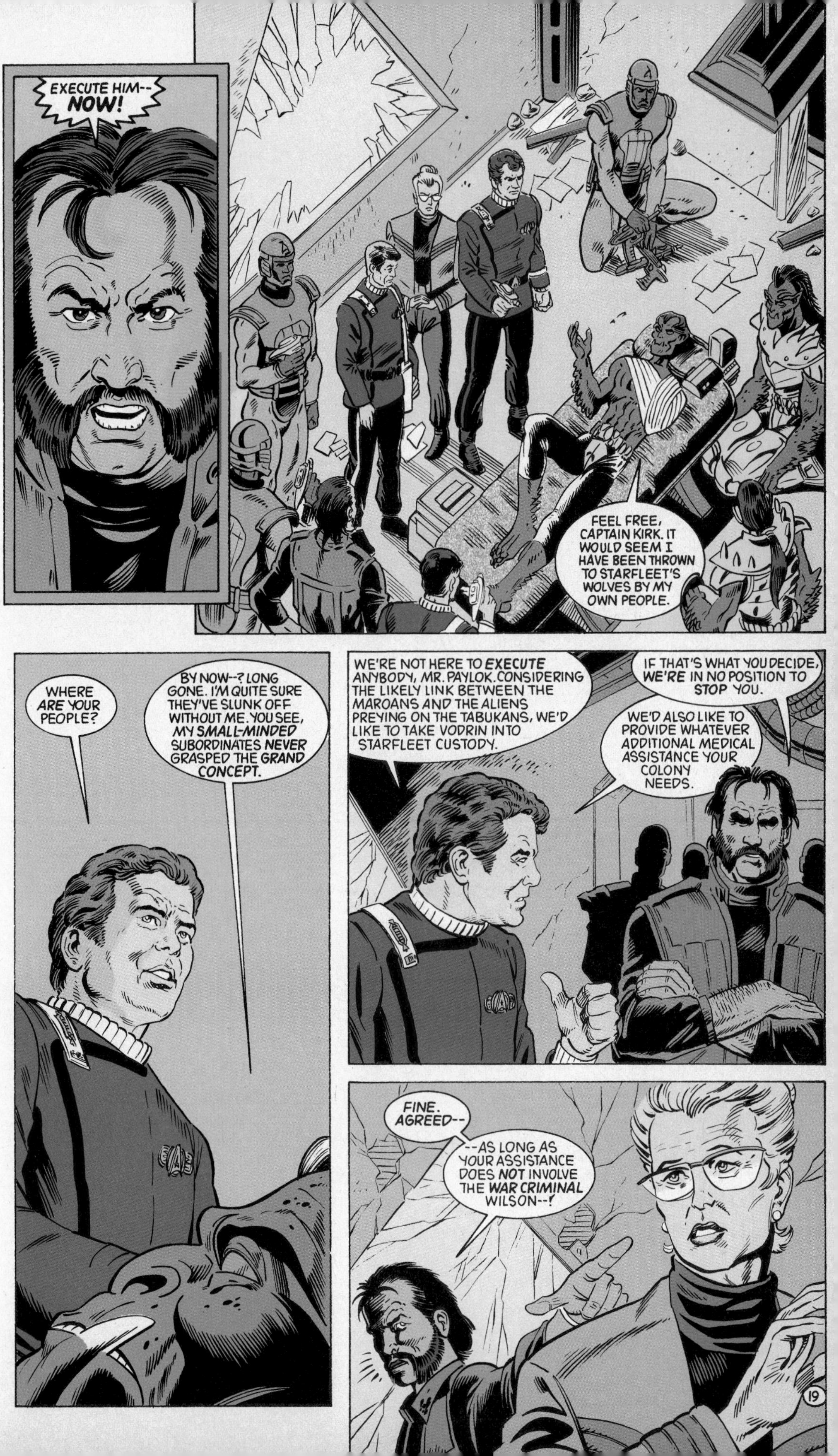

EXECUTE HIM-- NOW!
FEEL FREE, CAPTAIN KIRK. IT WOULD SEEM I HAVE BEEN THROWN TO STARFLEET'S WOLVES BY MY OWN PEOPLE.
WHERE ARE YOUR PEOPLE?
BY NOW--? LONG GONE. I'M QUITE SURE THEY'VE SLUNK OFF WITHOUT ME. YOU SEE, MY SMALL-MINDED SUBORDINATES NEVER GRASPED THE GRAND CONCEPT.
WE'RE NOT HERE TO EXECUTE ANYBODY, MR. PAYLOK. CONSIDERING THE LIKELY LINK BETWEEN THE MAROANS AND THE ALIENS PREYING ON THE TABUKANS, WE'D LIKE TO TAKE VODRIN INTO STARFLEET CUSTODY.
IF THAT'S WHAT YOU DECIDE, WE'RE IN NO POSITION TO STOP YOU.
WE'D ALSO LIKE TO PROVIDE WHATEVER ADDITIONAL MEDICAL ASSISTANCE YOUR COLONY NEEDS.
FINE. AGREED--
--AS LONG AS YOUR ASSISTANCE DOES NOT INVOLVE THE WAR CRIMINAL WILSON--!

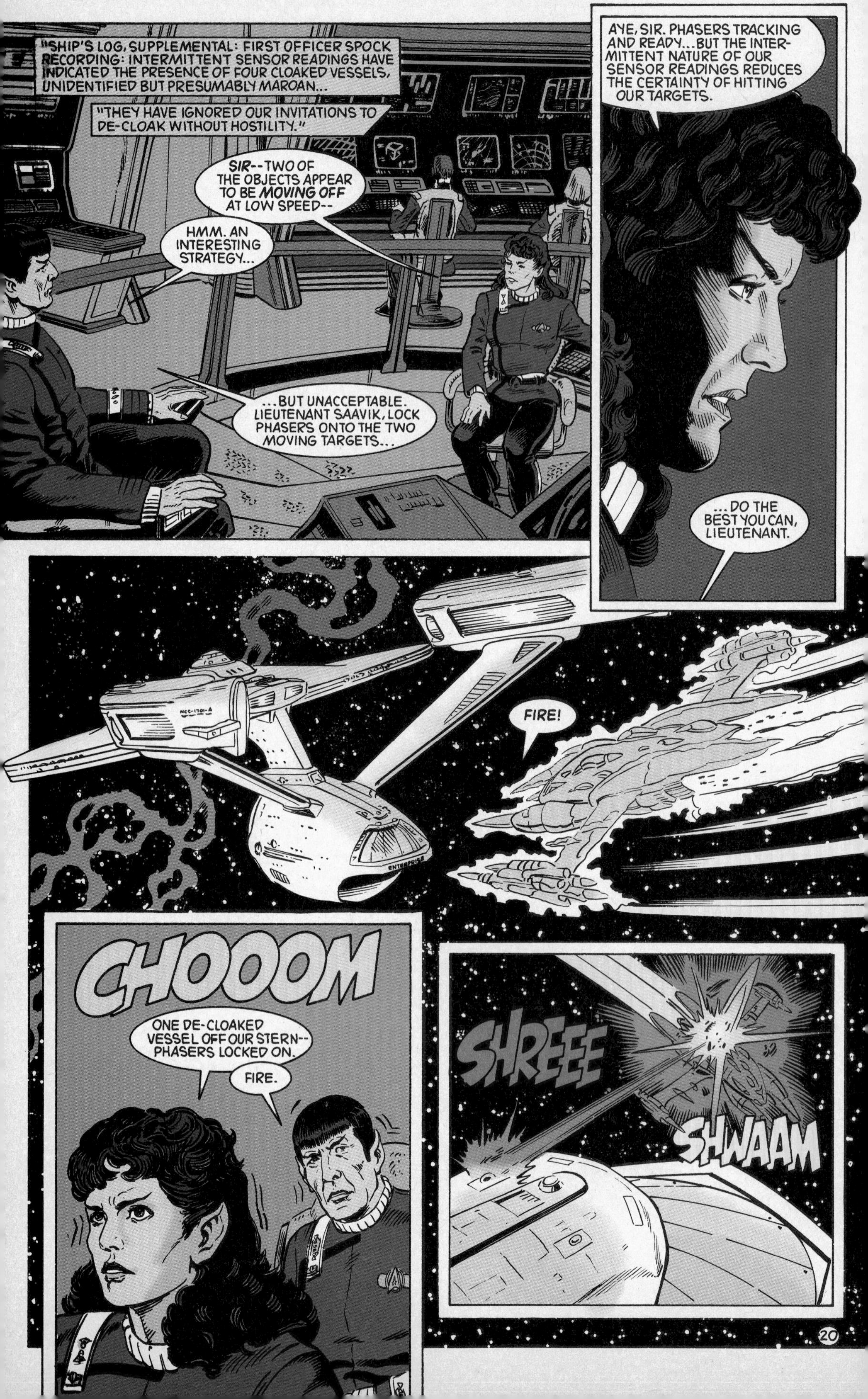
"SHIP'S LOG, SUPPLEMENTAL: FIRST OFFICER SPOCK RECORDING: INTERMITTENT SENSOR READINGS HAVE INDICATED THE PRESENCE OF FOUR CLOAKED VESSELS, UNIDENTIFIED BUT PRESUMABLY MAROAN...
"THEY HAVE IGNORED OUR INVITATIONS TO DE-CLOAK WITHOUT HOSTILITY."
SIR--TWO OF THE OBJECTS APPEAR TO BE MOVING OFF AT LOW SPEED--
HMM. AN INTERESTING STRATEGY...
...BUT UNACCEPTABLE. LIEUTENANT SAAVIK, LOCK PHASERS ONTO THE TWO MOVING TARGETS...
AYE, SIR. PHASERS TRACKING AND READY...BUT THE INTERMITTENT NATURE OF OUR SENSOR READINGS REDUCES THE CERTAINTY OF HITTING OUR TARGETS.
...DO THE BEST YOU CAN, LIEUTENANT.
NCC-1701-A
ENTERPRISE
FIRE!
CHOOOM
ONE DE-CLOAKED VESSEL OFF OUR STERN--PHASERS LOCKED ON.
FIRE.
SHREEE
SHWAAM

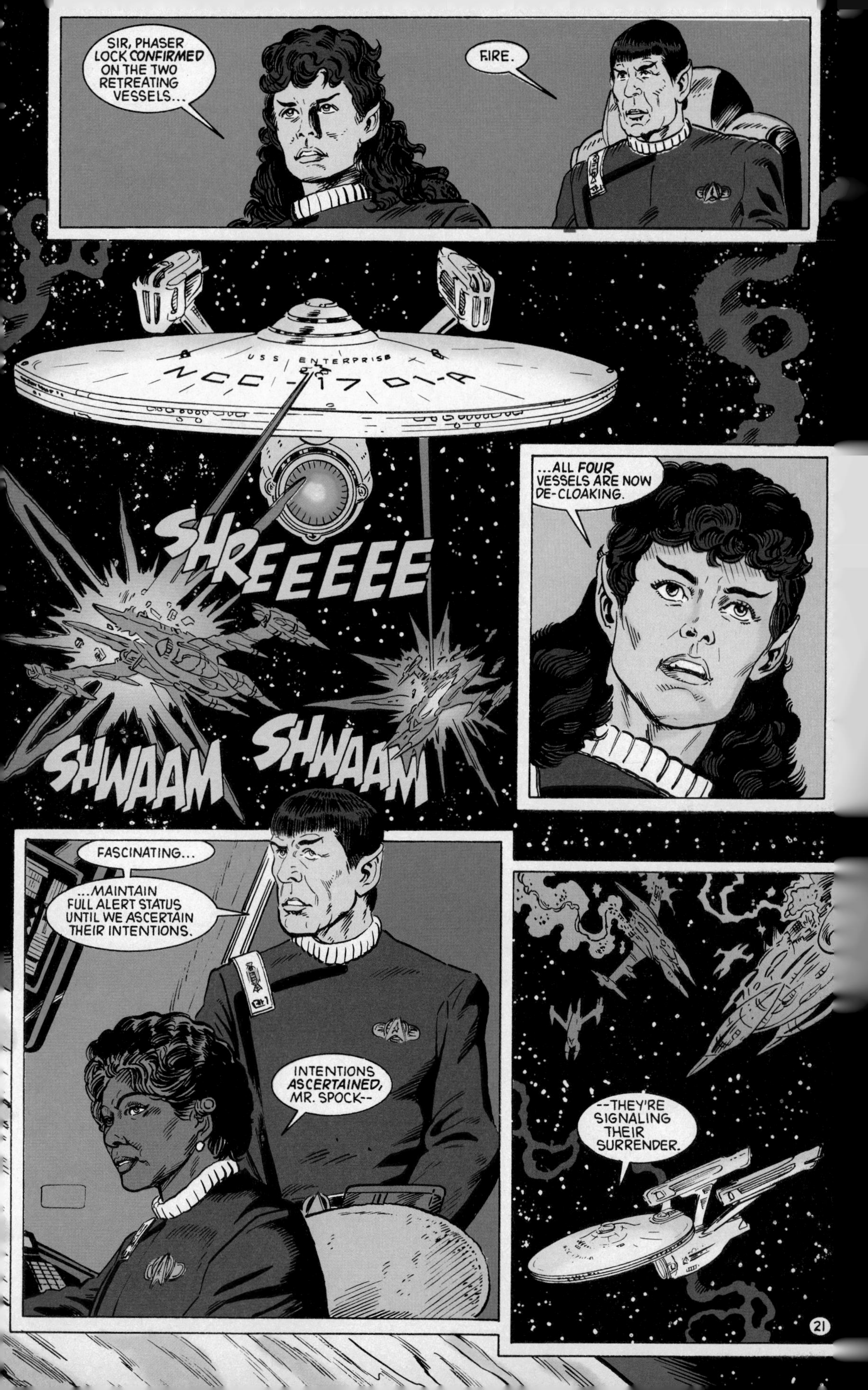

SIR, PHASER LOCK CONFIRMED ON THE TWO RETREATING VESSELS...
FIRE.
USS ENTERPRISE
NCC-1701-A
SHREEEEE
SHWAAM
SHWAAM
...ALL FOUR VESSELS ARE NOW DE-CLOAKING.
FASCINATING...
...MAINTAIN FULL ALERT STATUS UNTIL WE ASCERTAIN THEIR INTENTIONS.
INTENTIONS ASCERTAINED, MR. SPOCK--
--THEY'RE SIGNALING THEIR SURRENDER.

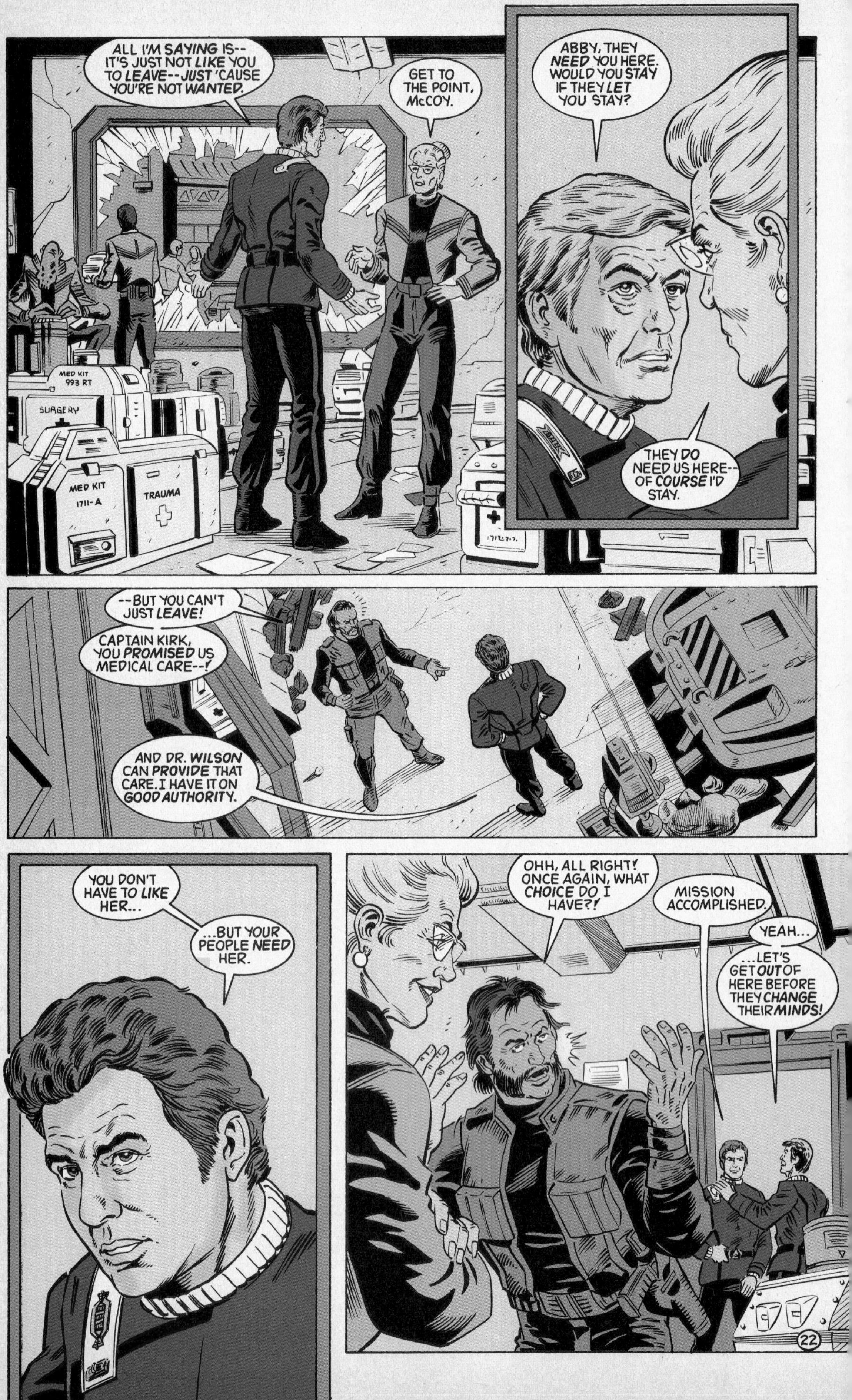
ALL I'M SAYING IS-- IT'S JUST NOT LIKE YOU TO LEAVE--JUST 'CAUSE YOU'RE NOT WANTED.
GET TO THE POINT, McCOY.
MED KIT 993 RT
SURGERY
MED KIT 1711-A
TRAUMA
ABBY, THEY NEED YOU HERE. WOULD YOU STAY IF THEY LET YOU STAY?
THEY DO NEED US HERE-- OF COURSE I'D STAY.
--BUT YOU CAN'T JUST LEAVE!
CAPTAIN KIRK, YOU PROMISED US MEDICAL CARE--!
AND DR. WILSON CAN PROVIDE THAT CARE. I HAVE IT ON GOOD AUTHORITY.
YOU DON'T HAVE TO LIKE HER...
...BUT YOUR PEOPLE NEED HER.
OHH, ALL RIGHT! ONCE AGAIN, WHAT CHOICE DO I HAVE?!
MISSION ACCOMPLISHED.
YEAH...
...LET'S GET OUT OF HERE BEFORE THEY CHANGE THEIR MINDS!
22

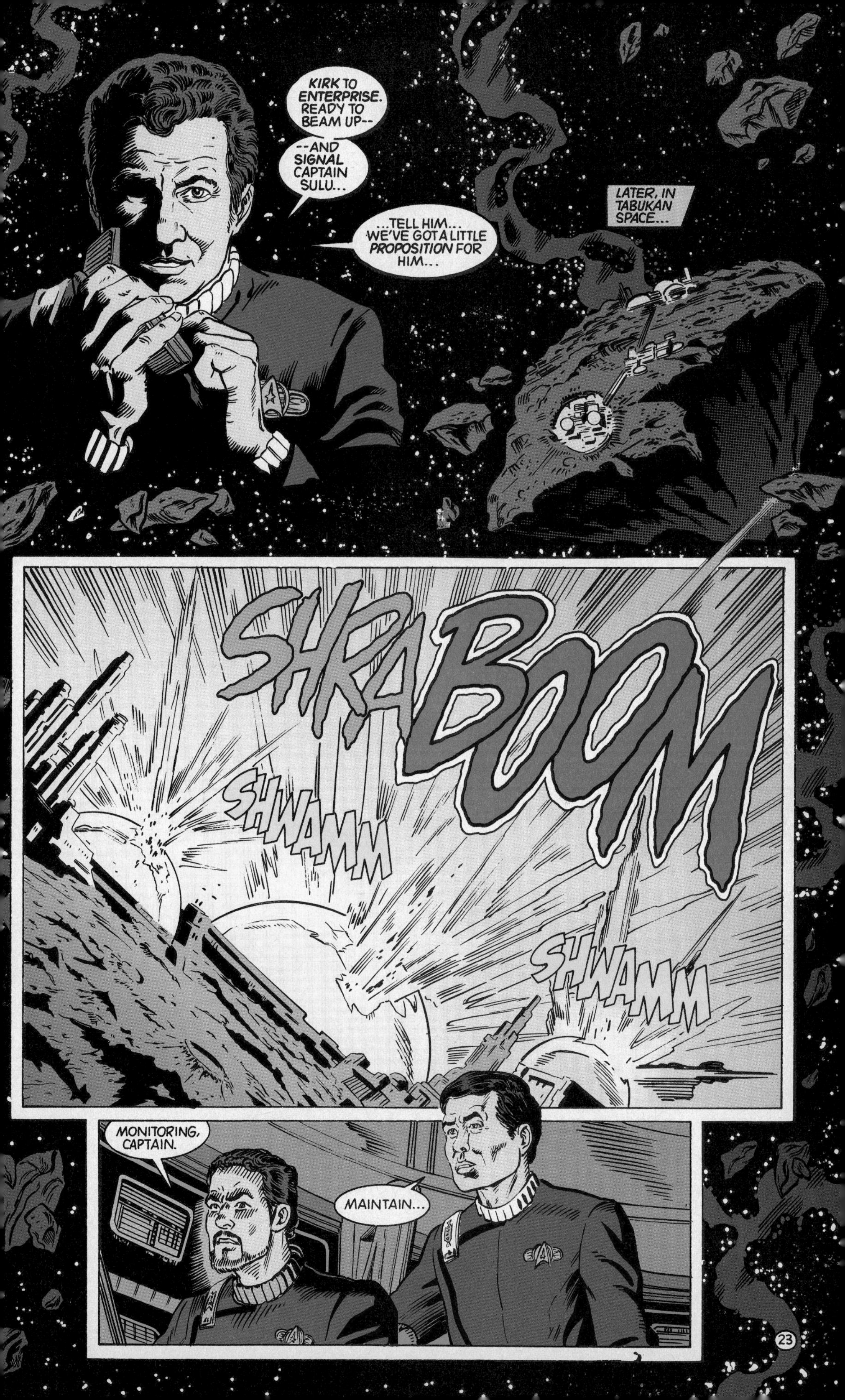
KIRK TO ENTERPRISE. READY TO BEAM UP--
--AND SIGNAL CAPTAIN SULU...
...TELL HIM... WE'VE GOT A LITTLE *PROPOSITION* FOR HIM...
LATER, IN TABUKAN SPACE...
SHRABOOM
SHWAMM
SHWAMM
MONITORING, CAPTAIN.
MAINTAIN...

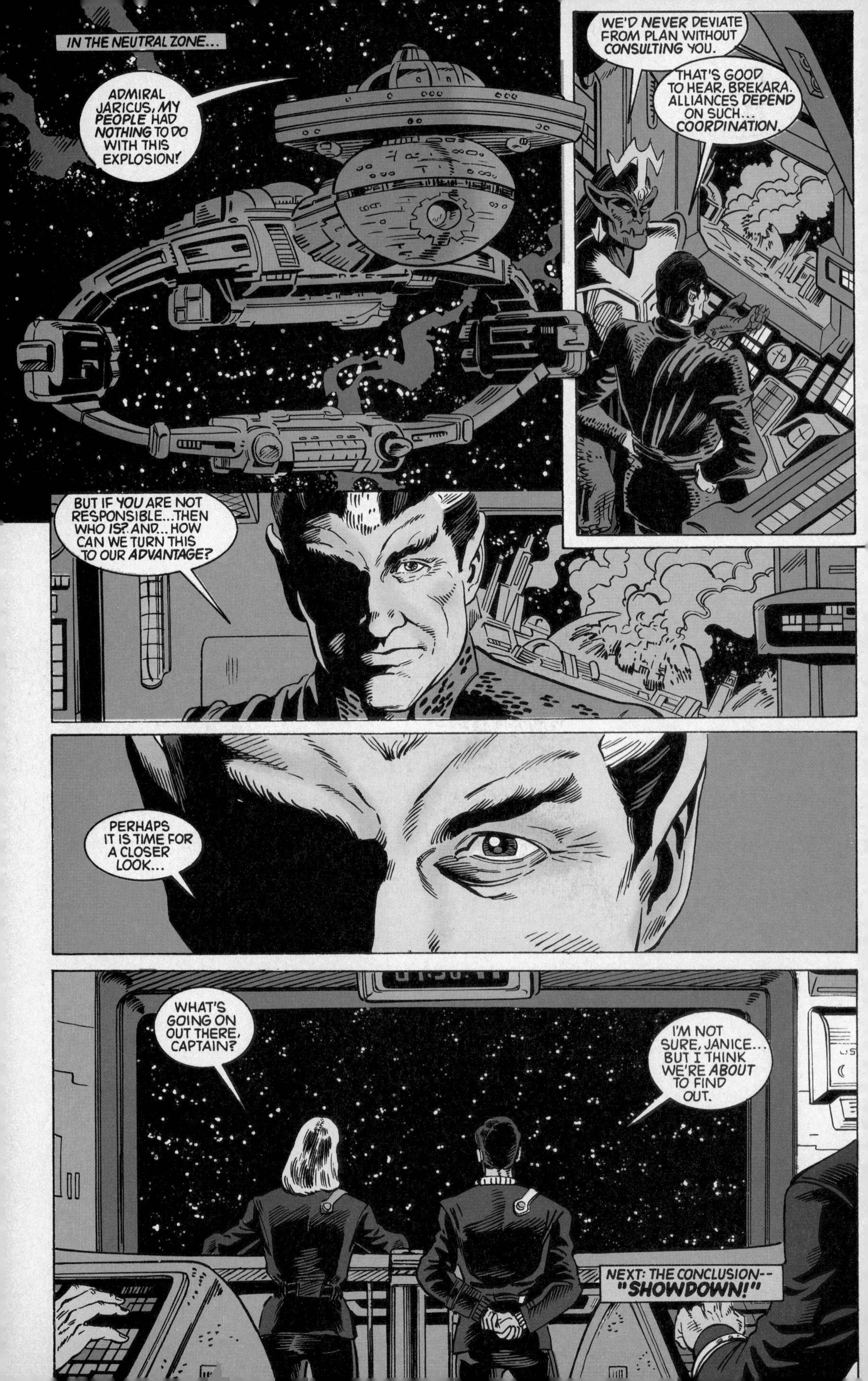
IN THE NEUTRAL ZONE...
ADMIRAL JARICUS, MY PEOPLE HAD NOTHING TO DO WITH THIS EXPLOSION!
WE'D NEVER DEVIATE FROM PLAN WITHOUT CONSULTING YOU.
THAT'S GOOD TO HEAR, BREKARA. ALLIANCES DEPEND ON SUCH... COORDINATION.
BUT IF YOU ARE NOT RESPONSIBLE...THEN WHO IS? AND... HOW CAN WE TURN THIS TO OUR ADVANTAGE?
PERHAPS IT IS TIME FOR A CLOSER LOOK...
WHAT'S GOING ON OUT THERE, CAPTAIN?
I'M NOT SURE, JANICE... BUT I THINK WE'RE ABOUT TO FIND OUT.
NEXT: THE CONCLUSION-- "SHOWDOWN!"

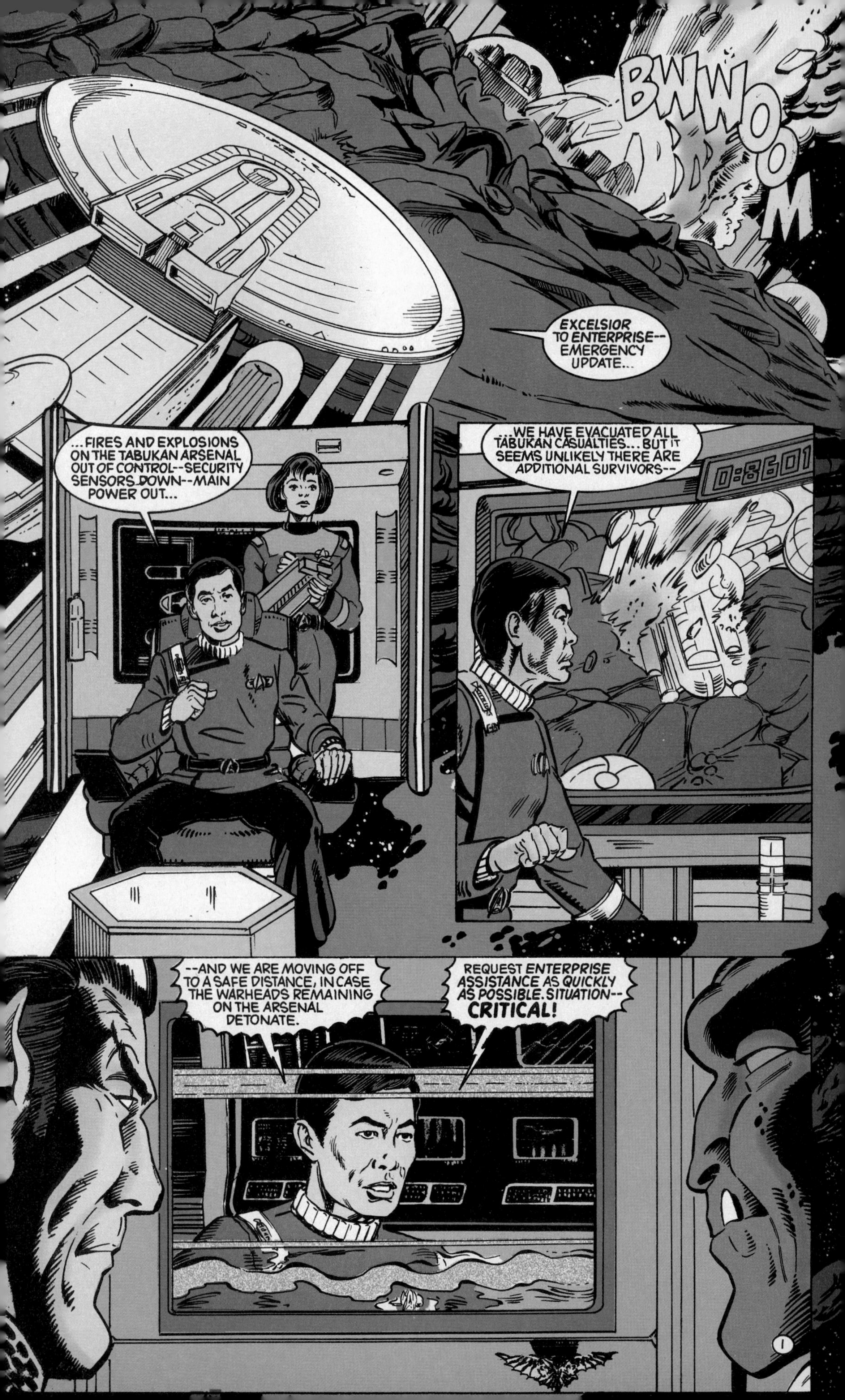
BWWOOOM
EXCELSIOR TO ENTERPRISE-- EMERGENCY UPDATE...
...FIRES AND EXPLOSIONS ON THE TABUKAN ARSENAL OUT OF CONTROL--SECURITY SENSORS DOWN--MAIN POWER OUT...
...WE HAVE EVACUATED ALL TABUKAN CASUALTIES... BUT IT SEEMS UNLIKELY THERE ARE ADDITIONAL SURVIVORS--
0:8601
--AND WE ARE MOVING OFF TO A SAFE DISTANCE, IN CASE THE WARHEADS REMAINING ON THE ARSENAL DETONATE.
REQUEST ENTERPRISE ASSISTANCE AS QUICKLY AS POSSIBLE. SITUATION-- CRITICAL!
1

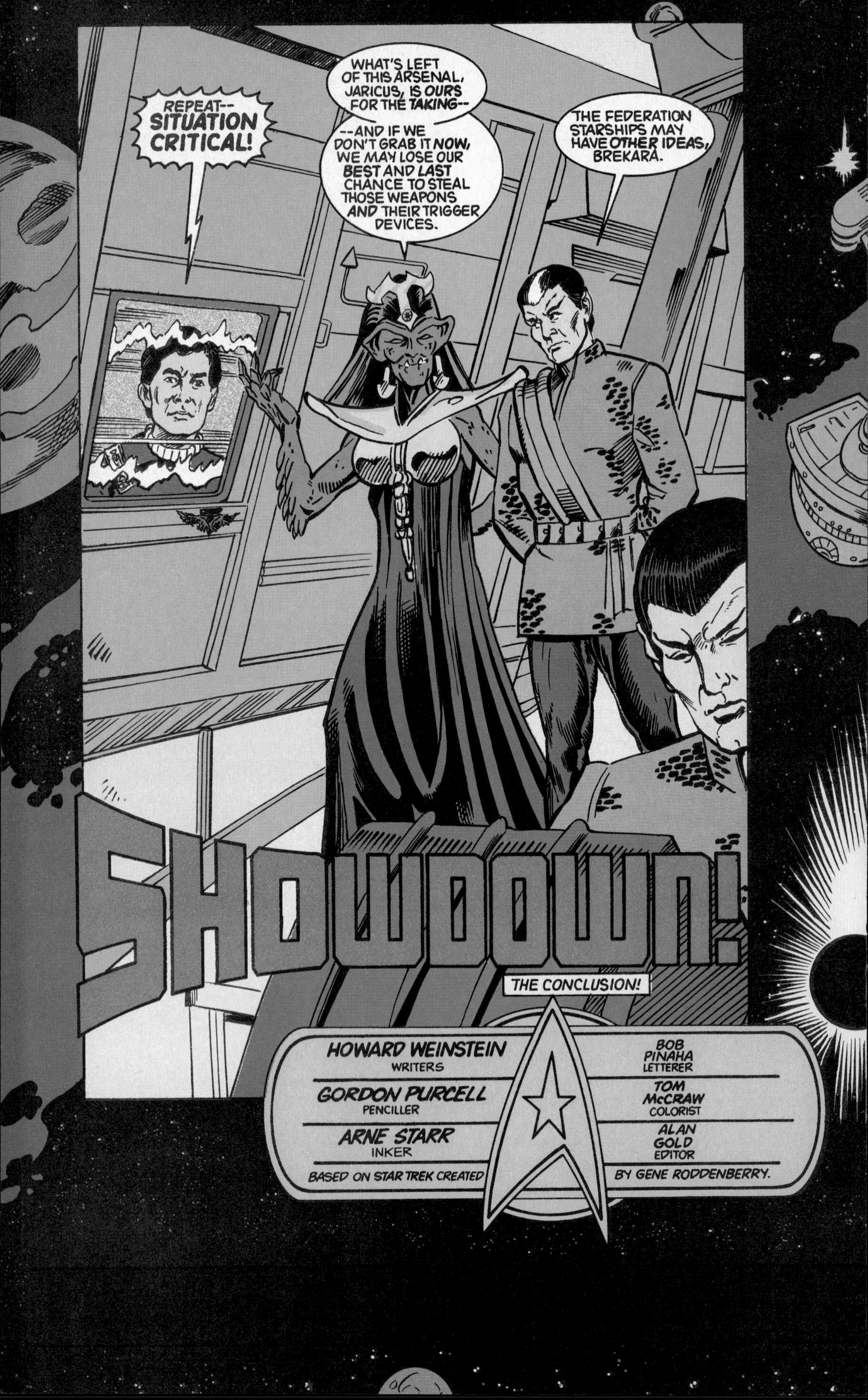
REPEAT-- SITUATION CRITICAL!
WHAT'S LEFT OF THIS ARSENAL, JARICUS, IS OURS FOR THE TAKING--
--AND IF WE DON'T GRAB IT NOW, WE MAY LOSE OUR BEST AND LAST CHANCE TO STEAL THOSE WEAPONS AND THEIR TRIGGER DEVICES.
THE FEDERATION STARSHIPS MAY HAVE OTHER IDEAS, BREKARA.
SHOWDOWN!
THE CONCLUSION!
HOWARD WEINSTEIN WRITERS
GORDON PURCELL PENCILLER
ARNE STARR INKER
BOB PINAHA LETTERER
TOM McCRAW COLORIST
ALAN GOLD EDITOR
BASED ON STAR TREK CREATED BY GENE RODDENBERRY.

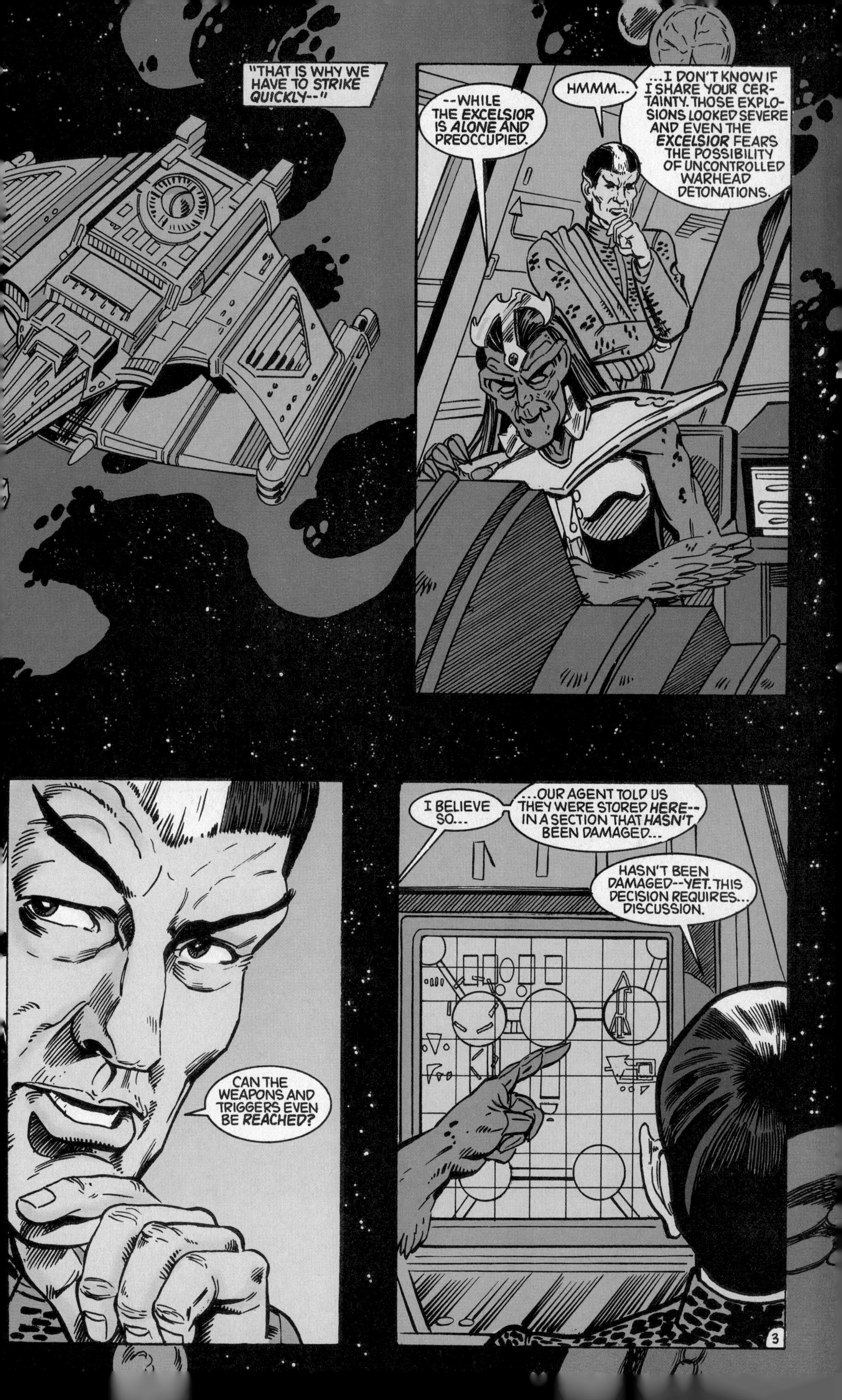
"THAT IS WHY WE HAVE TO STRIKE QUICKLY--"
--WHILE THE EXCELSIOR IS ALONE AND PREOCCUPIED.
HMMM...
...I DON'T KNOW IF I SHARE YOUR CERTAINTY. THOSE EXPLOSIONS LOOKED SEVERE AND EVEN THE EXCELSIOR FEARS THE POSSIBILITY OF UNCONTROLLED WARHEAD DETONATIONS.
CAN THE WEAPONS AND TRIGGERS EVEN BE REACHED?
I BELIEVE SO...
...OUR AGENT TOLD US THEY WERE STORED HERE-- IN A SECTION THAT HASN'T BEEN DAMAGED...
HASN'T BEEN DAMAGED--YET. THIS DECISION REQUIRES... DISCUSSION.
3

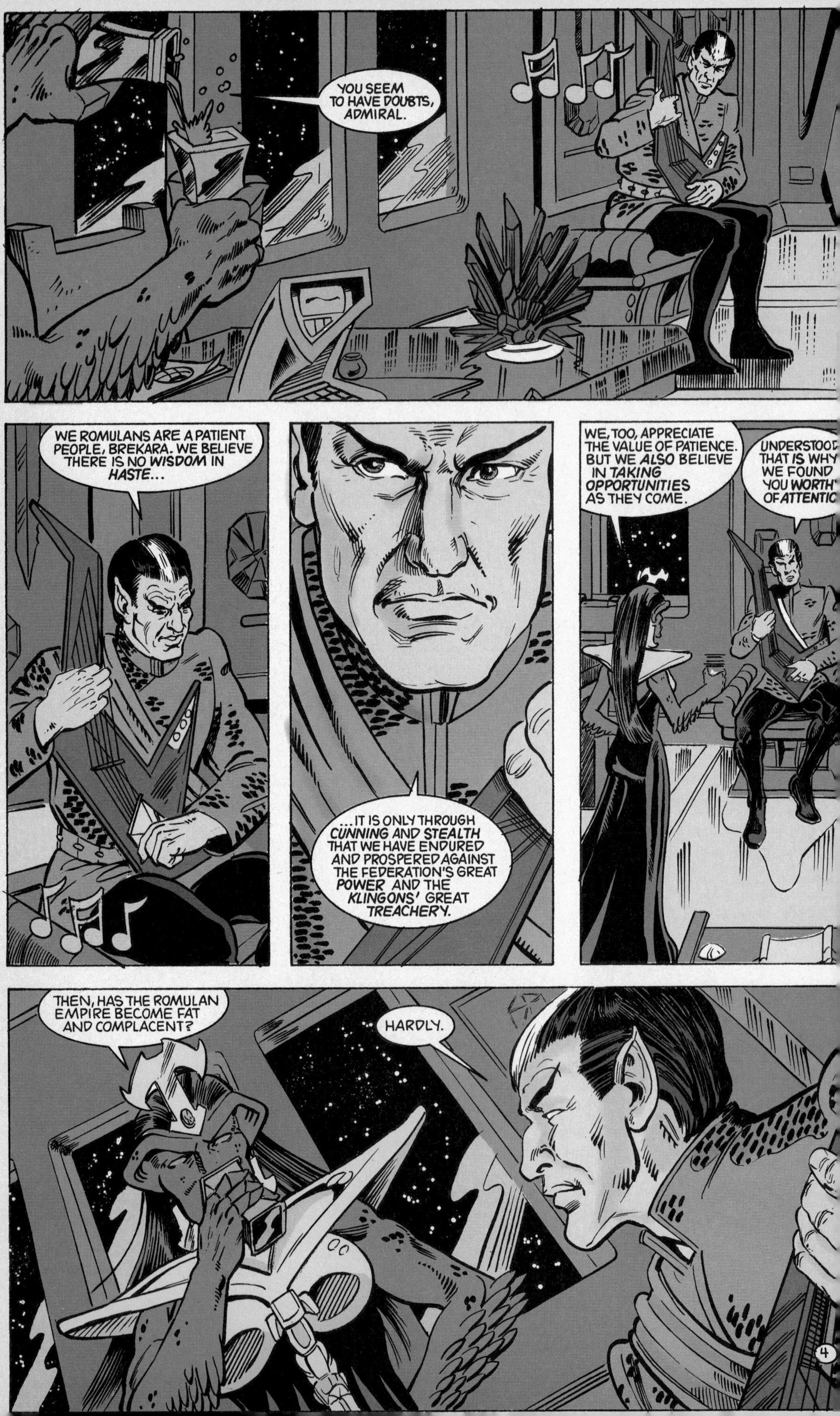
YOU SEEM TO HAVE DOUBTS, ADMIRAL.
WE ROMULANS ARE A PATIENT PEOPLE, BREKARA. WE BELIEVE THERE IS NO WISDOM IN HASTE...
...IT IS ONLY THROUGH CUNNING AND STEALTH THAT WE HAVE ENDURED AND PROSPERED AGAINST THE FEDERATION'S GREAT POWER AND THE KLINGONS' GREAT TREACHERY.
WE, TOO, APPRECIATE THE VALUE OF PATIENCE. BUT WE ALSO BELIEVE IN TAKING OPPORTUNITIES AS THEY COME.
UNDERSTOOD THAT IS WHY WE FOUND YOU WORTH OF ATTENTIC
THEN, HAS THE ROMULAN EMPIRE BECOME FAT AND COMPLACENT?
HARDLY.
4

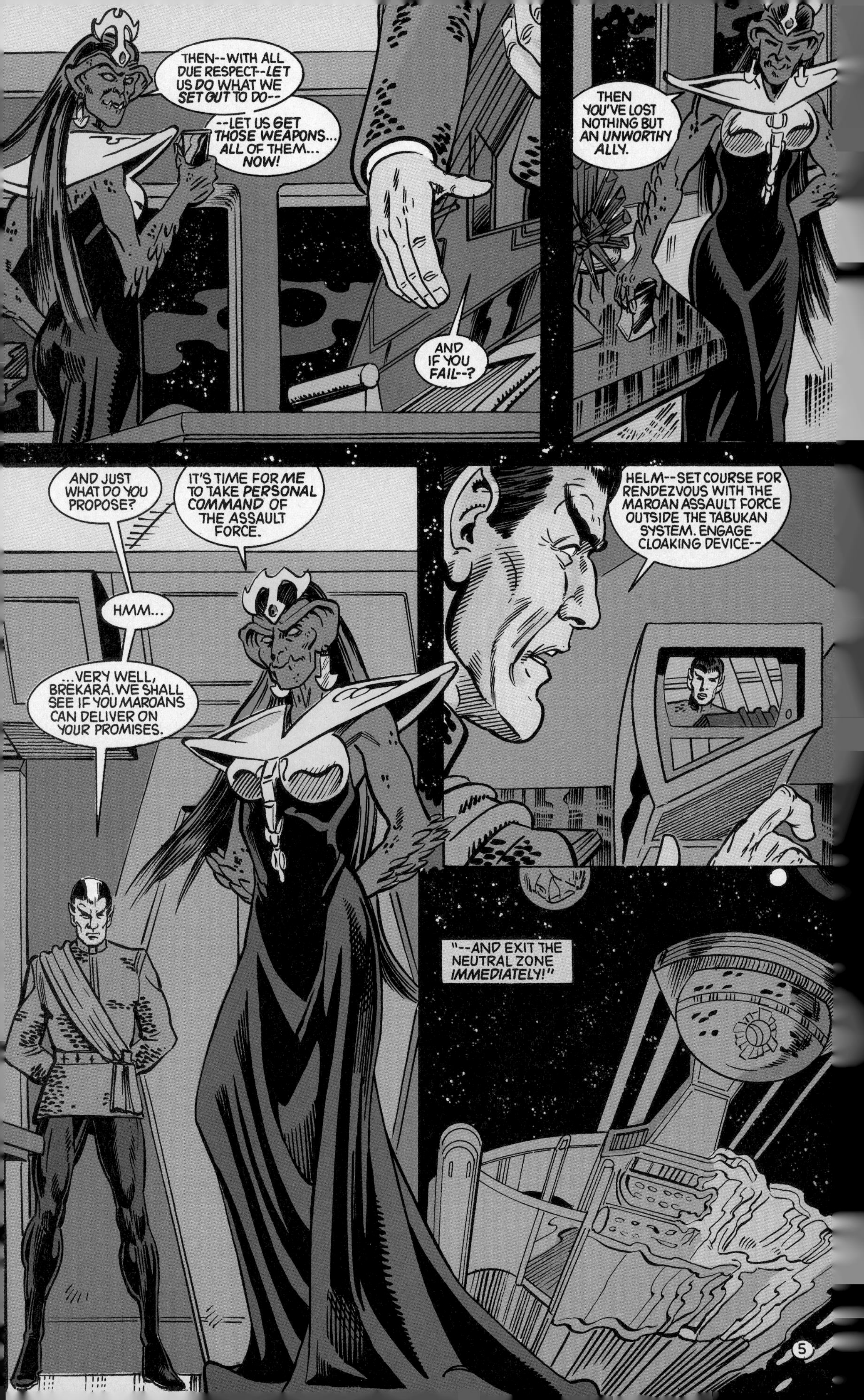
THEN--WITH ALL DUE RESPECT--LET US DO WHAT WE SET OUT TO DO--
--LET US GET THOSE WEAPONS... ALL OF THEM... NOW!
AND IF YOU FAIL--?
THEN YOU'VE LOST NOTHING BUT AN UNWORTHY ALLY.
AND JUST WHAT DO YOU PROPOSE?
IT'S TIME FOR ME TO TAKE PERSONAL COMMAND OF THE ASSAULT FORCE.
HMM...
...VERY WELL, BREKARA. WE SHALL SEE IF YOU MAROANS CAN DELIVER ON YOUR PROMISES.
HELM--SET COURSE FOR RENDEZVOUS WITH THE MAROAN ASSAULT FORCE OUTSIDE THE TABUKAN SYSTEM. ENGAGE CLOAKING DEVICE--
"--AND EXIT THE NEUTRAL ZONE IMMEDIATELY!"

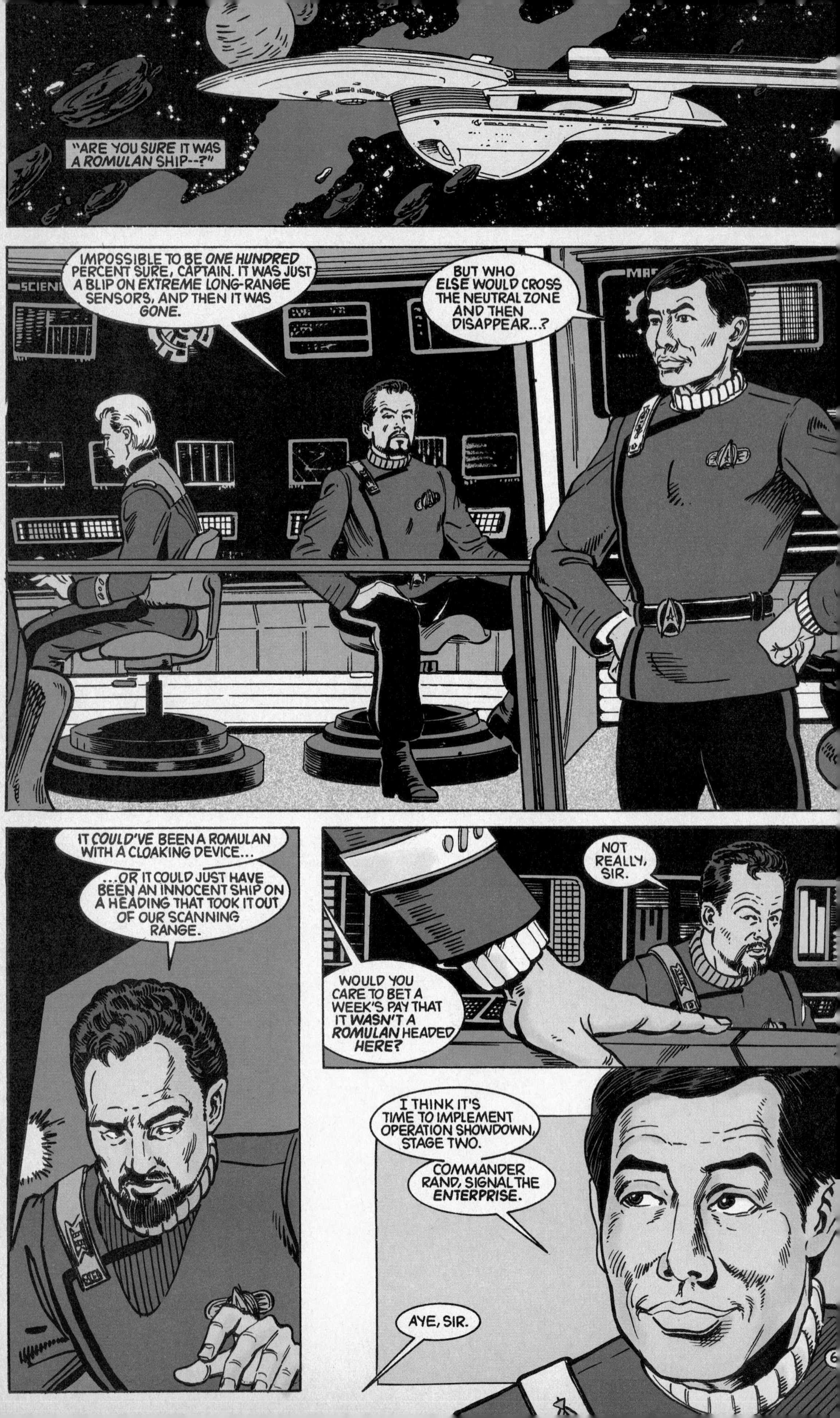
"ARE YOU SURE IT WAS A ROMULAN SHIP--?"
IMPOSSIBLE TO BE ONE HUNDRED PERCENT SURE, CAPTAIN. IT WAS JUST A BLIP ON EXTREME LONG-RANGE SENSORS, AND THEN IT WAS GONE.
BUT WHO ELSE WOULD CROSS THE NEUTRAL ZONE AND THEN DISAPPEAR...?
IT COULD'VE BEEN A ROMULAN WITH A CLOAKING DEVICE...
...OR IT COULD JUST HAVE BEEN AN INNOCENT SHIP ON A HEADING THAT TOOK IT OUT OF OUR SCANNING RANGE.
WOULD YOU CARE TO BET A WEEK'S PAY THAT IT WASN'T A ROMULAN HEADED HERE?
NOT REALLY, SIR.
I THINK IT'S TIME TO IMPLEMENT OPERATION SHOWDOWN, STAGE TWO.
COMMANDER RAND, SIGNAL THE ENTERPRISE.
AYE, SIR.

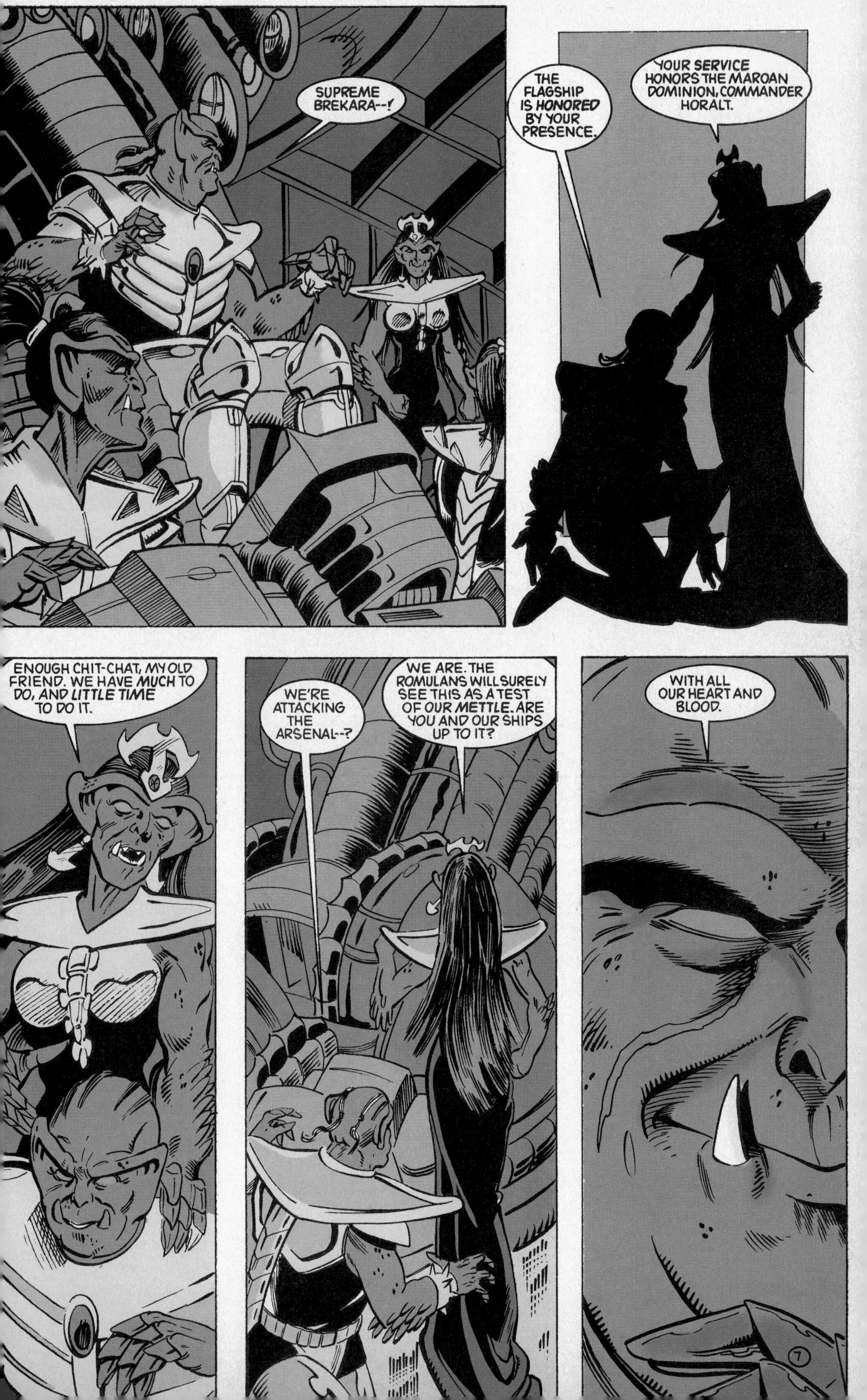
SUPREME BREKARA--!
THE FLAGSHIP IS HONORED BY YOUR PRESENCE.
YOUR SERVICE HONORS THE MAROAN DOMINION, COMMANDER HORALT.
ENOUGH CHIT-CHAT, MY OLD FRIEND. WE HAVE MUCH TO DO, AND LITTLE TIME TO DO IT.
WE'RE ATTACKING THE ARSENAL--?
WE ARE. THE ROMULANS WILL SURELY SEE THIS AS A TEST OF OUR METTLE. ARE YOU AND OUR SHIPS UP TO IT?
WITH ALL OUR HEART AND BLOOD.
7

LET'S HOPE IT DOESN'T COME TO THAT. NOW--LET'S SEE ALL THE DATA ON THE FEDERATION STARSHIPS--

SUPREME BREKARA--! A MESSAGE FROM NOBLE VODRIN--

OH--? IT'S ABOUT TIME THAT WAYWARD SON OF MINE SHOWED UP.

ON VISUAL.

CODE RED

THERE IS NO VISUAL SIGNAL, SUPREME BREKARA-- IT'S ON THE *CODE RED* FREQUENCY.

HMM. CONSIDERING THE PROXIMITY OF THE FEDERATION SHIPS, AN UNEXPECTEDLY WISE CHOICE VODRIN HAS MADE. DECODE--AND DISPLAY ON MAIN VIEWER.

YES, SUPREME ONE.

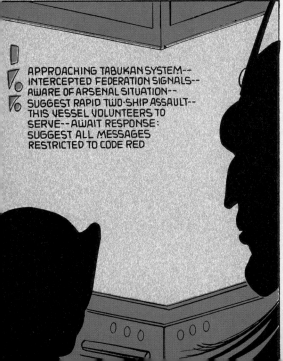

APPROACHING TABUKAN SYSTEM-- INTERCEPTED FEDERATION SIGNALS-- AWARE OF ARSENAL SITUATION-- SUGGEST RAPID TWO-SHIP ASSAULT-- THIS VESSEL VOLUNTEERS TO SERVE--AWAIT RESPONSE: SUGGEST ALL MESSAGES RESTRICTED TO CODE RED

EXACTLY WHAT I WAS THINKING, HORALT...

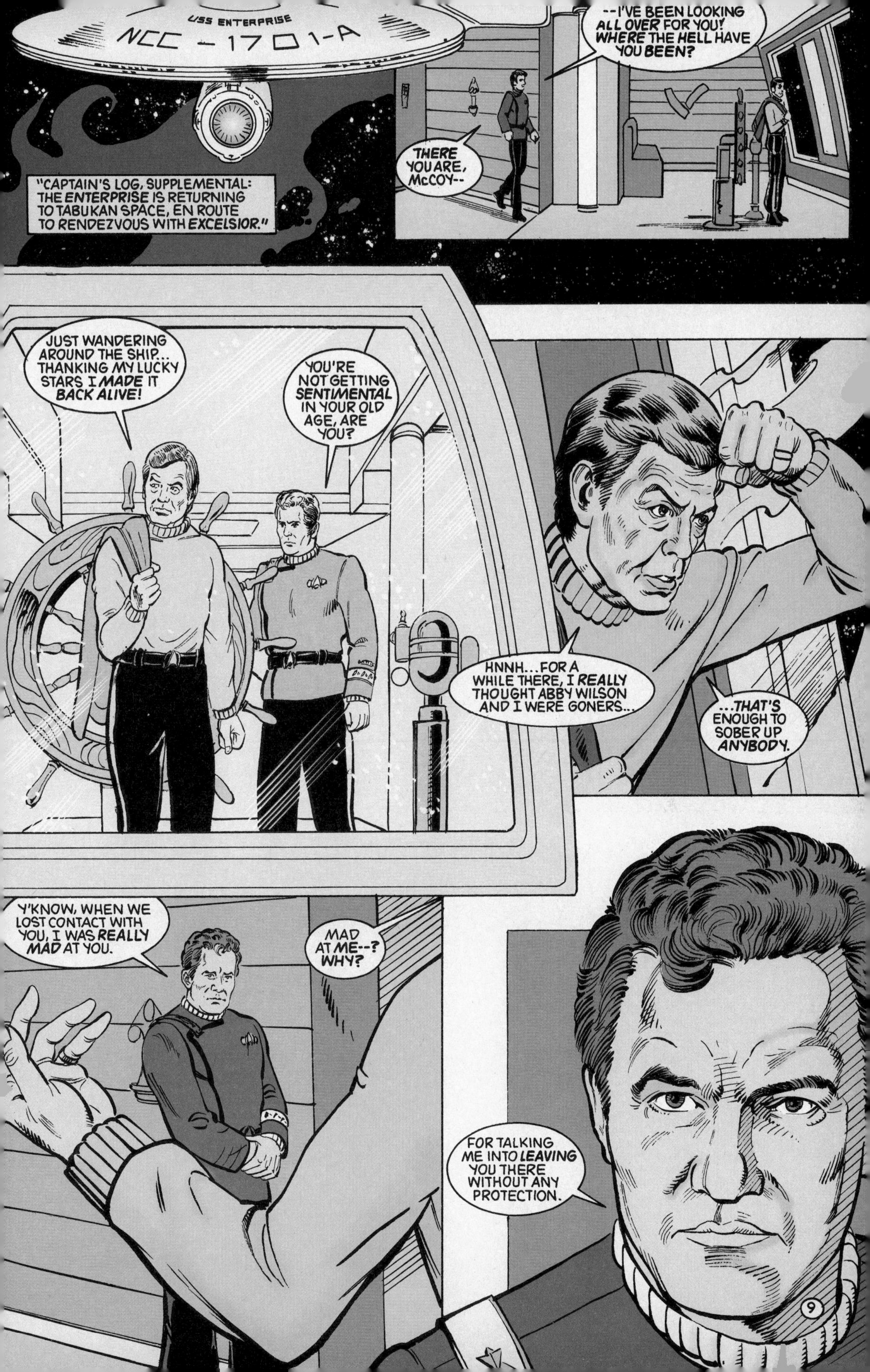
USS ENTERPRISE
NCC-1701-A
"CAPTAIN'S LOG, SUPPLEMENTAL: THE ENTERPRISE IS RETURNING TO TABUKAN SPACE, EN ROUTE TO RENDEZVOUS WITH EXCELSIOR."
THERE YOU ARE, McCOY--
--I'VE BEEN LOOKING ALL OVER FOR YOU! WHERE THE HELL HAVE YOU BEEN?
JUST WANDERING AROUND THE SHIP... THANKING MY LUCKY STARS I MADE IT BACK ALIVE!
YOU'RE NOT GETTING SENTIMENTAL IN YOUR OLD AGE, ARE YOU?
HNNH...FOR A WHILE THERE, I REALLY THOUGHT ABBY WILSON AND I WERE GONERS...
...THAT'S ENOUGH TO SOBER UP ANYBODY.
Y'KNOW, WHEN WE LOST CONTACT WITH YOU, I WAS REALLY MAD AT YOU.
MAD AT ME--? WHY?
FOR TALKING ME INTO LEAVING YOU THERE WITHOUT ANY PROTECTION.
9

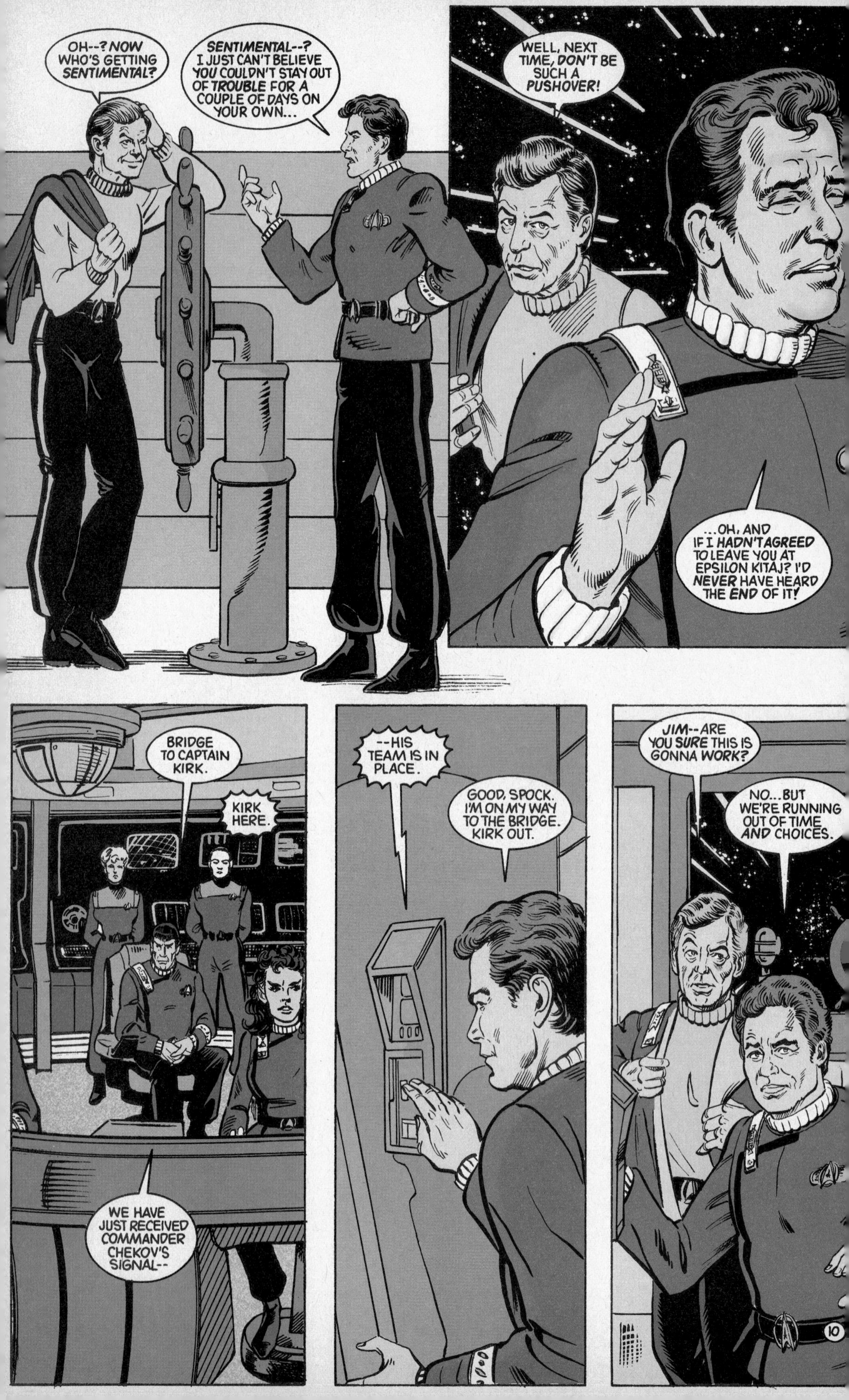
OH--? NOW WHO'S GETTING SENTIMENTAL?
SENTIMENTAL--? I JUST CAN'T BELIEVE YOU COULDN'T STAY OUT OF TROUBLE FOR A COUPLE OF DAYS ON YOUR OWN...
WELL, NEXT TIME, DON'T BE SUCH A PUSHOVER!
...OH, AND IF I HADN'T AGREED TO LEAVE YOU AT EPSILON KITAJ? I'D NEVER HAVE HEARD THE END OF IT!
BRIDGE TO CAPTAIN KIRK.
KIRK HERE.
WE HAVE JUST RECEIVED COMMANDER CHEKOV'S SIGNAL--
--HIS TEAM IS IN PLACE.
GOOD, SPOCK. I'M ON MY WAY TO THE BRIDGE. KIRK OUT.
JIM--ARE YOU SURE THIS IS GONNA WORK?
NO...BUT WE'RE RUNNING OUT OF TIME AND CHOICES.
10

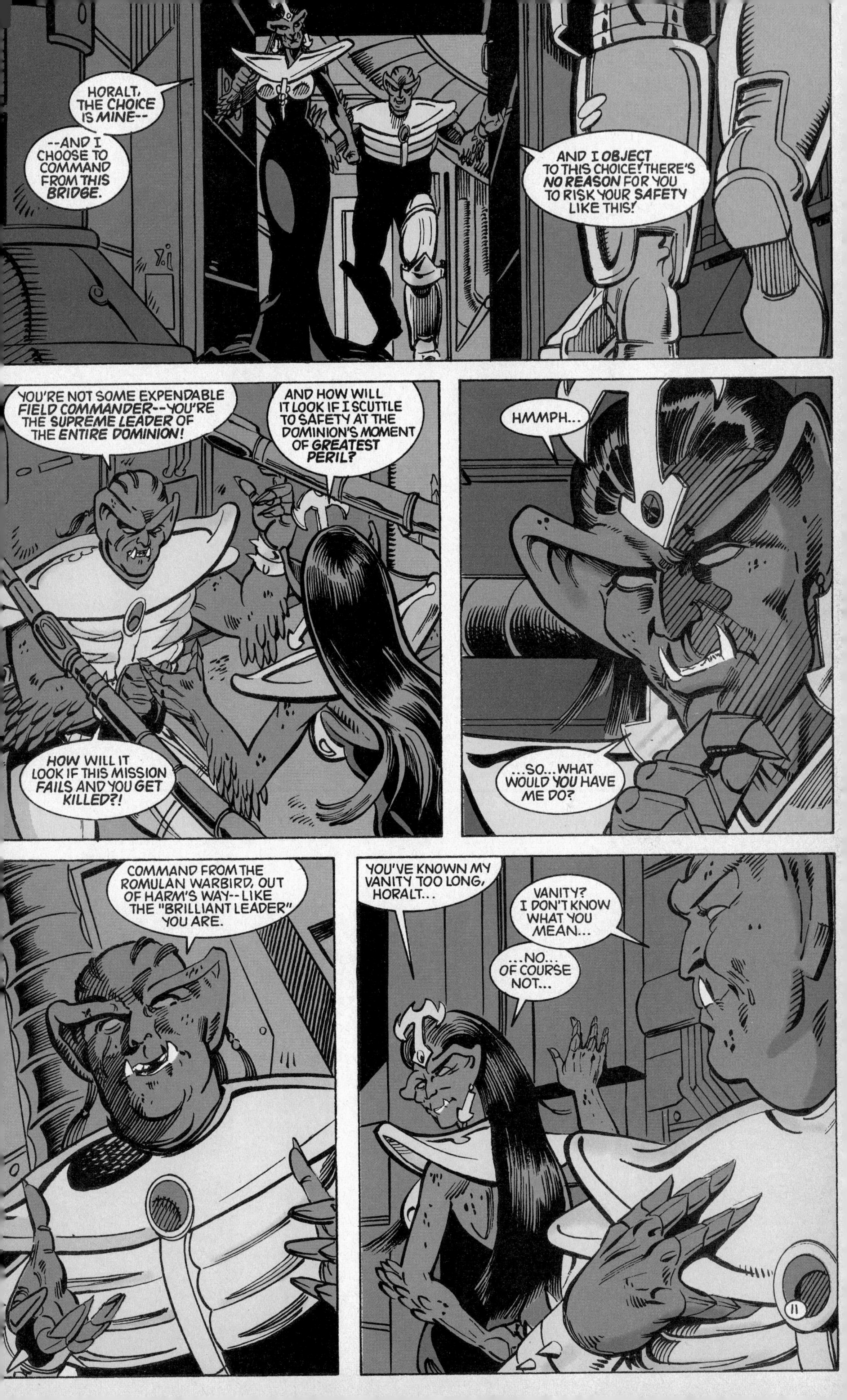
HORALT, THE CHOICE IS MINE--
--AND I CHOOSE TO COMMAND FROM THIS BRIDGE.
AND I OBJECT TO THIS CHOICE! THERE'S NO REASON FOR YOU TO RISK YOUR SAFETY LIKE THIS!
YOU'RE NOT SOME EXPENDABLE FIELD COMMANDER--YOU'RE THE SUPREME LEADER OF THE ENTIRE DOMINION!
AND HOW WILL IT LOOK IF I SCUTTLE TO SAFETY AT THE DOMINION'S MOMENT OF GREATEST PERIL?
HOW WILL IT LOOK IF THIS MISSION FAILS AND YOU GET KILLED?!
HMMPH...
...SO...WHAT WOULD YOU HAVE ME DO?
COMMAND FROM THE ROMULAN WARBIRD, OUT OF HARM'S WAY--LIKE THE "BRILLIANT LEADER" YOU ARE.
YOU'VE KNOWN MY VANITY TOO LONG, HORALT...
VANITY? I DON'T KNOW WHAT YOU MEAN...
...NO... OF COURSE NOT...
11

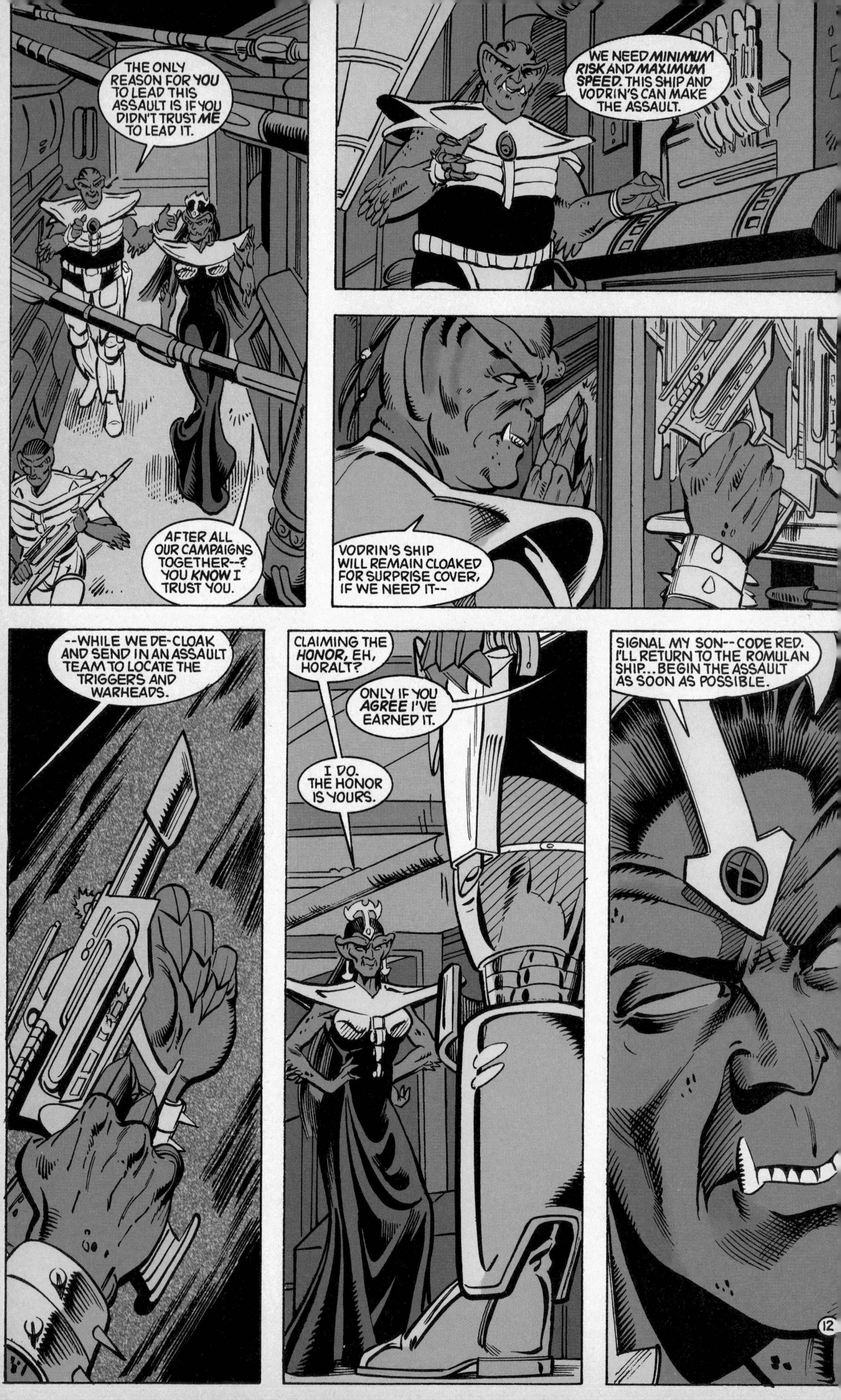
THE ONLY REASON FOR YOU TO LEAD THIS ASSAULT IS IF YOU DIDN'T TRUST ME TO LEAD IT.
AFTER ALL OUR CAMPAIGNS TOGETHER--? YOU KNOW I TRUST YOU.
WE NEED MINIMUM RISK AND MAXIMUM SPEED. THIS SHIP AND VODRIN'S CAN MAKE THE ASSAULT.
VODRIN'S SHIP WILL REMAIN CLOAKED FOR SURPRISE COVER, IF WE NEED IT--
--WHILE WE DE-CLOAK AND SEND IN AN ASSAULT TEAM TO LOCATE THE TRIGGERS AND WARHEADS.
CLAIMING THE HONOR, EH, HORALT?
ONLY IF YOU AGREE I'VE EARNED IT.
I DO. THE HONOR IS YOURS.
SIGNAL MY SON--CODE RED. I'LL RETURN TO THE ROMULAN SHIP... BEGIN THE ASSAULT AS SOON AS POSSIBLE.
12

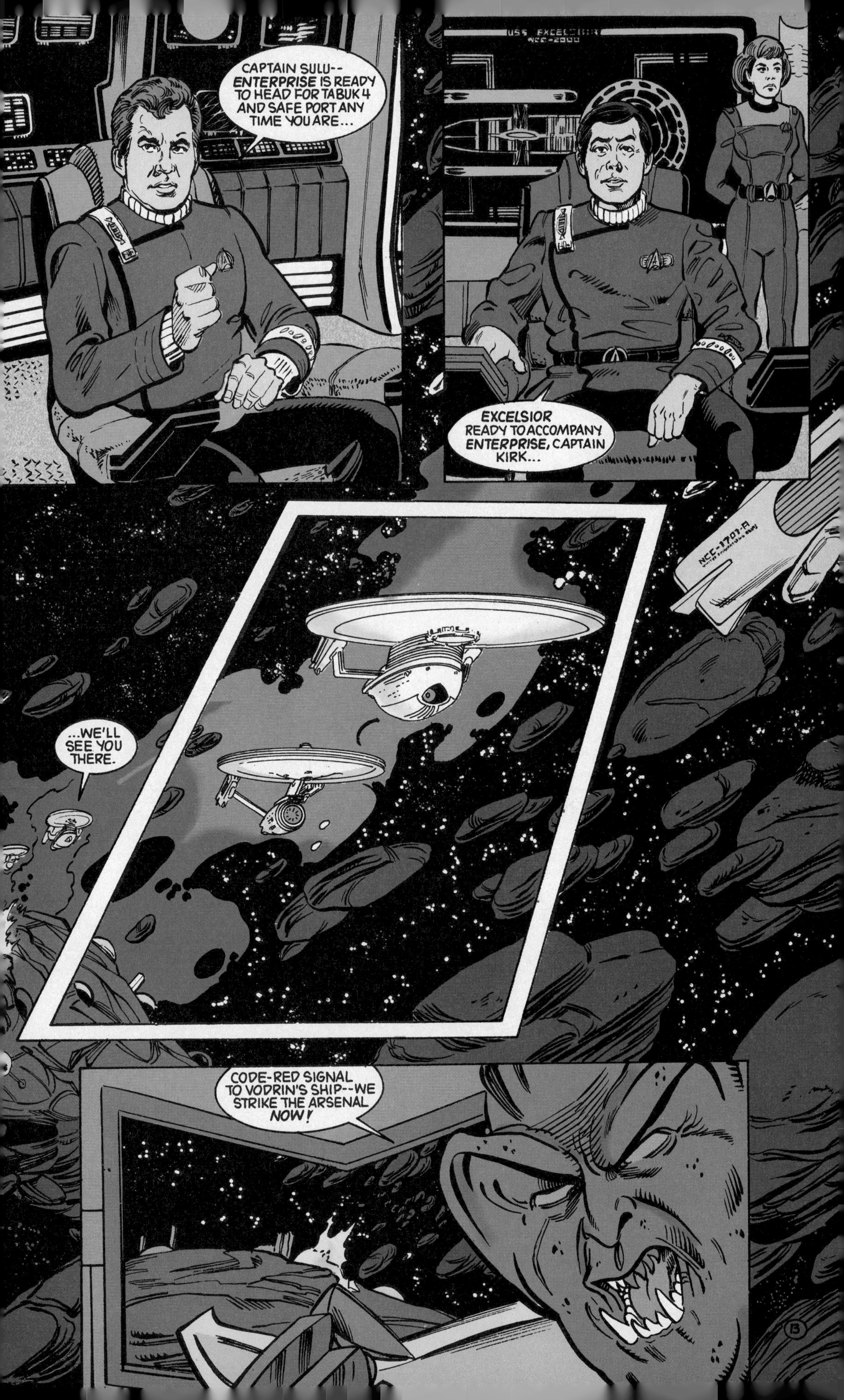

CAPTAIN SULU-- ENTERPRISE IS READY TO HEAD FOR TABUK 4 AND SAFE PORT ANY TIME YOU ARE...
USS EXCELSIOR NCC-2000
EXCELSIOR READY TO ACCOMPANY ENTERPRISE, CAPTAIN KIRK...
NCC-1701-A
...WE'LL SEE YOU THERE.
CODE-RED SIGNAL TO VODRIN'S SHIP--WE STRIKE THE ARSENAL NOW!
13

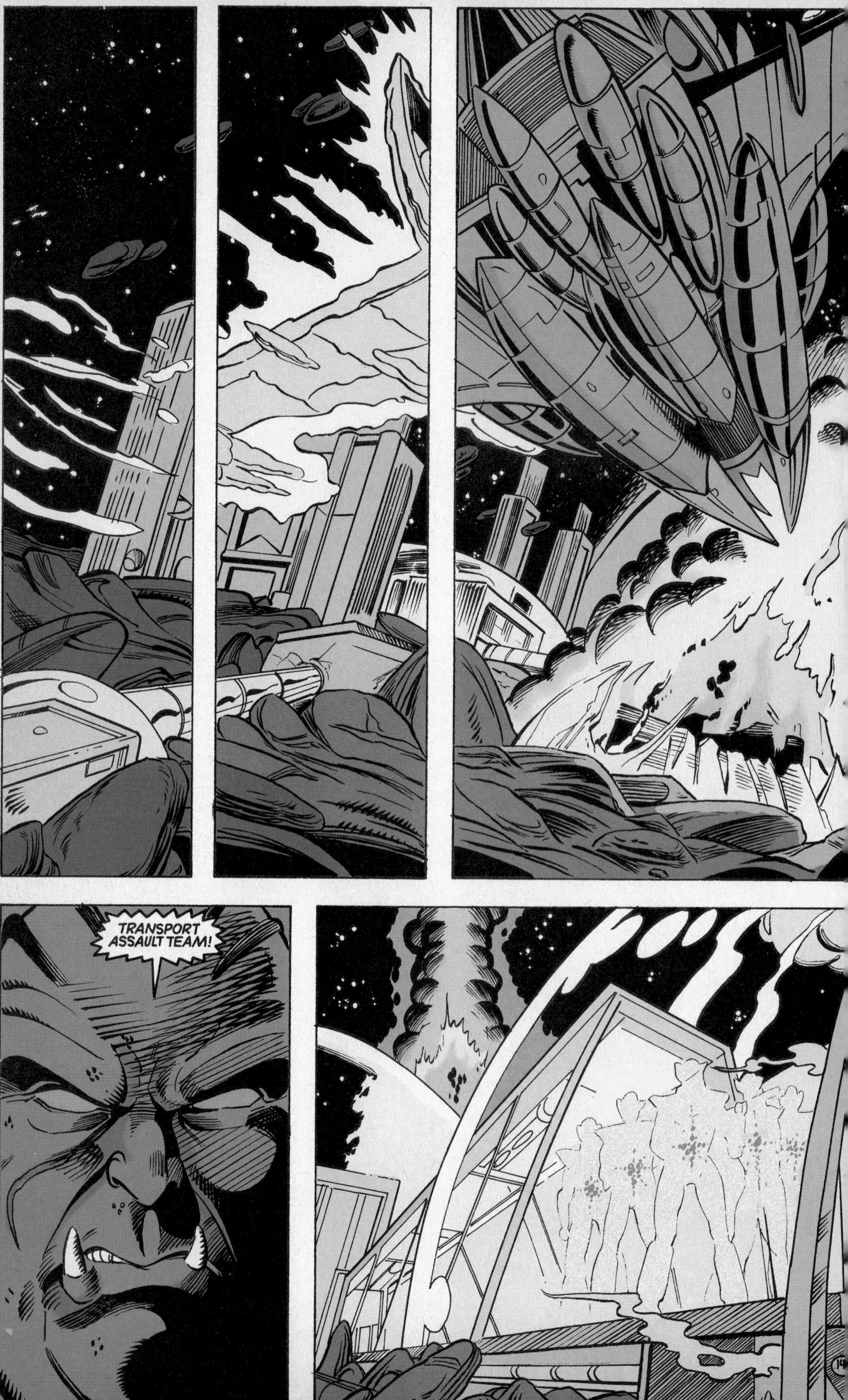
TRANSPORT ASSAULT TEAM!

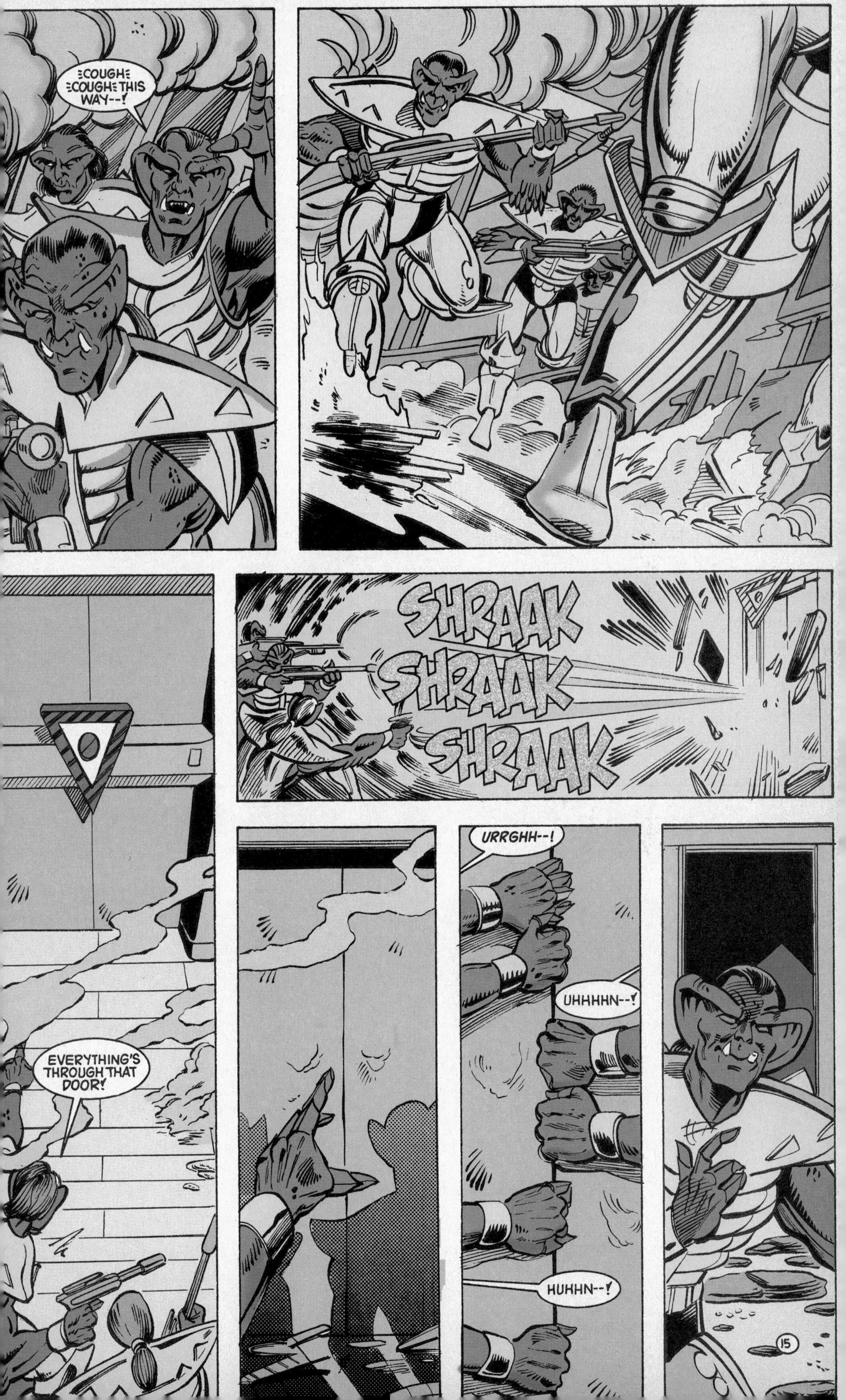
COUGH COUGH THIS WAY--!
SHRAAK
SHRAAK
SHRAAK
EVERYTHING'S THROUGH THAT DOOR!
URRGHH--!
UHHHHN--!
HUHHN--!

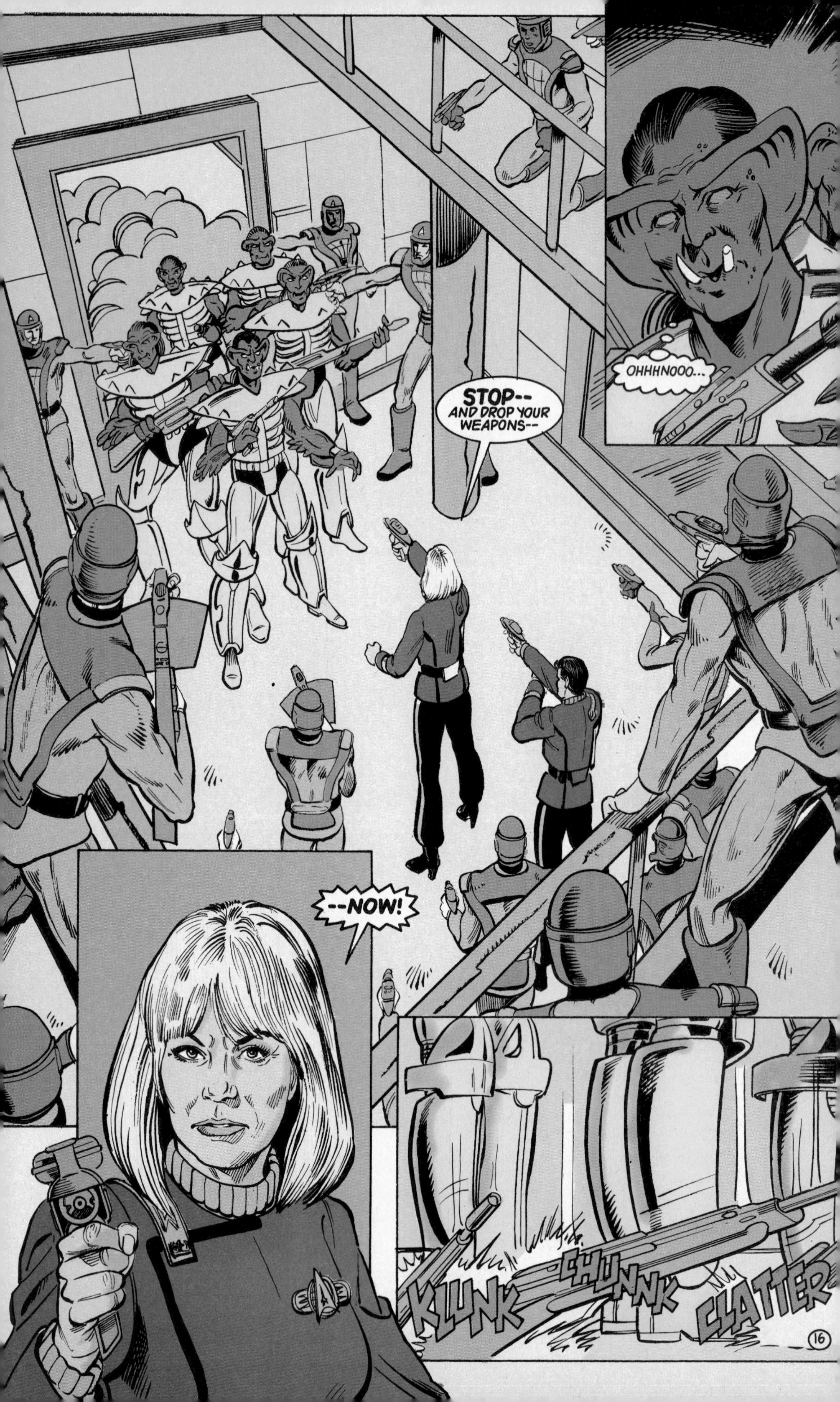

STOP-- AND DROP YOUR WEAPONS--
OHHHNOOO...
--NOW!
KLUNK
CHUNNK
CLATTER
16

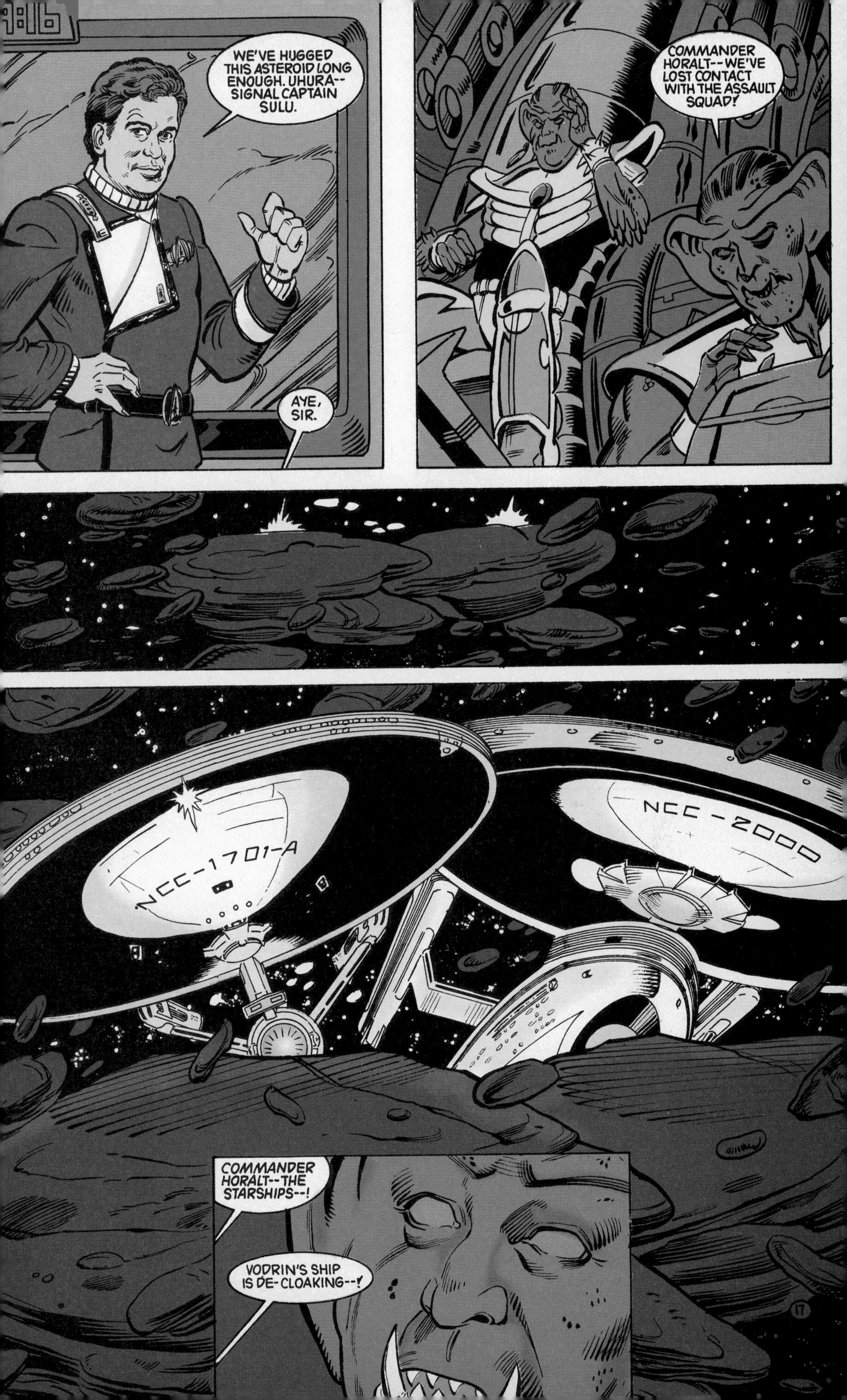

WE'VE HUGGED THIS ASTEROID LONG ENOUGH. UHURA--SIGNAL CAPTAIN SULU.
AYE, SIR.
COMMANDER HORALT--WE'VE LOST CONTACT WITH THE ASSAULT SQUAD!
NCC-1701-A
NCC-2000
COMMANDER HORALT--THE STARSHIPS--!
VODRIN'S SHIP IS DE-CLOAKING--!

VODRIN! **HELP US--!**

RECEIVING VISUAL SIGNAL--

ON SCREEN!

I AM AFRAID HELP VILL NOT BE POSSIBLE...

THAT ROMULAN SHIP IS HERE SOMEWHERE--

--AND I WANT HIM.

CAPTAIN--

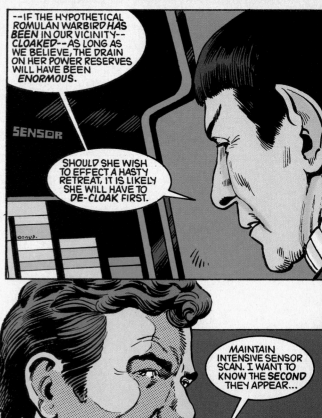

--IF THE HYPOTHETICAL ROMULAN WARBIRD **HAS BEEN** IN OUR VICINITY--**CLOAKED**--AS LONG AS WE BELIEVE, THE DRAIN ON HER POWER RESERVES WILL HAVE BEEN **ENORMOUS.**

SENSOR

SHOULD SHE WISH TO EFFECT A HASTY RETREAT, IT IS LIKELY SHE WILL HAVE TO DE-CLOAK FIRST.

MAINTAIN INTENSIVE SENSOR SCAN. I WANT TO KNOW THE **SECOND** THEY APPEAR...

18

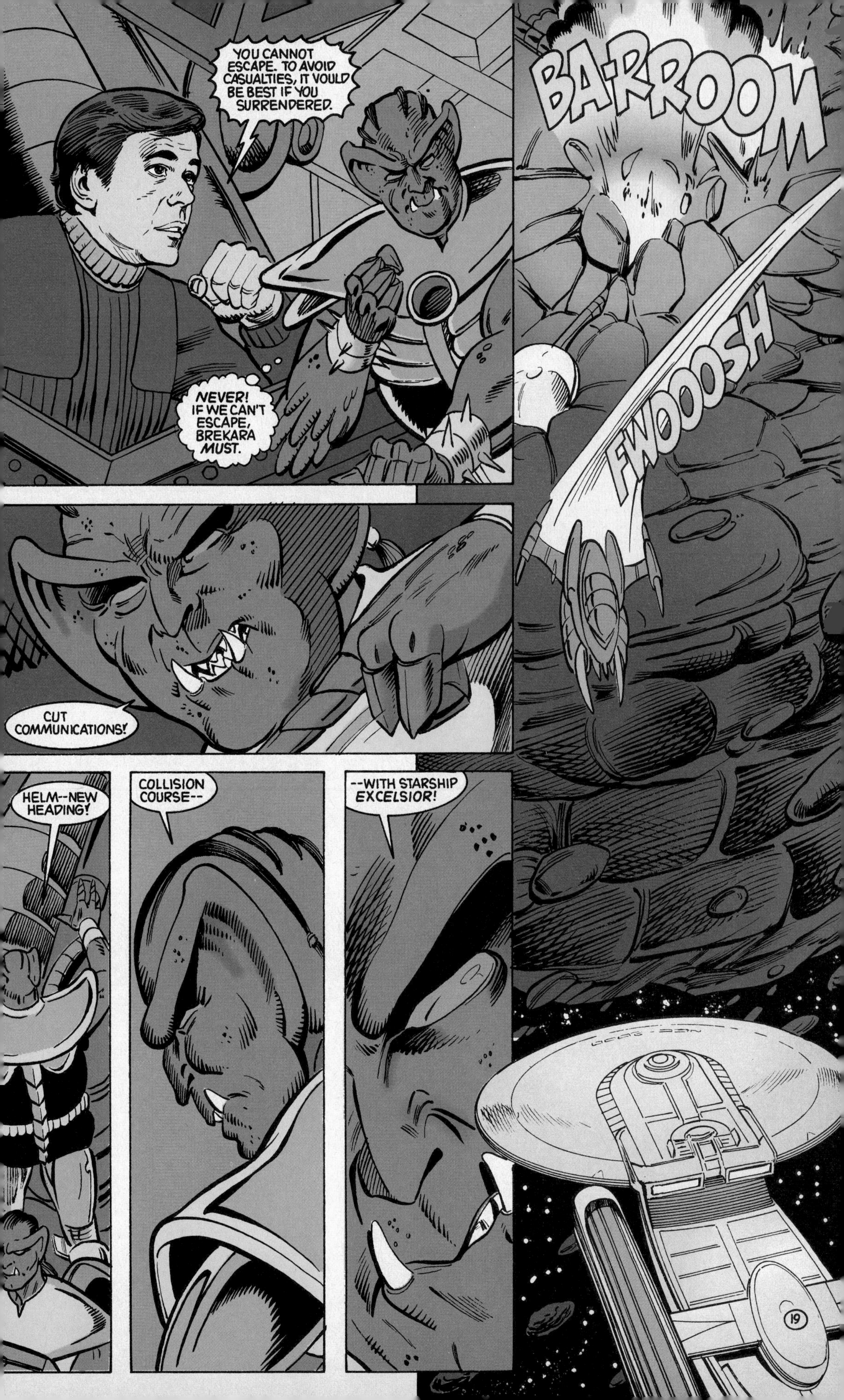

YOU CANNOT ESCAPE. TO AVOID CASUALTIES, IT WOULD BE BEST IF YOU SURRENDERED.
NEVER! IF WE CAN'T ESCAPE, BREKARA MUST.
CUT COMMUNICATIONS!
HELM--NEW HEADING!
COLLISION COURSE--
--WITH STARSHIP EXCELSIOR!
BA-RROOM
FWOOOSH
19

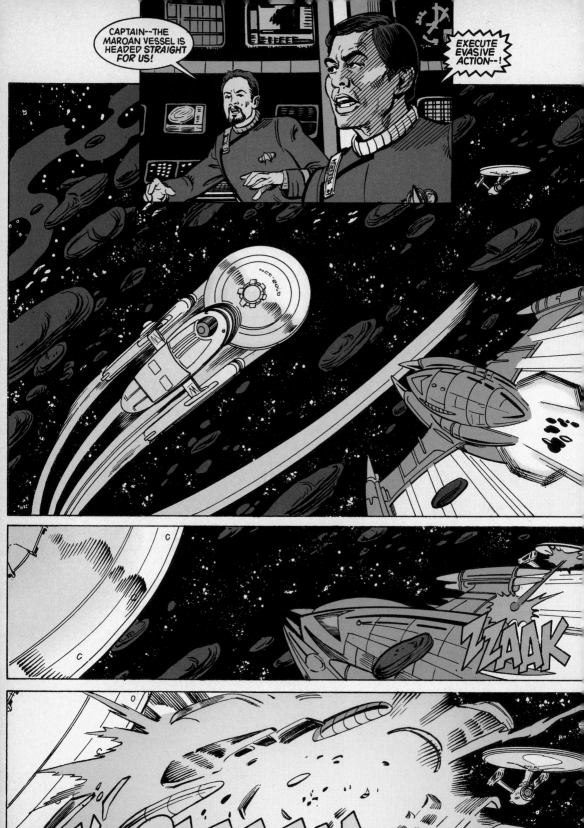

CAPTAIN--THE MAROAN VESSEL IS HEADED STRAIGHT FOR US!

EXECUTE EVASIVE ACTION--!

ZZAAK

KA·BLAAAM

20

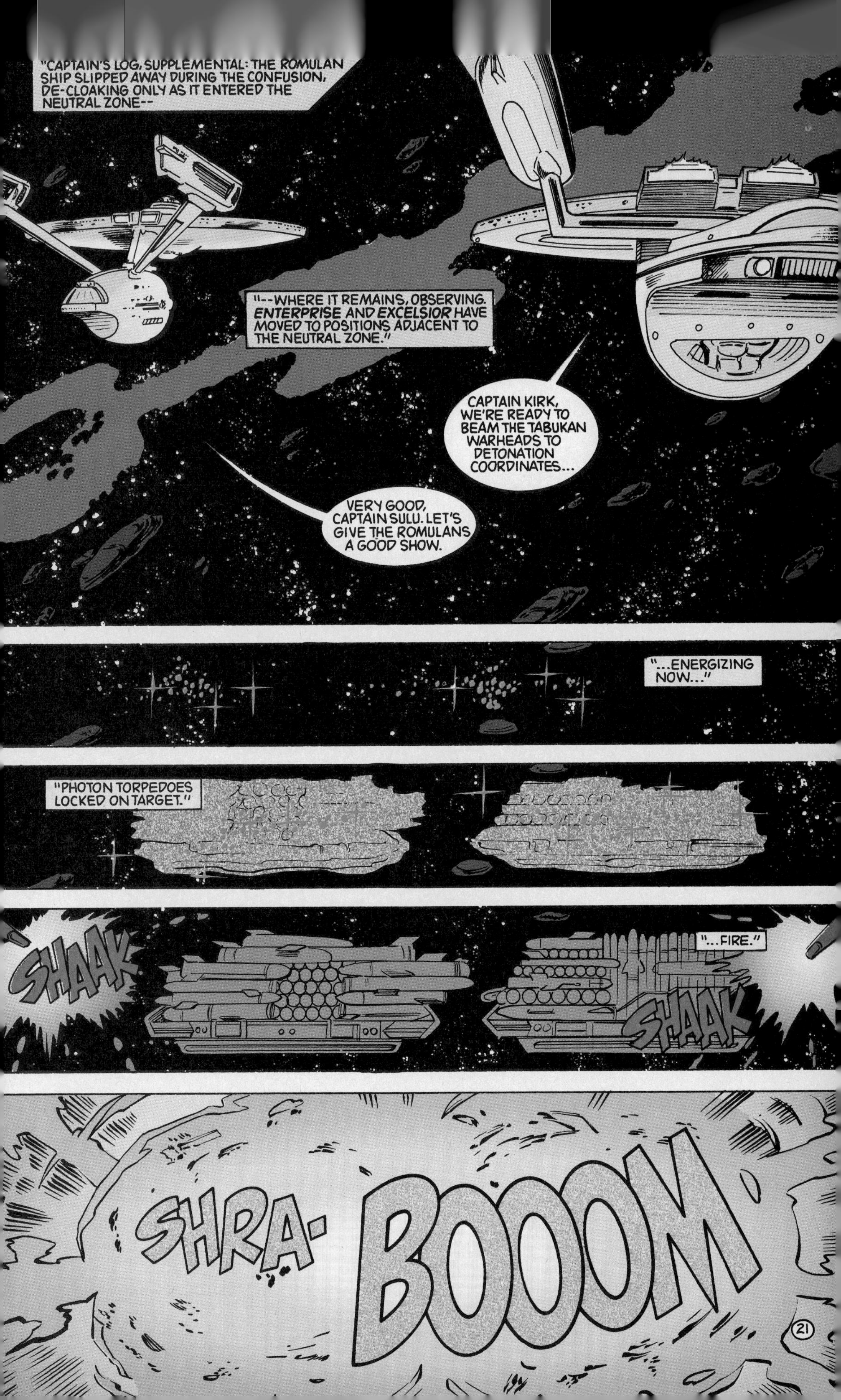
"CAPTAIN'S LOG, SUPPLEMENTAL: THE ROMULAN SHIP SLIPPED AWAY DURING THE CONFUSION, DE-CLOAKING ONLY AS IT ENTERED THE NEUTRAL ZONE--
"--WHERE IT REMAINS, OBSERVING. ENTERPRISE AND EXCELSIOR HAVE MOVED TO POSITIONS ADJACENT TO THE NEUTRAL ZONE."
CAPTAIN KIRK, WE'RE READY TO BEAM THE TABUKAN WARHEADS TO DETONATION COORDINATES...
VERY GOOD, CAPTAIN SULU. LET'S GIVE THE ROMULANS A GOOD SHOW.
"...ENERGIZING NOW..."
"PHOTON TORPEDOES LOCKED ON TARGET."
SHAAK
"...FIRE."
SHAAK
SHRA-BOOOOM
21

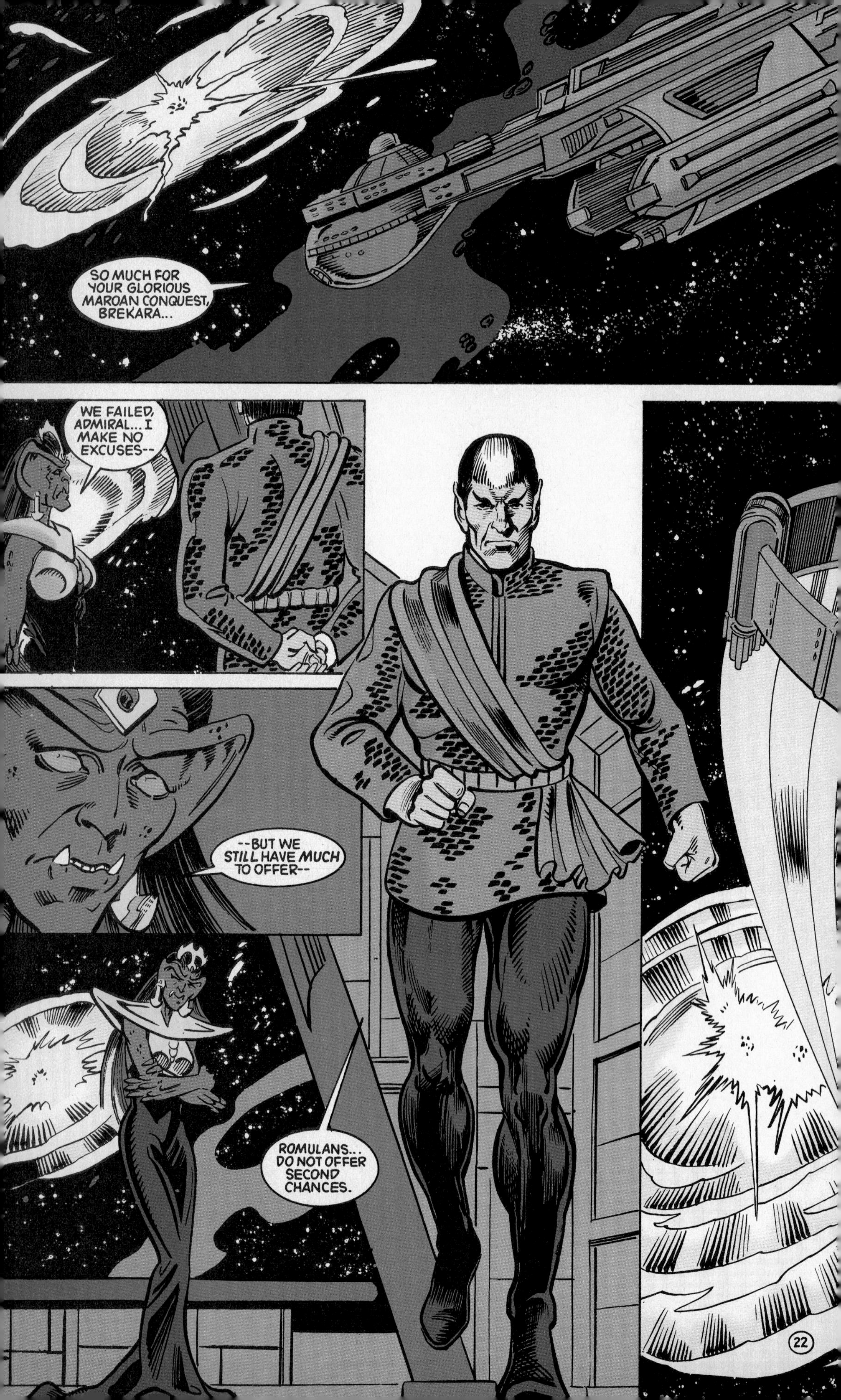
SO MUCH FOR YOUR GLORIOUS MAROAN CONQUEST, BREKARA...
WE FAILED, ADMIRAL... I MAKE NO EXCUSES--
--BUT WE STILL HAVE MUCH TO OFFER--
ROMULANS... DO NOT OFFER SECOND CHANCES.
22

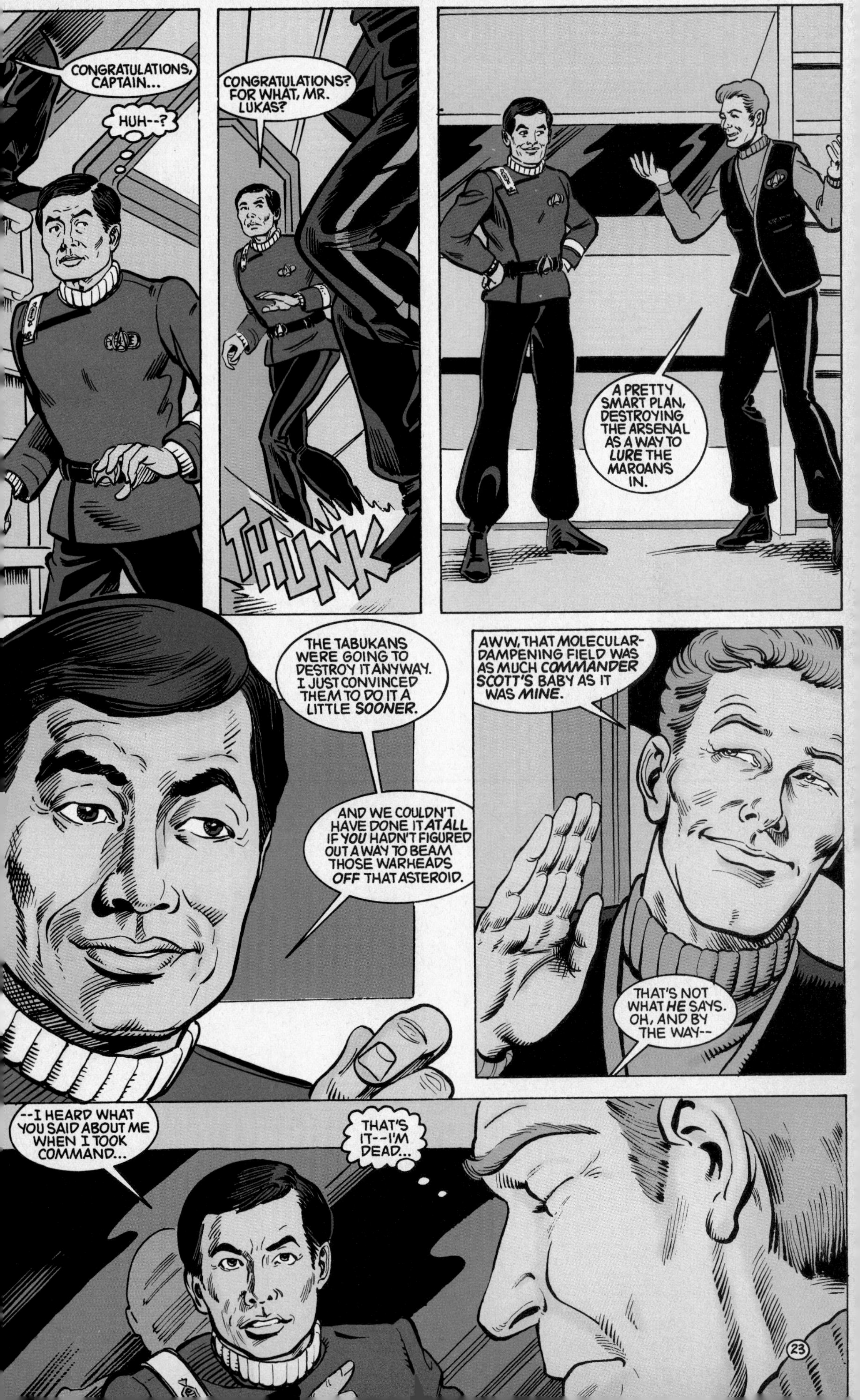
CONGRATULATIONS, CAPTAIN...
HUH--?
CONGRATULATIONS? FOR WHAT, MR. LUKAS?
THUNK
A PRETTY SMART PLAN, DESTROYING THE ARSENAL AS A WAY TO LURE THE MAROANS IN.
THE TABUKANS WERE GOING TO DESTROY IT ANYWAY. I JUST CONVINCED THEM TO DO IT A LITTLE SOONER.
AND WE COULDN'T HAVE DONE IT AT ALL IF YOU HADN'T FIGURED OUT A WAY TO BEAM THOSE WARHEADS OFF THAT ASTEROID.
AWW, THAT MOLECULAR-DAMPENING FIELD WAS AS MUCH COMMANDER SCOTT'S BABY AS IT WAS MINE.
THAT'S NOT WHAT HE SAYS. OH, AND BY THE WAY--
--I HEARD WHAT YOU SAID ABOUT ME WHEN I TOOK COMMAND...
THAT'S IT--I'M DEAD...

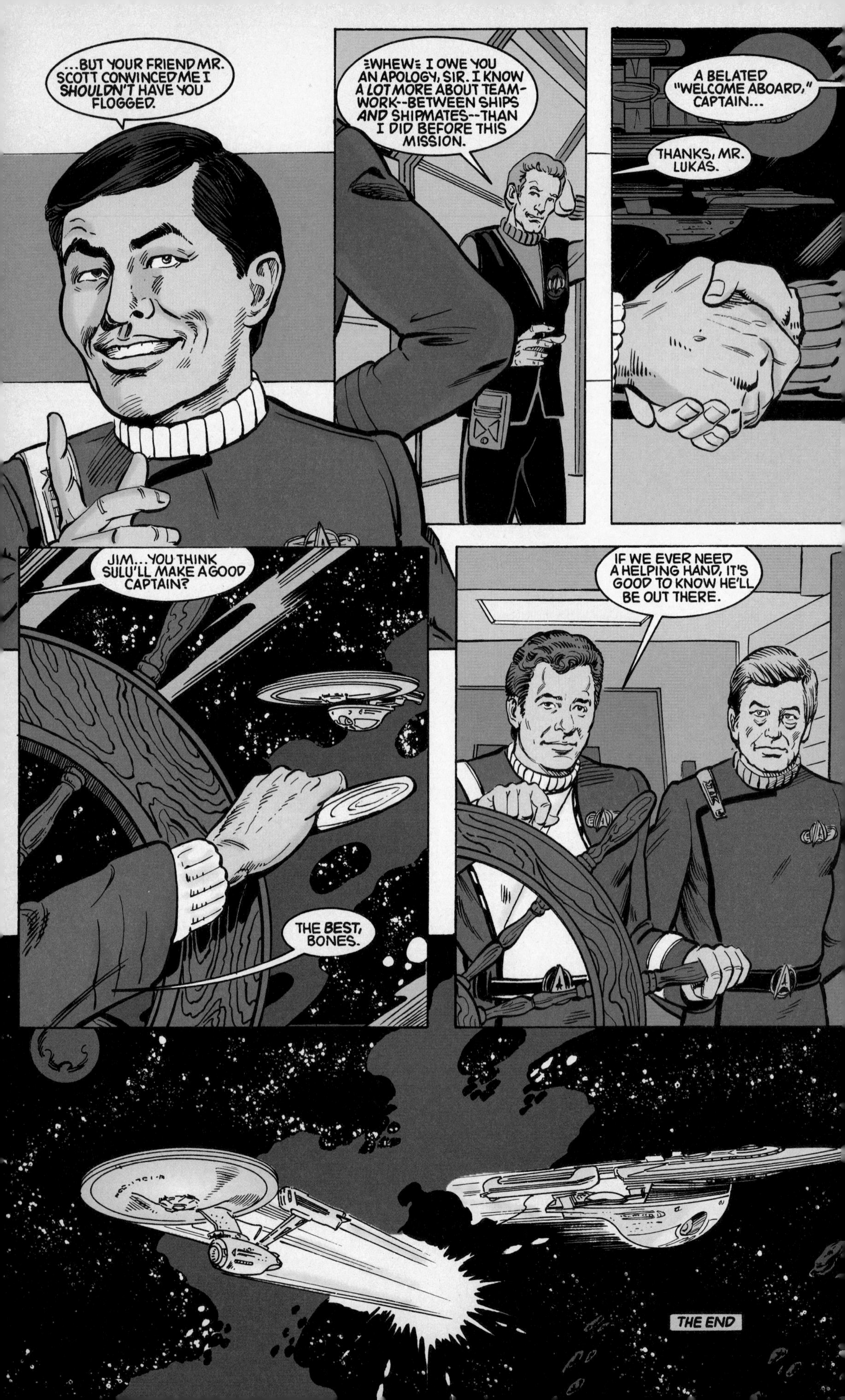
...BUT YOUR FRIEND MR. SCOTT CONVINCED ME I SHOULDN'T HAVE YOU FLOGGED.
=WHEW= I OWE YOU AN APOLOGY, SIR. I KNOW A LOT MORE ABOUT TEAM-WORK--BETWEEN SHIPS AND SHIPMATES--THAN I DID BEFORE THIS MISSION.
A BELATED "WELCOME ABOARD," CAPTAIN...
THANKS, MR. LUKAS.
JIM... YOU THINK SULU'LL MAKE A GOOD CAPTAIN?
THE BEST, BONES.
IF WE EVER NEED A HELPING HAND, IT'S GOOD TO KNOW HE'LL BE OUT THERE.
THE END

AFTERWORD

BY HOWARD WEINSTEIN

Ever since there've been *Star Trek* movies, I've wanted to write one. (Of course, I've also wanted Ed McMahon to find my house and give me that damned ten million dollar check he keeps promising me. But, even with Dick Clark helping him — and the detailed maps I keep sending — still no Ed, still no ten million bucks.)

And, somehow, I keep getting overlooked by the folks making *Star Trek* movies.

As the Rolling Stones sang in my youth, "You can't always get what you want." Alternately, "I can't get no satisfaction"...except *sometimes*.

This story is one of those times. Maybe I didn't get to write a *Star Trek* movie — but, within the comic-book format, it was our goal to have STAR TREK: TESTS OF COURAGE equal a movie in both size and scope.

For the past three and a half years, I've been lucky enough to be the regular writer of the "classic" STAR TREK series for DC Comics. One of the great things about this gig is the chance to tell stories that have not yet been told in all the original cast *Star Trek* episodes and films.

The incredible *Star Trek* saga has left open a wealth of continuity gaps to fill and dark corners to illuminate. With no budget limitations,

freed from the inevitable aging of actors, we're able to go back and forth in time and explore the lives of *all* of *Star Trek's* wonderful characters, with a level of detail simply not possible in TV or film formats.

One of these opportunities presented itself in the *Star Trek* movie series. Way back in *Star Trek II: The Wrath of Khan*, a scene had been written in which Kirk is being ferried to the Enterprise aboard a shuttle piloted by the redoubtable Commander Sulu. En route, Kirk confides to Sulu: "I cut your new orders personally. By the end of the month, you'll have your first command: U.S.S. Excelsior."

"Thank you, sir," says Sulu. "I've looked forward to this for a long time."

"You've earned it," Kirk says. "But I'm still grateful to have you at the helm for three weeks. I don't believe these kids can steer."

Unfortunately (for both Sulu and actor George Takei), the only part of that exchange surviving from page to screen is Kirk's last sentence. And Sulu remained at the Enterprise helm for *Star Trek III, IV* and *V*.

When *Star Trek V* was not the success its immediate predecessors had been, it looked doubtful that another original-cast movie would be made. Poor Sulu, it seemed, would slave away at that helm console for eternity.

Ahh, but *Star Trek VI was* made after all — and there, in the opening scenes, we found CAPTAIN SULU occupying the center seat of Excelsior. Not only that, but he finally got a first name — Hikaru. (Which he was *supposed* to get in a scene written for *Star Trek IV*, but the scene was cut... Hey, are you sensing a recurring theme here? If George Takei believed in conspiracies, we'd have to forgive him for wondering if somebody had it in for him.)

Especially for us old-time *Trek* fans, who lived through the original series' cancellation and the long wait for new voyages of the starship Enterprise, the movies have been special treats. But they've only come along once every two or three years, and there's only so much that can be packed into each one. They can't cover or explain everything. And now it appears that *Star Trek VI* was indeed the final film chapter expressly featuring the original crew of NCC-1701A, leaving us with a wealth of unanswered questions.

We could assume Sulu's parents were responsible for his first name — but what about his long-

delayed command? By the time we see him in *Star Trek VI*, he's already been captain for three years. What was his first mission like? How did his old shipmates react?

What did Sulu learn from all those years of observing one of the greatest captains in Starfleet history?

And what did the members of his *new* crew think of him? We didn't get to see much of that Excelsior crew in *Star Trek VI*. When we at DC Comics decided to tell this special story, Paramount Pictures allowed us generous latitude in creating flesh and blood officers to serve under Captain Sulu.

For instance, it seemed only fitting that Sulu would want an executive officer he knew and trusted. Since the movie placed Janice Rand on the Excelsior bridge as communications officer, we took the liberty of making Rand first officer as well — giving Sulu an old friend in whom to confide.

Before writing about Captain Sulu, I'd hoped to get some input from the one person who knows more about this character than anyone else — George Takei. Unfortunately, I didn't have a chance to do that. But I've had the privilege of knowing George for quite a while now, so I took some educated guesses at how he might have envisioned Sulu's early days in command.

This story originally appeared as a six-issue series (superbly pencilled by Gordon Purcell and Rod Whigham, inked by Arne Starr and Carlos Garzon, lettered by Bob Pinaha and colored by Tom McCraw). When the first three issues were ready, I sent them to George — and waited for his reaction. Knowing how busy he is, I had no idea when he'd get around to reading them.

But he must have been curious about how we'd treated his alter ego, because it wasn't long before I got a note. As I opened it, I thought: "George wouldn't have written back so fast *just* to tell me he'd *hated* the story... *would* he?"

He wouldn't... and he didn't. He loved it. And I'll confess right now I was one relieved writer. Nobody wants to offend a guy who's got all those phasers and photon torpedoes.

You may not have Excelsior's armaments at your disposal, but we sincerely hope you enjoy this story as much as George did, and as much as we enjoyed producing it.

March 1994

COVER GALLERY

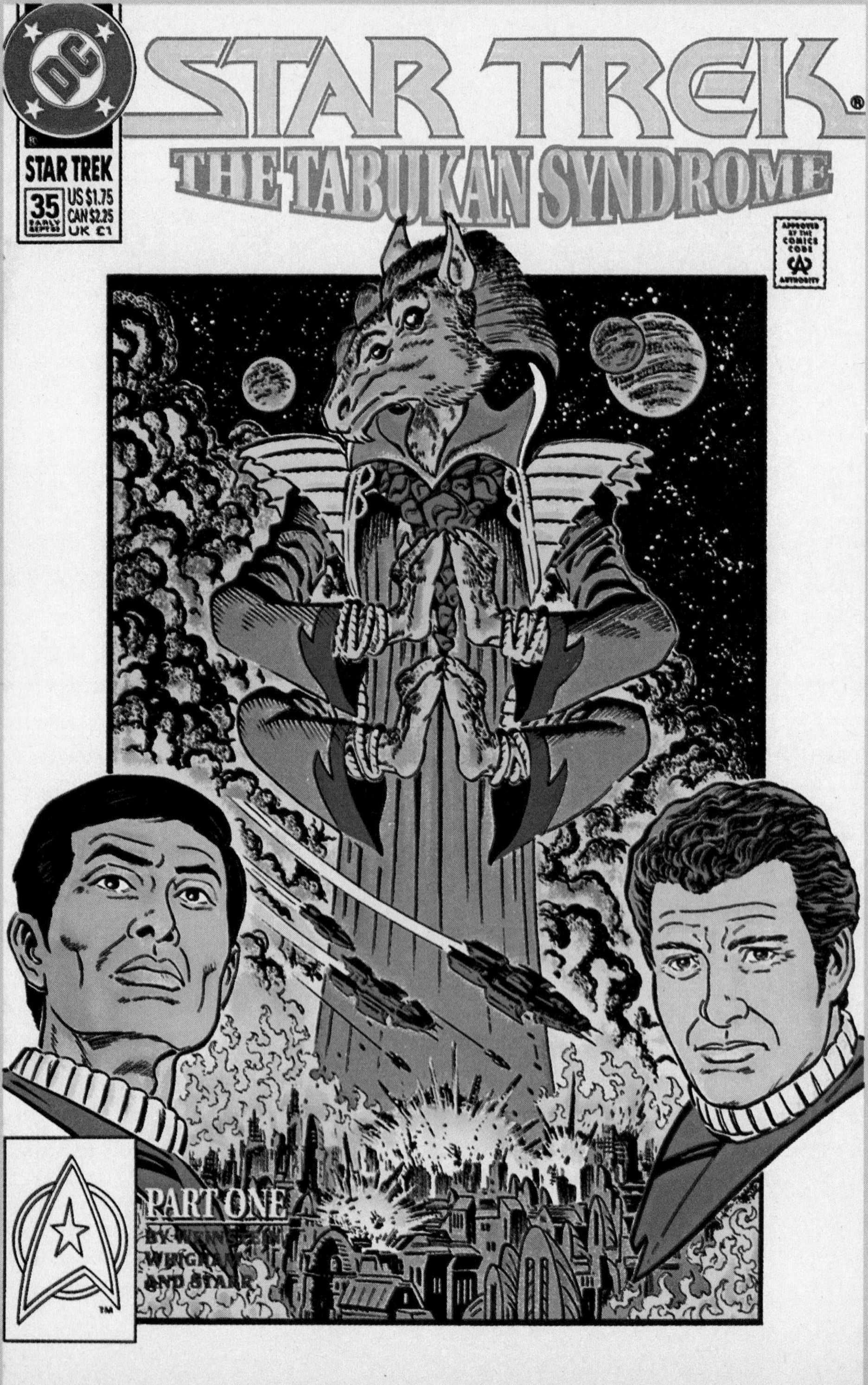
STAR TREK
THE TABUKAN SYNDROME
DC
STAR TREK
35
US $1.75
CAN $2.25
UK £1
PART ONE

STAR TREK
STAR TREK
36
US $1.75
CAN $2.25
UK £1
PART TWO
BY WEINSTEIN,
WHIGHAM
AND STARR
THE TABUKAN SYNDROME

STAR TREK
STAR TREK
37
US $1.75
CAN $2.25
UK £1
THE TABUKAN SYNDROME
PART THREE
BY WEINSTEIN,
PURCELL AND
GARZON

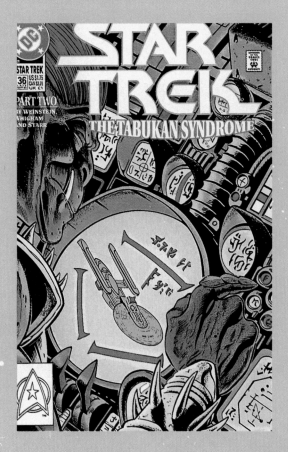

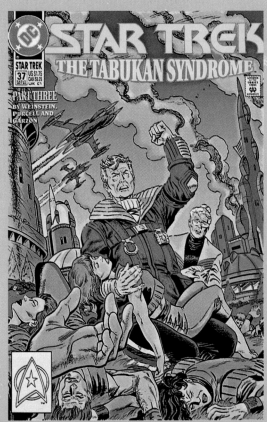

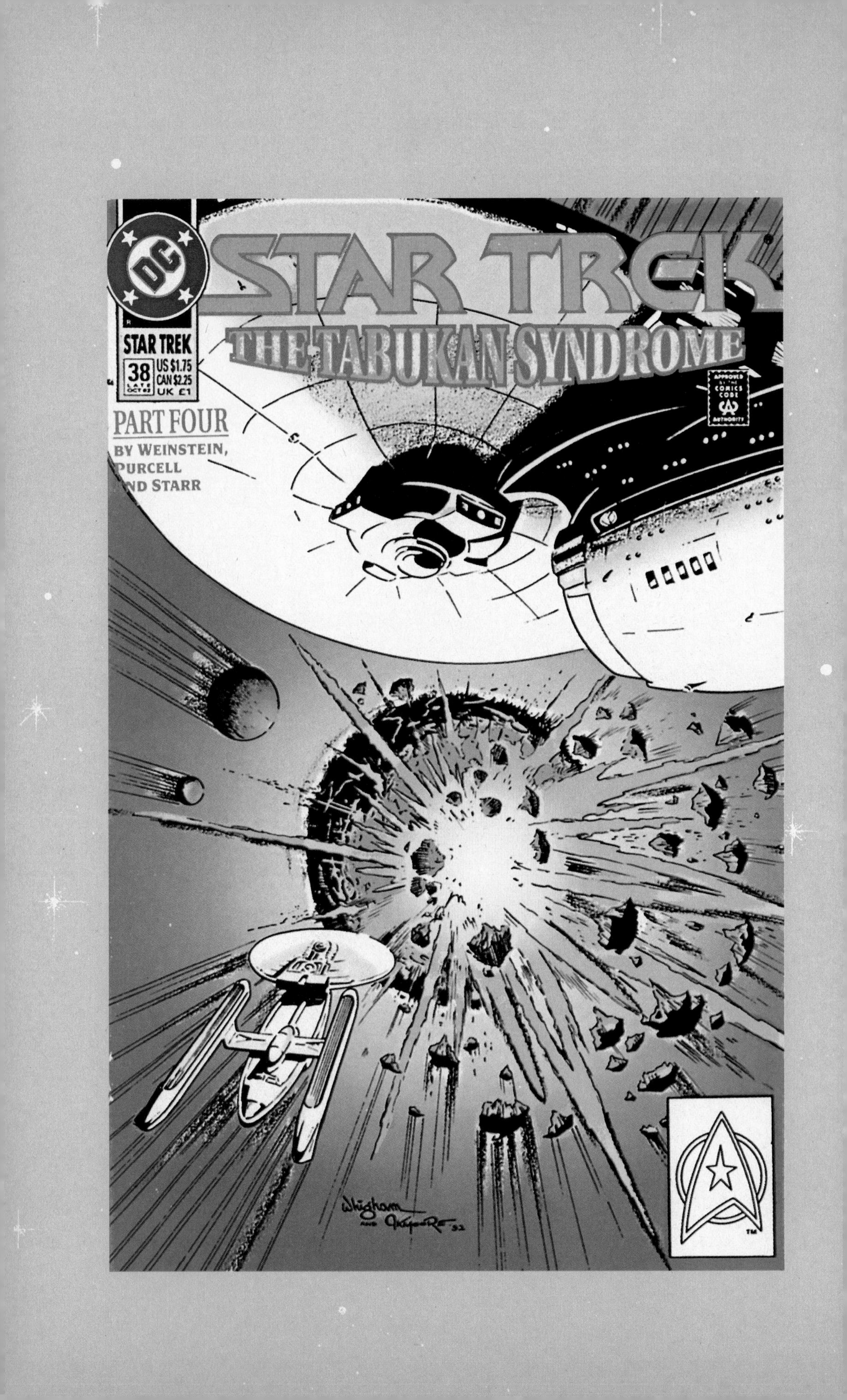
DC
STAR TREK
THE TABUKAN SYNDROME
STAR TREK
38
US $1.75
CAN $2.25
UK £1
APPROVED BY THE COMICS CODE AUTHORITY
PART FOUR
BY WEINSTEIN,
PURCELL
AND STARR
Whigham
AND McKENNA 92
TM

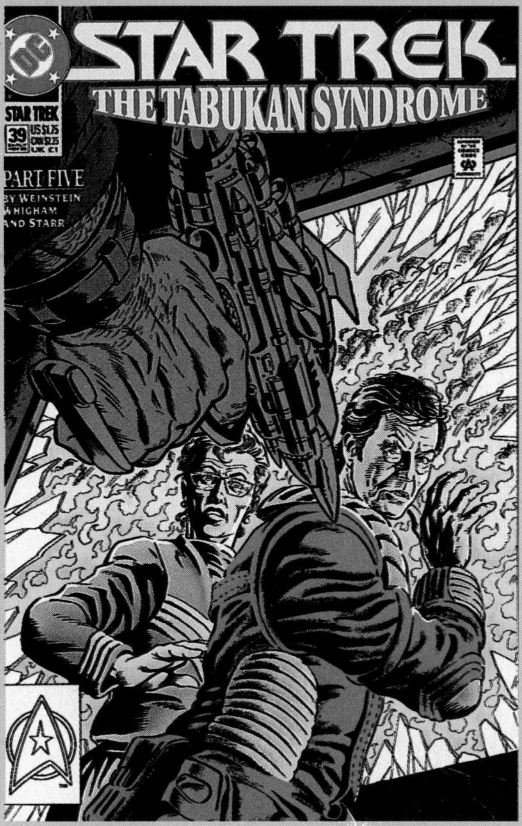
STAR TREK
THE TABUKAN SYNDROME
STAR TREK
39
PART FIVE
BY WEINSTEIN
WHIGHAM
AND STARR

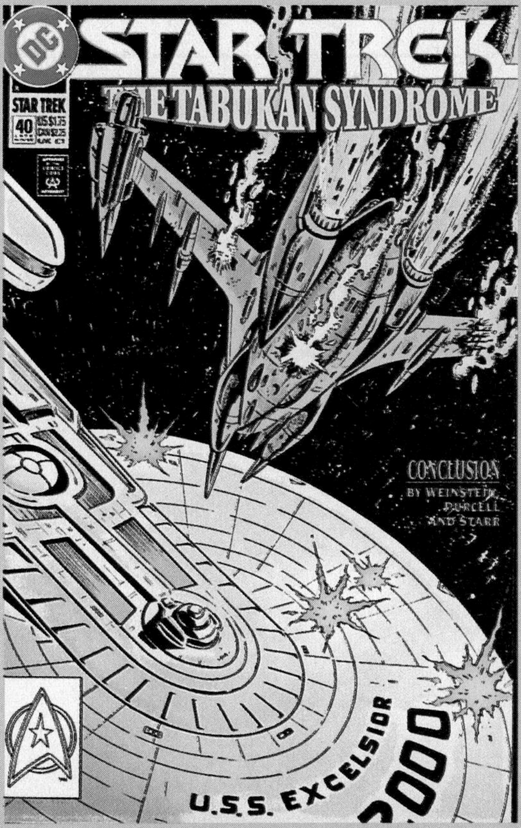
STAR TREK
THE TABUKAN SYNDROME
STAR TREK
40
CONCLUSION
U.S.S. EXCELSIOR

YOU CAN FIND MORE STAR-SPANNING ADVENTURES IN THE FOLLOWING BOOKS FROM DC:

STAR TREK: DEBT OF HONOR
Chris Claremont/Adam Hughes/Karl Story

STAR TREK: THE MIRROR UNIVERSE SAGA
Mike Barr/Tom Sutton/Ricardo Villagran

THE BEST OF STAR TREK
Various Writers and Artists

STAR TREK: WHO KILLED CAPTAIN KIRK?
Peter David/Tom Sutton/Gordon Purcell/Ricardo Villagran

STAR TREK: THE NEXT GENERATION—THE STAR LOST
Michael Jan Friedman/Peter Krause/Pablo Marcos

THE BEST OF STAR TREK: THE NEXT GENERATION
Various Writers and Artists